## PRAISE FOR

## A TIME TO LOVE AND A TIME TO DIE

"Finely drawn characters. Visually dramatic, tense and emotionally satisfying. This is one of the finest novels of the Great War I have read." — *Terence Culbert, former national broadcaster, producer and script writer for CTV.*

"Michael Joll, uses his consummate skill and research to show that amidst the savagery and brutality and the wanton sacrifice of hundreds of thousands of lives in the Great War, there was still hope, promise and an unquenchable desire to preserve the humanity in our species." — Ken Puddicombe, author of *Racing With The Rain*, *Junta* and *Down Independence Boulevard And Other Stories*.

"In this poignant story, Joll's often elegant writing stands in stark contrast with his unvarnished description of the brutality of trench warfare." —*Christopher Joll, former Life Guards officer, author and military historian.*

"…so realistic that one feels one is there, witnessing the…war campaign in France." — Catherine Gerasimov, United Nations interpreter.

"I'm mightily impressed." — Andrew Patenall, Professor Emeritus, English, University of Toronto, Ontario.

# OTHER BOOKS BY MICHAEL JOLL

Perfect Execution And Other Stories

Persons of Interest

# A TIME TO LOVE
# AND
# A TIME TO DIE

## Michael Joll

MiddleRoad | Publishers

*"Making Literature see the light of day."*

Library and Archives Canada Cataloguing in Publication

Joll, Michael, author

A Time To Love And A Time To die

Second Edition 20th July 2020

ISBN 978-1-9991365-7-4 (soft cover)


Cover Photographs courtesy of "Freeimages.com"
Poppy by Celia Enders
A Soldier Of The Great War by Yohan hmmm
Cover design by Ken Puddicombe

"Out of this nettle, danger, we pluck this flower, safety."

Shakespeare,  Henry IV, Part 1.

Table of Contents

# ACKNOWLEDGMENTS

My thanks and gratitude first, to my wife, Linda, who has suffered through the lengthy gestation of this novel going back to the day when it emerged as a stage play (never performed), a radio play (broadcast on Canadian public radio in 2007) and eventually through drafts without number before it reached publication in its present form. She still refers to this story by its original working title. I expect she always will.

To my editor, Kenneth Puddicombe, a writer and author of considerable talent as well as being an editor with a keen eye to what is needed and what is superfluous, my thanks. Editing is a laborious but vital process and Ken does it so well. I tend to throw in everything, including the kitchen sink. He throws out everything but the dish cloth, because that's where the story is hidden. "Just write the damn story," Tom Clancy said. And " If it sounds like writing, I rewrite it," said Elmore Leonard. Ken reminds me often of these words of writing wisdom.

To MiddleRoad Publishers for giving me the opportunity to bring this novel into the world, my gratitude. It has been, and continues to be, a great partnership.

My thanks to Terence Culbert, former national television producer, presenter and screenwriter for CTV in Canada and now an artist with a unique style of applying paint to canvas. Terence is guilty of encouraging me to write when he was old enough to know better. This novel, and the many stories that have come before its publication, are in part due to his insistence that I not quit.

To Christopher Joll, a prolific author, military historian and former captain in the Life Guards, Britain's foremost cavalry regiment, my thanks for pointing out the many egregious errors in matters military and historical that I missed. Without his timely intervention much of the premise for this story would have lacked the essential authenticity a novel of this type requires.

A big thank you to my many friends on Amherst island, Ontario, especially the late broadcasting legend, Stanley Burke, a self-confessed terrible actor but a man who had the unique ability to cut me down to size with a raised eyebrow and a soft growl.

To my scattered family, all of whom have contributed along the road in ways large and small in helping this story see the light of day, thank you.

And to Andrew Patenall, who may be a distant cousin but who has the presence of mind to deny any such connection, my thanks for taking a big part in the development of this novel from its early days as a radio play (he played the part of the character who later morphed into Rear Admiral, the Earl of St. Austell). Andrew is the only person who has terrified me, in large part because of his brilliance as a professor of English at the University of Toronto, but also because of his ability to see through BS and cut to the heart of a story. Forty years of teaching Shakespeare to hungover undergraduates will have that effect. I could never slip anything past him. His great, wry, English sense of humour always eased my annoyance at being caught flannelling in my writing instead of using *le mot juste*. I'm sure he would have failed me as a student, probably for cribbing my essay answers from the deliberate disinformation he had sown in Wikipedia for that very purpose. Andrew helped make me a better and more honest writer. He's too modest to take any credit for it. He taught me many lessons I haven't paid for. I remain in his debt.

To fellow members of the Brampton Writers' Guild, my thanks for your positive feedback and critique and your encouragement to continue whenever I felt like chucking in the towel.

My thanks to Brian Henry, who teaches creative writing at Ryerson University, whose second draft critique of this novel proved invaluable, and whose courses helped shape me into the writer I have become.

And to all those whose involvement I have not acknowledged by name, my apologies for the omission. It was not deliberate, but when you reach and pass a certain age the memory tends more to resemble a sieve than blotting paper. And if you are old enough to remember fountain pens and blotting paper, you know what I mean.

# 1. BOULOGNE

The glistening cobblestone streets of Dover were the last place Captain Haig-Mallory wanted to be. Not because of the steady rain that dripped off the flanks of the cavalrymen's horses and seeped through gaps in the men's waterproof capes, though that was miserable enough. To a man, they had all been in the army long enough to know that *waterproof* was a term used in a hit or miss fashion to suggest the material might, at a pinch, keep out a light drizzle for a short time. He spared no kind thoughts for the late Austrian Archduke, or the Kaiser; had it not been for them, in a week Harry Haig-Mallory would have been heading to the altar, anticipating the arrival of his bride-to-be.

Half an hour's ride had been enough to ensure the rain that ran down their necks off their caps saturated their battledress blouses and shirts. As wet as they were, however, the rain had failed to dampen the men's optimism for the task ahead.

When they reached their destination, Dover harbour, the open-sided sheds on the dock provided little relief from the weather while the regiment waited for the ferries to arrive. With their mountains of personal and ancillary equipment piled on the lee side of the sheds, the chill wind quickly cooled the men's enthusiasm. Some grumbled it was a taste of things to come. The more optimistic reckoned it was better than being shot at, though no one claimed to having ever been the target of enemy fire.

"It's a good sign," Haig-Mallory said to Lieutenant Merryweather, one of the young troop commanders in his squadron. "They're never happy unless they have something to grouse about."

Late in the afternoon, a long, hodgepodge convoy of ambulances with large red crosses painted on the canvas sides arrived at the dock and parked, nose to tail. Shortly after the convoy's arrival the first ferry nosed into the harbour from out of the gloom, rounded the breakwater and edged to its mooring. Two more followed. A ragged jeer sounded through the sheds as the first mooring line from the ferry snaked ashore. Moments later, the disgruntled troops watched stretcher bearers and uniformed nurses climb the gangways.

They did not have long to wait before the first of the long line of walking wounded straggled into an unsteady line at the top of the gangway. In ones and twos they snugged crutches under their armpits then lurched and slid down the wooden gangways to stumble ashore onto the rain-slick planks of the dock. From there they limped and hobbled their way towards the ambulances and queued up to be helped into the dark bowels of the waiting vehicles. Then followed stretcher cases, one after another for over an hour, all bloodied and many with stumps where limbs should have been. Harry took in the faces of his men as they absorbed the pain in the eyes of the wounded, at the heads wrapped in blood-soaked bandages stained with the dirt of battle.

"We shouldn't be surprised, Merryweather," Harry said, as he and the young subaltern watched the casualties make their way slowly across the dockside. "It's been three weeks already since the first shots were fired. But so many, and so soon?" He shook his head slowly.

The men looked on while the attendants stacked the wounded inside the ambulances in racks three and four high like so many lengths of cordwood. Huddled with a group of fellow officers in the lee of a mountain of baggage and equipment, Harry watched the shuffling, priestlike procession of the wounded. This was a face of war few had prepared for.

Harry came face to face with the harsh realization they were headed for France with the vast majority of officers like him, and the men they led — untested. He cast a glance at the men he was commissioned to lead and wondered how many would come back on a stretcher, how many would return unscathed, and how many would lie forever in France. It was a gloomy thought that refused to lift no matter how hard he tried.

While Harry's men waited for the ferries to unload their cargos of human suffering the wind increased in strength, the rain continued into the gloom of dusk and evening slid into night. One by one the ambulances left in the direction of the hospital, only to return empty a short while later to continue their grim shuttle. Cold, wet and miserable the men turned edgy until eventually, full of drugged and bandaged bodies, the last of the vehicles lurched away.

With the ferries finally emptied of wounded, the King's Imperial Hussars gathered their gear and prepared to embark. Long after midnight the three ferries cast off, headed for France. As the bow of the first ferry came around the end of the breakwater and out into the open sea, the full force of the gale blowing straight up the English Channel caught it full on the beam. The ferry staggered, its bow heaved then ploughed into the trough in front of the first towering wave. Cold bullets of salt spray blasted the unprotected men on the exposed deck. Harry held on to a brass rail in the first-class passenger lounge, convinced his war would be over before he ever set foot in France.

After what seemed like hours of physical and mental torture, Harry noticed the ship's motion lessen and he glanced through the porthole. In the dark, the imposing lighter grey bulk of the chalk cliffs of France loomed a mile or two away on their port beam. Boulogne could not be far off. This could only mean a blessed release from the twisting, heaving ferry, and the end of the revolting smell of the vomit and human feces the mountainous seas had not yet washed overboard from the exposed deck. He dared not think of the mess from the horses in the hold.

"And what lies ahead?" Lieutenant Merryweather muttered. He took a pull from his hip flask and offered it to Harry. Harry shook his head, in part to decline the offer, in part in wonder as to what they were doing there, all five hundred and forty-nine officers, non-commissioned officers and other ranks, about to disembark in Boulogne.

"Blowed if I know," Harry replied. "This wasn't supposed to happen, but it can't be any worse than this, can it?" Harry fell into silent contemplation.

After several moments, Merryweather gave Harry an odd look.

"What?" said Harry with a frown.

"I thought you said something, Sir."

"Probably just thinking aloud." He pointed at the quayside where the ferry was about to tie up. "I'm supposed to be getting married in a few days."

"Bad luck, Sir."

"Or bad timing. Suite at the Hôtel Georges Cinq in Paris for the honeymoon. Room service, drawing room, bedroom, even our own private bathroom. Wasted, thanks to the bloody Kaiser."

"With accommodation like that you wouldn't need to leave the hotel."

Harry scowled at his younger colleague.

"Sorry, Sir. Didn't mean it like that."

"I'm in France and she's still in America."

"Languishing, no doubt, Sir."

"I hope so, but it's not her fault."

"I don't think she can expect a postcard from you any time soon. *Having a wonderful time. Wish you were here.*"

"And I certainly don't want one from her in similar vein. In answer to your earlier question, Merryweather, this is what lies ahead." He pointed his swagger stick at the quay and the railway carriages drawn up parallel to it. "At least for the here and now. Best see to your men."

"Sir."

What that entailed was the logistical challenge of disembarking twenty-six officers and five hundred and twenty-three other ranks, most of them seasick, many so weakened they could barely stand. The officers ignored the shouts of the French officials ashore, and the swaying men fell in on the dockside by troop and by squadron, intent on making their way to the waiting trains.

With his squadron accounted for and aboard the first of the trains, Harry gazed wearily through his compartment window at the nondescript station buildings. With a long hiss of steam and a blast of the whistle, the engine clanked into slow forward motion. The sky lightened a little as they inched their way out of the shadow cast by the cliffs guarding the harbour. Low, rain-laden clouds scudded past the carriages. Each gust of wind drove the rain nearly horizontal and rattled the sides, roof and windows of the carriages like birdshot. In no time the windows steamed up on the inside with the collective breath of the officers crammed into what, in peacetime, amounted to first class compartments. In twenty-four hours, Harry calculated, they may have travelled twenty-five miles, from Dover to Boulogne. This, he surmised as he inhaled the acrid stench of coal smoke, the stink of stale armpit sweat, unbrushed teeth and the unmistakable, wet dog smell of damp wool of the uniforms worn by his brother officers, must be the new pace of war.

The train hissed, lurched and wheezed its way roughly south, away from the heaving misery of the sea and the memory of the nightmare crossing. They stopped frequently, sometimes for a few minutes, as a long-distance runner might while catching his breath; at other times for up to an hour, as if the race were over. Meanwhile the rain lashed a sodden, bleak landscape of sad, look-alike farms and hamlets, small, isolated copses and flattened wheat fields separated by hedgerows, flooded cart tracks and swollen, frothing streams.

Several hours later, with a prolonged hiss of steam, the train clanked to a halt. With much shouting and stamping of boots, the regiment alighted stiffly from their confinement onto a wooden railway platform. Stupefied by fatigue, and numbed by hunger, they gazed about them at a view of a rolling countryside that consisted entirely of bell tents as far as the eye could see, row upon row, field upon field, to the horizon and beyond.

Word soon spread they were but one unit in thousands, probably tens of thousands of troops in the nameless staging area for the British Expeditionary Force. Newspaper reporters had taken to filing their stories under the caption, *Somewhere in France*. To the men, *Somewhere* was here, wherever the hell *Here* was, and it was no use asking. And for how long? Don't ask. Surely, nowhere could be worse.

Harry had no idea where they were. Neither had he seen anything like this tent city. He shuddered. The sooner they deployed to the front lines the healthier they would all be. Only sickness lurked here.

The regiment spent one night at the staging camp where the men uniformly cursed the weather, cursed the mud and cursed the first infestation of lice. That done, they cursed France and they cursed the war, happy to have something to grouse about.

In the morning came orders to deploy.

A watery sun rose over the sodden staging camp when Harry's regiment gathered at the makeshift station for the next stop on their journey. It did not take long before their destination became public knowledge — Maubeuge.

"Never heard of it," one trooper declared.

"A dollop of donkey shit on the map of France," said another with authority.

"Who cares?" grumbled a third to general agreement it didn't matter a cuss where this particular dollop of donkey shit was, they were going to it.

The Hussars boarded their assigned train and waited. Eventually the engine came to life with huffs and wheezes. The train moved intermittently, sometimes several miles at a time, through railway stations that differed only in their names which no one could pronounce. Where they detrained had no station, no name; not even a wooden platform.

In the regiment's commandeered temporary headquarters, a tumbledown wooden barn that smelled of beaten earth, musty hay and mildew, Colonel Shackleton gathered his officers.

"We have intelligence," he announced, "that the enemy is advancing towards Mons with the intention of capturing and crossing the Mons-Condé Canal. If they manage to cross it, they'll have a clear run for Paris. Our job is to see they don't. The French in the centre of the line depend on us to protect their flank. We will not let them down, gentlemen. Any questions?"

A captain at the back of the barn raised his hand. "I take it, Sir, the Froggies aren't capable of looking after their own flank. Why are we supposed to be the ones to bail them out?"

"I know they're only Froggies, Edrich, but those are our orders. It is not up to us in the field to decide whether they're worth losing our own men over. People with a lot more gold braid than you or I will ever see make those decisions."

"Ours is not to reason why," a major muttered.

"No bloody balls, those Frogs," grumbled another, just loud enough to be heard and to mutterings of agreement.

"If there are no further serious questions, prepare your men to move out immediately."

In thin sunshine that flitted through scudding grey clouds the regiment fell in beside a gravel road that bordered a field of ripe barley. There they waited in stoic silence for someone to give an order. Harry nodded to the corporal major and his squadron moved off.

An afternoon's ride brought the four squadrons to a lightly wooded area to the rear of the Expeditionary Force's forward positions on the south bank of the canal. Harry dismounted and surveyed the scene to his front. Collieries, mine buildings and miners' cottages offered strongpoints. Slag heaps as high as any in England or Wales provided observation posts for supporting artillery fire. Through his binoculars he could make out some of the infantry's hastily dug trenches a couple of miles ahead.

"The Hun will have a surprise if he thinks this is going to be a Sunday afternoon picnic," Harry said to Merryweather.

"Not very sporting of the Hun to come through Belgium," Merryweather said.

"I think we're about to find out the Huns pay no regard to the rules of war any more than the rules of cricket."

"Fifteen rounds a minute from an infantryman's Lee Enfield and they won't know what's hit them," Merryweather replied. "The Germans will think it's machine gun fire."

"It works both ways. Our chaps will soon discover a horse and a sabre are no match for accurate rifle fire, or machine guns," Harry said gloomily and glanced at the sky. "Cloud and rain, by the looks of it. Could be worse. At least the horses won't overheat."

A rumble of guns, like distant thunder, drifted over the countryside. "Artillery," Merryweather said. "French or Belgian, I should think. I didn't see any of ours when we arrived."

"Let's hope they're not late for the show." A crackle of closer small arms fire rippled across the land. "Sounds like the infantry, rifles and machine guns," Harry said. "They must be at quite close quarters."

Lt. Merriweather frowned and turned to Harry. "When do you think we'll get involved, Sir?"

"Tomorrow. Or the day after. Or whenever Generals Allenby or Smith-Dorrien decide to commit us. Possibly never. Look to your front. Is this great cavalry country?"

"I see what you mean, Sir. Not exactly open countryside, is it? Too many hedges and ditches and not much flat ground. Way too many places for enemy marksmen to hide and pick us off. Good fox hunting country, though, if you like the jumps." He glanced at Harry who raised an eyebrow. "I ride with the Quorn at home."

Harry nodded. "I'm glad you paid attention in class, Mr. Merryweather. One day you may find yourself in my position asking the same question of a young officer. Now see to your men and be prepared to move out at a moment's notice."

Merryweather saluted and jogged back to his troop headquarters.

They did not have long to wait. At dawn the next day the German artillery bombardment began. At 9:00 a.m. came the first German infantry assault, concentrated to the right of Harry's position where the canal took a shallow loop to the north and back, forming a salient.

"It's the Royal Fusiliers taking the brunt of it, Haig-Mallory," Shackleton said as he put his field glasses down for a moment. He raised them again to his eyes and grunted. "And the Middlesex, the Hampshires and the Gordon Highlanders."

Harry trained his own binoculars on the fighting, at least two, probably closer to three miles away. "If they take the bridges, Sir, they'll have to call us in. The men will give a good account of themselves."

"Are they ready, Haig-Mallory?"

"Raring to have a go at the enemy, Sir. But they're raw. They need blooding. This'll give them an excellent chance to show their mettle."

"Stay with me, Haig-Mallory. I need my adjutant at my side to keep an eye on the things I may not see when I'm leading the charge."

"Of course, Sir."

"Meanwhile, make sure the men and horses are properly fed and watered. We may not have time later on."

Harry called a trooper over. "Colonel's orders. To all squadron and troop commanders. Early lunch and pack provisions for twenty-four hours."

"Sir!" The trooper snapped a salute and fled from the sight of his commanding officer and his adjutant.

At 3:00 p.m. Colonel Shackleton looked up from the dispatch received moments earlier. "General Allenby has ordered a retirement of all troops across a broad front, Haig-Mallory. We're to take up a defensive position to the rear of the infantry, which will take up new positions south of Mons." He pointed to the map in his hand. "As soon as we're told to move out, we will reform here, on a line south of the Valenciennes-Maubeuge road. Our regiment will form the centre of the line of reinforcements."

"I'll pass the word. I don't think it'll be a popular move, if you don't mind my saying, Sir. I think the men really want to get to grips with the enemy and give them a taste of Sheffield steel."

"As Major Shaw-Bingley reminded us a short while ago, though I am not sure he meant me to hear it, *Ours is not to reason why*, Haig-Mallory."

"*Ours is just to do and die. And into the valley of death rode the six hundred.* Or something like that. You'd think we'd learned something in the Crimea."

"Quite so. And long before that. Meanwhile we wait for the order to retire. Or advance. In the confusion of battle they're often one and the same thing."

They waited for the order which did not come until the early hours of the following morning. They moved to defensive positions. New orders arrived within minutes — the 2nd Cavalry Division, which included the King's Imperial Hussars, would get their chance to fight a rearguard action against the German infantry advance.

Nearly five hundred and fifty men on horseback moved forward under cover of darkness to a position in a heavily wooded area of oak, beech and elm trees and thick undergrowth north of the Valenciennes road. A runner reported back shortly after dawn. "The enemy 'as reached the canal, but they 'asn't crossed it yet," the breathless young trooper reported. "The engineers 'as blown all the bridges." He took a deep gulp of air. "The infantry passed through my position a short while ago." He sucked in another breath and hopped from one foot to the other. "The Bedfords mostly, Sir. And I recognized the flashes of some of the Duke of Wellington's Regiment. All very orderly, Sir, like they was out for a bit of shopping in the High Street."

"Won't be long, Haig-Mallory," Shackleton said once the runner left. "They'll get their blooding whether they like it or not."

The men chafed. They honed sabres that needed no sharpening. They polished leather and brass until it gleamed fit for the King's inspection. The NCOs knew it was better than having a bunch of idlers gossiping, spreading rumours, stoking fear and waiting for an order that still might never materialize.

Late in the afternoon word reached them: the Germans were already in Élouges, directly in front of them.

"I see them, Haig-Mallory." Shackleton pointed to figures about a mile ahead of their position. "Pass the word to A Squadron to mount and wait for my command."

"The other three Squadrons, Sir?"

"Major Kerslake and B to remain in reserve with C and D. Take command of A with Merryweather under you. We cut. We thrust. We absolutely do not give chase, no matter how tempting the opportunity. That's how we lost the battle of Hastings. Leave a few survivors to spread fear. Understood?"

"Sir." Harry saluted and left on the run.

The smell of saddle and harness leather and horse sweat drifted into Harry's nose. He heard the occasional quiet whinny from down the line but for the most part the horses stood still, barely moving a hoof. He found the waiting the hardest on the men's nerves as well as his own. Pressure built on his bladder. This would be his first taste of action, and virtually to a man theirs also. But for years they had trained and practiced until the charge was imprinted on their brains as second nature. No need for heroic speeches. They had a job to do — Germans to kill, as many as possible while they incurred minimal casualties of their own.

From their concealed position they watched the vanguard of the enemy infantry saunter unopposed down the paved road half a mile away. Some of the Germans advanced with their rifles slung over their shoulders; some carried them loosely in one hand. They gave off the air of self-assurance, of cockiness, with the smell of victory in their nostrils. And who could blame them? A few, perhaps more wary, less experienced or more scared than their brothers, held their rifles at the high port.

The Germans fanned out a quarter of a mile from the edge of the wood when they reached the Valenciennes road, elevated two or three feet above the surrounding countryside with ditches and hedges on either side. Harry estimated perhaps a hundred men, no match for his eager troopers, not with the surprise of an ambush hitting them where it hurt most. He grinned.

Shackleton raised his field glasses to his eyes. Harry saw his forehead furrow. Shackleton lowered the glasses and handed them to Harry. "Tell me if you can see any machine guns."

Harry squinted through the lenses. "No," he said. "I don't see any."

"Good. Nor did I. If there's one thing I fear as a cavalry officer, it's machine guns. Catch us out in the open on a charge and they'll make mincemeat of us in no time flat." He turned his attention to the advancing German infantry. "Make the most of this, Haig-Mallory," he said without turning his head. "It may be our one and only chance to act as cavalry."

They waited for the leading section of German infantrymen to advance across recently reaped wheat fields. When the Germans reached within a hundred yards of the woods, Shackleton raised his sabre high over his head. Every trooper held his breath. The bugler put his bugle to his lips, wet them and looked to his side for the word. Shackleton nodded, pointed his sword at the enemy and yelled, "Charge!"

# 2. THE MARNE

The bugler blew the charge, loud, clear and without waver.

Close to one hundred and sixty cavalrymen yelled in unison as they broke through the undergrowth at the edge of the wood. Bugles blared as they charged across the stubble field at a full gallop with sabres held high.

Caught by surprise, it took several seconds before the bewildered German soldiers reacted. They fumbled rifles, dropped some, cocked bolts and pointed their weapons in the direction of the charging cavalry. A few managed to fire a round before the English horsemen fell upon them.

Harry closed in on the nearest German soldier and swiped backhand at him. The shock up his arm as his sabre's blade bit into bone surprised him. He heard a scream and saw the German drop to the ground. Blood spurted in a fountain from a severed artery. Time stood still while Harry watched enthralled as the man's feet drummed the earth feebly while his arm spewed blood into a widening pool beside him. With a final twitch the man lay still. His bloody, severed hand, flesh, bones, sinews and ligaments stuck out like a hedgehog's prickles from the wrist. For what seemed forever Harry remained in his saddle, fascinated and at the same time revolted by the sight of the first man he had ever killed, a man who once had a mother and a father, brothers and sister most likely, perhaps a wife or a sweetheart. And now, Harry realized, the nameless man lay dead, because I killed him.

A bullet missed Harry's cheek by a hair's breadth, leaving a long scorch mark on his skin. He wrenched his attention from the dead man to the German who had tried to kill him. He saw the man work the bolt and raise his rifle. Harry drove his spurs into his horse's flank. The horse reared and plunged forward. Harry drove the point of his sabre through the man's eye before he could fire. The blade shuddered as it hit the bone of the socket. The shock drove up his wrist. Harry pulled out his blade and, in a detached manner, took note of the grey brain matter stuck to the blade and the dark red of the man's blood flowing from the tip. "Nothing personal, old chap," he muttered. This time he did not watch the German die but urged his horse into the thick of the enemy infantrymen.

Through the clash of steel and gunfire he heard individual shouts and screams, the neighs of frightened horses and hooves crashing on the dirt and churned-up stubble. Fury drove him to cut and slash at every German he could find. Ribbons of blood flew over his head with each arcing sabre slash. His blade juddered and his wrist jarred as time and again English steel struck German bone. A warm, slippery flow of bright arterial blood ran under the sabre's pommel, across his knuckles and trickled up his wrist. He wiped the blood from his sabre on his trouser leg, then turned his mount in a tight circle. Out of the corner of an eye he saw a German with his rifle at his hip take aim at him.

I'm dead, flashed through Harry's mind. Stupid, careless, thoughtless clot, not searching for danger signals. He faced his killer, spurred his horse and yelled. The German fired. The percussion of the shot rang in Harry's ears. The bullet missed. Harry lunged at the grey-clad soldier. He swept his sabre down towards the German's head. The German braced himself and thrust his bayonet. Harry saw the thrust in time, adjusted the arc of his own sabre slash, and parried it. He swept the rifle and bayonet aside and, in one fluid motion slashed the blade of his sabre against the man's exposed neck. The German fell to his knees, his hands clawing at his throat as dark blood spurted into the air from the severed jugular vein. He pitched forward. The toes of his boots drummed uselessly on the red earth beneath him. Harry turned his horse. Out of the corner of his eye he saw the man lie still.

Harry lunged at another Hun. He heard the man's blood gurgle in his throat, imagined it drain into his lungs before it spewed onto the ground as frothing vomit. The man twisted and fell face up. For a moment Harry wondered if the German would bleed to death or drown in his own blood. He wrenched his thoughts away when he heard the bugle sound the recall and sought the bugler to regain his bearings. He reined in his horse and turned it. The horse reared and pawed the air for a second before its front hooves returned to earth with a thud. Harry shuddered at the sound of cracking bone. A glance told him his horse's hooves had crushed the head and body of the fallen enemy soldier. The German, who would now neither bleed to death nor drown in his own blood, was past caring. Harry dug his spurs into the horse's flanks. The horse hurdled the body on the hoof-churned, bloody earth and raced back toward the woods.

A few steps ahead of him Harry saw the figure of a dazed young officer reeling like a drunkard before he fell backward on top of his dead horse.

"Mr. Merryweather," Harry called out as he slowed to a canter. "I see you are unhorsed. My hand, Sir, and a lift back home if you wish."

A grin spread over Merryweather's face. "Indeed, Sir, I do find myself disadvantaged."

Harry leaned over. With one hand he clasped the subaltern's forearm and hauled him up. "Take my stirrups, Mr. Merryweather, if you please, and hold on to me."

"In return, Sir, I shall act as your rearguard should some Hun decide to take a pot shot at us."

"Most sporting of you," Harry shouted over his shoulder. With a yell he raked his spurs against his horse's flanks. The horse leaped forward and galloped to the safety of the trees.

Harry reined in the horse and dismounted. It was only then that he realized his entire body trembled like an autumn leaf. Could it be fear? Or relief that he had survived his first battle unharmed? Is this what it's like for everyone after a battle? He recalled his first fist fight behind the squash courts at Marlborough school. He had won, skinned his knuckles and suffered a cut lip, but the other boy had gone down gasping for air after a punch to the solar plexus. He recalled shaking, not for a moment, but for minutes, perhaps for as much as an hour after the fight ended. It's only like this after a battle if you survive, he decided with a tight-lipped grimace.

"Corporal Major," he called out.

"Sir!"

"Roll call and casualties, if you would."

"Sir. Already done, Sir. Two horses lost, Sir. Trooper Smith 898 has a sprained ankle and wrist when he was unhorsed. And you, Sir."

Harry looked puzzled and shrugged. "Carry on, Corporal Major."

"Very good, Sir." The NCO saluted and turned. "You, you and you," he yelled, pointing to three troopers who had failed to make themselves scarce. "Lookouts. Anything moves, report on the double."

Life in a cavalry regiment quickly returned to normal, with the senior NCOs running the show, as it should be, as it had ever been since the days of the Norman Conquest.

Harry reported to Shackleton immediately and snapped up a bloody salute, his fingers already sticky with drying, congealing German blood. "Any prisoners, Haig-Mallory?"

"None, Sir. A handful managed to run before we retired. I estimate their casualties at ninety killed or wounded. We can retrieve the wounded for interrogation if needed."

"They'll only slow us down." He thought for a moment. "Not a bad afternoon's work."

"For a bunch of first timers, not at all bad, Sir. I can hardly believe what we accomplished, the damage we did, without losing a single man. The power of surprise and the cavalry, I expect, Sir."

Shackleton remained silent for several moments. "I saw what you did out there, Haig-Mallory. Not only what you did to the enemy, but for Merryweather. You probably saved his life. No question a Hun marksman would have picked him off if you'd left him out there. We're going to need all our officers before this is over. I'm putting you up for a medal."

"Sir…?"

"I don't know which. It won't be the big one. I'll see what I can get for you. The new one, the Military Cross, if I can." He pointed at a gash on Harry's thigh. "You're uniform's a mess. Get it cleaned up and get that wound seen to by the MO and wash the blood off your hands and face while you're at it. You look perfectly ghastly."

Harry peered down at the blood on his hands and thigh. "I hadn't noticed. It must have been a bayonet. I should take more care. It's ruined a perfectly good pair of breeches."

"Have your soldier-servant take care of the repairs."

Harry opened his mouth to reply when the pain hit. He clamped it quickly shut with a grimace. "The MO, you said, Sir. A good idea. A stitch or two. If there's nothing else pressing at the moment?"

*

In the makeshift Headquarters tent that evening, the assembled officers heard the order to move out. Le Cateau was the word. That was the where of it. The when? Nobody knew for sure. The purpose? Hold the front line on the old Roman road from Le Cateau to Cambrai. Be the eyes and ears of the infantry. Seek, find and harass the enemy with ambushes and sneak attacks at every opportunity – charge, cut, thrust and retire. Avoid dug-in German positions and their machine guns. Hit and run.

Run. "Not with this leg," Harry muttered. A spasm of pain lanced through his thigh and throbbed with each heartbeat. He decided not to put weight on it. In spite of the dozen stitches it took to close the gash he refused to use a cane or take anything for the pain. He told himself it would be better in a day or two, though at that moment he didn't believe it. If he had to run, at least it would be on horseback, not on foot. He spared a thought for the poor bloody infantry.

*

The following day rumour reached Harry: they were to abandon France and leave it to the French to carry the fight alone. When that rumour proved false they heard of plans to build a stockade, a redoubt, and fight to the last man. Then came the renewed call to head for the Channel ports. Then to concentrate their defenses north of Paris, on the Marne, and repulse the German advance within sight of the spires of Notre Dame Cathedral and the Eiffel Tower.

Colonel Shackleton called an impromptu meeting. "The rumours we have all heard, gentlemen, and which are far more intriguing and interesting than the truth, are, like the vast majority of rumours, false." He looked for relief in the anxious faces of his officers and found little. "We have orders to continue our sorties at squadron strength against vanguards of the enemy infantry. We will probe, attack and vanish into the woods before the Germans have a chance to mount any serious counterattack. In other words, all the stuff we've bloody well trained to do all these years."

The regiment followed orders, but always retreating, towards Paris and away from the English Channel. Mile after mile they fought a little war against the Germans who had no answer to the cavalry's tactics. Ambush, kill, demoralize and disappear. Repeat until ordered to stop. Nothing personal, Fritz, but rather you die for your country than I for mine. In the days following their first charge they lost not another man or horse. Some of the men regarded themselves as invincible. The more superstitious crossed their fingers. A few prayed.

*

On the first Saturday in September, with Paris barely thirty miles behind them, the German bombardment began. Well to the rear of the front lines, Harry finished his mug of tea and evaporated milk under the shelter of the large canvas awning that served as regiment headquarters.

"It's make or break this time," Shackleton said. "Let's hope it's not a repeat of Custer's Last Stand."

"We're ready as soon as they drop the flag," he told Shackleton. "We haven't fired a shot in days and the men are a little testy at having to spit polish their leather while the rest of the Expeditionary Force and the French take it on the chin."

"Our turn will come, Haig-Mallory." Shackleton put his mug down on a folding camp table and lit a cigarette. He sucked in the first drag and exhaled with his eyes closed. Harry saw the slight tremor in his CO's hands and the deep lines around his eyes and mouth. The obligations and the strain of command, Harry knew, took their toll on senior officers in a way the lowest private soldier would never understand. "Today, tomorrow or next year. We won't go down without a damn good fight."

"The French won't take kindly if we run for Calais, Sir."

Shackleton regarded Harry closely. "There will be no running for the Channel Ports. They're cut off. If we lose this battle," he said in a slow and measured tone, "we lose the war. The Empire will collapse like a leaky balloon and I suspect our way of life will change irrevocably, probably forever. Whitehall and Berlin will come to an accommodation, which won't sit well with the French. It's our job to make sure it doesn't happen."

Harry looked thoughtful for a moment. "The Hussars won't let England down, Sir. England can count on it. We have never surrendered, and we never shall."

"So there's no misunderstanding, Haig-Mallory, there's no contingency plan in case things go against us. We're here till the end."

"England's worth fighting for. So is France."

"You have to admit though, the Hun may be a savage soldier, but he's not excitable like the Frenchies. He'll give you a brutal, but honest fight. Not like the Boer in the last one."

"You'd know more about that than I, Sir."

"Take it from me, the Hun's brave, he's dedicated and he's disciplined. He won't turn tail and run. You can't trust our allies any further than you can see them with both hands on the table. Sometimes I wonder if we're fighting the right enemy."

"The French say we're only here still because our line of retreat to the Channel's cut off, otherwise we would have turned tail and run long ago."

"Not true on either count," Shackleton snapped, but his voice failed to carry conviction. "Anyway, how do you know what the French think?"

"I read French at Oxford, Sir. I speak it passably well. For an Englishman. My stepmother is Swiss, as was my mother."

"No harm in speaking French. As long as you don't become a Frog yourself."

"No chance of that, Sir. French beer is terrible, even worse than German muck."

"Damn good wine, though."

"Yes, Sir. Damn good wine."

*

Stand to, half an hour before dawn on the fifth day of the battle, saw the men bleary-eyed, sleep-deprived and irritable. Some shaved their leathery, furrowed faces in the pre-dawn dark. Most did not bother. They preferred to wait for the squadron corporal major to bellow, "Never in my life have I seen such a slovenly bunch of idlers and shirkers who have the audacity to call themselves professional soldiers." This usually preceded breakfast. And breakfast was still an hour or more away, after stand down if they were lucky and the Germans didn't attack again.

"Corporal major can't fire us all," one wag grumbled.

"He can fire me any time. I'm sick of this. It's not fun anymore."

"It'd leave him fighting the Huns on his own."

"I'd like to see him try it," said someone a bit further down the line.

"I'll hold his coat," offered another, holding his arms out like he was a bullfighter.

"And I want a front row seat in the stalls."

"Look to your front you horrible little man," a corporal of horse snarled, "or I'll jump on you from a fucking great height and wrap my fucking rifle around your miserable fucking neck. Cut the cackle. You sound like a bunch of bloody hens in the hen house, and about as fucking useless as a fucking Frenchman in a whorehouse."

And so it went, up and down the line until, with the sun fully up for half an hour, the order came to stand down. It now seemed unlikely the Germans would interfere with the start of their day, and even less likely their own generals might throw a spanner in the works with the order to advance before breakfast. All morning and into the afternoon the regiment stood down. The men nervously pissed their tea into sumps in trenches if they couldn't make it to the stinking latrine in time. And all the while they waited for the call to advance to the front line. Or stay where they were. Or retreat.

The call came in the evening, after the second stand to and stand down of the day. Grumbling at having their beauty sleep interrupted by inconsiderate officers, they joined four columns of British infantry and artillery in their march toward the River Marne. As night fell, they moved through the reserve line of French *poilus* in their faded baggy red trousers and blue jackets with both sides spitting and cussing at each other,

When they crossed the river at noon the following day, they found only a few weary German prisoners-of-war guarded by wary, silent French soldiers. The line seemed strangely quiet to Harry as he advanced on horseback at the head of his squadron. "The Huns are pulling back," came the word. Morale picked up. The clouds of dust the cavalry kicked up seemed less dry and bitter to the men. Whenever they rode through French positions, brass jingling and leather squeaking, the *poilus* greeted them with enthusiasm, if not exactly as conquering heroes, then at least with slightly less distrust.

"How far?" became the question of the moment.

"Berlin?" one trooper suggested.

"Beyond Reams, or something, so I heard," said another. He looked around at the dumb faces of his comrades. "What? I don't fucking know how to pronounce it any more than you, you daft twat."

"Is it in Germany?"

"Must be. Sounds Hunnish."

As Harry discovered, *Beyond Reims* was accurate. The Germans dug in on the heavily wooded crest of a ridge on the far side of the River Aisne. "Any sensible man would take one look at their defenses and decide this might be a good time to start peace talks," Harry said to Shackleton when they established their encampment later that night.

"Sensible men are in short supply in Whitehall," Shackleton replied. "And presumably Berlin. But don't say I said so." He slipped his field glasses into the leather case and turned his horse towards their makeshift camp.

That night, in the solitude of his tent, Harry's thoughts turned to Athena, back in America, and realized with a guilty start he hadn't spared her more than a passing thought in the rush of war, deployment in the field and their first battle. Then the retreat from Mons and the near annihilation of the French and British armies on the Marne. That had been too close for comfort and how they had been spared any involvement was beyond him. In the quiet of the night he only now realized how tense he had been since their arrival in France; that his mind had been focused on the here and now, in particular the imperative to staying alive.

He wondered if this was a taste of things to come, pushing Athena to the back of his mind while he concentrated on his duties. But one day, he promised, one day he would return to England and marry her. When the war was over. And the way things were going, it didn't look like that would be by Christmas, unless the Germans had other ideas and they could all go home.

He interlaced his fingers and placed them behind his head while he stared at the canvas above his head flapping occasionally in the light breeze. He heard the stamp of sentries' feet and their soft calls of "All quiet, Corporal." He closed his eyes and thought of Athena, beautiful Athena, and of all that had transpired in the turbulent two months since they first met in Washington.

- 19 -

# 3. ATHENA

"Mr. Forrest Bryan and Miss Athena Fenhagen."

Harry turned his head to peer down the receiving line at the newest set of invitees to the British Embassy in Washington: Two more Americans, he had no doubt, destined to pass through his well-ordered life as casually as pebbles tossed onto the mirrored surface of a mill pond. And like the pebbles, equally without question, they would leave scarcely a ripple in his life as they sank without trace, which would suit him just fine. Out of the corner of one eye he glimpsed a beautiful young woman in a white ball gown. She seemed to be accompanied by a balding, bland-faced man in immaculate evening dress, a man who affected a studied, bored look as he waited with evident impatience to be introduced to Sir Cecil Spring Rice, the British Ambassador.

"Athena Fenhagen, of Cleveland, Ohio, Mr. Ambassador," Harry heard her say as she curtsied. The British Ambassador took the offered hand and kissed the fingertips.

"My wife, Lady Florence," the ambassador said, nodding to the woman at his side. Athena smiled and curtseyed for the introduction, then it was the First Secretary's turn to introduce her to the next person in line. "Major General, Sir Neville Trevor-Bailey," the First Secretary said. The major general bowed stiffly, little more than a stoop of his shoulders and a slight nod of his head. "I'm the Military Attaché here at the Embassy. May I present Captain, the Honourable Hereward Haig-Mallory of the King's Imperial Hussars? Captain Haig-Mallory is my aide-de-camp."

Harry held the offered hand with delicacy. He elevated his gaze from her elbow length, white kid gloves to her off-the-shoulder white silk gown and her delicate pendant, diamond and pearl earrings. He took in the matching diamond and pearl necklace that rested on the firm, pale skin above the modest swell of her breasts. A dainty filigree of gold wire and tiny pearls held her dark brown hair in place where her dresser had swept it up to the top of her head. A hint of exotic perfume reached him and imprinted itself indelibly in his memory. He admired the light sprinkle of freckles on her cheeks on either side of her small, pert nose that turned up ever so slightly at the tip. Her clear blue eyes seemed to return his smile but surely a woman as beautiful as she could only be mocking him. Nevertheless, he knew he was a lost cause. She was no pebble and he no longer a placid mill pond. He held his breath. The heat rose from the back of his neck to his face as it always did when he was nervous. He decided to do his utmost to convince Miss Athena Fenhagen, of Cleveland, Ohio, that she could complicate his calm and predictable life any time she chose. And now would be a good time to start.

"I'm glad you are able to celebrate Midsummer's Eve with us, Miss Fenhagen," Harry said in as formal a tone as he could manage. He found himself barely able to contain the nervous stammer that threatened to turn him into a gibbering wreck and render the lie to his outward polish. "I hope you will do me the honour of placing my name on your dance card." The last words came out in a rush, but he congratulated himself for not stuttering in the presence of such beauty.

He saw Athena scrutinize his immaculate scarlet and black mess uniform, cut and fitted by John Jones, his military tailor in Saville Row. He could see his face reflected in his boots, and he'd stood extra close to his razor before he'd left his room that evening. He accepted he was no classic Greek god but prayed nonetheless that he had left a good first impression on her. He tried to read her thoughts, to find out if he had scraped a pass mark. Or if he would find himself humbled and insignificant in the presence of this Aphrodite. A single glance of appraisal from her unsmiling lips told him he had failed.

Then Athena smiled. She averted her eyes for a moment as she flicked her gaze on Forrest. He saw her wrinkle her nose, very slightly. She cocked her head and regarded Harry with a raised eyebrow. "I have only just arrived, Captain Haig-Mallory, and my card is empty."

"That is hard to believe."

She glanced to her side. "I believe we are holding up the line, Captain."

Harry realized he still held Athena's hand. With reluctance he bowed and released it. She moved on without another word. He wondered if a hint of a smile flirted with her lips before it vanished. Could it have been an invitation to dance with her more than the once required to fulfill a social obligation? How could it be? In her sight he must be as  insignificant as he was fifteen years ago on his first day at Marlborough School. A goddess like her must think him as enticing as boiled tripe with Brussels sprouts. And as lowly as something phlegmy typically found in a Petrie dish in the biology lab at school.

His attention followed her as she made her way to the end of the receiving line. The First Secretary cleared his throat and announced, "Mr. Forrest Bryan," in a loud voice. Harry's mind jerked back to the present and he shook the offered hand. "The son of the Secretary of State," Harry said. "An honour indeed."

"Here in place of my father, and Miss Fenhagen's escort for the evening." Not a trace of warmth accompanied either the forced smile or his voice. Without another word, Bryan followed Athena down the line towards the ballroom, its drapes pale blue and gold silk to match the watered silk wall coverings. Crystal stemware glittered in the light shed by the electric chandeliers. Silver gilt cutlery gleamed. Blue and gold-rimmed, fine bone china place settings sat on spotless white napery. Harry watched Bryan seat Athena at a table and immediately beckon a waiter. He clamped his jaw shut and wrestled his attention from Athena Fenhagen and the aroma of freshly baked bridge rolls to the next couple in the receiving line.

Try as he might to catch a glimpse of her, he did not see Athena again until after dinner and the speeches. When the dance orchestra struck up the first bars of a Strauss waltz, Harry edged towards her. "May I have the honour, Miss Fenhagen?" He forced the words out with his bow in the hope that she might not notice his nervous stutter or see his face turn the colour of his mess jacket. She offered her hand and lowered her gaze.

"You dance well, Captain Haig-Mallory," she said as they swung through the second corner of the waltz. "Hereward, I believe Sir Neville said. What an unusual name." She clutched his arm as they glided through the third corner and failed to relax her grip as he guided her through the next steps.

"Named after Hereward the Wake," he said, once they reached a series of steps that required less concentration on his part. "A Saxon outlaw who led rebellions against the Norman invaders. Possibly a template for Robin Hood. You would deem him a patriot, naturally." He smiled.

"Naturally." She moved closer. Harry adjusted the position of his hand on her waist to accommodate her unexpected and welcome proximity.

"I am known to all and sundry as Haig-Mallory, and as Harry to family and a few close friends. And, I hope, to you."

"Captain Hereward Haig-Mallory. Harry."

"Of the King's Imperial Hussars." He relaxed a little now that the ice was broken and he could navigate his way through the floes with a little more certainty. "We are one of the oldest English cavalry regiments and part of the king's personal bodyguard. We're quite famous, at least in England."

"No doubt, or you would hardly be in Washington. And it's Athena, if you intend to dance with me more than once. Miss Fenhagen makes me sound like a maiden aunt. I have one of those. I do not wish to be reminded."

"Athena," he repeated. "The Greek goddess of something, but I can't remember what."

"The daughter of Zeus and the goddess of many things, including wisdom and war."

"Appropriate, I'm sure."

"Of the Cleveland, Ohio Fenhagens, Randolph and Minerva," she continued, as if Harry hadn't interrupted. "Not as grand as the Haig-Mallorys, no doubt, but the equal to any man, as my father would say, if not better."

"Minerva. I'm on firmer ground there. The Roman equivalent of Athena."

"Correct. And what does Captain, the Honourable Hereward Haig-Mallory do at the British Embassy?" Athena lingered in his arms at the conclusion of the dance while she waited for an answer.

"I'm aide-de-camp to the Military Attaché."

"So he said. Which means?"

"I'm his general factotum."

Athena arched her eyebrows.

"In true army fashion I do what I am told, when, where and how, and I don't ask why. I fetch and carry, and try not to forget things, such as where the Attaché left his spectacles, or his attaché case, or the name of the next Very Important Visitor. I've no one to boss around and no real decisions to make. I'm a sort of household servant, only at the Embassy. In an army uniform. Very ordinary, really. Quite menial in fact."

"You're funny, Captain Haig-Mallory. I always believed Englishmen were insufferable bores."

"So you've met my father." Harry laughed. The orchestra struck up the first notes of a Lehar waltz. "Shall we dance? If your card is not yet full, of course," He held his arms out.

"Two in a row, Captain Haig-Mallory? Why, that is somewhat presumptuous."

He frowned. "I apologize. I.., er..., I shouldn't hog you to myself." He silently cursed the return of his nervous stutter and his red ears.

"However, it's early in the evening and I find my card still has gaps," she said without either a glance at her card or an attempt to move from the dance floor. "Forrest, my escort this evening, seems to have deserted me in favour of the card table." She nodded in the direction of a foursome playing cards in a corner near the bar. "I can't complain. It allows me to pursue my own interests unhindered."

"Mr. Bryan?" Harry held his breath while he waited for a reply.

She wrinkled her nose, this time without any attempt to hide her evident distaste. "Forrest is a dozen years older than me. Our fathers are acquainted. He stands to become enormously wealthy and probably very powerful in the government one day. And he's as boring as a bath sponge."

In spite of her frosty tone of voice, her glance led Harry to believe his name might be on the race card for the Athena Fenhagen maiden handicap sweepstakes. And he would gladly give anything to take on the role of her bath sponge. One glance at the son of the American Secretary of State convinced Harry the bookmakers would not handicap too severely his own chances at wooing the beautiful Athena Fenhagen. If she were inclined to be wooed by a lowly captain.

At the conclusion of the dance she rested her hand lightly on the three pips of a captain on Harry's lapel, then brushed his single row of miniature medals. "How did you earn these, My Lord?"

"Not for doing anything courageous, I assure you. And it's my father who is My Lord, except to family. I'm plain, the Honourable Hereward, second son of a Cornish admiral who, through neither fault nor merit of his own, inherited an earldom. I'm unlikely to inherit either the title or the fortune. Forrest is obviously way out of my league in every respect."

Athena put a finger to Harry's lips. "Hush," she whispered. "Don't worry about Forrest. I'm sure he's quite glad there's someone to take me off his hands while he plays poker."

Harry looked stunned. "But…," he managed before he remembered to close his mouth. He cocked his head. "Do you fox trot?"

"Certainly. I hoped you might ask." They stepped into the dance which, to gather from the few couples on the dance floor, was not as popular as one might have been led to believe. "As you may have guessed," she said, "it's not Forrest's dashing good looks that cause some women to swoon. It's his access to power and, of course, his money. I believe he knows I'm immune to those twin charms."

When the orchestra took a break, Harry escorted Athena to her table. Bryan looked up from his card hand and gave Athena an imperious, dismissive wave. "Don't mind me, Athena. Help yourself to Champagne." He returned to the examination of his hand and the pot on the table top. He played his hand and raked the pot towards him.

Bryan glanced around the table of men, leaned back in his chair and squinted over his shoulder at Harry. "Haig-Mallory, isn't it?"

Harry nodded.

"I'm not much of a dancer. Can't stand it, to be honest. A waste of time. Vertical substitute, I call it, and a poor substitute for the real thing." His companions guffawed. A look of horror spread across Harry's face as the blood rushed to the surface. He touched Athena's elbow and led her away from the table.

"What an appalling thing to say!" Harry lowered his voice but failed to hide his abhorrence at Bryan's remark.

Athena shrugged. "That's Forrest all over. Unlike his father, he'll never make it as a diplomat."

Harry shuddered. "He shows no regard for your sensibilities."

Athena laughed. "You sound like something out of Jane Austen or the Brontë sisters."

"I bow to your greater judgement on the subject, not having read either. Although," he added hastily, "I'm led to believe their heroines displayed good manners, which is more than I can say for Mr. Bryan."

"It would be bad manners to discuss Forrest behind his back. However, I'll be quite forthright. We do not have a relationship of any sort, least of all one which I believe he implied."

Harry's face burned.

"There's no need to look so embarrassed, Harry. I may be from Cleveland, but I am not naïve. I attended Vassar."

Harry looked blank.

"A liberal arts college? I spent four years there unchaperoned. Do I shock you?"

"I don't know what to say."

"We American women are not shrinking violets. I continue a long tradition of women who know what we want and fight for what's right. In short, I'm your average twentieth century American woman."

"You will never be average, Athena. Not to me"

Athena blushed and fanned her face with her hand. "How long will you be at the Embassy?"

"It's a one-year secondment. I return to England in August."

Athena squinted at him. Harry didn't know what to make of the inquisitorial look.

"Would it be possible to see you again before I leave?" he stammered. "I have at most two more months in Washington."

She studied him for several seconds as if he were a chloroformed moth pinned to a collector's board. Harry took a step back. Failure stared him in the face. Athena stuck her hands on her hips.

"Captain Haig-Mallory, if you hadn't asked, I should have been forced to make enquiries of my own, starting at your reception desk. A single, unaccompanied lady enquiring after a certain Captain Hereward Haig-Mallory, requesting an appointment to see him, possibly alone, might cause diplomatic eyebrows to twitch."

Harry let out a loud exhale. "But not enough of a diplomatic incident to cause the recall of both ambassadors, I hope. Or to send a gunboat up the Potomac."

"Your lot did that once, a hundred years ago. Don't think we've forgotten."

"I remember something about the incident from my history books. If I recall it required a lot of white paint on the Presidential mansion to cover up the fire damage, and the truce signed on American soil."

"Touché. However, if you force me to go through with my threat it might possibly result in the early recall of the aide-de-camp to the Military Attaché." She offered a smile and half turned her head. "I'm in Washington until the end of the month, then back to Cleveland. My hotel, the Martha Washington, is for women only."

"Of course."

"So perhaps we might meet elsewhere, in public maybe, where we wouldn't gather unwanted attention."

"For afternoon tea, perhaps."

"Something like that."

"The Hay-Adams Hotel? Four o'clock this coming Sunday? They hold a tea dance there. If you're not otherwise engaged, of course."

"If I find myself otherwise engaged, I shall disengage myself," Athena said. "And now I'm about to get the essential and perfectly timed headache.

Perhaps you would be kind enough to take me to Forrest's table so I can have him arrange for his driver to take me back to my hotel?"

"Of course." Harry hesitated. "I can't say I'd be delighted to escort you to Mr. Bryan's table. That couldn't be further from the truth. However, I shall do as you request and languish alone for the rest of the evening." He kissed the offered gloved fingers.

"Are you sure you've never read Jane Austen or the Brontë Sisters, Harry."

"Quite. I hope they're not as boring as Sir Walter Scott's novels."

"Those appeal to a different reader. One with a great deal of time on his hands and little better to occupy it. Though I gather he was a favourite of Queen Victoria."

"That may explain something, but I've no idea what."

Harry escorted Athena to Bryan's table of ill-mannered boors. "Thank you for the dance, Miss Fenhagen," he said, as he relinquished the hand he had held since the end of their last dance. "I do hope to see you again should you have occasion to attend on the Embassy."

Athena smiled and curtseyed. "Should the occasion arise, Captain Haig-Mallory," she replied in a cool voice, and turned to Forrest Bryan to ask for the motor to be sent round and take her back to her hotel.

For once Harry found himself in uncharted waters, and what might happen next, he could only guess. What he did know, however, was that he was under starter's orders in the Athena Fenhagen maiden handicap sweepstakes, and he thanked his lucky stars he was a damn good rider. He had a week in which to press his case and hopefully persuade her to extend her stay in Washington a little longer.

As he watched Forrest escort Athena to the front doors of the Embassy, he made a mental note to look up Jane Austen and the Brontë Sisters and find something of theirs to read before Sunday.

# 4. THE ARCHDUKE

Forrest's chauffeur delivered Athena to the front door of Martha Washington Hotel. Instead of asking for the key to her room at the reception desk, Athena chose a deep-cushioned armchair in the hotel lobby. She took a cigarette from a pack in her small evening reticule, placed it in a long, retractable, ebony and silver holder and struck a match from the matchbook on the table in front of her. While she smoked, she debated her next move. A taxi to the Hay-Adams would only take a few minutes, but would Harry be there? Or would he still be at the Embassy, debriefing — wasn't that the word they use in the army? — the high and low points of the ball with fellow staff members? Or if he wasn't required, could he have snagged some little serving girl from the kitchen staff only too flattered to be bedded by an English Lord? No. Please, not the latter. That wouldn't be very gentlemanly but, at least, according to Forrest, altogether perfectly normal and accepted behaviour among the British aristocracy. Which, she suspected, was little different from most American men of wealth. She shut her eyes and screwed them tight. She tried to imagine Harry with a scullery maid or cook's helper in a small, locked room at the back of the Embassy kitchen, receiving what he no doubt considered his due. Her imagination drew a blank. Maybe he wasn't like that at all.

She contemplated the taxi again. It would hardly be proper for her to arrive at Harry's hotel, this late at night, unaccompanied and unannounced. She realized then she had no idea where Harry lived. He had mentioned the Hay-Adams hotel, but that was no guarantee he stayed there. The British didn't have an army barracks, so she figured he probably lived at the Embassy. She could hardly return there to make enquiries at the reception desk, if it were still open. Even less could she ask to be directed to Captain Haig-Mallory's rooms, where she would find him alone and throw herself at him. He would think her a trollop, a hussy, a courtesan — once he had had his fill of her. And when she discovered just how inexperienced she was in the arts of the bedroom he might cancel his invitation to tea on Sunday afternoon.

She wondered what he looked like in ordinary clothes rather than the formal, glamorous uniform he wore for the ball. In his everyday army uniform. Or in civilian clothes. Or better still, without clothes at all. She suppressed a grin at the thought. Delicious, she admitted. She examined the lipstick smear she had left on the cigarette holder. Harry hadn't kissed her. He hadn't tried to kiss her. Hadn't even suggested it might be on his mind, so now her lipstick was a film on a length of ebony rather than on his lips. "What a waste," she whispered, then glanced around the empty lobby to see who might have heard. Only the night manager, a woman, stood behind the reception desk with her back to Athena, ignoring her. She stubbed out her cigarette and discarded the butt in the circular ashtray of heavy green glass on the table. The hotel management disapproved of smoking, and of women who smoked. As if to emphasize their point, the hotel rooms came without ashtrays, although they left matchbooks and ashtrays in the lobby. How thoughtful of them, Athena thought. She stuck her tongue out at the woman's back

She decided to go to the library in the morning and do some research on Harry's family. She was sure someone there would be happy to help. Once she had been able to confirm that he was who he said he was — as if the Embassy would mislead her — she would be able to take whatever steps she thought prudent to continue their relationship. Or walk away before she got in too deep, none the worse for the experience. She stopped for a moment. Relationship? What relationship? Four hours at an Embassy ball without even a hint of a kiss can hardly constitute a relationship by anyone's definition. She snorted. At least Forrest had tried to kiss her. But not at the Embassy. That would not be proper. Not in public and certainly not as the son of the Secretary of State.

She sighed. Four hours! You've known him four hours. What are you thinking? She stopped in mid-stride as she headed for the elevator. She knew what she was thinking. If the research at the library went well, she could wait until Sunday for the payoff. Her father's expression. She got in the elevator. The gate rattled as it closed behind her and the elevator took her at a snail's pace to the fourth floor.

She undressed slowly until she stood naked in her room. She retrieved her nightgown from beneath her pillow and held it against her body while she examined herself in the full-length mirror on her wardrobe door. She let the nightgown slip slowly down her front until her shoulders were fully bared to the lamplight. Then a little more until her breasts were exposed. She let go of the nightgown and regarded the pile of white cotton at her feet as if it were an alien thing, devoid of form or shape or known purpose. She stepped over it — the chamber maid would pick it up when she tidied the room and made up the bed in the morning.

Between the cool sheets, her mind swirled in time with the waltzes she and Harry had shared. She saw them by a moonlit, dappled sea that lapped quietly at their feet over warm sand. Then they were in an English castle with battlements. And a moat. Empty suits of armour in the oak paneled hall watched them make love on a tiger skin on the flagstone floor in front of a blazing log fire. They were always naked and entwined. Their bodies glistened from their urgent lovemaking. It didn't matter where, as long as it was with him.

Athena tossed and turned in bed, unable to get Harry out of her mind. As long as her thoughts were glued to him, sleep evaded her for hours. In the dark she couldn't see the clock, or her watch, but she knew it had to be past three o'clock. She fell asleep sometime before dawn with images of their lovemaking burned into her mind.

*

Harry lounged in a leather armchair towards the rear of the spacious, ornate lobby of the Hay-Adams Hotel, listening in to the buzz of the men's conversation around him. The assassination of the Austrian Archduke, Franz Ferdinand that morning seemed to the topic of the afternoon. Hardly surprising really, he thought. The news had arrived by cable, wasn't twelve hours old yet and it was mostly speculation anyway. It would probably be in all the newspapers tomorrow and on the bottom of the birdcage by Tuesday. He had been called into the Embassy that morning after breakfast and briefed on what they knew, which was precious little.

The Archduke was dead. So was his wife, both assassinated by a Serbian anarchist by all counts. So what? It was common knowledge the Balkans were nothing but a festering boil in need of lancing. Every nation and religion in that cesspit loathed and distrusted the others, had done for more generations than most people could count, but this could hardly be the scalpel that would solve the problem, could it? Why on earth would the Archduke visit that hellhole in the first place? And take his wife with him, for heaven's sake? Asking for trouble. And he found it. What could he expect? Served him right. Given that the situation had nothing to do with Britain, in Harry's opinion the briefing had been a complete waste of time.

He lit a cigarette and leaned back in his armchair. He glanced at the clock. Still a few minutes to go until Athena arrived. If she chose to arrive at all. An attack of nerves gnawed at his entrails. By now he had convinced himself that she had come to her senses, had second thoughts and stayed in her hotel. He had had no contact with her since the ball. And of course it wouldn't be proper for her to come unaccompanied. But she'd agreed. It might as well have been her suggestion.

Dressed in his Number Two khaki uniform with gold braid looped through his epaulette and medal ribbons on his chest, he stood out from the other patrons in the lobby. The crowd of mostly men wore black frock coats and starched white shirt fronts. The hatted, older women dressed in dove grey, lilac or black. He shouldn't be hard to spot, he thought. The moment he finished the cigarette and stubbed it out he saw Athena enter the hotel through the main door. He rose to greet her, waved discreetly and made his way across the lobby. Athena took his offered hand and held it while Harry kissed her fingertips.

"I hope I haven't kept you waiting," she said.

"Not at all. Tea?"

"Which is why I'm here, if you recall, Captain Haig-Mallory. And maybe a dance or two?"

"And afterwards perhaps a stroll?"

"Two minds with but a single thought." She laughed and wrinkled her nose. He decided he loved the way she wrinkled her nose and was about to comment when a waiter approached.

"Captain Haig-Mallory? This way, please. We have your usual table reserved."

"The waiter seemed to know you," Athena hissed when they were seated. "Do you come here often with other ladies?"

"I have a room here."

Athena glared at him and set her mouth in a narrow, prim line. This isn't going too well, she thought. Maybe it would be best to duck out now, rather than waste an afternoon with someone who turned out to be a charlatan.

"Sorry. Badly phrased, but true," Harry said hastily. "There's no room at the Embassy. Hence the room here. The hotel is conveniently placed for the Embassy and junior officers don't rate a suite. The powers that be set in authority over us have to remind us of our lowly status within the hierarchy and keep us in our place. And so, yes, I frequently dine here. Alone."

"I see." She relaxed her school ma'am look and the frost thawed somewhat.

"They make one of the better cups of tea in Washington. The Darjeeling is especially good, as is the Earl Grey…"

*

"You said the other evening you're the son of a Cornish admiral," Athena said, as they strolled past the White House after tea and several dances. She didn't let on that her research at the library had confirmed this snippet of his family history. "I'd love to visit Cornwall one day." With one hand she held her parasol over her head to keep the sun off and swept the hem of her sky-blue skirt up and away from the dusty sidewalk with the other. The movement revealed a glimpse of silk stockinged ankle that lasted a little longer than necessary, but she made sure it was long enough for Harry to notice. A tease, she knew. An invitation even. But only if he proved worthy, which she had yet to determine.

Harry turned and studied Athena, close up and in daylight. The woman at his side was more graceful and lissome than any he had known, far more beautiful than the one he had held in his arms and danced with only five nights ago. And he had thought then that there could not be another woman in the world more beautiful than she. Her smile radiated warmth and humour. Her pale skin possessed an alabaster translucence. Her dark hair shone in the late afternoon sunlight and her blue eyes sparkled beneath the wide brim of her spring hat. He drew in a deep breath.

"You sh... sh... shall, if you wish." He fell silent, cursed the nervous stammer beneath his breath, and counted the cracks in the paving stones as they walked. Athena did not interrupt his study of Washington's sidewalks. "I've known you for five days," he finally said, and exhaled loudly. "And I know with absolute certainty I don't want to leave Washington without you."

"This is a bit quick and unexpected, Harry." She stopped, turned to face him and twirled her parasol slowly over her head. "As much as I'd like to visit Cornwall, I have to consider my options. Imagine — an unmarried lady crosses the Atlantic without a chaperone in order to visit an unmarried gentleman at his home in England. Scandalous! It would create an uproar, even in Cleveland."

"But still not enough for gunboats up the Thames or the Potomac, I hope."

"Not quite that scandalous. Not even questions in Congress or Parliament, but eyebrow-raising at the very least."

"But your parents...?"

"My parents were broad-minded enough to let me spend four years at University and the past four months in Washington on my own. I assured them they could rely on my sense of good judgement."

"I see." Harry hoped against hope she had indeed exercised good judgement. At least up until now. Though that did not explain her stepping out with him this afternoon, alone.

"My mother's always had the grace never to ask what I'd been up to at Vassar, though she could probably guess. She's never actually said anything, but I think she might have been a bit modern in her day. Even bold. It's hard to think that about one's parents, don't you think? Squidgy-squirmy." She didn't give Harry time for thought or a reply. "And if I did go to England, my father would merely caution me to be on the lookout for charlatans, rakes and other assorted rogues…"

"… But not cavalry officers."

"Especially cavalry officers, and to avoid them all as if they carried bubonic plague."

"Perhaps you could travel with your parents. Or at least with your mother."

"Why? Have her lead me astray? That I can do without any help. I'm alone with you right now, unchaperoned, aren't I? The first option is far more adventurous. And no witnesses." She grinned wickedly. "When did you have in mind?"

Harry did not trust himself to speak. Athena shot him a penetrating stare. "Or have I misunderstood your intentions? You are asking me to marry you, aren't you? Not something less conventional? What would my parents say if they thought that was what was on your mind?"

Harry swallowed audibly before he nodded dumbly. He gathered his wits slowly, trying to calm the quaver he was sure would find its way into his voice at any moment. If only he could stop his knees shaking. "We only met for a few hours on Tuesday evening," he said.

Athena's eyes flashed angrily. True, she thought, and very quick even for these days, but also thought better of voicing her opinion. She folded her parasol and drove the tip onto the sidewalk. This, she thought, was going downhill faster than the Wells Fargo stage trying to outrun a bunch of bandits. Perhaps Harry was a weakling after all. All mouth and no pants. But he was so damned handsome it would be a waste not to find out which he was. Still, he did infuriate her with his shillyshallying. And his nervous stammer. She jammed a fist against her hip. "So I did misunderstand what I took to be noble intentions, but which I now understand to be no more than… than… a ploy to gain my trust and affection before you discard me like a dishrag in favour of… of some inbred English lady earl." She snorted. "Which are you beneath your civilized façade, Captain Haig-Mallory — charlatan, rake or rogue?"

Harry took a step back. "N… Neither." He gathered himself. "I mean none. Please hear me out."

"I'm waiting." She glared at him and pouted.

"I knew immediately I set eyes on you I wanted more than anything in the world to marry you. Right there on the Embassy dance floor if we could have found a minister or whatever it takes to get married in America."

"You expect me to believe you?"

"Yes. Because it's the truth."

Athena breathed heavily. "Three hours, four at the most on Tuesday, and not two more today. And on that basis, you want to marry me?"

Harry gulped. "Yes. Without question."

"You don't know anything about me. I could be a congenital idiot for all you know."

"You can't be. You went to Vassar."

"So I said. Did you check?"

"No, Absolutely not. I had no reason to."

"A good thing too. You can trust me, Harry. Or would you feel happier hiring a Pinkerton's detective to follow me and check my bona fides. Huh?"

Harry spluttered incoherently.

"And by the same token I know virtually nothing about you," she added darkly.

"There's little more to tell. I'm really quite ordinary. What you see is pretty well what you get. I confess to occasional bouts of inertia whenever someone's not looking, and I'm not particularly ambitious. If those are faults, I plead guilty."

"There are worse faults. An inability to sit still and ruthless ambition would be quite off-putting."

"I know all I need to know about you. You could be a foundling, an orphan for all I care. You are everything I could possibly desire. You're the most beautiful woman I've ever seen, let alone met. You're charming, witty, intelligent, educated. And beguiling."

Athena harrumphed. "Only beguiling? Not bewitching?"

"Both."

Her anger melted as fast as a sherbet in August. "You're funny." She laughed.

"What's so funny about a chap falling in love with a beautiful woman, even if it is a bit quick?"

"Only an idiot believes in love at first sight." She hesitated. "Then I met you." She let her hand fall on his sleeve. "I knew as soon as I saw you in the receiving line you were the one for me. I guess that makes me an idiot with a degree from Vassar after all."

"And I was certain you were the only one for me."

"But men fall in and out of love all the time, don't they?"

Harry looked as if about to offer a rebuttal. Athena jumped in quickly before he had the chance. "It's different for a woman."

"I bow to your greater knowledge in such matters. I haven't had the opportunity to examine the phenomenon in great detail. I've never felt this way before about anyone."

"Silly, isn't it," she said. "Being so certain about something when we hadn't exchanged more than a word or two? I've already told Forrest I need not see him again."

"Gosh."

"He took it well, no protest." She unfolded her parasol, snapped it open and twirled it gaily over her head.

"Did he suspect?"

"Probably. Though not about you. I said and did nothing to suggest I might be open to becoming his next flavour of the month. I don't believe *au revoir* came as a complete surprise. It was as I suspected. There are other anchorages for him, snug harbours, willing arms and open legs."

Harry covered his mouth.

"I'm sorry, Harry. Did I embarrass you? A bit too forthright?"

"You took me by surprise with your candour."

"You forgot to mention accuracy. I wished him well." She linked her arm through Harry's and pulled him toward her.

Her perfume drifted into his nose. He recognized it as the same she wore to the Embassy . "I love your perfume. I find it intoxicating. I can't get enough of it."

"It's French. Parfum des Champs-Élysées by Guerlain. It was a gift."

"From a handsome admirer, no doubt."

"Some might think him so. Actually it was from a middle-aged man of means. A lady doesn't buy perfume for herself."

"Oh."

Athena left the needle in a little longer before she confessed, "My father gave it to me before I left Cleveland." She smiled. "He said it was to keep charlatans, rakes and rogues at bay. And gentlemen. They're the worst of the lot, so he says. My mother agreed."

"You can tell him it didn't work on me."

"But it worked on everyone else." She gave Harry a playful shove.

"I read Jane Eyre the other night. She was a very determined young woman. A bit like you, I should think. I hope you take that as a compliment."

They continued their stroll along the National Mall. The trees had outgrown their new, pale green leaves; the blossoms of spring long since spent and blown away. The earth in the flower beds smelled damp after the rain shower that morning and the flowers heady with the scent of summer promise. "And I want to be married in Cornwall, in your local church. I don't want a big, fancy wedding with everyone assuming I only married you for your title, and you for my money."

"I don't have a title, other than Captain, and the Honourable." He turned serious. "And I was absolutely unaware you had money." He pointed to a park bench. "Let's sit for a while."

"Enough to keep me in the Martha Washington Hotel for a few months," she said as she smoothed her dress over her knees and the hem of her dress over her shoes. "And a dress allowance. My father owns Fenhagen Iron and Steel. There's nothing glamorous about foundries and steel mills, but it's how we Fenhagens have earned our living since my grandfather arrived from Holland. Van den Haag, I think they say in Dutch. Or something like that. I don't speak Dutch. From The Hague in English, which the people in Immigration wherever it was he landed sixty years ago wrote down as Fenhagen."

"Your parents were both born here?"

"Yes. Both born and raised in Cleveland. Nothing fancy about either of them."

"What else?"

"Not much you might consider unusual, except my mother's aunt married into the Greek royal family, though I only have her word for it. I'm an only child. My father doesn't spoil me, but he sees that I don't lack essential creature comforts."

"Like the aforementioned dress allowance." Harry thought for a moment, wondering how much to impart. There were things his commanding officer didn't know, and best kept that way. But Athena seemed different. Prickly, perhaps, on the surface, and probably with good reason. He hadn't exactly covered himself with glory this afternoon. It was so damned easy to get off on the wrong foot and so hard to correct. But he decided to be open and honest with her. If she married him, she deserved to know all there was that contributed to who he was. But perhaps not all at once. Even now, years after the event, some things he would only confide with her once he was certain of her affection.

# 5. PILLOW TALK

"My family's among the wealthiest in England," Harry said. "I receive my army pay and allowances, and a more than adequate income from my father, commensurate with my army rank. It's designed to ensure I don't appear a pauper among my peers in the regiment. It's my older brother, Ernest who will eventually inherit. I have to stay in his good books if I wish to remain comfortable."

"I hope you get along with him," Athena said.

Harry laughed. "I'd say we get along as well as most brothers. I don't imagine he'll cut me off and leave me to starve when my father's name finds itself in the Obituary page of the Times."

Athena put her hand on Harry's arm. "I don't mind if you're a pauper. You're a prince to me. My prince."

Harry covered Athena's hand with his. He hesitated. "Will you marry me, Athena Fenhagen?"

Tears welled in Athena's eyes. She fished out a lace handkerchief from her purse and dabbed her eyes and nose. Only moments ago she had decided to break off any attachment to Harry. Now everything was back to where she had hoped it would be before she set foot in the Hay-Adams a couple of hours ago. "Yes," she whispered between sniffs.

"It's usually good weather in *Roseland* at the end of August and into September."

Confusion clouded Athena's face. "*Roseland?*"

"It's what we call our house, *Roseland Place.* It's near St. Just, which is a small village, little more than a hamlet really. We own it."

"Own what?"

"The village of St. Just. And several other villages and hamlets on either side of the river and a few thousand acres of farmland. I'm not sure how many. And some properties in London."

Athena linked her arm possessively through Harry's. "Gosh! Isn't that what you say in England?"

"*Wow* works just as well." He gazed at her face again.

"Can we live there?"

"I can probably persuade my father to let us have a room to call our own. It's not as if we don't have several to spare."

"With a large four-poster bed?"

"If you want one."

"I want."

"It shall be done, My Lady."

"Oh, Harry, will it really happen?"

"Of course. Say the word. Hopefully we can arrange the wedding for the last Saturday in August at St. Just's."

"That church, St. Just's? Where is it?"

"It's a short walk from our house. It's old. Bits of it go back to Norman times. But it's not in the least grand. If you'd rather, we could be married at Windsor Castle. Or in Cleveland, if you'd be more comfortable there."

"No. I said I don't want anything fancy. St. Just's will suit me more than well enough."

"I think you'll like it in England. If not, we can always live here. I hope you'll be happy in either place."

She looked into Harry's eyes. "You do love me, don't you, Harry?"

"More than you can possibly imagine. And tomorrow even more."

"Then say it. I want to hear it."

"I love you, Athena Fenhagen, with all my heart."

"And I love you, too, Hereward Haig-Mallory." She pulled back a little and gave him a puzzled look. "Do you have a middle name?"

Harry looked surprised. "Three. Charles Arthur Edward. And yours?"

"It's Matilda. I don't like it. I only use it on official forms. Let's find someplace quiet so you can tell me all about yourself. Right from Day One, if you can remember that far back."

"If you insist."

"I do. I ought to know something about the man I'm going to marry."

"In case you change your mind?"

"Absolutely!" She saw him wince. "Only joking. Not a chance."

"And I about the Fenhagens of Cleveland. But not all at once. Perhaps one snippet a day until I sail." He glanced around at the fast thinning crowds on the Mall. "It's getting chilly. The hotel lobby? I'm sure we can find a quiet, out-of-the-way corner while we wait for dinner. If you will do me the honour of dining with me."

They rose from the bench on the Mall and made their way back to the hotel. On the steps of the Hay-Adams Harry took Athena in his arms and kissed her on the lips. They broke apart. "It's getting a bit late," he said. "Perhaps we should postpone the voyages of discovery until, say, tomorrow. I'm loath to do so, but I ought to hail a taxi to take you to your hotel."

She pushed him away playfully. "Is this the brush-off? Are you having cold feet or regrets at your hasty proposal of marriage?"

"No," he spluttered. "I was only thinking of your propriety, of what people might say if they see us together well into the evening."

She looked at him and waved a hand dismissively. "I'm not leaving the hotel until I know all about you. Should I stamp my foot?" She grinned. "Besides, no one knows me in Washington."

"You can hardly stay here until all hours of the day and night. What would your parents say?"

"My parents don't need to know, any more than yours do. Shall we skip dinner?"

"Gosh. Are you suggesting what I think you're suggesting?"

"You're remarkably quick on the uptake, Captain Haig-Mallory."

"By the skin of my teeth I finished Oxford with a first in French."

"Which only means you're very good at French. I know this is incredibly fast, even for these days, but I want to see what else you're very good at."

"Such as?"

Athena glanced down. Her gaze hovered over Harry's trousers. She looked back up again. "Before I marry you, I plan to take full advantage of my lack of chaperone to make sure you're a gentleman who gives as much as he receives. Or do I need to make myself clearer?"

Harry managed to convert a smirk to a grin, then a grin to a smile. "I got it first go. Are you sure?"

"I know what I'm doing."

"In which case I'll ring down for Champagne, a bucket of ice and two glasses, and practice my excuse for showing up late for work tomorrow."

*

Athena lay back on the pillows, her face flushed and her hair disheveled. The scent of their lovemaking rose from the sheets where it mingled with the aroma of Harry's sweat. It made for an unforgettable combination, one she knew she would carry in her memory and in her heart all her life. Harry lit a cigarette and passed it to her, then lit one for himself. They smoked in silence, staring at the ceiling. After they stubbed out the cigarettes, Harry poured more champagne.

"You must think terrible things of me, Harry," Athena murmured. "I'm twenty-four. I'm not sure what you expected. As you discovered, I'm no Athena Parthenos."

"Who?"

"Athena the Virgin in ancient Greece."

"Greek wasn't my strongest subject at school."

"They named the Parthenon after her."

"Quite an honour. She must have been a real beauty." Harry lay silent for a while. "I hope I didn't disappoint you," he said.

"You didn't. What you did to me I'll never forget."

"There are some things not covered in the Army basic training manual that…"

"You learn on field exercises?"

"You're very perceptive."

"I'm told Grandfather Fenhagen fought with the Union forces. So did my mother's father. I'm not totally ignorant of the army life." She hesitated. "I hope I didn't disappoint you."

"You were beyond my wildest imagination."

"You imagined us making love?"

"Ever since we met."

"I never suspected making love could be so wonderful." She downed the last of her glass of Champagne. "In spite of what you may think, I'm not as adventurous as I seem. I'm certainly no Moll Flanders."

"I've not met her either. One of your heroines of literature?"

"Neither a heroine of mine nor a rôle model."

Harry polished his silent image as he appraised Athena in the light of the bedside electric lamps, taking in every curve of her slender body. She held the empty glass out. "If you're pouring."

Harry regarded her, reclining next to him with the covers pushed down to her knees. In his eagerness to please, he tipped the bottle too far and too fast. The froth bubbled over. Champagne dribbled from the stem of her glass and trickled through the valley between her breasts. She watched for a moment as the pale liquid ran towards her navel. It pooled there, then overflowed, spilled out and flowed down to the tangle of glistening dark hair. She downed what remained of the Champagne in her glass, then turned to Harry and whispered, "Lick it off."

The empty bottle leaned to one side in the ice bucket. The room lay in darkness. They lounged against the pillows once more, their cigarette smoke curling to the ceiling. The smell of their lovemaking hovered over them.

"So, Captain Haig-Mallory. Take me back to the beginning."

Harry cleared his throat and shut his eyes, the better to conjure up the memory, and how best to explain it. Should he share that incident in his life with Athena? Did it matter if he did? Or didn't? He loved her, of that he was certain. She deserved to know, no matter how painful it may be to dredge up the past. He hesitated. "It was in April, eighteen-ninety-nine," he said uncertainly. "It was not an event I will ever forget. It changed my life, or at least its direction. I was nearly thirteen…"

*

His father, then a commodore in the Royal Navy, sat at his desk in his study in *Roseland Place*. The mullioned, diamond-leaded panes of the windows of the dark-paneled room provided a partial view of the formal rose garden that sloped gradually in terraces to the stone wall beyond which a short promontory separated *Roseland* from a tidal creek off the Carrick Roads. Harry's father held a letter that bore the crest of the Royal Naval College, Dartmouth, at the top of the page. As he read the letter a second time his face turned a deeper red, then purple. He slammed the single sheet of paper face up on his blotting pad and exploded.

"Tregarrick!"

The butler entered the study seconds later. "My Lord?" The plummy baritone rose from his perfectly polished shoes.

"Tell my son, Hereward, I wish to see him immediately."

"Yes, My Lord." The butler left the study silently, knowing full well from long experience, the use of the name Hereward, rather than Harry, forecast a full Force 8 gale ahead for the youngster. He closed the door with a soft click. Moments later his discreet knock on the door interrupted His Lordship's deliberations. "Come!" The door opened and Harry's slender form slid into the room. Tregarrick closed the door and left the boy alone to face whatever it was that had infuriated the commodore.

"Yes, Father? You wanted to see me?" The boy's piping treble quavered. Nevertheless, he held his gaze steadfast on his father. The watery April afternoon sun shone through the windows behind his father's desk. He knew from illustrations he'd seen of sailing ships the panes were the same as those in an admiral's quarters below the poop deck of a ship of the line. The smell of furniture polish rose to Harry's nose. Surreptitiously he cast his sight around his father's study, at the paintings of naval battles, of a portrait of Lord Nelson, the scratched and water-damaged wooden box containing his father's first sextant. The dry, salt-stained leather case that held his father's high-powered binoculars sat on a bookshelf where it always sat. Harry's gaze returned to the west facing windows and the mounted telescope that was aimed at the Carrick Roads and the distant shore. Everything in the study screamed ROYAL NAVY.

With his face still mottled with rage, Harry's father regarded his son and his quaking knees as the boy stood at attention before him. Harry could guess what lay ahead. He expected it, the inevitable. The course he had embarked upon, charted a year ago after careful deliberation, he believed was the only one open to him. With the decision came foreseeable consequences, amongst which included the caning that would follow. The only unknown was how unpleasantly painful and noisy the next few minutes would prove to be.

He knew he deserved his father's hiding. If he was thrashed to within an inch of his life there would be no doubt his father had rumbled his scheme. If it proved to be an ordinary caning, such as the headmaster of his prep school routinely handed out, then Harry knew he was in the clear. If so, the true motive behind what had prompted the letter now brandished like a weapon in front of his nose, remained his secret.

Harry focused on the early budding roses in the garden and the rhododendrons and azaleas in full bloom. When they failed to make a permanent imprint on his mind, he tried to focus on England's prospects against Australia in the test cricket series due to start in June.

"I don't want to see you," the commodore yelled. "If I had my way I would never set eyes on you again."

"Yes, Father."

His father held the letter aloft and waved it. "This arrived from Dartmouth a few minutes ago. It says you failed the entrance exam. It says your grasp of mathematics is appalling and unlikely to improve even under their tutelage. In short, Harry, the Royal Navy will not accept you. They have turned you down. There is no second chance. You are unacceptable to them."

Nothing further escaped his father's lips but Harry knew there was more to come. He began a study of his shoes while he waited for a count of five. "Yes, Father," he said in a small voice without looking up, scarcely able to contain his glee. He hoped England would win the series.

"Don't you *Yes, Father* me, you snotty-nosed whippersnapper," his father roared. "There has been a Haig-Mallory in the Navy since before the days of Drake. We have served England proudly for centuries."

Harry turned from the general study of his shoes to the specific study of his toecaps. His father's voice rose. "We owe our prominence as a family to the Navy. The Navy only takes the best, the most promising of all the applicants as midshipmen. Then the Navy molds those snotties into thinking men, capable of precise navigation by sun and stars and of calculating a fire pattern that straddles the enemy with the first salvo. I expected you to be among them."

His father paused, then lowered his voice. His next words carried menace. "You have let me down," he said slowly, enunciating each syllable with care. "You have let the family down. In short, you have disgraced us. I am more than disappointed in you." He paused again to let the words sink in. "I am furious," he yelled.

Harry's knees trembled. Australia always sent a strong team. They would be tough to beat, even on English soil. A tear trickled down his freckled cheek. He sniffed, once and shifted his study from his toecaps to a detailed examination of the intricacies of his shoe buckles.

"Do you have any idea what this means?" Harry's head snapped up. He briefly contemplated his father's thunderous words. Did his father suspect the truth? That his failure was deliberate? Either way, a lie now would hardly make things worse, and a lie was better than admit the truth.

"No, Father." Harry's voice quavered. It seemed the safest response in the circumstances, even if untrue. He braced himself for more to come.

"It means the end of the line for a Haig-Mallory as a naval officer in the service of England and the Queen. Oh, I have no doubt the Navy would take you on as an Ordinary Seaman." Sarcasm sweated from the pores of each word. "But this letter means you can never be an officer in the Royal Navy."

His father drew himself up to his full height. "You have failed, Harry. You are twelve and you stare failure in the face. There is only one thing for it. You shall have to follow you equally useless brother and go to Marlborough School. From there you will go into the Army. Hopefully it will make a man of you, though I have my doubts. Do you understand?"

"Yes, Father."

"Now bend over so I may flog you, as you so richly deserve."

"Yes, Father." Harry meekly bent forward over the back of the visitors' chair in front of his father's desk.

With a thin cane, the commodore delivered six of the best over Harry's bony backside. With each stroke Harry focused on the test match at Trent Bridge only six weeks away. With the first stroke of the cane he hoped W.G.Grace would be on form. With the second that Grace and C.B.Fry would be able to blunt Australia's pace attack. With the third came the hope that Ranjitsinhji would come through in the middle order with his renowned stroke-making. With the fourth and fifth strokes he prayed for a fast, true wicket so England's pace men could wreak havoc with Australia's vaunted batsmen. With the sixth he hoped England would win the series and retain the ashes.

"I hope that taught you an object lesson in the consequences of failure. Now get out of my sight before I decide to flog you again."

Harry scuttled out of the study and narrowly missed colliding with the well-upholstered form of Tregarrick. "I shall send tea and supper up to your room, Master Harry," the butler said, quietly. "It might be safer if you spend the rest of the day there. It will blow over, you'll see. I believe your father plans to return to Plymouth after breakfast tomorrow. I will signal the all clear."

"Thank you, Tregarrick," Harry said, while he rubbed his backside and sniffed. He wiped his hand across his nose and down the pants of his sailor suit. "Perhaps the sports section of the newspaper when my father has finished with it? There may be something on cricket that will help take my mind off things."

He spent the rest of the day in his bedroom. The six thin, red welts on his backside made it difficult to adopt any position but prone on his counterpane. His future lay ahead. Cloudy, to be sure. But at least it would not include Dartmouth. That was enough to bring a painful smile to his face.

*

Athena turned to Harry. "So, about the math exam."

"You need maths to get into Dartmouth. No maths, no engineering, no navigation, no gun laying, nothing. My father was furious."

"So you said. Weren't you any good at math?"

"I was all right, better than at Greek, but it was never my strongest subject."

"But surely you must have had some warning your math wasn't up to scratch. You could have gotten extra tutoring, surely?"

He smiled. "Not a word. Amazing."

"So, you went from a C student to an F overnight?"

"It took some doing."

"What?" She edged away from him. "Don't tell me. You deliberately failed the math exam? I don't believe you."

"Mea culpa. But that's exactly what I did."

"But why?"

"It was the only way I could think of to avoid going to Dartmouth. I couldn't face life in the Royal Navy. And to refuse my father at twelve would have got me nowhere."

Athena slumped back against her pillow. "It was that bad, huh? At twelve. Wow!"

"Please don't let on to anyone, least of all to my father. I suspect he's still furious with me."

She shook her head. "I promise." She leaned over him. Her breasts dangled inches from his face, an invitation to play. "Do you think…?" she whispered.

Harry's mind spun. "Do I think what?"

"Do you think you might have anything left? Apart from energy, I mean." To make herself absolutely clear she reached down and found what she wanted. "Oh, Harry. I do believe you do."

*

While a bleary-eyed Harry tried to function at work, Athena wrote to her parents the next day to inform them of her intention.

*… I have met a young English army officer attached to the British Embassy. He is the son of Rear Admiral, the Earl of St Austell. He returns to England at the end of August and I will stay in Washington an extra month to keep him company. He has asked me to marry him. I have agreed. I am delirious with happiness. We will be married in England on the last Saturday in August. I hope father will give me away and that you, mamma, will stand as the mother of the bride. I am sure you will love him, and yes, he is tall, dark and handsome…*

Her mother's reply only amounted to, *Congratulations. We look forward to the trip to England,* which she followed with, *In the meantime enjoy yourself, dear.* Athena frowned. What did her mother mean? Had she figured out that her daughter had been more than stepping out with Harry? That they had shared a bed and had every intention of doing so as often as possible until Harry was due to return to England? If anything, the loaded comment, the enjoinder to *'enjoy yourself'* could really only mean one thing — her mother was under no delusion as to her daughter's romantic antics. If anything, it confirmed her suspicions — that her mother had been no virgin on her wedding night, with or without the help or connivance of her father. Her father only wanted to know if he needed to wire more money.

*

"This assassination of the Austrian Archduke," Athena said over dinner a couple of nights later. "It won't affect you, will it?"

"I can't see how. Our chaps at the Embassy call it internal house cleaning. It has nothing to do with us. They'll settle their differences in the time honoured Balkan way by killing each other in the most gruesome ways they can imagine. Then we'll all move on as if nothing had happened."

"That's a bit callous of your *chaps*, isn't it?"

"Perhaps, but it doesn't alter the truth of the matter."

"But what if you do have to go back before August? Where does that leave us?"

"No change of plans in the works," he said and tried to reassure her by patting her hand. She snatched it away. "Allow a week for the crossing, and if we get a special licence if they won't waive the reading of the banns, you'll be walking up the aisle on your father's arm on the twenty-ninth of August." He leaned back. "Army wives have to become accustomed to separation. It comes with the job." He frowned.

"What's the matter?"

"I wonder if Demelza will remember me. I've been gone a year."

Athena returned the frown. Who's Demelza? An old girlfriend? One of the servants? An older woman who taught him all she knew about making love? If Harry mentioned her, it couldn't be that bad. Could it? She swallowed the bait. "Who's Demelza? Should I be jealous?"

"My clumber spaniel. My parents gave her to me as a puppy when I passed out from Sandhurst. Army officers often have a dog, usually a Labrador retriever. I love her with all my heart, as only an Englishman would love his dog but, being away most of the time I don't see much of her."

Athena squeezed Harry's hand. "I'm sure she'll remember you, your smell if not your face. If you love her with all your heart, how much do you love me?"

"Even more than I love Demelza."

"Right answer, Captain Haig-Mallory."

# 6. SECOND THOUGHTS

For the next two weeks Athena and Harry spent their spare time and every night together. Athena passed her days, when she wasn't busy gathering her trousseau from the finest of Washington's stores, researching Cornwall in the encyclopedias at the Library of Congress and the Smithsonian. Meanwhile, Harry read the week-old Times and Daily Telegraph newspapers as well as the American dailies and digested the news from Europe. It was one thing, the editorials concluded, for the Austrian Archduke to allow himself to be assassinated, foolish and even careless of him — a prudent person would anticipate how easily that could happen on a visit to the Balkans. It was another matter entirely for Germany, France, Great Britain and several lesser nations to allow themselves to be dragged into this sordid little affair involving foreigners from Eastern Europe. That was, the editorialists concluded, the sort of thing that happened behind squalid little Greek restaurants in Soho, not on the world stage.

Serbia, the papers said a few days later, needed to be taken to the headmaster's study and thrashed, and about bloody time too, a notion even the yellow press seemed to agree with. Then reports of the existence of a complex filigree of bilateral and multilateral mutual defence treaties surfaced from the bog of diplomacy, treaties that would kick in should one nation be foolish enough to take up arms against another. The treaties, as one correspondent to the editor of the Times wrote, were harder to follow than the three-card trick. And equally crooked.

In a matter of days after the assassination, before even the state funerals for the archduke and his wife — an unfortunate, if unintended victim — sabres were being rattled in diplomatic scabbards, threats and counter-threats uttered, and war plans retrieved from archives and dusted off in case things devolved from bad to worse.

Harry, and indeed most of Britain believed a diplomatic solution would result. Meanwhile, sensible nations decided to mobilize their armed forces as a precaution, even if mobilization would inevitably be understood as an unofficial declaration of hostilities, if not outright war. War, he reasoned, would surely be confined to the Balkans. It could hardly involve the Great Powers. He was still optimistic about a diplomatic resolution when he was called into General Trevor-Bailey's office on the morning of July 15th.

"Sorry to be the bearer of bad news, Haig-Mallory," the general said with a mournful look on his face. Harry wondered what the news could be. A death in the family? A complaint from a member of the Washington public who may have seen him and Athena together in inappropriate circumstance? There was nothing else he could think of.

"You're being recalled effective immediately. The situation in Europe seems to be going downhill rather quickly, and indeed ominously." The general cleared his throat. "We're hoping for the best, naturally, but we have to prepare for the worst. You're needed back home with your regiment. We've booked your ticket on the train for Friday afternoon and your passage from New York on Saturday. Not much time to tie up any loose ends but can't be helped." He paused. "Under the circumstances."

*Tie up loose ends?* What did Trevor-Bailey mean by that, Harry wondered? "And, *Under the circumstances?* Did he know about Athena? Perhaps they had not been as discreet as he believed.

The general rose from behind his desk and extended his hand. "Good luck."

Harry shook the offered hand then stood back to salute. No hat on, he reminded himself in the nick of time. He placed his hat firmly on his head and gave the general a proper, quivering, salute. "Thank you, sir," was all he could think to say. He did an about turn and made his way out of the general's office.

In his own office, he tidied his things and placed them in a cardboard box. There wasn't much to gather that didn't belong to the Embassy. He travelled light, as the Americans were fond of saying, and there was very little in his office of a personal nature to take home. He phoned the Martha Washington hotel only to be told that Miss Fenhagen was out and not expected back for some time.

"Damn and blast!" He exploded as soon as he had put the receiver back in its cradle. He needed to talk to Athena, give her the news and make alternative plans for the next couple of days.

That evening they met as planned without having contacted each other during the day. Harry regarded Athena across the dinner table from him in the Ebbitt Café on 15th Street. Her skin seemed to glow in the candle light. Her face radiated happiness. Her dress, the one she had worn to the Embassy ball, enhanced her modest bust. The alabaster skin visible at the tops of her breasts as they floated provocatively above the gown's bust line with each breath she took, shone with vitality.

She blinked. A puzzled, half-smile, half-frown flitted across her face and forehead. "What? Why are you looking at me like that, Harry?"

"I'm admiring your beauty and wondering what I might have done in a past life to deserve you."

"Don't go all Hindu or Buddhist on me, Harry. It's not like you. You're always so plain and straightforward."

Harry gulped. "Are you sure you want to go through with this?" He held his breath.

Athena opened her eyes wide. "What do you mean?"

"You are the most beautiful woman in Creation. You wear your heart on your sleeve. I don't deserve you."

Tears welled in Athena's eyes. She held them back for a moment. "Are you saying you don't want to marry me?" She covered her face with her hands. Her tears spilled down her cheeks onto the tablecloth. "Am I nothing more to you than two weeks of bedroom fun and games before you push off back to England without me?" Her chest heaved. She dabbed at her face with her table napkin. "Because if so, I'll leave right now and you'll never see me again. Is that what you want?" She buried her face in her hands.

Harry reached out to take a hand. "Don't touch me!" she hissed, and turned her face away.

Harry gulped. "It's not that, Athena. I love you, desperately. There's nothing in the world I want more than to marry you. I want to spend the rest of my life with you, but look at what you're facing if you marry me."

She pulled back the corners of her mouth in a snarl. "And what's that I haven't already figured out?" She turned back to face him. Twin red spots lit her cheeks.

"You're going to leave your parents behind."

"*Quelle surprise*, as they say in French," she said, making no attempt to disguise her sarcasm. "Every bride does that. It comes immediately after saying, I do without making a mess of it, and right before the obligation to satisfy her husband in bed that night. Followed by the mess of having children."

"You probably won't see your parents for years. They may grow ill in that time."

"I'm not a doctor or a nurse. They can afford both," she snapped.

Harry hesitated. "My family, well, it's… it's different from yours."

"How?"

"My family's English."

"No way. Another surprise. I thought they might be Hottentots."

"Which isn't necessarily a good thing from an American standpoint," Harry said, ignoring the barb. "My father's a bully, at least that's how he acts some of the time. I've told you that. The Dartmouth entrance exam wasn't the first time he caned me, or the last. But he wasn't always like that. When he was home on leave, and later on dockyard duty, he used to play football with Ernest and me in the garden. He knew I was more interested in cricket, so he'd sometimes bowl to me for hours, overarm like I was a grown-up, not underarm as he might to a child, to help me with my batting. Then I went off to Marlborough School and all that changed. He never went to sea again. Most of the time he and my stepmother ignore each other. They certainly don't share a bedroom. Mostly he lives in London."

"Hmm. Do go on." The scorn in her voice was not lost on Harry.

"My older brother, Ernest…"

"What about him?"

"He lost an eye in a shooting accident when he was about twelve. Apart from that, well, you could say he's not academically inclined."

"But he's not a lunatic. I take it he can read and write."

"No. I mean, yes. He can read and write. We went to the same school. Though that may not speak too well of the school. He was in the Remove form."

"What's that?"

"It's where those who are not too swift up top put in the required hours to justify the school fees without holding back the brighter boys."

"So, you have a brother who's a bit on the not too bright side."

"Yes. My sister, actually my half-sister, Cecilia, is very bright. She's at Cambridge, studying to become a doctor."

"What's wrong with being bright? So am I."

"I know you are, but you're not a socialist. Cecilia has strange ideas about equality."

"I'm American. We believe in equality," she snapped.

"Cecilia may even be a suffragette, but she hasn't positively declared for them. I think it's only a matter of time before she does something silly and embarrass the family."

"Like marrying a foreigner?"

"Yes. No. Not like that. Making speeches about equality for women, for example. Or living with an artist and not trying to hide the fact she's not married to him."

"A bit like we've been living these past two weeks."

"No. Yes. I don't know what to say. At least we're planning to get married."

"Are we? Just a moment ago I thought you weren't too sure what you wanted."

"I'm absolutely sure. I'm not sure you're sure. Does that make sense?"

"No. So, to recap, your father's a tyrant, he and your stepmother rarely speak to each other, your older brother, the heir to the family title and fortune is a bit of what you English call a twit, and your sister's a suffragette who wants to work for fairness and equality among all of mankind. Is that it?"

"Yes." He leaned back in his chair. The waiter interrupted by arriving at that moment with their entrées and placed them in front of them. He stood back and bowed his head to Harry.

"Is there anything else, Sir?"

"I've changed my mind about the wine."

"I'll have the sommelier attend immediately, sir."

The sommelier arrived and Athena sat back in her chair, glaring at Harry while he ordered the *Krug Champagne* rather than the *Veuve Cliquot*.

"If you want to chuck it in before it's too late, I wouldn't blame you. Tell your parents you've had second thoughts about me and leaving America."

Athena snorted and blew her nose on her table napkin.

"I have a clean handkerchief if you'd like one."

She grinned sheepishly. "Too late for that now." She shoved the napkin out of sight onto her lap.

"I'm sorry I made you cry. That's the last thing I'd ever want to do. But if you want to take some time to rethink …"

Athena gave Harry a withering glare. "I don't give up easily."

"You still want to marry me after all that?"

"I'll think about it. I'll let you know over breakfast. And if you want to know, I'm not hungry and I've got a headache." She turned away from him. "You can have the doorman call a cab to take me back to my hotel. I need to sleep. You can enjoy the Champagne on your own." She rose to leave.

Harry took a deep breath. "There's more," he said, choking over the words.

"Oh, yeah," Athena snapped. "Such as?"

"I've been recalled to England."

Athena's face paled to alabaster. She sat down heavily, gulped once, then a second time. "Why?" she croaked.

"The situation in Europe. I only found out this morning. I called your hotel but you were out. They need me back in England."

Athena took a deep breath as she digested the information. "When do you leave? How much time do we have?"

"I leave for New York on Friday, sail next day. So two full days and nights."

Tears trickled down Athena's cheeks. She dabbed at them with her table napkin and sniffed. "What about our wedding? What will become of us?"

"I see no reason to change our plans. I expect this will all blow over in a week or two."

"But they won't send you back to Washington, will they?"

"They've told me my replacement's already been told not to pack. I expect if the situation doesn't change, they'll send over someone they can spare, a junior Royal, for example. Someone with lots of gold braid who knows his manners. One who they'd prefer not to stick his head in harm's way if things don't turn out the way we think they will. One of the king's nephews possibly."

"Meanwhile they expect you to risk your life instead of him." She snorted. "If that's the case, I don't think much of your Royal Family."

"I was due to go back next month anyway. It's a few weeks earlier now. That's all. It's a false alarm. Nothing will happen, you'll see. There's no need to reschedule the wedding. You can sail with your parents in the middle of August. I'll personally meet you at Southampton dock and take you to Cornwall where your parents can chaperone you for a week. To make sure we don't misbehave." He smiled encouragingly. "If you still want to."

"That's a lot to think about." She sighed heavily and rose. "You'd better call me that cab. I'll sleep at my hotel tonight. I'll let you have my decision in the morning, if I've come to one."

Pale faced, Harry rose and beckoned for the waiter. "A taxi, if you would," Harry said. He watched Athena follow the waiter to the restaurant entrance before he lost sight of her. "I can't blame you for calling it a day," he mumbled, as he resumed his seat. The last thing he wanted was Champagne, but they had hardly touched the bottle. He poured a glass and elicited a frown from a passing waiter who hastened to the table. "And a large Scotch whisky chaser," Harry said. He looked down and saw his hands shake. He downed the Champagne in one long swallow and waited for the whisky to arrive.

In his room at the Hay-Adams Hotel, Harry lay on his back with his hands behind his head. He stared at the dark ceiling and the slowly circling fan eddying the hot, humid air while he wondered if it was too late to back out now, with the wedding little more than six weeks away. It would hardly be fair on Athena. But how fair would it be having to leave her for weeks or months at a time while the army decided where to send him next, and the time after that? The situation in Europe wasn't particularly worrisome, but if it deteriorated until one side or the other painted itself into a corner and found hostilities the only way out, he'd have to go. To France most likely, until it all blew over.

He knew these were merely excuses to mask his own doubts. The real heart of the matter was; did he love Athena enough to marry her, to tie himself to one woman for the rest of his life? She was beautiful, certainly. The most beautiful woman he'd ever set eyes on, and he'd told her that, many times. He couldn't believe the things she got up to when they were in bed together. But inevitably, that would change as they grew older and lovemaking was no longer as exciting as it was now, snatched daringly, if not quite in broad daylight, at least after work had ended for the day. And perhaps because it was stolen, illicit in the eyes of society, it heightened the experience. Experience. Athena had obviously had sex before they met, though she hadn't disclosed any details of the lucky man — or men. He could hardly blame her. She was twenty-four and blisteringly good looking.

He acknowledged he was no paragon of virtue either. Nellie, the tweenie with whom he'd lost his virginity at seventeen had been impressed by the attention he paid to her. She had left him in no doubt about her desire to please her master's son in the best way she knew how. And she certainly knew how. When prompted, and with Harry's promise never to tell Tregarrick or any of the other servants, she told him she had discarded her virginity in the bushes at the end of the school playing field one summer's evening when she was thirteen. And frequently since. He had given her ten shillings, a small fortune, for her trouble. And every time since, until they were caught. She was sacked on the spot. His father winked. His stepmother acted horrified and Ernest seemed jealous. Only Cecilia had remained in the dark, being away at boarding school at the time. Harry had made a mental note to be more circumspect in the future.

And while he was at the Royal Military College, Sandhurst, with London less than an hour away by train, Lady Maude Howard had taken him under her wing while her husband was away on diplomatic service. She was old enough to be his mother, and indeed was the mother of one of the Princess Royal's ladies-in-waiting. He had been eternally grateful for his education under her tutelage which he had put to good use on several occasions since graduating from Sandhurst. And now there was Athena.

He had given Athena the opportunity to back out. He scolded himself for taking the coward's way out by inviting her to make the decision rather than being man enough to make it himself. As the ceiling seemed to loom ever closer to his chest and his mind whirled with indecision, not to mention the entire bottle of Krug, he decided he did want to marry her. More than anything else in the world. Athena was beautiful. He'd never find anyone as imaginative as Lady Maude, but Athena came close. About nine and a half out of ten when measured against the yardstick of Lady Maude. And a definite eleven out of ten for looks. Yes, he decided, he'd go through with it. If she would still have him. And if she no longer wanted him, it would be the biggest, stupidest thing he had ever done. Or ever likely to. And if she refused to have any more to do with him, he couldn't blame her. He had been impulsive when he had asked her to marry him. But he didn't regret it. He reached over but Athena wasn't next to him for the first time in two weeks. "What a bloody mess," he muttered as he cursed his foolishness before he drifted into a restless sleep.

"I thought about what you said last night," Athena said over breakfast at a café they frequented rather than be seen together in the hotel dining room. She sipped her coffee before taking a bite of warm, buttered raspberry muffin. "You might like to know I still love you, in spite of what you told me."

Harry brightened. The clouds parted. The sun peeked through.

"And I want to marry you, and into your weird family. And leave America and my parents. That is, if you still want me to." She raised her eyebrows and stared at him. She had lobbed the tennis ball firmly back into his court. It was decision time and the challenging look in her eyes told Harry she knew it.

Harry's shoulders slumped.

"Oh, dear," she said. "Was that the wrong answer? You don't want to go through with it, do you?"

He saw the tears build beneath her lower eyelids. "I'm incredibly relieved," he said. He put his coffee cup back in its saucer. "I know it was precipitous me to ask you so soon after we met, and I'm so glad you said yes. I hoped you wouldn't change your mind over the past couple of weeks, after getting to know me better, and realizing I'm far less than an ideal potential husband. I needed to make sure you understood you still had an option… you know, to reconsider." He leaned forward across the small round table. "I want to marry you more than anything else in the world. Please say *Yes* again."

"Yes, Harry. Nothing for me has changed since the first time I saw you, and I've put last night behind us. I'll come with you to New York then I'll go home to Cleveland and start packing. I hope there'll be room in the caboose for all my trunks and suitcases."

Harry beamed. The waiter looked at him quizzically. "More coffee, Sir?"

# 7. POSTPONED

Six days after sailing from New York, Harry disembarked at Liverpool. His ocean liner, the *S. S. Lapland*, failed to hit an iceberg, run aground, collide with another vessel, suffer engine failure or have to fly the quarantine flag, all of which he was certain would happen. The next day he reported for duty at Horsefield Barracks in Bristol, a working cavalry officer again.

He glanced around his commanding officer's office while he waited for Colonel Shackleton to look up from the paperwork that littered his desk. Nothing he could see in the cluttered office appeared to have changed since he left for Washington. He sniffed the air, redolent of furniture polish and stale pipe tobacco smoke. He glanced down surreptitiously. At his feet lay the same threadbare strip of carpet in front of the desk that had been there a year ago, and the onyx pen and ink set centred on the blotting pad on the CO's desk sat exactly as he remembered them.

Colonel Shackleton screwed the cap onto his fountain pen, laid the pen aside and looked up.

"Permission to marry, Sir." The words gushed out of Harry's mouth the moment he snapped his quivering salute to his side, and before he even thought to exchange the customary greeting with his commanding officer.

"Denied, Haig-Mallory," Colonel Shackleton said in a bored voice and turned his attention to the sheaf of papers he had just pulled out from a desk drawer. Harry's mouth gaped. Shackleton placed the papers on his desk and focused on Harry. "Why on earth would you want to get married? You don't have to, do you? I mean, you haven't been careless or anything while you were away, have you?"

"No, Sir. Nothing like that."

"At least we're over the first hurdle." Shackleton's voice carried some hint of warmth this time. Harry hoped perhaps it wasn't going to be an absolute *No*, after all.

"After all, captains may marry, Sir."

"With their CO's consent, may I remind you?"

"We were hoping to be married at the end of next month, in Cornwall," Harry said, on slightly surer footing this time. "You're invited of course. She'll be coming over with her parents. They have their passages booked from New York. It would seem a pity for them to have to change their plans."

"Americans, are they?"

"Yes, Sir. Quite well-to-do. Her father's an industrialist, from Ohio. Her mother's related to the Greek royal family."

Shackleton's head snapped up. "I didn't know the Greeks had a royal family."

"Not as prominent as ours, of course. Minor Royals, you could call them. Her mother has an aunt who married one of them."

Shackleton sniffed. "The Balkans. Not the most stable of places to come from. Which is why you're here, may I remind you."

"Oh, the aunt's not from there. She's American through and through for generations. It's the aunt's husband who's Greek."

"For a moment I thought she might be a direct descendant. Nevertheless, mark my word, marrying foreigners is fraught with dangers and split allegiances."

Harry ploughed on. "No scandal in the family."

"You're suggesting she's a suitable wife for a cavalry officer, are you?"

"Absolutely, Sir."

"One can't be too careful these days, Haig-Mallory. Some officers make a habit of falling under the spell of women who come from parts of the world with distasteful regimes. Or they make a fool of themselves over actresses and chorus girls. Captain Blamires comes to mind. The next thing is scandal."

Harry nodded. This was not going as well as he hoped.

"The Fenhagens are a model of propriety, Sir."

"If she's as virtuous as you say, then she's wholly unsuited to becoming a soldier's wife. Still, if you insist on marrying, I suppose you'd like some leave to prepare for the wedding and a honeymoon." He sighed, but the grin below the black bristly moustache gave the game away.

"If I can be spared for a short while, Sir."

"We've got along without you for a year, Haig-Mallory, though I can't think how we managed. I think we can get along without you for another couple of weeks or so. What's the date?"

"August 29th at St. Just's-in-Roseland. I've already sent a telegram to the vicar and he's confirmed time and date for us. Honeymoon in Paris, then back to soldiering."

"I look forward to receiving my invitation. You're due some leave after your stint in Washington. Twenty-one days enough? A week before the day and two weeks after?"

"That will be…" He let out the deep breath bottled up inside since he stepped into the colonel's office. "Thank you, Sir. She won't let us down. She's beautiful. I know you'll love her." Harry paused for a moment's thought. "I should probably spend a day or two at home to make the final arrangements for the wedding," he said. "To see my mother and father so they can see I'm still alive. Anything important scheduled for the next few days?"

"Nothing on the calendar, unless the Kaiser has other plans." Shackleton glanced at his watch. "If you leave now you've still time to get a late train. You can pick up you railway warrant from the duty officer's desk on your way out."

"Thank you, Sir. Then perhaps I won't have to go down again until a day or two before the wedding, so I don't miss it. That wouldn't go down too well."

Shackleton gave a non-committal grunt. "Report to Major Kerslake when you get back. You can take over A Squadron. We're going to have to spend the next couple of weeks or so getting you accustomed to soldiering again after the cushy life in Washington. Once Merryweather's back from leave he'll take over A and you'll take over as adjutant from Captain Shaw-Bingley. He's being booted up to major effective the first of August. Carry on." He reached for the sheaf of papers.

"Thank you, Sir." He was about to salute before he left when he saw Shackleton scrutinize him as if sizing him up on a first meeting. "This trouble in Europe, Haig-Mallory."

"Yes, Sir?"

"I doubt if anything will come of it, but we can't be lackadaisical. Don't stray too far from where a telegram might reach you. Just in case. Perhaps you might leave your honeymoon address with Major Kerslake before you leave for the wedding."

"The Hôtel Georges Cinq in Paris. I'll provide Major Kerslake with the telegraph address."

"One other thing, Haig-Mallory."

"Sir?"

"Your evaluation from General Trevor-Bailey in Washington. Top marks. Well done. Glad to have you back in the saddle."

"Thank you, Sir." He snapped up a salute.

*

Harry had hardly set foot in *Roseland* when he received the telegram signed AUTH COL SHACKLETON STOP ALL LEAVE CANCELLED EFFECTIVE IMMEDIATELY.

"Bloody Hell," Harry yelled and crumpled the telegram in his fist. He immediately apologized to his mother who was in earshot, as was most of the household. There was nothing for it. Return on the first train in the morning, cancel, or at the very least postpone the wedding indefinitely. And prepare for the worst — war with Germany.

He sent a telegram to Cleveland, hoping it would arrive before Athena and her parents left for England. He wondered what Athena's response would be. Would she think this was simply an excuse not to get married? Was he backing out now with a case of cold feet? She would no doubt be spitting mad and have every right to be. And how would her parents handle it? He couldn't guess. Perhaps with a sigh of relief that their daughter wasn't about to run off to England to marry a cad? They hadn't given him that impression, though. He and the Fenhagens had corresponded, as only right and proper as he was about to uproot their daughter and cart her off to England for, hopefully, the rest of her life. They seemed genuinely to approve of her choice of husband, even though he would never inherit his father's title or the estate. To judge by what Athena had told him, and from reading between the lines in Mr. Fenhagen's letters, they didn't seem to be social climbers and seemed about as unsnobbish as any American he had met. *Minnie and I are Republicans*, Randolph Fenhagen had written, not that Harry knew the difference between a Republican and a Democrat; only that both parties existed in a state of permanent agitation with each other. Harry had had the presence of mind not to request further enlightenment. *Her mother's family has been here since before the War of Independence and her father was an ordinary working man with enough get up and go to become a success. English titles aren't high on our list of priorities, but if one day Athena should become a lady earl, or whatever you call them, I'd neither be disappointed nor tell her to hand it back.*

Harry was in a sour mood at dinner, primed by three generous tots of his father's best single malt Scotch whisky and fueled by a glass of hock with the fish and one of claret with the beef. Once his sister, Cecilia and his stepmother had retired to the drawing room, Tregarrick, the butler placed the decanter of Port on the table in front of the earl. Tregarrick dismissed the footmen and placed himself on the other side of the dining room door, where he could no doubt hear every word that was said over the Port.

Harry ignored his brother, Ernest, and turned to his father. "As you may have noticed," he said, "I'm not in the best of moods this evening. My last dinner *en famille* for who knows how long, and nothing but speculation about the prospect of war and the postponement of my wedding. I've sent a telegram to Cleveland but I shall have to write to Athena and give her the news. That might be the most difficult thing I've ever had to do."

"If you hadn't chosen a foreigner, you could be married on your next leave."

Harry rounded on his father. "You married a foreigner. Twice, if I recall, and neither successfully, to judge by the way you thought to impregnate Cecilia's mother while still married to mine. My mother's premature death must have come as an enormous relief."

His father's head jerked up. Ernest looked from one to the other as if he were watching a tennis rally. "I'll have none of that talk in my house, and least of all at my dinner table."

Harry bit his lip and clamped down hard on his teeth. The muscles in his jaw rippled while he fought to control his temper. "I won't apologize for my words, Father. They're out, said, and meant." He was sick of apologizing to his father, but he knew the dinner table was not the place to wage war with family. That was why houses such as theirs had studies with stout doors behind which frank words could be exchanged.

His father's face turned a mottled red. He pointed at Harry with a cheese knife. "It won't blow over, you know. It'll be a shooting war, mark my words."

"I'm fully aware of that," Harry snapped at his father in spite of his resolve not to let his temper get the upper hand.

"If you hadn't failed your Dartmouth entrance examination you might be in command of a destroyer by now instead of riding off to France to get yourself blown off your horse."

"At least I'm not shirking my duty."

His father regarded Harry with open hostility. "What do you mean by that remark?"

"You know very well. Pax Britannica. Forty-five years in the navy without ever seeing a shot fired in anger."

"You contemptible whippersnapper!" Harry's father leaned on the arms of his chair and made to rise to his feet. His mouth opened and closed as if he were a fish gasping for oxygen. Spittle ran like a thread from top to bottom lips. Ernest's expression suggested he was also a fish floundering on the beach with the tide out.

"Sit down. I haven't finished yet, Father," Harry's voice, though low, was filled with menace. His father sunk back in his chair as if he had been slapped in the face. "You were directly responsible for our mother's death." He nodded at Ernest. "You can't blame anyone but yourself. You held the reins when the carriage toppled on her." He paused to let the words sink in. "You haven't done an honourable thing in your life. I doubt that you ever will."

Harry rose and threw his table napkin onto his side plate. He knew he had lost his temper. The words were out, in front of Ernest. There was no taking them back. No apology would smooth the ruffled feathers. He would have to live with the consequences, whatever they might be. The loss of his allowance, perhaps. A pauper had no life as a cavalry officer. He doubted if this spat would blow over, any more than the likelihood of war would evaporate. "Now, if you will excuse me, I'm off to fight a war, something you have managed to avoid all your service life. Please say goodnight to mother and Cecilia for me." He grabbed a crystal tumbler and the decanter of Scotch whiskey from the sideboard and headed for the door.

In the doorway he turned and looked at his father with undisguised animosity. "Like most bullies," he said quietly, "you're weak, cowardly and contemptible." He saw Ernest open and close his mouth without making a sound. Harry turned his back on the two of them and closed the door behind him with a soft click.

*

Telegram in hand, Athena stomped through the living room and into her father's study, a room she rarely visited uninvited. She waved the offending piece of paper at her father and slammed it onto his desk. Her father, somewhat taken aback at this unusual behaviour, removed his eyeglasses and placed them carefully on the desk top. He looked up at his daughter without uttering a word.

"It's off," she hissed. "It's off," she shouted, pointing at the telegram.

Randolph Fenhagen raised his eyebrows. Athena screwed the telegram into a ball and threw it in the general direction of the wastepaper basket. "You can unpack. Completely. And mamma. The wedding's off. Postponed. Cancelled. I don't know which."

"But from what you tell us and from his letters he seems such an agreeable young man," her father said. "Sincere. I'm sure he loves you. Maybe it's simply a case of the jitters. He'll get over it, you'll see. There'll be another cable tomorrow confirming everything."

"No, there won't. It's not Harry. It's Germany. Or England. Or both. I don't know which. Harry's leave is cancelled indefinitely. They're mobilizing, preparing for war. He'll be gone to France in days and no idea when he'll be back. If it's war, I may never see him again. If I do I might not recognize him as the man I said goodbye to two weeks ago. It's so bloody unfair."

"It is, as you say, dear, bloody unfair, though you might want to tone down your choice of language in front of your mother."

Athena opened her mouth to retort. Her father held his hand up. "I know your mother's heard far worse, and used it on occasion, but still…I'm sure she'll be very upset at this turn of events, as we both are. You, we, will have to adjust to the situation, see what transpires and make the most of whatever's left after the smoke has cleared. You know you have our backing in whatever you choose to do. Now, let's tell mother together. She'll want to make alternative plans for the summer."

Athena gritted her teeth, balled her hands into fists and snarled as she stomped out of the study, following her father in search of her mother. They found her mother in the small drawing room in a window seat with a book open on her lap. She looked up when her husband and daughter burst into the room. Minerva Fenhagen closed her book and picked up her cup and saucer. She sipped her tea and waited.

"Athena has something to say, Minnie," her husband said. "And you may want something stronger than Darjeeling when she's finished."

Minerva Fenhagen regarded her daughter with a stern but not unfriendly face and put her cup and saucer on the occasional table at her elbow.

"The wedding's off," Athena blurted out. "Indefinitely."

Her mother waited for further explanation. She did not have to wait long. When Athena finished, her mother stood and smoothed the front of her dress. "You're right, Ralph. This news calls for something more substantial than tea. Bourbon, I think. And a stiff one. And don't ring for the Hedges. I wouldn't want it getting back to the servants' hall that there's anything amiss that would require whiskey, especially before dinner."

Too late. A light tap on the door, a slight cough, and Hedges, the butler slid into the room. "A cablegram rarely precedes good news, Sir. I anticipated a restorative might be in order. Two glasses or three, Sir?"

"Three, I think, Hedges," Athena said. "And leave the stopper off the decanter when you've finished. We can refresh our glasses ourselves as needs be."

Hedges glanced deferentially at his employer who gave a slight nod. "Very good, Sir."

"I didn't know you drank whiskey, Athena," her father said once Hedges left the room.

Athena studied her shoes before looking up with defiance in her eyes. "I've been drinking your whiskey since I was sixteen, Father."

Randolph Fenhagen roared with laughter. "I'm glad I didn't father a Goodie-two-shoes for a daughter." He clapped a hand on Athena's back. "Good for you. Any other confessions you'd like to get off your chest? No? Perhaps best left unsaid. I never did go in for that Catholic nonsense about confession being good for the soul."

The first round of whiskies vanished in double quick time and the glasses quickly replenished. "We have no option but to sit and wait to see what transpires in Europe," Minerva said, starting on her third stiff Bourbon and seeming unaffected by the first two. "If nothing happens, if it's simply a precaution while cooler heads prevail in London and Berlin, you'll be at the altar in time for Christmas. Maybe even Thanksgiving." She glanced pointedly at Athena's belly. "Assuming there's no reason for undue haste."

Athena's father looked away and studied the wallpaper frieze over the door.

"I'm not pregnant, Mamma. I can reassure you of that."

"I'm glad to hear it, dear. Until you're married, if you can't be good, be careful I always say. And even then it often pays to plan ahead." She looked at her husband for confirmation.

"Quite. Quite," he said. "Neither of us expected you to be a nun while you were in Washington."

"Or at Vassar," Athena's mother chipped in.

"We're glad you were sensible about things. Time enough for a family later on, if that's what you decide on. Though speaking for both of us, I think we'd prefer the traditional order, if you can manage it. A wedding before we become grandparents."

Red-faced, Athena didn't know where to look. She drained her glass and set it down with a bang on top of the drinks cabinet. "I don't think there's much chance of either in the near future." She turned to her mother. "I'm going to change for dinner. If you hear any strange, loud noises, it'll only be me kicking the hell out of the trash can in my room. And I won't need any help dressing."

She stormed off, stomping her feet on each stair tread and slammed her bedroom door.

# 8. WAR

Harry sat at the breakfast table the following morning, hungover, still furious with his father and only a little less with his own behaviour at dinner. He could not blame it entirely on drink. He had bottled up his anger for so long that he had often wondered if he would ever let it loose. Then he'd allowed emotion to overcome his better judgement. But, for the first time in his life, he had stood up to his father and put him in his place, not with fists but with words. In the long run he knew words cut deeper, in spite of that idiotic saying about sticks and stones.

He pulled out his pocket watch and checked the time. He didn't wish to leave *Roseland;* he hadn't been there more than a few hours, it seemed, but neither could he feign ignorance of the telegram. Honour and duty bound, he had to leave within the hour if he were to reach Horsefield Barracks the same day. Then what? Pure speculation, which got him nowhere. But his regiment was of the highest calibre and reputation. He could not believe they would be held back in reserve if there was fighting to be done.

Unable to face hot buttered toast and marmalade, the kippers or the devilled kidneys and scrambled eggs on the sideboard, Harry chewed half-heartedly on a piece of dry toast. He was about to go to war, and that could only mean with Germany, in France most likely. The Germans surely wouldn't ignore Belgium's neutrality and invade through there. No, they would come through Alsace and Lorraine, like they did in 1870, no matter how tempting an advance might be across the unfortified borders between Germany, Belgium and France.

"We'll miss you, Harry," Cecilia said, breaking the heavy silence.

He looked up. "It won't be for long, I'm sure. A precautionary measure. Best to be prepared rather than sorry."

"It's a pity about having to postpone the wedding."

"We went through that last night. Nothing new to add. Once the situation in Europe's cleared up we can rearrange it." In spite of his pounding temples, he tried to sound bright and positive. "Otherwise you might be married before me."

"Don't be gloomy, Harry. I don't have any desire to get married and leave the cushy life here. Who in her right mind would swap all this for washing her husband's dirty underclothes and socks, cooking, cleaning and dealing with shit-filled nappies?"

"Even as a doctor you intend marrying down, I take it?"

"Inevitably, these days, if you marry for love, not money. Otherwise I'll be doing the rounds of what passes for society in Cornwall in the hope of snagging someone from the County." She wrinkled her nose, but it did not have the same effect on him as when Athena did it. "They're mostly as inbred as Pekinese and as bright as donkeys. Even finding a clueless one will prove a monumental task."

"That's quite the revelation for someone who's not twenty-one yet."

"Anyway, the old order won't last forever. This war, assuming there is one, will probably see its death. Then women will get the vote, and you men won't like it."

Harry inspected his fingernails. He cleared his throat. "I have an unpleasant suspicion you might be right, at least in some respects. I think the world is going to be turned upside down before any of us gets much older."

Cecilia smiled smugly and sipped her tea while Harry drank his coffee in silence. At nine he threw his napkin onto the tablecloth and rose. "Time to go. I have a job to do. I hope mother is up and dressed in time to say good bye." He glanced over at the butler. "Tregarrick, please have my bags ready in the hall in five minutes, and have Rhodes bring the Daimler round to the front."

"Very good, Sir."

Rhodes, the Earl of St Austell's chauffeur, drove the Daimler with care up the gravel driveway. As a mark of respect, Tregarrick and as many of the servants as could be spared from their duties gathered on the front steps of *Roseland* to wish Harry good luck. He hugged his tearful sister and stepmother while Rhodes waited impassively with the door held open. Harry noticed his father's absence from the steps. Just as well, he thought. They both might have difficulty feigning civility to one another. And Ernest was probably still sleeping off his hangover this early in the day.

Harry decided he should say something encouraging before he left. With a lump in his throat and his heart beating fast, he said simply, "I'm sure I'll be back before long. If it comes to war, they don't stand a chance. It'll probably all be over by Christmas."

With those few words, Captain, the Honourable Hereward Haig-Mallory climbed into the back of the car, settled into his seat and set off to war. He raised his leather-wrapped swagger stick in salute as Rhodes engaged gear and eased the car down the driveway, past the venerable spreading Cedar of Lebanon, and on towards the gates.

"Horsefield Barracks I take it, Sir?"

"If you would, Rhodes."

Harry turned and peered through the rear window. The family remained on the steps. His stepmother cried into a handkerchief and Cecilia waved until the car turned out of the gates and onto the St Austell road. Rhodes stared straight ahead at the deserted road. His eyes never strayed to the rear-view mirror until he broke the silence a few minutes later. "All being well, Sir, you should be in Bristol in time for dinner. Something to look forward to, I dare say." Without waiting for a reply he slid the glass partition closed.

By the time they were through Exeter, Harry's headache had moved to the top of his head, though his temples still throbbed. He pressed his fingers against the small locket on the chain around his neck, the locket that contained Athena's colour tinted miniature portrait and a lock of her hair she had given him before he left New York. He vowed he would carry it forever. He would be buried with it if need be. He would make a note of his wishes in his journal before he retired for the night in his room.

This was no way to prepare to go to war, he told himself with disgust at the maudlin sentimentality that had settled over him. He resolved to do the best he possibly could to lead his men in a manner befitting a cavalry officer. They could depend on him to use his best judgement and all his training to ensure their safety in so far as it was humanly possible. It was the Hussars' way. It was the only way he knew. He would not let his men, or his regiment, down.

Several hours later, Rhodes swung the Daimler off the road and came to a smooth stop at the white painted barrier in front of the guard house at the entrance to the Cavalry Depot. The Hussar at the gate sprang to attention with a crash of hobnails on tarmac and snapped up a quivering salute when he saw the uniformed figure of an officer in the back.

Rhodes wound down his window. "Captain, The Honourable Hereward Haig-Mallory," he announced, as the soldier glanced into the rear of the car and verified the identity of the passenger. He raised the barrier, crashed to attention once again and snapped up another salute as the Daimler purred past on its way to the commanding officer's office.

When Harry reported for duty, Colonel Shackleton came straight to the point. "Still no declaration, Haig-Mallory," he said. "War may yet be avoided, though I think it unlikely. It always seems to fall to old men who have never experienced battle to send young men abroad to do the killing for them. And the dying. Perhaps if they'd seen the brutal face of war, they might choose to act more prudently and with greater circumspection."

"Yes, Sir." Harry could think of nothing more to add.

"And don't say I said so."

"No, Sir."

"I have no idea if or when exactly we'll be off, or where we'll be going, other than most probably to France. We can leave tomorrow if we have to. My best guess is they'll send as many infantry as they can to France as fast as they can cram them onto the boats, then the artillery. I suspect the cavalry might be the last to go." When Harry looked puzzled, Shackleton said, "They can cram five infantrymen onto the boat for every cavalryman and his horse. Probably more if they try."

At the mention of a boat, Harry's face turned white. Of course, he should have anticipated a sea voyage across the Channel. They weren't going to ride across. He examined Shackleton's youthful face, the familiar clipped black moustache, black hair and dark eyes in the hope he might find a clue to any hidden meaning behind the words. He found none. Harry took Shackleton's words with a straight face and refused to let his frustration show. He was certain now that he could have spent more time at home. Perhaps even time enough for a wedding, though a honeymoon might have had to wait. "I see," he said in the end.

"I doubt if you do, but that's by the by. I believe this war will be different from anything we've ever fought or even prepared for before, and nothing like South Africa. But I may be wrong."

Shackleton paused to let his words sink in. Harry knew Shackleton was rarely wrong, which was one reason why he was the youngest lieutenant colonel in the brigade, moneyed, naturally, and of a good family but with a reputation of being cast from a different mould from most senior officers. And to top it all, Shackleton was little older than himself. "We'll have to soldier on as best we can, no matter the circumstances, think on our feet and be prepared to improvise when necessary."

Harry nodded, but remained tight-lipped.

"I know it's sacrilegious to say this, Haig-Mallory, but I think the cavalry might have had its day. We're no match for machine guns and accurate artillery fire. A glorious way to die, of course, charging the enemy at a full gallop with sabres drawn, but even more futile now than it was in the Crimea. It's not what any of us really wants deep down, is it?"

"No, Sir. Not as a first choice."

When Harry offered no further comment, Shackleton sighed and said, "We always seem to fight today's war with yesterday's tactics. Time marches on. Sadly, the army only marches." He looked Harry squarely in the eyes. "Again, not a whisper I said so. It would be unseemly for a captain to be put on jankers."

Shackleton allowed a hint of a smile play with his lips. "There's a briefing after dinner for all officers. That is all."

A sense of foreboding settled over Harry on his way to the mess. Germany was mobilizing. France already had. Britain and her allies had responded in kind. There had still not been a declaration of war and there were hopes, growing fainter by the hour, that war might yet be averted, but the realization sank in that a country mobilizing was effectively a country already at war.

*

On the 4th of August news broke with Colonel Shackleton's announcement at breakfast. "Our ultimatum expired at eleven o'clock last night," he said. "Germany has not responded. We are therefore at war, gentlemen."

A shot of adrenalin pumped through Harry's veins and he was aware of the first hint of dampness in his underarms. War. So it had come to that. He might easily be killed, he thought, though that was not the cause of his immediate fear. He was about to be tested, severely, in the face of real guns, real bullets and real soldiers intent on killing him. What would happen if his response were found wanting? Disgrace certainly for conduct unbecoming of a Hussar Officer. And he would be unworthy of Athena. He sucked in a breath of cigarette smoke-filled air and held it. His hands shook. He tightened them into fists until the trembling passed. He exhaled quietly. Even if it meant his death, he vowed he would not let anyone down, least of all Athena.

Harry watched Shackleton scrutinize his officers' faces; expectance, excitement and enthusiasm on the subalterns', through varying degrees of disinterest and boredom on the more senior. "We break camp tomorrow at o-six hundred hours," he said. "The King's Imperial Hussars will form part of the Household Cavalry Composite Regiment. We have orders to sail for

France. Ensure your men are ready."

The regiment rank and file received the news with cheering and excitement. Off to France, there to drive the Germans all the way back to the Rhine and beyond, demoralized and completely outmatched by the best of the British cavalry. Five hundred and forty-nine officers, non-commissioned officers and troopers together with six hundred horses, including remounts made ready for their short ride to the railway station. Shackleton was right, Harry thought ruefully. Counting the tack, harnesses, arms, ammunition and a mountain of ancillary equipment, their regiment needed at least five times the ship space as the infantry.

The newspaper banner headlines the next day confirmed that Britain was at war. The Times' merely stated BRITAIN AT WAR in two-inch block capitals reserved for the announcement of the Second Coming of Christ. The Daily Telegraph's fuller headline proclaimed, GREAT BRITAIN AT WAR WITH GERMANY, as if its readers had been out of touch with world news the past month. Harry only had to skim the first paragraphs to confirm there was nothing he didn't already know.

Two seemingly interminable stop and start days later the regiment disembarked from the troop train at Dover and rode to their camp on the chalk downs above the town. There they waited under canvas for two weeks while the last of their equipment straggled in. When not shrouded in fog, they could see the French coast and the cliffs at Cap Gris Nez across the English Channel. So near, they felt as if they could reach out and touch France. And yet so far, not in distance, but in time, which moved at the army's own rhythm and pace. In France, and wherever else they might end up, virtually all of the rank and file who had never been outside England would face an alien way of life. And danger, no matter how good they proved to be at killing Germans.

*

The Fenhagens sat down for Sunday dinner on the ninth. "Harry told me the English have a cold dinner on Sundays," Athena said. "They give the servants the afternoon and evening off so they can go to the evening service at church." Her mother looked at her with disbelief on her face. "As many as can be spared," Athena added hurriedly. "Everyone gets at least half a day off every week. Most of them take it on Sunday. Which is why it's a cold supper with the cook at church. And they serve themselves like it's a buffet."

"I've no doubt you'll get used to the way they do things there after a while," her mother said. "Whenever that may be."

Athena looked away with her lips compressed in a narrow line.

"Funny people, the British," her mother continued, unperturbed. "Not like us at all.”

“It happens when you marry a foreigner,” her father said. “Perfectly natural Athena should want to fit in with them. Goodness knows they haven’t shown much inkling to do things the American way. Nice people, I’m told, but a bit stuffy, stuck in their ways. They’ll lose their empire if they’re not careful. Maybe sooner than they think. Germany’s no pushover.”

“You’re making me nervous, Papa ,” Athena said. “Harry will be over there any day now. He sent a cable last week.”

“You didn’t tell me,” her father said.

“It was only two words. We’re off. Three if you count love. And four if you include Harry. He didn’t say where or when. I wish I knew where he was.”

“Military secrets,” her father said. “We’ll know when you do, if you tell us. And if the censors allow him to be more explicit. Anyway,” he glanced at his wife, “I’d lay a dollar on it being France.”

“We were supposed to be getting married in less than three weeks and honeymooning in Paris. If you’re right, Papa, it may well be he’ll be there without me. It’s so unfair.” She looked at her mother. “See? I didn’t swear. But it makes me want to spit.”

“Neither of which is becoming of a lady at the dinner table. It seems you will have to reserve both for the baseball diamond,” her mother said.

“According to the paper, the Cleveland Naps won yesterday.” Her father sounded happy. “They beat the Boston Red Sox.”

“Far too little, far too late, Papa,” Athena said. “The Naps are woeful. They play like they’re taking a nap whenever the ball’s in play. The smart money’s on the Philadelphia Athletics.” She reached over and touched his sleeve. “Don’t worry. Cleveland can’t get any worse. They’re rebuilding. Again. And there’s always next year.”

# 9. A TIME TO LOVE

"Harry's in France." Athena looked up from the hastily scribbled one-page letter in her hand. "He can't say where but they're under canvas for the time being," she said to her mother over coffee in the morning room. Athena's cup sat in its saucer with the untouched contents cooling by the minute. She read the letter a third time. "He says nothing much is happening. It's all *Hurry up and wait*, which he says is typical of the army. They usually only see the enemy at a distance." She put the letter down. "I wonder what he means by *usually*. Do you think he's already been in action?"

Her mother put down her coffee cup. "I wouldn't read anything into one word, dear. I have to admit the news in the paper isn't exactly encouraging, not after the defeat at Mons, but let's look on the positive side. They and the French held the Germans at bay before they could reach Paris and then pushed them back towards Belgium. And Harry's alive, or you wouldn't have his letter. He's unhurt and obviously in good spirits to judge from what little he says. I'm sure he can look after himself."

"I'm still worried about him, though, Mamma. His regiment's top drawer. They'll be in the fighting for sure. Oh, Mamma, I do hope he's all right." Tears welled in Athena's eyes. She dabbed at them with a napkin and sniffed, once.

"As we both do, dear. He'll be all right, I know it. And you'll be walking up the aisle on your father's arm, and back down on Harry's before you know it. Now, drink your coffee before it's stone cold."

*

Over the following days and weeks the brigade in which Harry's regiment formed a small part followed the infantry as it set about a sluggish advance in a roughly northerly direction. By November, they found themselves encamped in the grounds of the Château Gran'ville outside the village of Ste-

Marguerite-des-Lys-Gran'ville which straddled the unmarked border between France and Belgium.

Like so many villages in northeast France the regiment passed through, the unremarkable commune of Ste-Marguerite-des-Lys-Gran'ville more closely resembled a large hamlet surrounded by farms. An abundant harvest, most of which the villagers had successfully hidden from the Germans, had largely escaped purloin during the German retreat. In turn the local inhabitants were inclined toward generosity in their hospitality towards their new occupiers. They also profited from the sale of fresh food to augment the unappetizing tinned rations of the British soldiers.

The villagers, for the most part old men, young boys and women, laughed good naturedly at the Tommies. In return, and without a word of French between them, Harry's men attempted to beg, buy or otherwise scrounge food for their messes and wine for their tables. How long the bonhomie between the English and the locals would last Harry would not guess, but he suspected it might end with the first unrequested pregnancy. Knowing his men and their legendary ability to charm their way into the inner confines of a nun's habit, he estimated a honeymoon of perhaps three months. By then he anticipated they would have deployed to the front, for now bogged down around Ypres, and his men would have dodged the bullet of paternity.

Late in the morning of Boxing Day, with the fog of alcohol and his hangover by then largely dissipated, Harry wandered away from the château. The idea was to stretch his legs and get a breath of fresh air untainted by the stink of spilled beer and stale wine in the officers' mess. Without a plan or a destination in mind, he followed a low stone wall to a gap where a gate had once hung. He passed through the gap and crossed the churned mud and goose droppings of a farmyard, heading towards the farmhouse. With an annoyed honk and an undignified flap of wings, two white geese hurried out of his way.

"Papa?"

Harry stopped and turned. A red-headed, freckle-faced child of about three regarded him with thumb-in-mouth curiosity. He smiled and shook his head. "*Non, chérie. Pas ton père.*" A woman in her mid-twenties, he guessed, with bright red hair like the child, hurried from the farmhouse door and snatched the child away from harm. Harry noticed the woman's green eyes and pale, freckled face, like the child's, and wondered at her heritage. He quickly took in her beige, spun wool blouse buttoned up the front to the neck, and heavy wool, ankle length dark brown skirt beneath a white cotton apron. She held the skirt up away from the dirt with one hand. He noticed the wooden clogs on her feet, and her ankles and calves, though wrapped in thick wool stockings, were bared to view.

"You have a charming daughter," Harry said in French, as the woman he took to be the child's mother turned a protective back on him.

"You speak French?" Her voice registered surprise as she turned to face him. The child wriggled in her mother's arms and slid to the ground.

"I am probably the only one in my regiment who does."

"Did she ask if you were her father?"

"Yes. Why?"

"She asks every soldier she sees. She knows her father is a soldier, but he's been gone since the mobilization. I'm sure she wouldn't recognize him if he walked up to her like you did."

"It must be hard on her."

The woman shrugged. "She knows nothing else. Sophie is not yet three."

"I am Captain Haig-Mallory. I'm the adjutant. We've taken over the Château Gran'ville for our headquarters. I don't think we've met before, at least not formally, but I believe you have business dealings with our squadron quartermaster corporal on behalf of the commune. Am I right?"

"Yes, Captain. I hope I am of service." She brushed her hands on her apron. A slight movement suggested the smallest of curtsies.

"We greatly appreciate the supply of fresh meat, fruit and vegetables. Keep up the good work."

Harry tipped the peak of his hat with his swagger stick and turned to leave.

"I am Solange Grenier," she said. "This is our farm." She swept her arm behind her to indicate the dilapidated stone buildings and the surrounding pasture.

"Your husband is at the front?"

"Yes. A *poilu*. As the mayor of Ste-Marguerite he said it was his duty to set an example."

"Is he safe? Do you hear from him?"

"I receive letters occasionally, but he is not much of a writer. I have not seen him since the mobilization in July, nearly six months. We are on our own here these days, for how long, who knows? *C'est la vie*." She shrugged. "We have become accustomed to it."

Harry could not determine if an implied invitation, for friendship, for help or for protection lay hidden in her words. "If I can be of service, Madame," he said, "please allow me."

Solange gave him a broad smile and took Sophie by the hand. "*Le Capitaine parle bien le français, n'est-ce-pas, chérie?*" She looked down at her daughter, who buried her head in her mother's apron. "I don't know why she has become shy. It's most unlike Sophie." She smiled again. "We must go. We have chores to complete before supper."

*

In the days and weeks following Christmas, Harry oversaw Solange's work as the go-between when the regiment needed to purchase local goods, mostly to ensure the mark-up was fair to both sides and her commission was earned and paid.

In late February, as Harry approached the smallholding, he smiled inwardly at the prospect of a few minutes with Solange before business intervened.

"Captain Haig-Mallory," Solange said after she'd shooed Sophie out of the kitchen. "You have been kind to me. And your men have been good for us in the village. I would like to show my appreciation and gratitude."

"There is no need," Harry said, skeptical of what she had up her sleeve and what might be in it for her if he agreed.

"But there is," she said hastily. "It is not out of politeness. I want to invite you to dinner. Perhaps on Sunday. I think you are not too busy on Sunday evenings."

"We don't fight Germans on Sundays. It's in the rule book." He laughed and cast his suspicions aside. "I'd be delighted and honoured. May I bring something?"

"No, but thank you. I have all I need here. At six? You can help me give Sophie her supper and put her to bed. She has told me she wants you to read her a bedtime story. Will you do that?"

"Of course. I'd love to."

*

After her supper on Sunday evening they put Sophie to bed. Harry read not one, not two, but three stories. Then he read the first one again, exactly as he read it the first time, down to the last inflexion of his voice. This, Solange explained, was of the utmost importance when one is not quite three.

With lamp oil in scarce supply, and the farmhouse without electricity, dinner by candlelight was a welcome expedience. They did not reach the cheese course. Either by design or by happenstance, a bottle of table wine banished any lingering inhibitions. Without a word, Solange rose from the table, took Harry's unprotesting hand and led him up the creaking stairs to her bedroom beneath the eaves.

"The weather…," Harry said, breaking the awkward silence with the first thing that sprang to mind once he had closed the door.

"My husband…,"

"This is not a situation…," Harry stammered.

"The news from the front…" Her voice sounded breathless and husky. The tops of her breasts quivered with each slight movement beneath the plain wool blouse. Harry noticed the top two buttons had come unbuttoned at the neck.

"I have ever found myself in…,"

"Is always bad…,"

"With a married woman… I'm sorry. I interrupted you."

"I have never been attracted to another man, Capitaine 'Arry." She touched her neckline and undid another button. The movement set her breasts trembling. She rounded her shoulders to emphasize her cleavage. Her blouse gaped open to reveal a white petticoat and narrow pale blue satin ribbons. There was little left to Harry's imagination. She smiled, then pulled her shoulders back. The outline of her nipples bulged against the cloth as if the petticoat didn't exist. There was no doubt left in Harry's mind, had there been any at the outset that he was not in her bedroom to admire her wedding portraits.

Solange's perfume, which he had not noticed before, rose to fill Harry's head with a mix of sultry eastern spices and a hint of musk. "Except for Pierre-Auguste," she added, hastily. "Not as I am to you. It is hot in here, is it not?" She fanned her face with her hand. Her breasts shimmied. More perfume wafted his way. She fluttered her eyelashes and edged her hot body closer to Harry. She touched his forearm. Goosebumps ran up his arm. "He is at Verdun. I have not heard from him in over four months. You know how it is for a French soldier at the front."

"I do." Harry touched the warm skin of her arm. "May God grant your husband a safe journey through the war."

Her voice trembled. "It is my daily prayer. There will be no retreat from Verdun. Our men, my husband, will live or die there, but they will never yield a centimetre of French soil to the Boche."

"In the meantime…"

"Yes, in the meantime…" She caught her breath. "You need to take comfort as much as any man, where you can." She turned her head away demurely. "I understand a man's needs. Fulfillment…"

"No more than for a woman, I assure you." He held his breath, sensing the electricity crackle across the small gap that separated them like the tips of a spark plug. If he touched her now he was sure they would both receive an electric shock.

She crossed to the other side of the small room. On a chest of drawers of unfinished wood beneath a mirror stood a sealed bottle of Cognac and two glasses. She held up the bottle. "A Cognac, Capitaine 'Arry? I find it helps me to sleep in the long, cold nights when I am alone."

Harry decided Pierre-Auguste's wife did not appear in the least upset at her impending betrayal of her husband. If anything, she sounded excited at the prospect of adultery and determined to make the best of her situation. He could not, in all conscience, disappoint her.

"A small Cognac would be most welcome. But there are better, and far more pleasant ways to achieve sleep when one is alone, *n'est-ce-pas?*" Harry smiled. The look in her eyes when she returned his smile spoke of mischief.

"You have guessed my secret, Capitaine 'Arry."

"I think it is no secret. A girl must do whatever she can to get to sleep when she is alone. And too much Cognac can dull the senses." He felt the blood hammer in his ears. "And may I call you Solange? Madame Grenier sounds so formal when we are alone and…"

"But of course." She poured a generous amount of Cognac into the two tumblers. He took his Cognac in one hand and sniffed it. "One sip," he said, putting the glass to his lips. "The rest I shall save for later."

She turned her back to him. "I can confide in you, Capitaine 'Arry?"

"Certainly. You already have once this evening." He ran his hands gently across her shoulders and over her rounded breasts. He cupped them lightly, feeling them swell and her nipples harden beneath his palms. He heard her sharp intake of breath, her soft moan. He released her breasts, undid the last of the buttons on her blouse and slid it off her shoulders.

"I do not expect to see Pierre-Auguste again."

"He is a brave and gallant soldier." The blouse fell to the floor.

"He will die before he dishonours France."

"I understand." He unbuttoned the skirt. It fell from her hips to the strip of carpet beside the bed. She stepped out of her slippers. The buttons up the front of her petticoat provided no challenge. It followed the skirt to the floor.

She wore nothing else. She turned her back to him. He kissed the crook of her neck. Her skin crawled with goosebumps. Her nipples stood out from her breasts, stiff with arousal no less that from the chill of the unheated bedroom.

"It is same for you, for England," she breathed as her chest rose and fell with her mounting excitement.

"We share the same commitment to our countries." His hands registered the shiver of anticipation running through her body. He cupped her breasts while he kissed her ear lobes, her neck and her shoulders. He hastily slipped the chain and locket from around his neck and slid it into his trousers pocket. Solange turned to face him and tore his jacket from his shoulders, undid his tie and collar and unbuttoned his shirt. She flung the shirt on top of her discarded clothes. He pulled off his woolen undershirt, threw it down beside his shirt and stood in front of her with his braces dangling by his side, breathing heavily. She placed her hands on his chest, fingering his chest hair. She touched his nipples.

"You like that?"

Harry groaned with pleasure. He stripped off the rest of his clothes and stood before her, fully aroused and as naked as she. Solange laughed gaily and pulled him onto the bed. He tumbled on top of her and wrapped his arms around her. His mouth sought hers. She returned his kisses with passion.

"We should not hurry," he whispered in her ear. "We have all night before us."

"We have time for mutual exploration, Capitaine 'Arry." She whimpered with pleasure and held his head against her breast while his hand explored the intimate crevices of her body.

"*Là. C'est là, chéri,*" she gasped. Moments later her body stiffened. She dug her finger nails into Harry's shoulders, took a sharp intake of breath and held it for a moment. "*J'arrive. J'arrive,*" she cried out.

"The bed is noisy," Harry said, once she stopped squirming. "And so are you. We should be careful. We don't want to wake Sophie. What would she say if she found us together like this?"

"Sophie is too young to understand anything. Besides, she sleeps through thunderstorms. She will not wake until seven tomorrow. And I could not prevent myself from expressing my pleasure." She wriggled beneath him and clasped his hand to her breast. "You are so good, 'Arry. It has been so long."

"Too long for both of us, I think," he whispered in her ear. His hand strayed down without resistance and found what he sought. Moments later Solange's body stiffened, followed in seconds by muted squeals and grunts and a convulsive thrust of her hips. She relaxed, then took him and guided him inside her.

"That was the first time since Pierre-Auguste left for the war," she murmured afterwards, as she lay relaxed beneath him, her arms and legs wrapped around him in tight embrace.

"I won't say a word if you don't. We have our hands full with the Boche. I don't need an angry husband to contend with as well."

Solange giggled. "My handsome Capitaine 'Arry. You are too good to me. It is a pity, but like my Pierre-Auguste, you will soon leave me." When she rose from the bed Harry thought the night was over. But she hurried over to the dresser and returned with their cognacs and a pack of cigarettes. She drew one from a pack. "A smoke with our cognac?"

"Please. I left mine at the château. A *disque bleu?*"

"*Oui.* A cigarette is good after making love, *n'est-ce-pas?*" She struck a match and lit two cigarettes, inhaled hers deeply and expelled the smoke before passing the other to Harry.

The aroma of their lovemaking seeped from beneath the duvet to mingle with the pungent smell of French cigarette tobacco smoke. Harry stared at the low, angled ceiling beneath the eaves and decided, under different circumstances, he could become quite accustomed to this arrangement, uncomplicated as it was. Neither party needed to do more than enjoy the other's company and the benefits they gained. Pierre-Auguste need never know, any more than Athena. They lit another cigarette and smoked and sipped cognac in silence until they stubbed the cigarette butts out. He pulled the feather comforter over them. Cold, feeble light from the crescent moon glinted in the frost-filled air beyond the window. For a soldier in wartime, he thought, this is about as good as it gets.

"Can we do it again? Make love to Solange?"

Harry reached down. "Like this?"

"Yes. And after you will enter me again?"

"Of course. Once is never enough."

"If only Pierre-Auguste understood that."

A spike of guilt flashed through Harry's mind at the thought of betraying Athena's trust in his good behaviour while they were apart. He suppressed the thought in an instant and concentrated on the moment, the paramount need for human contact. And if Pierre-Auguste discovered his wife's adultery, it would remain between the two of them to resolve the issue. He and his regiment would be long gone by then. A bit callous on his part, he thought, but war changed the rules of engagement. And hanged for a sheep as hanged for a lamb, he thought as he resumed his attention on Solange and her soft, warm body.

# 10. SOLANGE

Each visit to the Grenier farm brought Harry a deepening attachment for Solange, and for Sophie, whom by now he looked upon as something like a daughter. He managed to convince himself that before long there would be a swift and clean, no remorse parting. They would both move on. He to a wife, when the war allowed; Solange to another lover. Or, if she were lucky, back to a husband and a modicum of stability and security in her life.

After a while he would spare them little more than the occasional thought, wondering what became of them, before this intermission in his life faded to oblivion. Both would forget him, Solange more deliberately but perhaps less easily than Sophie. If Pierre-Auguste returned from the war and resumed his place as head of his family, eventually the grind of unrelenting hard labour would take its toll on that neat, trim body. Her hair would lose its lustrous red sheen and turn grey. Her face would become lined from worry, work and poverty. Her waist and legs would thicken and her lovely breasts would sag. It would take time, but for a woman in her situation it would inevitably happen, and quicker than most. He didn't want to see her like that, ten, fifteen, twenty years from now. Better to cherish the memory of the present than to contemplate the bleakness of her future.

*

*My dearest Harry,*

*It is hard to believe it is almost a year since we met. So much has happened to you since then but little of interest takes place in Cleveland, and probably just as well. I am sure you have more than enough excitement in your life for both of us.*

*My father's secretary of many years retired at the end of December. I have taken her place until he finds a suitable replacement or, better still, I find myself in England as Mrs. Haig-Mallory. The arrangement must be to father's satisfaction as he hasn't sacked me yet.*

*If my father should pass on before we marry, at least I will have some knowledge of how the company works. Just think: one day you could be an American industrialist and husband of the owner of one of the bigger iron and steel manufacturers in the country. I hope that day is long coming. My father enjoys robust good health, as does mother, so the chances of becoming a steel magnate, or selling my inheritance and living like the idle rich with a villa on the French Riviera and a mansion in England are probably many years away...*

*Stay safe,*

*Love,*

*Athena*


Harry reread Athena's last letter and a scalpel of guilt sliced through him every time his thoughts dwelt on Solange and not on Athena. Now, in mid-April, with both armies locked in a vicious stalemate around Ypres, barely a dozen miles distant, he wondered what the future would, could, possibly hold for them with a war and the Atlantic Ocean separating them. He tried to put the question out of his head while he concentrated on his letter to Athena, expressing sentiments that were clearly lies, living the life of a fraud. It was silly, he knew, but falling as he had for Solange would only make their eventual parting not bittersweet, but simply bitter. She had become more than a passing whim, a brief interlude while away from Athena. But part they must, and with the final page of the book, mercifully the words, *The End* would replace the messy complications of their continuing relationship.

He put his pen down and screwed the cap back on. His diary entry for the day and the regiment activity log could wait until after the ink dried on his letter to Athena. And that way he could spend more time with Solange and Sophie. Yes, he decided, it was better to live for the moment, and the future be hanged. Death, he was certain, dogged him over the horizon, at the front, as it stalked all those whom fate had led there. He would probably find himself deployed to the Salient around Ypres within days rather than weeks or months. They had hung around Ste-Marguerite too long already, doing nothing to help win the war. And once they left he would never see Solange, or Sophie, again. The fortunes of war would make the decision for him, the responsibility for the inevitable parting would rest on the shoulders of other, nameless, faceless individuals. It would not take an act of courage on his part to turn his back on Solange when the time came. But it was convenient.

*

Harry's soldier-servant knocked on the door to his room that evening, shortly after his return from supper with Solange and Sophie. News of a briefing by the colonel after breakfast the following day was the word. The soldier tapped the side of his nose, a hint that the briefing may even contain word of their future deployment. Harry knew better than to bet against information emanating from any batman, a more reliable conduit of intelligence than coded wireless signals from high command.

Colonel Shackleton stood the officers at ease the next morning with, "Be seated, gentlemen." He looked around the room at the faces of his officers. "You may smoke. The big picture is as follows. Both sides have dug in along a line that runs from the Swiss border with France, to the southern end of the North Sea and the Straits of Dover. Currently, Nieuport is in our hands. Ostend remains in theirs. Should that change, I'm confident the General Staff will see fit to inform us."

Titters of laughter followed this snippet of military intelligence.

"Speaking of the General Staff, they have decided that we, along with the Horse Guards, Dragoons, Lancers and the other cavalry units, are obsolete in this kind of modern warfare." He held his hands up in mock horror as the entire officer corps present loudly booed the news. "With both sides dug in and living in trenches with little give or take on either side, those in the know have decided that horses don't fare well in trenches. Poor stabling conditions, I suspect, coupled with a lack of paddocks in which to exercise. It's one thing getting over Beecher's Brook. It's quite another extricating oneself from the ditch on the other side should you find yourself unhorsed in the process." He regarded his officers sternly. "As no doubt many of you have discovered after an ill-advised flutter on the favourite in the Grand National."

A short ripple of laughter ran around the room before the faces of the officers turned glum. "Please try to contain your joy, gentlemen. Those placed above us possess far more wisdom than we mere front-line soldiers will ever acquire. Although they have not come right out and said so, my only conclusion is they, whoever they are, intend to unhorse us, and use us as common foot soldiers."

Another chorus of boos greeted him from the body of the room.

"And no gentleman goes into battle unmounted." Those present thumped the tabletops in approval. Shackleton held his hand up for silence. "Which means, at a stroke of a pen, we are no longer gentlemen. Which also means, for some of us, nothing has changed."

Laughter greeted him this time as the officers winked and nudged each other.

"Those of you who consider it undignified for a cavalry officer to march into battle may wish to consider a transfer to another branch of the army. The Royal Horse Artillery and the Royal Flying Corps come to mind as units where opportunities for transport of a kind other than one's feet may still be available. Flying, I'm told by those who have survived the experience, is good, clean fun."

He looked around the room to see if any of the officers gathered showed any inclination to learn to fly. "No? What an unadventurous lot we are. Those of you who wish to remain as officers in the Hussars should order stout boots next time you are home on leave. In the meantime, it becomes imperative you get the men fit with lots of cross-country running and route marches." Groans rose from the body of officers recalling the cross-country runs of their schooldays. "And above all, marksmanship. I have no timetable for any change in our role, gentlemen, nor how the Chiefs of the Imperial General Staff intend to implement it. I think I can assure you though, it is not a question of if, but when we become part of the Poor Bloody Infantry. That is all. Dismissed."

The officers stood to attention as Shackleton left the room before they burst into a cacophony of questions, but as none knew any more than the other, the questions quickly devolved into speculation and argument. Harry knew, come what may, he would remain in the Hussars. It was all he had wanted since he had deliberately failed his Dartmouth entrance exam. He was a Hussar for life, and he hoped, not solely for his own sake but for Athena's as well, it would be a long life, though the casualty reports from the front offered scant comfort.

He was sure by now that Athena must have read of the figures and seen the names printed in the British press and reprinted in the American newspapers. She had every right to be worried, as had every parent of a son in France. From what he'd read, the British Expeditionary Force, the professional army that landed in France in August 1914, one hundred thousand men including his regiment, had virtually ceased to exist a year later. Nine in ten lay dead, or wounded, or prisoners of war. He had heard the French had suffered worse than the British. He hoped Germany and its allies had lost proportionally. Survival, he was sure, was nothing more than a pious hope, something to cling to in dark moments when all else failed. He knew it was only a matter of time before his name appeared in the Times casualty list. He would become a statistic. And Athena would read his name and know their life together had ended before it had begun.

*

After lunch, Harry continued his letter to Athena, set aside the evening before by his visit to Solange:

*…How I long to see you again, to see your face, to touch your hair, your skin and kiss*

*your lips. More than that it would be indelicate to say.*

*We chafe at the bit here, wondering why we are here and not somewhere else where we might be of more use. Time will tell, I suppose. The villagers are kind and treat us well, augmenting our rations with fresh produce — for a price, of course! In return we help repair their homes, barns and farm machinery. It works out well for all concerned. If we are still here for the harvest, no doubt many of the men will be volunteered to help. I think some will be sorry to leave. The quiet country life seems to suit them but we are all slaves to our duty...*

He left the envelope unsealed for censoring by the colonel. His carefully crafted letters contained both the broad and the specific truth, but omitted much that should not find its way into any soldier's letter home to a loved one. He was secretly glad Athena lived in America where she was unlikely to bump into anyone he knew who might have uncovered his affair with Solange. He thought he had managed to keep that part of his life undetected, but he could never be sure. Before long, Solange would become part of his past, buried with the rest of his memories, pleasant and unpleasant, with no reminders.

In truth, Harry's war remained unusually, even ominously, quiet. From the Château Gran'ville they could sometimes hear an artillery barrage if the wind blew from the east, not uncommon those winter and spring months, but the order never came to deploy to the front. The first consignment of infantry pattern boots arrived for the men in April. By the end of May most of the rank and file had boots that fitted, and coarse woolen infantry uniforms began to trickle in to the squadron quartermaster corporal's store. With the arrival of the uniforms, as far as the men were concerned, their lives as cavalry had reached a dead end of usefulness.

*

Colonel Shackleton called a meeting of all officers before lunch one day in early July. "It's been eleven months since the declaration of war," he said, "and we haven't fired a shot in anger since The Marne. And hardly any then. Some of you might wonder why we are here." He looked around the room at their blank faces to gauge their reaction. "Or perhaps not. However, I shall keep you in suspense no longer." He picked up his glass of water, held it to his lips and drank slowly, then scratched his head before inspecting his nails. A titter of laughter rippled through the body of officers. "We had it wrong all along." He took another sip of water. "Orders have come down from on high, gentlemen. We are to return to England in two days for mounted ceremonial duties at Buckingham Palace and Windsor Castle. No lesser personage than King George the Fifth signed the order. He wanted the best, so the best he got. Us."

He ran a finger across his moustache. "For those of you who have forgotten which end of a horse points forward, riding lessons will be available before we embark."

A temporary stay of execution, Harry thought, as the officers filed out of the mess. The year's casualties had amounted to Smith's sprained ankle and wrist, his own bayonet wound, and two lost horses, all at Le Cateau. Their luck couldn't hold forever, and he knew they'd be back, to face death somewhere on the western front, probably sooner rather than later. Until that day, like the Greek gods, he'd accept his own temporary stay of execution and make the most of it. Perhaps, he thought, Epicurus had it right after all – *Eat, drink and be merry, for tomorrow we may die.* Convenient, Harry concluded, for those who did not believe in life after death. And at that point he wasn't sure where he stood on the issue.

He bellied up to the bar and signed the chit for a Scotch and soda. He'd miss Solange, he thought as he took his first sip and savoured the way the whisky ran across his tongue and burned its way down his throat. At least for a while. Why, he asked himself again, was he having an affair with the wife of a French soldier? That first night together had spoken only to their need for sexual satisfaction coupled with opportunity. But over time their relationship had developed until now it had become as much an affair of the heart as of the body. At least, for him. It could even be love, but if it were, it was completely different from how he reacted to Athena in the first heady days of their romance.

With Solange it had taken time to reach a point in his life where he found himself lost in thought at the bar in the officers' mess, immersed in an existential contemplation of his future beyond the day after tomorrow. He asked himself if it were possible to love two women equally, yet differently, at the same time. Or if he actually did. Perhaps his love — and he was certain this was love, not a passing infatuation — for Solange ran deeper than that for Athena. Or maybe that was only because Solange was here, in the present, a few hundred yards and not an ocean away. And who could resist Sophie? An ache in his heart caused him to grimace and he looked around surreptitiously, hoping no one had noticed. Perhaps he wanted a family of his own more than he ever suspected. Was that it? Was Sophie the attraction? He thought about it for a moment. No, he decided. Solange was the true object of his affection. Sophie was the icing on the cake, but she was not his daughter, not a child of his making. She was Solange and Pierre-Auguste's daughter. She belonged to them.

He swallowed the rest of his Scotch in one gulp and placed the glass on the bar top. Why couldn't this have been an ordinary, uncomplicated affair? All that could come of it was at least one, and possibly two broken hearts.

"Another one, Sir?" The mess orderly held the Scotch bottle up. Harry pushed the glass across the bar and signed the chit. A few more of these, he thought, and bugger the doubts that consumed him.

*

Poignant leave taking in the village by the men left women sniffing into handkerchiefs or crying unashamedly. Most of those with swollen bellies that spoke of carelessness by both parties would eventually have to offer explanations to those absent husbands fortunate enough to return home. Further farewells prompted another round of amorous clinches. *One for the road*, a frequent excuse, would no doubt lead to further pregnancies on top of those duly noted and accounted for.

"Is it true, 'Arry? You are leaving us?" Tears welled in Solange's eyes as she twisted her apron in her hands.

"Yes." A lump swelled in his throat as soon as he acknowledged the fact. "The day after tomorrow."

"Do not worry about us," she said as she turned her head away from him. "We will be fine. We will have one last dinner together tonight and we will make love. Then we will part without tears or regrets. You will go off to fight the Boche and then return to England when you have defeated them. You will marry and have lots of children and be happy. And Pierre-Auguste will return and life will continue in Ste-Marguerite." She turned back, no longer able to contain the tears.

Harry took her in his arms and held her close until the shudders running through her body subsided. "I wish you and little Sophie only happiness, always and forever." He kissed her, softly and gently on the lips and fought back the tears brimming in his own eyes as they clung to each other. "I love you," he wanted to say. "I will return after the war." But he could not find the words, perhaps because they weren't true, no matter how deeply he believed them today. He was engaged to be married to Athena, and he would marry her, if he lived long enough. That was the promise he had made to her and he would not break it. No matter the temptation.

"I have received news of Pierre-Auguste," Solange said quietly and with sadness in her voice. "He is a prisoner of war. That is all I know. But at least he is out of the fighting. I hope they will treat him well."

"I'm sure they will, Solange. Whatever we may think of the Germans, deep down they are like Frenchmen and Englishmen — decent, honourable human beings."

At least, he hoped so, for all their sakes. In spite of the gas attacks at Ypres that had claimed thousands of British, French and Belgian lives and blinded so many more. The wide gap left in the front line was where he and his men ought to be, fighting, not preparing to return to London, unscathed amid all the allied carnage. Perhaps the rumours about German soldiers bayonetting Belgian babies and pregnant mothers was more than a rumour after all. Perhaps he was wrong about the Germans. Perhaps they were anything but decent and honourable. How could they be when they used chlorine and mustard gas? But he couldn't express his thought to Solange whose husband was now a statistic; a number, not a name in a register. Prisoner of war. File closed.

Harry was thankful Solange had failed to notice his shiver at what would he was sure would come to pass.

He took her cool, dry hand in his and let her lead him upstairs for the last time.

# 11. THE GENERAL

On their arrival at Dover, Colonel Shackleton called Harry into the CO's temporary, bare-bones office in Dover Castle. The smell of stale pipe tobacco smoke from the last incumbent lingered in the air and leached from the grubby curtains and threadbare carpet. Shackleton stood behind a scarred wooden desk that bore the burn marks of untended cigarettes. Papers, files and folders littered the desk and overflowed from the dilapidated filing cabinets. A map of the Western Front hung from the eau-de-nil gloss-painted wall behind him.

Harry glanced at the impassive face of newly promoted Captain Merryweather, ramrod straight next to the CO's desk. He scowled at the young man with the third pip on his shoulders, occupying his own rightful position as adjutant on any formal occasion. He looked, Harry thought, all too cozy beside their commanding officer. Harry wondered what he might have done to offend the colonel. Nothing came to mind. His men and his junior officers were all up to scratch. Could there be a problem with the censoring of the letters? Or a complaint from the women of Ste-Marguerite-des-Lys-Gran'ville? From Solange even? Did Shackleton know about Solange?

"Colonel," Harry said in a clipped, military voice as he snapped his salute to his side.

His face betrayed his concern at being called into the CO's office without explanation.

"At ease, Major," Shackleton said.

Harry hardly heard his CO in his confusion. "I beg your pardon, Sir?"

"Major Haig-Mallory, congratulations! Your promotion has come through, and well deserved too, I must say."

Harry started to say something when Shackleton interrupted. "There is one drawback, though. While we're all spit and polish at Windsor and Horse Guards, you'll be leaving us, temporarily at least."

A puzzled look creased Harry's forehead and wrinkled the skin at the corners of his eyes.

"After some leave and a chance to buy new uniforms, you'll be back in France as liaison officer between Field Marshal, The Viscount French and the French General, Lanrezac, with whom the Field Marshal has a particularly prickly relationship."

Harry arched his eyebrows and opened his mouth, then thought better of it.

"Frankly, I don't envy you, but your experience as aide-de-camp in Washington, as well as your ability to parler the old français was duly noticed, and not only by me. Most of us can barely mutter something about the plume de ma tante, and yet you can gabble away with the natives as if you were to the manoir born, so to speak."

"As children we spoke French at home when my father wasn't around"

"I won't ask at which Frog bordello you learned the more colloquial lingo, probably not a delicate question, and I doubt it came from your mother or your stepmother. Anyway, whether you like it or not this is a very important job that's landed in your lap. Mess it up and you'll truly be in the consommé. There are lots of top-level people wandering around France unable to talk to each other, and if the people who plan things can't understand each other, things will get buggered up in a hurry. You know how it is."

Harry knew exactly how it was. He'd been in the army since he was eighteen.

"How long is this detachment for?"

"Haven't the foggiest, old man. Six months to a year at least if you don't botch it. It's an excellent career opportunity, and there's no question you're the right man for the job. I understand your opposite number on the French General Staff is also a major, School of Artillery, same as Napoleon was. Of course I don't trust the Frogs any more than any other sensible Englishman would. They're so bloody…, well, French, if you know what I mean. Not like us at all. I suppose they can't help it." He gave Harry a quick smile then turned serious.

"You have a priceless advantage, Haig-Mallory. You understand their double-dealing treachery and their whoremongering mentality, and hopefully you can read between the lines. Stay on your toes at all times. Watch your back. That's the only advice I can give you. What you pick up in their unguarded conversations, every inflection, every nuance in what they say, could be of vital intelligence to the higher-ups."

"I'll do that, Sir."

"And don't underestimate Major General Horrocks-Smythe, your new CO. He may be the oddest-looking fellow you'll ever meet, but he doesn't miss a thing. He's a fine judge of character and want of it. Be on your guard with him is all I can suggest. One thing you will discover, he sounds old school. It's a bluff. Don't be fooled by what he says. He's only testing you, probing for your response and trying to expose any weakness. He doesn't tolerate yes-men. Don't waffle. We have too many wafflers in the army as it is. Tell him what you believe and be prepared to back it up with hard facts. Behind his unique exterior is one of the sharpest, and most adaptable military minds we have."

"Thanks for the warning, Sir. About the General, I mean."

"I gather the King is particularly interested in your reports. I may be wrong, but I don't think His Majesty trusts our present allies any more than Wellington did his at Waterloo. The Duke was probably only too thankful he was fighting the French, not having them as allies." Shackleton uttered a light cough. "Anyway, it's a staff job, part liaison, part spy, a bit more gold braid and such. I know your kit will be up to standard. Make sure you have plenty of everything, mess kit especially. You'll be assigned a new soldier-servant on your arrival. An Englishman hopefully, but if he's a Froggie, he's probably a spy for their high command. And you can bet your pay your counterpart is. Any questions?" Shackleton raised his eyebrows for a second. "Good. Splendid. Merryweather has your rail pass. Good luck. See you in a year possibly."

Shackleton reached out and shook Harry's hand. Harry took a step back, came to a proper, thunderous attention and snapped up a quivering salute.

Still at sea with the turn of events, he could think of nothing more eloquent to say than, "Thank you, Sir." He did an about turn and marched out of the office, followed by Merryweather. As soon as the door closed behind them Merryweather pounded Harry on the back.

"Congratulations, Harry. Delighted you got the promotion. By the way, could you let me have the mess accounts before you leave?"

Harry's heart sank. "Of course, Reggie," he groaned. "Never my favourite task, but at least they're up-to-date, though whether they're accurate or not is another matter. I'll get them for you."

*

A week later, at *Roseland*, Cecilia squinted at Harry. "Why's there a caterpillar under your nose? Or did you forget to wipe your mouth after the Brown Windsor soup at lunch?"

Harry's finger instinctively touched the hair sprouting from his upper lip.

"I'm growing a moustache."

"What on earth for?"

"There's nothing in Kings Rules and Regulations that requires majors to have moustaches, but I don't know one who doesn't. I'm following tradition."

"It makes you look old and grumpy," Cecilia said. "Not in the least bit dashing."

"Get used to it. I shall shave it off when I retire."

"It might make you look distinguished," his stepmother said, though her voice failed to carry conviction.

"Athena won't like it," Cecilia said.

"The way the war's going I might be retired before I see her again."

"Buck up, Harry," Ernest said. "I know the war's been dragging on for a year but it won't last forever. Athena will be over here on the first liner out of Cleveland, breaking down the church doors and demanding to get married on the spot."

"Cleveland's five hundred miles inland, Ernest."

"Oh."

Cecilia turned to her mother. "When did father say he might be back, Mother?"

"Only that it won't be until the end of next month at the earliest. He's going to miss the grouse season for the second year in a row. What is the world coming to?"

"The world's changing, Mother," Cecilia said. "And not a moment too soon. I've decided not to go back to Cambridge." She looked around the table to gauge the reaction. Her announcement elicited only disinterested faces. "It'll be years before I qualify as a doctor. I'm determined to do something useful for the war effort before it's too late. I'm learning to drive. Rhodes is teaching me, on one of the farm lorries if you must know, not the Daimler or the Lanchester. I don't think he's too happy about it. I intend to become an ambulance driver and battlefield nurse once I qualify."

"Well," Harry said. "That is a turn up for the books."

"I heard yesterday Westminster Hospital has accepted my application and because of my studies at Cambridge they've granted me advanced standing, so two years rather than three." She turned to Harry. "But I don't ever want to see you in my hospital tent, Harry. Not even for an ingrowing toenail or a moustache removal."

"Good for you, Cecilia. Does father know?"

"Good God, no. I haven't seen him for ages in any case. Besides, I'm of age now and there's nothing he can do to stop me."

"Other than cut off your allowance, dear," her mother said.

"Only if he finds out. And that'll only be if one of the three of you at this table blabs. In which case I can promise the culprit an extremely delicate operation with a rusty, blunt scalpel without the benefit of anesthetic."

"Blabs about what?" Ernest said.

"Precisely, Ernest. This conversation never took place, understand?"

"What conversation? Even I understand that. My lips are sealed."

"Mother?"

"It's not something I'd bring up in conversation, dear. Not that your father is likely to ask how you're doing at Cambridge. You know he doesn't approve of women at University."

"And don't look at me," Harry said. "I am the model of discretion. I'd have to censor any reference to nursing school in any case. When can we expect you in France?"

"Two years from now at the most. I expect they'll accelerate the course, given the need for battlefield nurses during a war. So perhaps a year, or eighteen months at the most."

"In time to help turn the tide with one final push, then."

"Or sooner."

"We're all proud of you, Cecilia," her mother said. "I know I am."

*

Before he left *Roseland*, Harry penned a short letter to Athena:

*…There is no chance of home leave for Christmas this year, and it will likely be next summer, August if I'm lucky before I am scheduled for any. If you still love me, could we marry then? If you have had a change of heart, I will understand and bear my loss with stoicism. If you still wish to throw your lot in with an English soldier, do you think it unwise and unsafe to cross the Atlantic until war's end? I try not to think of another disaster like the 'Lusitania.' I don't think my general would spare me for a few weeks while I travel to Cleveland to get married. He would probably offer some feeble excuse such as there being a war on, and anyway, I would still have to bring you back with me to Cornwall.*

*I cannot wait a moment longer before I see you again. I visualize us married, snatching what happiness we may when we are together and preferably alone, like we did during those days and nights in Washington I'm not allowed to mention. Until then, all I have of you are memories, and what is bound up in the locket I wear around my neck night and day…*

He screwed the cap back on his pen thoughtfully. He hoped Athena believed his words as much as he wanted to believe them himself.

*

After his short leave, barely enough time to be measured for and take delivery of his new uniforms, Harry spent two hours with a viselike grip on the handrail of the cross-Channel ferry. He was sure that the steamer, with him and several hundred men aboard, would at any moment be hit by a torpedo and sink with all hands. His conviction remained until his anticlimactic return to France and terra firma. Two hours and a train journey later, he reported to General Horrocks-Smythe at Corps Headquarters in Amiens, not without some trepidation, never having reported directly to an officer of such exalted rank during his service career.

In the tradition of The King's Imperial Hussars, Harry stood over six feet tall in bare feet. When he rose to greet Harry, the spare frame of Major General, Sir Claude Archibald Pendragon Horrocks-Smythe towered a good eight inches above him. His head reminded Harry of a farm silo, a tall cylinder with pale grey eyes close together, separated by a thin, beaky, hawk-like nose. The general's immaculate uniform tunic bore four rows of medal ribbons on his tunic, which included, Harry noted, the striped, blue and burgundy ribbon of the Distinguished Service Order.

During the brief interview Harry saw his new commanding officer appraise his spit-polished Sam Browne, the carefully sponged and pressed khaki uniform and glossy cavalry officer's boots. Harry stood stone-faced, like a mannequin in his tailor's window. He knew the general's inspection would go into his service record before the hour was out. He hoped he passed muster.

Horrocks-Smythe cleared his throat and called for his adjutant. An impeccably dressed, sandy-moustached young captain entered the room and crashed to attention. "Sir." To Harry it sounded like a bark.

Horrocks-Smythe turned his attention back to Harry. "Luncheon is at thirteen hundred hours." The general's luxuriant, nicotine-stained, walrus moustache hovered above thin lips and bobbed in time with every word he spoke. "Captain Benaud will show you to your office once you have unpacked. Report back here at fourteen hundred hours. Any questions?"

Harry could think of none. "No, Sir."

"I should hope not. Everything was in plain language. Even the lowest private soldier, or an Australian like Captain Benaud here, should be able to follow them." He turned his back on Haig-Mallory. The interview was over. "Show Major Haig-Mallory to his quarters, Benaud. That is all. Carry on."

*

Harry couched his first letter to Athena a week after his arrival in France, in an upbeat manner.

*...I am far from the front lines, warm and dry. I might as well be back in Washington, except here I fetch and carry and do everything in English and French. And, of course, you're not here.*

*My French counterpart, Major Jean-Marc Honoré St. Hillaire de Fougault-Cassegrain, to give him his full and rather splendid name, speaks passable English which he likes to practice on me when his superiors are not listening. Why that should be I do not know.*

*Rather like my late mother, Cassegrain claims to have had a Marquis in his family right up to the Revolution, when, like my mother's, his Marquis managed simultaneously to lose both his estate and his head.*

*Thankfully my French is in top notch shape. I had plenty of opportunity to use it the last time I was in France as no one else in the regiment spoke a word of it. Cassegrain tells me I have an excellent French accent with a hint of Swiss about it. He is helping to bring me quickly up to snuff with the local colloquialisms that Oxford failed to provide.*

*I have to admit we do dine well. The chefs attached to our hosts, the French General Staff, are every bit as good as those at the Georges Cinq in Paris. We will stay there one day, my sweetheart, when the war is won. It is only a little over a year ago we were planning our honeymoon, but it seems like a lifetime has passed. I long to hold your hand again, to feel the touch of your finger tips on my face. I shall wait, for as long as it takes, to hold you in my arms again...*

*

Within a month of his return to France, General Staff HQ moved closer to the front line. "Ste-Marguerite-des-Lys-Gran'ville, Haig-Mallory," Horrocks-Smythe announced after breakfast. "Or however they pronounce it. I understand you know the area well, so let's hope your familiarity with the area proves beneficial."

Ste-Marguerite-des-Lys-Gran'ville. Harry's stomach lurched at the news. It would prove impossible to avoid Solange in the small village. Besides, her farm lay adjacent to the grounds of the Château Gran'ville, so it was only a matter of time before he ran into her. The prospect scared him yet exhilarated him at the same time. Had Solange already taken another lover? No matter how circumspect they had been, inevitably rumours would one day circulate about her affair with the English Captain Haig-Mallory. By the time Pierre-August returned and discovered her infidelity, Harry calculated he would be long gone from Solange's life, and their relationship, if not forgotten, at least shunted down a branch line to a distant siding.

In spite of his misgivings, a frisson of excitement at the prospect of seeing Solange again ran the length of his spine and, with a bee-like buzz, settled in his stomach. Unless there was someone new in her life, could they rekindle their relationship? And if so, how could he keep their affair hidden from the omniscient Horrocks-Smythe? Or from Cassegrain, who seemed to make it a point of honour to discover everything possible about Harry? And from Athena?

"No point in putting it off." Harry caught himself in conversation with the mirror during the morning shave a week after the move.

"I have a couple of things to attend to in the village," he told Cassegrain. "I'll skip lunch. I'll be back by two." Cassegrain's eyebrows shot up but Harry refused to rise to the bait.

Harry took a circuitous route to Solange's farm and arrived unannounced. He knocked on the door and a few seconds later Sophie opened it.

"*Maman,*" she called. "*C'est Capitaine Harry pour toi.*"

Solange came to the door, wiping her hands on her apron. "I did not believe her," she said. Tears pooled in her eyes and spilled down her cheeks. "It really is you. I never thought I would see you again. Please come in. We are having lunch. Soup and bread, but say you will share it with us."

"I'd be delighted," Harry said, and winked at Sophie. "As long as you eat all yours, and grow up to be tall and strong and beautiful like maman."

"I will." A summer shower of fat raindrops fell from the September sky. The drops dampened the dusty, hard packed earth of the farmyard and lent it that particular smell unmistakable for any other. Sophie grabbed Harry by the hand and pulled him into the dark, stone-walled kitchen. Solange grabbed a box of matches from the kitchen drawer and struck one. Harry blew it out.

"But it is so dark in here," she protested.

"Lamp oil is scarce. Besides, your face glows enough to light up the whole house."

"Shh! Do not let Sophie hear you." She pushed Harry away and pointed to the table. "Sit while I fetch some soup and bread."

"I only have half an hour," Harry said.

"How long will you be in the village?" Solange said over her shoulder, as she busied herself with a bowl and ladle. She cut a slice off the loaf, put it on a plate and handed it to Harry.

"I don't know. You know how it is in the army. Here one day, gone the next without warning. But with luck we should be here several months."

Solange turned to Sophie. "Drink your milk, then you can run upstairs to your room and play until the rain stops." She turned to Harry. "I find the milk sour, but Sophie finds nothing wrong with it."

Sophie drained her glass and rose from the table. "*Au revoir, Capitaine Harry.*" She skipped off.

"Actually, it is major now. A promotion." He pointed to the crown on his shoulder tabs and touched his moustache.

"Congratulations. And the moustache suits you. Most distinguished."

"Thank you. That's not what my sister thinks."

Solange looked down at her hands, folded in her lap as if in prayer. "It is funny about the milk," she said, quietly. "It was the same when I was carrying Sophie. It tasted sour then, too." She looked up. "I … I am carrying our child."

Harry's stomach lurched. Goosebumps ran the length of his arms. "You caught me by surprise. I don't know what to say."

"You do not have to say anything. It is a simple fact of life. And life becomes complicated sometimes."

"When is the baby due?"

"If I am right, Sophie will have a brother or a sister to play with around Christmas."

Harry did a quick mental calculation. The timing was right. Their first night together, or shortly after? She must have suspected, probably even knew she was pregnant before he left in July. Why didn't she say anything? He didn't doubt he was the father, unless she had another lover tucked away. He immediately dismissed the thought as unworthy. He glanced at her belly. The loose clothes and pinafore hid the bulge, but on careful examination he could see she was expecting.

"I have received bad news," Solange said quietly. "Unfortunately, it is official. Pierre-Auguste was wounded before he was captured. He died of his wounds in the prison camp."

"Oh, dear God," Harry said.

"I did not really believe he would ever come home. At least he will never know about us." ı

Harry thought for a long moment. "I will not abandon you. I will do everything I can to support you." He hesitated, wondering if he should come clean about Athena. "I have a confession," he said before further thought could intervene and change his mind.

"What is it? Do you wish to tell me?"

"I have a fiancée. An American."

"I see." Solange's shoulders sagged. "I am not surprised such a handsome man as you would have a fiancée. I hoped… But, alas, I always knew it could not be. After all, I am only a Belgian peasant, the widow of a tenant farmer on land owned by the Sieur de Gran'ville. You are an English milord."

Harry put his hands on her shoulders and hung his head. "I made a promise, a commitment to her. We were supposed to be married in August last year, but the war made it impossible. Then I met you and life became more complicated than either of us could imagine, even without the baby. She does not know about you."

"And you should not tell her. She does not wish to know about me. And I do not wish to know about her."

"But what happens in the meantime?"

Solange shrugged. "*C'est la vie*. It is messy sometimes. If you wish, we will enjoy each other's company until you leave. Then Sophie will forget all about you and we will continue as before, only with three instead of two."

Harry shuffled his feet, struggling to find the right words to express what he needed to say. "With Pierre-Auguste alive I never thought we might marry," he mumbled.

"Nor I." She hesitated and looked away. "If Pierre-Auguste returned one day, we would pick up the pieces and bury the past. He is… was, a forgiving man. Now, he will not return, but even without the baby coming." She patted her belly. "The war makes things too uncertain."

"And I am a front-line soldier. It would be too much to be widowed twice." How noble a gesture, Harry, he thought, to put Solange ahead of him, and how easily the most insincere of words flowed.

Solange grabbed Harry and clasped him to her body. "I love you, 'Arry. I will never forget you, as long as I breathe."

"And I will never forget you, or Sophie. And our baby. You will always hold a special place in my heart. And I will never tell my fiancée about you, I swear. It will be our secret, to die with us when we are old and wrinkled." He paused. "We may not marry in any case. I have been gone more than a year."

"Then she would be a fool," Solange said. "Who would not want to marry you?" She clung to him and wept onto his shoulder while she swayed in his arms. The aroma of the kitchen, of the bread and the vegetable soup simmering on the stove mingled with the scent of her body and drifted into his brain. From there they found their way into his memory.

Harry regarded Solange with a serious expression on his face. "I will have to live with this deceit for the rest of my life but, as you say, life becomes messy sometimes."

"We make it so with our choices."

"I don't regret a thing."

"Neither do I."

"I don't even know if I still love her."

"I am certain you do. If you did not love her, you would not have told me."

"You might be right, but I'm still not sure. I won't know until I see her again. Only then will I know if I can pick up the threads of a relationship. Perhaps it is frayed beyond mending. Like me, she is alone all this time. And if she is like me, she may have been reckless and found someone new, someone who comes home to her after work every night. Someone who will love her instead of me. Someone who is not a soldier in a time of war."

Solange pushed Harry away. She wore no make-up other than some face powder which she left smeared on his uniform when she lifted her head from his shoulder. She tried to brush the powder away with her fingertips but only succeeded in rubbing it into the cloth. She pulled a face.

"You superiors will know you have been seeing a woman." She gave a light laugh.

"How?"

"The face powder on your shoulder. It is not your colour." She looked away, at the stove, at the uneaten lunch on the table, at Sophie's empty milk glass.

Harry drew her back to him. She rested her head on his shoulder. Her chest rose and fell with her laboured breathing and he knew she was crying silently. He rubbed her back. "We will manage," he whispered in her ear.

She broke away and held him at arm's length. "We will. For me it will not be the end of the world. I will never reveal the identity of our baby's father, I promise. And I have no need of money, now or ever."

"But it will cost money to have the baby. The doctor, or the midwife, medicines for the pain."

"I had none last time. And the midwife is my aunt. I can trust her to keep my secret. So, you see, everything will be fine." She spun him around and pointed him at the door. "You have to go back to work. I must not keep you. Now go. I will see you again soon." She gave him a gentle shove. "On Sunday?"

At the door Harry turned. "I want to see you again, too."

"You will. We will have dinner together, every Wednesday and Sunday, like before. Only the two of us, after Sophie has gone to bed. It is best if she does not think of you. I do not want her to connect us, or to suspect somehow you are the father of her brother."

"A brother?"

"I suspect so. I hope so, so he will grow to be big and strong and handsome like his father."

"And if it's a girl?"

"Then she will be beautiful like her mother. With red hair and freckles."

Harry smiled. "I will be happy with either." He frowned.

"What is the matter, my handsome 'Arry? You are not happy?"

"I enjoy seeing Sophie. It will hard having to avoid her, but I think I understand. I know she will forget me. Sad for me, but true." He kissed Solange on the forehead. He closed the farmhouse door quietly behind him.

# 12. LADIES' NIGHT

It was the last Saturday in September, 1915, Ladies' Night at the Lakewood Masonic Lodge on Detroit Avenue. Randolph Fenhagen brought a young man over to their table. "May I introduce you to Lester Morgan?" He nodded to the young man at his side. "His father is something to do with Pittsburgh Steel."

"Chairman of the Board," Lester Morgan said. "As Mr. Fenhagen well knows." He laughed. "I'm still learning the ropes. One day, if he considers me worthy, he plans to pass the reins to me. If he considers me not up to snuff, I shall have to find something else to do with what I've learned thus far."
 "Rather like Athena, here," her father said. "Destined to fill my shoes one day if she doesn't run off and marry that English fellow I gather she's rather fond of."

Lester Morgan took the gloved hands of Minerva and Athena Fenhagen in turn and kissed the fingers.

"A pleasure," he murmured. He wore no gloves. Athena glanced at his hands and saw the Masonic ring, the same as her father wore. She looked at his face. He smiled. With a slight nod she returned the smile. "And mine," she said. Athena's mother stole a glance at her daughter and her eyebrows twitched fractionally before she looked away.

Lester Morgan lowered his gaze to Athena's hand which, by now, he had released. Beneath the white glove the setting of her engagement ring bulged. "Mr. Fenhagen tells me you're engaged to be married. May I offer my congratulations to both you and the extraordinarily lucky man?"

Athena smiled. "Thank you, Mr. Morgan. We were set to be married in August of last year but my fiancé had to return to England to fight in the war. He is a cavalry officer, a major in the Hussars."

"I have heard of them. A regiment with an enviable reputation for the calibre of its officers and for its outstanding bravery in the field. I can wish him only the best of fortune and pray he comes through this unpleasantness unscathed."

"I believe the war is a bit more than unpleasant, Mr. Morgan. From the reports in the newspapers I don't think it an understatement to call it beastly. Still, Harry, my fiancé, is seconded to the Generals Staff somewhere in France and, he says, until next August at the earliest if all holds true, agreeably far from the dirt and danger of the front lines."

Lester Morgan turned to Athena's father. "May I have permission to ask your daughter to dance, Sir?"

Randolph Fenhagen laughed. "Athena is over twenty-one and hasn't asked my permission for anything for several years. Maybe you should ask her yourself."

Lester Morgan turned his red-faced attention to Athena. "May I ask you for the honour of a dance, Miss Fenhagen?"

"You may."

He held out his hand.

"I said, in answer to your question, that you may ask. I'm still waiting."

Morgan's face turned redder. Mr. Fenhagen smirked. "That's Athena for you, Morgan. Her own person, and an English major."

"No need to ask, Mr. Morgan. The answer is yes. I was hoping you would ask. My mother will tell you my father is not the most eligible or accomplished of dance partners."

The small orchestra struck up a waltz and Morgan took Athena in his arms. "You dance well, Miss Fenhagen," he said.

"It's Athena, except in front of my parents. And I am out of practice."

"I find that surprising."

"My regular dance partner is in France, if you remember. I've not danced with anyone since he left. Except now with you, of course."

"And it's Lester, except in front of your parents."

Athena laughed. "Don't think for a second you can fool them with the formal act. They can see right through both of us. Now, will you hold me a little closer? It's easier to follow your lead that way."

Two waltzes and a quickstep later they returned to the Fenhagen table. "You're back so soon?" her mother said.

"She's tired of having her toes trodden on," Morgan said.

"That's not the way I saw it," Minerva Fenhagen said, and laughed. Her mother placed her hand on Athena's arm. "Go and enjoy yourself, dear. It's the first time in over a year I've seen you look happy." She turned to Morgan. "I wouldn't want to be stranded in a desert with you, Mr. Morgan. We're dying of thirst."

"Champagne?"

"Anything but the non-alcoholic fruit punch."

"Coming right up." He left and headed for the bar.

Minerva Fenhagen held her fan over her mouth. "He's good looking, isn't he?"

"Average, I'd say."

"A lot more than that, Athena. Not to be dismissed. Your father says he's running Erie Steel, the Pittsburgh Steel subsidiary in Cleveland. I'd say he's a young man to keep an eye on."

"Mamma. I'm engaged to be married to Harry. I'm not two-timing."

"I never suggested you should. But it might be wise to have more than one string to your bow. Or should that be more than one beau on a string? Should you find a good-looking, wealthy and well connected young American ultimately more to your liking than your dashing English cavalry officer, then that will be your decision alone. You know you will always have our blessing. Particularly if you make the right choice. Ah, here comes Mr. Morgan with life-saving refreshments." She winked and patted Athena's hand.

Athena and Lester danced for most of the remainder of the evening. Fifteen months and, she made a quick mental calculation, two days since she'd first danced with Harry. Lester danced well. He seemed more self-assured than Harry. He might even be a little better looking and about as tall. Of course, Harry had been in military mess dress and Lester was only in white tie and tails, but still…

When she thought no one was watching them, she reached up and touched the small scar near Lester's eye.

He smiled and put his mouth close to her ear. "Nothing heroic, I'm afraid. Lacrosse. When I was at Yale."

She kissed her fingertips and touched them to the scar. "All better now," she said.

Lester tightened his grip around her waist and piloted her through a three-point turn. "Definitely better," he said, and smiled at her. They were in a corner of the dance floor, alone for a moment. The music stopped. She stood on tiptoe and kissed Lester, briefly, on the lips. She had no idea why she succumbed to the impulse. She hoped no one saw her, least of all her parents.

She stepped away from the arms of Lester Morgan and saw the frown on his forehead. "I'm sorry, Lester," she whispered. "I don't know what came over me. I've embarrassed you. Please forgive me."

"There's nothing to forgive, Athena. It never happened, if that's what you want. Or you can do it again as often as you wish and I won't mind in the slightest. Of the two options, I much prefer the second. As your father said, you are your own person."

Athena looked for her parents. They were not on the dance floor nor at their table and she and Lester were the last couple on the floor. "I wonder if my parents have gone home already," she said. "It's quite late. I think most of the members have left." The hall was quite empty. As if to confirm her diagnosis, the orchestra began to disassemble their music stands, fold up their sheets of music and put away their instruments.

"I'll check with the cloakroom attendant," Lester said. He returned a minute later shaking his head. "She was just packing up to go home. She said they left half an hour ago. They left word with her that I was to take you home."

"Oh," Athena said. "I wish they'd told me."

"I have an automobile. I'll gladly take you home."

"They'll be expecting me for breakfast, Lester."

The frown appeared on Lester's forehead again, then disappeared. "Are you suggesting, I mean, am I right in thinking what I think you're suggesting, Athena?"

A slight blush lit up her cheeks. She had heard Harry ask that, fifteen months ago. Was history really about to repeat itself? "You tell me what's on your mind?"

"Well. I mean I hardly know you and it's awfully sudden. I mean… Actually, I don't know what I mean."

"It's Saturday night. Neither of us has to work tomorrow, right?"

"Right."

"We could find a club and drink Champagne and go dancing until they throw us out and then you could drive me home. Or we could skip all that and you could drive me home right now. Or you could drive me, to your home perhaps, and then back to my home in time for a bath before breakfast." She hesitated, then brushed her breasts lightly over his forearm. "Pick one."

"We have a house on Euclid," he said slowly. "It's nothing like as grand as yours, I'm sure. My father keeps it for visits by senior management rather than use a hotel. And for me while I'm here. He hires extra staff when needed. I told my staff to take the night off. They have their quarters separate from the main part of the house."

"So it's unlikely we'd be disturbed?"

"Pretty unlikely."

"Option three, then?"

Lester Morgan placed his hand in the small of Athena's back and guided her to the cloakroom. "Wait here while I get the automobile."

Athena shot him an odd look.

"I do my own driving," Lester said. "It's more exciting."

A few minutes later Lester pulled up in front of the darkened Masonic Lodge in a gleaming, white Buick Model 10 with the canvas top down and folded away. The night was warm and humid with the sulphurous smell of foundry smoke hanging in the still air. Only suffused moonlight penetrated the light ground mist that hovered beneath the haze. Few street lamps were on and most of Cleveland's homes lay in darkness. Lester put the gear in neutral, hopped out and held the passenger door open for Athena. She gathered the skirt of her gown and accepted Lester's helping hand to mount the step into the automobile.

"Impressive," she said, as she made herself comfortable and adjusted her wide brimmed hat. "A lot sportier than my father's automobile. His is a sedan."

"It's made for, and I quote the manufacturer, *Men with real red blood who don't like to eat dust.*"

"I take it that's you?"

He nodded. "Yes, ma'am. Sixty miles per hour in top gear and…"

"I hope it has brakes, Lester," Athena said, interrupting the stream of mechanical information she was sure was about to follow.

"Oh, yes. It has those. And they're quite good. I can stop in next to no distance, even going downhill." He put his hand on Athena's knee and gave it a light squeeze. She gave him an encouraging look.

"But no higher," she said. She didn't have to add, *Yet,* even though that was precisely what she wanted. But not in the driveway of the Masonic Lodge. She squeezed her thighs together. She was sure Lester understood her intention without her saying anything.

He put the car into gear. "How about I take you for a spin before we head home? Show you what it can do."

Lester let in the clutch and the Buick jerked forward. With another squeal he turned hard and fast onto the asphalt of Detroit Avenue. Athena clung onto the door handle to prevent being thrown out of the vehicle as the tires bit into the turn and held the line. Lester straightened the car and hit the throttle. The Buick surged forward and they sped away through the deserted Cleveland streets. He braked hard and turned onto Euclid, heading for his home. They drove fast along Euclid until they approached East 105th Street and the red traffic light. Lester didn't slow.

"Don't you have to stop for a red traffic light, Lester?" Athena screamed.

"Not unless there's a cop there. Fun, huh?" He accelerated.

"Lester," Athena yelled into his ear.

"What?"

"Stop."

"What?"

"I said pull over and stop. Right now. I want to go home."

Lester slowed and came to a stop a quarter of a mile from the intersection. "What's the problem, Athena?"

"You're the problem." She couldn't control her trembling body. "You're reckless. You could have had us both killed back there. If you kill yourself, that's one thing. If you take some innocent person with you, that's entirely different. Now take me home. Slowly."

Lester put his hand on Athena's thigh. She brushed it off. "Don't do that," she hissed. "Keep your hands off me. If I want you to touch me, I'll be sure and tell you. Which will be next time it snows in Brazil." Lester engaged gear and drove Athena slowly home in petulant silence. He stopped the Buick in front of her father's house, put the gear in neutral and applied the handbrake. He didn't offer to help her out.

"I don't need to see you again, Mr. Morgan," she said with her voice hard and now under control. "If you treat your lady friends the way you drive your automobile, you don't deserve either. Good night."

Athena turned her back and mounted the front steps of her parents' home. She unlocked the door, entered the hallway and closed the door behind her without looking back. She heard the vehicle drive away with a screech of tires and leaned against the door, seething with rage and trembling with fright. "What in God's holy name could I have been thinking?' she muttered. "Oh, Harry, I'm so sorry. Forgive me, please. You don't know how much I miss you. I promise I'll never do that again. I'll be true to you, always. I swear."

She hung her hat and cloak in the hall closet and made her way to the kitchen at the back of the house. Grateful that she had learned something useful during those years spent at Vassar, she put that knowledge to good use and brewed a pot of coffee. When she had poured a china mug full she set herself down in a Shaker-style, hard back wooden chair at the kitchen table. She shivered in the cold kitchen. To warm herself, she sipped the coffee and clutched the mug in both hands until the shivering eased. She heard a noise and looked up, startled.

Her mother stood in the doorway in her nightdress and dressing gown. "I heard you come in," she said. "Is everything...?"

"I'm fine. Mr. Morgan drove me home. He... He's a wild man behind the wheel of an automobile. He didn't stop for the red traffic light at One-Oh-Fifth. I thought we'd both be killed. I told him to drive me home."

"I don't know what you were doing in that part of town with a young man you hardly know, and it's none of my business." Her mother sounded cool.

Athena put her hands to her face and burst into tears. "We were going back to his house," she sobbed. "For a nightcap. Before... I knew what I was doing. So did he. I feel so awful, like I betrayed Harry. I'm stupid. Stupid. Stupid." She banged her fists on the table.

Her mother put a hand on Athena's shoulder and gave it a slight squeeze. "You're not alone, Athena. We are all tempted from time to time. The reasons vary, but loneliness is a common thread. Sometimes we succumb to the temptation. Sometimes we manage to resist it. While I'm here, and your father's snoring his head off upstairs, there are a couple of things I should tell you. And it's probably not what you're dreading. It's far too late for that."

"All right. Let me have it, Mamma."

"Don't ever tell Harry about tonight. He doesn't want to know. He has enough on his plate being a soldier in a war without worrying about whether you still love him or have been unfaithful."

"I wasn't unfaithful. Not completely. And I won't tell him. But isn't honesty in a marriage a good thing?"

Minerva Fenhagen shot her daughter a curious look. "A husband doesn't need to know everything any more than a wife does. And what he doesn't need to know won't hurt him if he doesn't know. But if he finds out, be honest and never try to justify what you've done. Excuses only make it worse."

"Nothing happened with Lester, but I had every intention of making sure it did. At least at first."

"Sometimes it's too late to change your mind over a bad decision. You were lucky tonight and no harm's done."

"I've told Lester Morgan I won't be seeing him again."

"I'm not surprised."

Athena's coffee had grown cold. She stared at the puddle of brown liquid in the bottom of her mug. "I think I've had enough coffee," she said. "I think I'll go to bed. You've put my mind at ease, Mamma. I think I shall sleep well. And I won't say a word to anyone about anything they don't need to know. Ever." She smiled, rose and gave her mother a hug and a peck on the cheek.

"I'm glad I could help. It's one of the things mothers can still be good for, even at your age. As one day you will discover for yourself."

# 13. MADELEINE

Harry slipped away from the Château Gran'ville whenever he could to snatch time with Solange after Sophie was in bed. Over the months Solange's belly grew until it looked as if it were about to burst. Her hands, feet and legs swelled with the pregnancy. Her face rounded as the due date approached. Her first contractions came while Harry was at the farmhouse on December 14th.

"It is best if you do not stay," Solange said to Harry. "Please go and fetch my aunt. I will be in good hands. *Tante* Claudette delivered Sophie. Perhaps in a week it will be safe to return." She shoved him gently out of the farmhouse door into the frosty night.

A day later, a daughter, Madeleine, greeted the world with a lung-emptying howl. Harry cried when he heard the news, though whether they were tears of joy, regret or heartbreak he could not tell. From then on it was with mixed emotions that he stole away at night to visit Solange. They both knew their relationship had a finite end date. Only the timing remained unknown. It could hardly be beyond his present assignment which was due to expire at the end of July, if Shackleton's estimation was correct. Harry hoped fervently that the break, when it came, would be swift and clean. But since Madeleine's arrival he sensed a barrier encroaching on their relationship, as if Solange did not want to draw any closer to him. They had not made love since early November. He wondered if they ever would again.

No matter how much he longed for their old relationship to return, he grew to accept that it never would. "Women are strange creatures, Harry," his father once said, not long before Harry started at Sandhurst. "Nobody really understands them, least of all know what it is they want. They get married. We give them security. Then they have a baby or two. That's usually when things start to go off the rails. They get moody and withdrawn. They become preoccupied with the baby. They don't have time for you. They're not like us at all once that happens. It's a woman thing. Don't try to understand it. Better simply get used to it and find something else to occupy your time and energies, if you know what I mean."

When she and Harry were together, Solange turned her attention to Madeleine every few minutes; a feed here, a nappy change there, a cry, a hug and a rock of the cradle. Harry did everything he could to show her how much he loved her and the baby, but to no avail. She seemed permanently distracted and at times tired to the point of exhaustion, "with looking after the baby, taking care of Sophie and running the farm, my 'Arry."

"I want to help," he told her. "Tell me what I can do. You refuse money, but there must be something I can do instead."

"There is nothing we need or you can do. We have to accustom ourselves to the fact you will leave us one day soon and we will never see you again. We have to fend for ourselves once more, like we used to before you entered our lives."

"We can marry. It's not too late. I can write to my fiancée and tell her I'll marry you."

"I do not think your General will let you marry me, not with our differences in rank."

"I can ask. If I phrase it right, I'm sure he'll approve." It sounded good, though Harry had his doubts that General Horrocks-Smythe would entertain the idea of one of his hand-picked staff marrying a peasant woman whom he had carelessly managed to get pregnant. And his father would have apoplexy which, in Harry's opinion, would look good on him and only serve him right.

"No, 'Arry. As much as I love you, I will not let you do it. We were destined to meet and fall in love and have a baby, but we were never meant to marry. It could only end in disaster — for all of us."

"But I love you, Solange, and Sophie and Madeleine. I want you to be with me forever, as a family."

She turned her head and hurried away. "The baby is crying," she said over her shoulder. He heard the catch in her throat that paired with the lump in his. "I must see to her."

He opened his wallet and took out every banknote he had. He found a scrap of paper, the back of a mess bill, and scribbled, "It is all I have tonight. I will bring more every time I see you. Please take it, if not for you, then for Sophie and Madeleine." It did not appease his conscience, but as she had refused all other offers of help it was something more than *Hello, goodbye, it was nice knowing you.* But not much.

*

Ralph Fenhagen called Athena into his office after lunch on a Monday early in February. "You're chomping at the bit. What's eating you?"

"Nothing."

"Over a long-married life I have learned than when a woman says nothing, little could be further from the truth. What is it?"

"Harry. I'm worried sick about him."

"Understandable, but worrying won't make him any safer."

"I know, and I try not to. If I didn't have this job to take my mind off things I'd go crazy worrying about him."

"You can hardly go to him in the middle of a war and ask him to come home before he does something silly. Or brave."

"But there must be something I can do. Why aren't we fighting alongside the English and the French? Why can't America do something other than sit on the sidelines when our oldest friends and closest allies are dying in France and Belgium?"

Ralph Fenhagen steepled his fingers and rested his chin on the finger tips. "I have friends, well, more like acquaintances but we know each other better than some, people who have influence in the government."

"Like who?"

"The Astors. The Vanderbilts. The Rockefellers. A couple of others though they're not as well connected in Washington. If I were to give you letters of introduction, would you like to go to New York and plead your case, our case I should say, on all our behalf, and see if you can persuade them to put some pressure on President Wilson to stop fence sitting. I can also give you letters of introduction to our senators and our representative."

"Would you? I mean, that would be really helpful. If only one of them would have a word with the President that could set the ball rolling."

"Consider it done, Athena. You don't need a chaperone at your age and I dare say no one will mind too much if you travel without one. You can stay at the Martha Washington hotel in New York and the one in Washington. Take next week off. I'll survive for a few days without you." He smiled. "Go on. It's for you. And for Harry."

"If I weren't in the office I'd throw my arms around your neck and kiss you, Papa . Thank you so much. I'll do everything in my power to convince everyone that we need to stand shoulder to shoulder with England and France."

*

Athena took the train to New York the following Sunday, and to

Washington on Wednesday. She returned to Cleveland on Saturday, exhausted and furious. After venting her frustrations on her father within minutes of her arrival at home, she sat down to write to Harry.


*...I have been to see to all of my father's wealthy and influential friends in New York. I begged them to intervene with the President our behalf of England and France, to persuade our government to enter the war on the side of our allies. I have even written to Mr. Walter Hines Page, a friend of father's and our ambassador to London, asking him to try and put pressure on Congress and President Wilson, a Democrat. I believe Mr. Page to be a committed anglophile. I have not yet received a reply from him.*

*I might as well have been speaking to a parrot. Every one of them said the same thing: 'When the time is right,' or 'Not right now, there is no mood to enter a European war,' or, 'It's not our fight.' It was so frustrating.*

*Helen Astor, John's widow — he went down with the Titanic if you remember — was polite, but distant. Alfred Vanderbilt Jr. whose father died when the Germans sunk the Lusitania, hardly gave me the time of day. I thought if anyone would bear a grudge against the Germans, it would be him. But no. And Grace Vanderbilt, Cornelius's wife, was charming but would not commit to intervening on my behalf. The Rockefellers didn't even acknowledge receipt of my father's letter of introduction and refused to acknowledge my presence. And John Rockefeller is a Republican, for Heaven's sake! So rude of him. If that's what money does to a man, I'd rather be a pauper. I could say something very nasty about their whole family, but I won't. The most suitable language would be most unladylike. You will have to teach me how to say what I want in French so that I can say, 'Pardon my French.'*

*After New York I went to Washington and virtually camped outside the offices of both our Ohio Senators, hoping to get to see one or the other. My father's letters of introduction failed to persuade either of them to see me. Their flunkies always told me the Senators were 'too busy'. I had pinned my hopes on Senator Harding as he is a Republican, a friend of father's and a man with supposedly Presidential aspirations. I was greatly disappointed by his response. God help us if he ever becomes President.*

*Senator Pomerene is a Democrat, though and, as my father has mentioned, we are Republicans. Besides, father does not know Senator Pomerene personally. Being from Ohio, my father lacks insider influence in Washington so as such he can be of little benefit in their re-election bids. I suspect both regard me as only a woman, an overly bold one at that, without a vote, of no consequence and deservingly put in her place. I am beginning to understand your sister Cecilia's affection for the suffragette movement. If women ever get the vote here I am seriously thinking of becoming a Democrat, in spite of our family tradition. However, I do love my father and would hate to disappoint him.*

*I even went to see Mr. Bryan, the Secretary of State, Forrest's father, if you remember. My father knows him quite well, but he refused to see me. Maybe Forrest didn't speak too kindly of me after we parted but I can hardly be the first woman who has dumped him. Or, I hope, the last.*

*Our District Representative in Congress at least agreed to see me, but, in spite of his promises he offered nothing to help the cause. He is a Democrat after all; Ohio is solidly Democrat and the Republicans control the House. If he is defeated in the elections in March I will have to start over, and a lowly Representative really is the ground floor in Congress.*

*I have exhausted all the possibilities. I know no one else to turn to...*

*Stay safe, Harry,*

*Love,*

*Athena.*


Harry read and reread the letter. Bless her, he thought, she was trying to help in the only way she could. He lingered over the last words: *Stay safe, Harry.* She always ended her letters with these words. As if the alternative was a choice worth contemplating, for her as much as for him. A pang he recognized as longing shot through his heart. In spite of everything, there was still something there. Perhaps all was not lost.

*

During his precious few off-duty minutes during the spring of 1916 Harry allowed his mind to meander occasionally from his letter writing to Athena to the daffodils and tulips, the fragrant purple-red camellias and the Lenten roses growing in the gardens of *Roseland* at that time of the year. He longed to be there, strolling the garden paths or the lanes of St. Just with Demelza; anywhere except in Ste-Marguerite. The war continued just over the horizon, around Ypres. He was safe, for now, staying safe as Athena asked while others didn't. His turn would come, of that he had no doubt, and staying safe would no longer be an option. Until then he could imagine *Roseland* as he remembered it in spring, full of early flowers and birdsong, the hedges in leaf and branches swollen with nests, meadows green with new grass and yellow with dandelions. The villagers would turn the dandelions into delicious wine to tide them over until the elderberries ripened. Nothing wasted, not like here in Flanders, where the wasteland stretched beyond his imagination.

Ultimately, perhaps inevitably, his thoughts always returned to Solange. He had no doubt he loved her and probably always would in some way. But she had made it clear they had no future together, no matter how much he might wish it. It was up to him to end the affair and to find the silver lining for both, rather than let it peter out. Soon, he promised himself repeatedly. When he was man enough to make the break, to move on without a backward glance. Sooner rather than later, he promised, to give his heart time to heal before he returned to Athena.

*

Glad to be dry and indoors on March 26th, rather than in a waterlogged trench, *Somewhere in France*, Harry drummed the clip of his fountain pen cap against the edge of his desk in time to a beat in his head only he could hear. His letter to Athena had stalled. His mind wandered to Solange, Sophie, and Madeleine. In frustration he tossed his pen onto the blotting pad and saw the ink splatter onto his letter. Now he would have to start it over again. He wondered if that might be an omen, a call for a new start. He looked up from his desk and marveled at the power of the equinoctial gale that threatened to blow Ste-Marguerite off the map. The cold, hard rain, driven horizontal by howling winds, lashed the château's lead-paned windows in its attempt to wash away what the wind failed to accomplish. The weather was as foul-tempered, perhaps worse, than what they had experienced in August of '14 when they first crossed the Channel and set foot in France. He picked up his pen again, drew in a deep breath and forced himself to concentrate on rewriting his letter.

*...I have finally received news that my posting here will officially end on July 3st. I have hardly had a day away from work since I arrived and the powers that be have told me that I shall receive three weeks leave effective August 1st. If you still feel the same way about me as I do about you, would you like us to be married then?*

*The 5th would be the best day. It is a Saturday, which will allow us two full weeks together before I have to return to my regiment. If that is too soon, the 12th would be good. As I imagine it will be a small wedding I don't think the 12th will inconvenience too many. I doubt if anyone will be grouse shooting this year. But the sooner, the better, is my choice. What do you say, my sweet?*

*

Athena read Harry's letter three times before she told her mother about it. "Keep it for dinner," she told Athena. "Then tell us together. I will act surprised. I want to see your father's face when he gets the news. I don't think he will be overjoyed to lose you at the office but I know he won't do anything to prevent you from going over to England to be married." She touched Athena's wrist. "I'll make sure we have wine with dinner even though it's only Thursday. A celebration demands a glass or two."

"Wine?" Randolph Fenhagen said when a decanter of claret appeared with the beef course.

"When Cook told me what she had prepared for dinner I decided I wanted a glass to go with it. It won't hurt you to have a glass on Thursday any more than it hurts you when you have a glass on Friday or Saturday. Now, be a dear and pour us each a glass."

Athena sipped at her wine and placed the glass on the table. Her mother gave her a look of encouragement. "I have received news from Harry," Athena said.

"All is well, I hope," her father said.

"The best news possible, Papa. Harry will be home on leave in August and asks if we can be married then."

"I see," her father said, and cocked his head as he looked from mother to daughter. "And what have you told him?"

"I haven't replied yet. The letter only arrived this afternoon."

"You have learned well in the short time you've worked with me."

"Why do you say that?"

"Only a fool rushes in where wise men fear to tread. Isn't that a proverb? Examine all the most likely ramifications of a decision before finally settling a course. And a wise general never goes into battle without an escape plan. Just in case."

"You don't sound enthusiastic, Papa."

"I only want what is best for you, and that is your happiness every day for the rest of your life. Do you still love your Englishman as much as you did two years ago?"

Athena glanced at her mother, a silent plea for guidance. Her mother said nothing.

"I have asked myself the same question daily since we parted, Papa."

"And what is your answer?"

She hesitated, took a sip of wine and placed the glass squarely on its coaster. She swallowed. "No." She paused again, picking her next words with care. "I don't. Not in the same way. How can I? I haven't seen him for nearly two years. I have his photograph but I can't love a photograph. I don't have him. I can't see him as he is, today, now, as if he were across the table from me, having dinner. I can't touch him, or smell him. I can't hear his voice or taste his lips. I'm in love with Harry, Papa. But it must be like being in love with a ghost, someone who isn't real. He's a memory, an idea. That's what I'm in love with. And I must make it real. And to do that I must go to him and stay with him for the rest of our lives."

Randolph Fenhagen regarded Athena with a stern gaze. "You are a lot smarter than I gave you credit for," he said, slowly. "We change daily. The changes may not be noticeable, but they are nevertheless real. And our ideas and attitudes change as well as our bodies. You fell in love with Harry two years ago after a courtship of barely three weeks. In spite of the time you spent together, I doubt if you could possibly have gotten to know him completely. And since then, he will have changed, as you have. He will have seen, and possibly done, things in the war that he may never wish you to know about. He may be proud of his accomplishments. He may be ashamed. I suggest you never ask. He will confide in you only when he decides to. If he ever does. And that takes trust, which is perhaps the most important ingredient in any relationship, especially marriage." He sat back in his chair and gripped the arms.

"And I agree with your father, Athena, in every respect," Minerva said. "Do you intend to go to England to be married?"

"I promised him, Mamma. I won't go back on my word."

"Even if that turns out to be the wrong decision?"

Athena sipped more wine, buying time to formulate her answer. "Father says a wrong decision is better than no decision. Isn't that right, Papa?"

Randolph Fenhagen nodded.

"A bad decision can be replaced by a better decision," she continued, undaunted. "Indecision can be fatal. It provides the enemy with the advantage of seizing the initiative. And inflexibility is often as bad as indecision." She looked at her father for confirmation.

"Quite right. And you should go to the top of your class."

"What will you tell Harry?" her mother pressed.

Athena took another sip of wine. "That I will go to England and that we will be married in August of this year, and that you will both come with me like we originally planned."

"Good," her father said. "That's settled. But I don't think it wise for us to risk an Atlantic crossing. It will be bad enough to lose you to a husband half the world away. But if the Germans decide they don't want us in England, and all three of us discover to our cost that we can't swim as far as Ireland, we will all be drinking seawater." He raised his glass. "Congratulations, Athena. I'm very proud of you for sticking by Harry all this time. Right, Mother?"

Minerva Fenhagen beamed. "They say you can never go home. But there will always be a door open for you."

"I'll make it work, Mamma. I'll do everything in my power to make Harry proud of me, as a wife and as the mother of his, our, children someday. I won't give him any reason to doubt my love for him. Ever."

"It will take some getting used to having a warm, smelly body next to you in bed again, Athena."

Athena blushed. Without looking at either of them, her father hurriedly picked up his wine glass and disposed of the contents in one long swallow.

"But persevere, dear," her mother said. "He's worth it."

Randolph Fenhagen picked up the decanter. "Another glass, Minnie?"

*

Athena's reply arrived in late April … *August 5th, with all my heart...*

Harry should have been overjoyed instead of drained. He asked himself repeatedly how she could still be in love with him after all this time apart. Was it too late to tell her he'd had a change of heart? That he'd fallen in love with somebody else? That he could no longer love her as she deserved? That in fact she'd been right two years ago, that she was nothing more than a summer romance he'd said goodbye to on the dock in New York? We don't know each other anymore. How much more is there to know? How open do we want to be? We could both be making the biggest mistake of our lives if we go through with the marriage.

In the end, with trepidation and a sense of foreboding Harry took the plunge and wrote his last letter to Athena from Ste-Marguerite at the end of June:

*…I shall be here until the last day of my assignment before I get leave. I shall have three weeks in which to try to act like a civilized human being, which will be hard as I have spent my entire adult life as a soldier.*

*I hope sailing schedules from New York make the 5th possible for the wedding. If the vicar insists on posting the banns again, I am sure I can persuade him the church roof still leaks when it rains and is in need of costly repairs, to say nothing of the wheezy organ. In any case all you have to do is show up at the appointed time and place.*

*I doubt if there will be enough time for you to write back to me here. With the war, the post is not as reliable as it once was. A telegram to Roseland with your answer will suffice...*

# 14. ROSELAND

For three months they had been fiendishly busy. The big one, the push that would end the war and drive Germany to surrender took all their waking hours at the Château Gran'ville. The Somme was the word. It would dwarf the Marne by comparison. Every spare soldier in the British Empire would hurl himself at the German front line, blast through the reserve trenches and into the open countryside beyond. They would cripple the Germany army and bring Germany to her knees, begging for mercy. Division by division withdrew from the front line to the rear to practice the attack, then took the place of the next in line to rehearse. Everyone knew July 1st would be the date that would go down in history as the greatest British victory of all time. Morale was sky high. Nothing could stop them now on their march to Berlin.

Privately, Harry also was aware that if everyone in the allied trenches knew the date of the attack, undoubtedly so did the Germans. As if the unprecedented, week-long allied artillery barrage hadn't been warning enough.

On the night of June 30th, up and down the front line, Tommies held their breath as the barrage overhead reached a crescendo. No one slept. They would scramble from their trenches at first light, charge across no man's land and attack the devastated German positions.

The Kings' Imperial Hussars led the attack and advanced into a wall of German artillery and small arms fire from which they never recovered.

The British and American newspapers tried to put a positive spin on the news but few believed them. For all of July the attacks continued. For all of July the Germans defied them, openly jeering at the retreating British soldiers from the top of their parapets as attack after attack failed.

After breakfast on the last day of July, a sombre Major General Sir Claude Archibald Pendragon Horrocks-Smythe, CB, DSO, *Clap* as he was known behind his back and never to his face, summoned Harry into his spacious, but cluttered, office. Horrocks-Smythe cleared his throat a number of times and his walrus moustache bobbed as he dredged up the words he needed.

"Haig-Mallory."

"Sir?"

The general glanced around him and at glared at the closed door as if defying anyone to interrupt him before he had finished offloading whatever was on his chest. He cleared his throat. "Seeing as we're alone, I can tell you the Frogs have decided to award you some sort of gong for your efforts here. Not sure what it is yet. It'll have to be cleared through the usual protocol channels. Croix de Guerre probably. Or the Légion d'honeur, however you pronounce it. Something of the sort."

Horrocks-Smythe grunted and cleared his throat. "As you know, junior staff officers do not normally deserve awards merely for showing up for work every day and carrying out their assigned duties without proving a complete clot." He stared at Harry for several moments, as if inviting a reply, preferably along the lines of, I can always decline the honour.

Harry missed the clue. "I understand completely, Sir," he said hastily, filling in the blank air. "But at least I won't be around to be kissed on the cheeks."

Horrocks-Smythe sighed. "Quite so. Ghastly show they make of that sort of thing."

"Obviously they never received a proper Public School education."

"You were Marlborough, I believe." Clap stroked his moustache. Harry knew there was no belief about it. Clap undoubtedly had the complete contents of Harry's file, down to his marks at the end of each term at Marlborough, permanently etched in his brain.

"Wellington, myself." Harry wasn't sure how to interpret the harrumph that followed the statement. Did Clap consider Wellington to be superior to Marlborough? Or vice versa? He could not think of anything to say, so waited out the silence. He glanced up at the cigarette smoke floating like a thin layer of cirrus a few inches below the ceiling. He wondered when the other shoe was about to drop. Had Clap discovered his affair with Solange? Or her pregnancy, of which he would no doubt heartily and noisily disapprove? Harry scrutinized the impassive face for a clue. He came away empty-handed.

Horrocks-Smythe cleared his throat with another loud harrumph. "We'll obviously have to do something to match their gong, whatever it turns out to be. Protocol, you understand. We don't want to set a precedent, but we can't have the Froggies outdoing us in the gong department, can we now?"

Harry shuffled his feet. Horrocks-Smythe forestalled the reply. "Not your fault, of course. They forced our hands, you understand. You'll be notified what it is in due course."

"Yes, Sir."

"One last thing, Haig-Mallory."

Here it comes, thought Harry, and braced himself for the verbal body blow. "Sir?"

"I'm sure you remember your Greek lessons from the otherwise squandered days of your youth."

Greek? Solange maybe. But not Greek. He wondered where this change of tack might lead. "Not my strongest subject, Sir."

"Nevertheless, you will recall it was Socrates who named the four virtues. Prudence, Justice, Fortitude and Temperance. It takes all four to make a good officer. He said Prudence was the most important of them all. He called it, *The perfect ability to make right decisions.* You will do well to remember that."

At that moment Harry was sure Clap knew about Solange, but he was damned if he was going to admit it. Horrocks-Smythe glanced at the wall clock then back at Harry. An awkward silence fell until Clap harrumphed again. "Report to Brigade HQ in Bristol on the twenty-first for assignment," he said brusquely. "No doubt you will be back here, or somewhere nearby, before long. Carry on."

Harry came to attention and snapped up a salute. The interview was over. Horrocks-Smythe's last words sounded rankled. They held no warmth, no thanks for a thankless task well done, no extension of his duties, no handshake and no good wishes for the future. The French medal had obviously annoyed the general. Not all medals were well earned, Harry knew, but they should all carry at least some merit, not merely awarded to match protocols. Or not proving to be a complete clot.

*

While Harry packed his two suitcases and small trunk, his mind returned to last night, the last he and Solange had spent together. They had not made love, but had said their tearful farewells, adieu, this time, not au revoir, in the kitchen. Sophie was in bed when he tiptoed upstairs to her room and stood beside her, watching her untroubled sleep. He kissed her forehead without waking her, and stroked her thick, red hair. Cradled in her mother's arms, Madeleine latched onto his finger and would not let go. His daughter. Her clutch brought a tear to his eyes and, before he turned his head away, he saw tears brim also in Solange's eyes. He wondered if it was sadness at their parting, the end of their relationship, or the uncertainty of a bleak future as a widow with two young children. Or could it have been love, perhaps, a love she no longer wished to acknowledge or express, but could not relinquish?

"Go," she had said. "I do not want your money. Go. Do not look back. We will not be here." She pushed him to the door and over the threshold. He heard her slide the bolt home, an act of finality, of no second thoughts. It was over. He had been tempted to leave money under a stone jar of flour, but she never once took her eyes off him, as if she knew his intentions. It's to help raise the children, he wanted to tell her. But he could not bring the words to his lips.

He turned his back on Solange and his infant daughter in the certain knowledge he would never see any of them again. As he trudged towards the château a flash of artillery fire on the horizon broke into his thoughts of what might have been and could now never be. He stopped and straightened into a soldierly bearing while he watched the war continue without him many miles distant. He counted the seconds after the first flash while he waited for the rumble and calculated the distance as if he were reckoning the approach of a thunder storm at home. Many seconds later the low thump of the guns broke the stillness of the night, twelve, perhaps as much as fourteen miles away. Had the ground trembled beneath his boots? Or had he imagined it?

His head swam. His legs buckled under him and he grasped a fence post. He rested his forehead on folded hands and let the tears fall until there were none left. A black cloud of wretchedness hung over him. He had lost her, gone as assuredly as his mother had left him. He wondered if their parting had served some cause that he could not comprehend, had appeased some god whose existence and purpose had yet to be revealed. Or whether it would simply leave a temporary vacuum from which they would both move on with other people to fill their lives.

He pushed himself away from the post but could not bring himself to let go. He tried to stand fully upright, but his knees refused to obey. His breath came in the ragged gasps of a runner at the end of a long, grueling race. Behind eyes closed to block out the night, a momentary veil of red and a deeper darkness settled upon him. He suppressed the primal urge to wail his grief for all the world to hear. The world, he knew, did not care. The world had troubles enough of its own.

The smell of damp earth and the bitter scent of stinging nettles and summer phlox crushed beneath his boots drifted into his consciousness. He straightened, a soldier again, put Solange behind him and marched the last few hundred yards to the château.

*

Within an hour of the conclusion of his meeting with General Horrocks-Smythe, Harry had his railway warrant in hand and was on his way home. He stopped at the vicarage and handed the parish priest, Father Jean-Paul Migot, most of his French and Belgian money. "I regret, Father, the time has come for me to leave Ste-Marguerite-des-Lys. I doubt I shall ever return. Please see that those in the parish in most need benefit from what little I have in my wallet, especially the widows and children." The priest nodded his thanks with a faint, knowing smile. Harry shook the priest's hand and without another word climbed into the waiting staff car.

While he spent the next few minutes on the station platform, the thought struck him: perhaps he understood now what Horrocks-Smythe meant when he spoke of prudence being the perfect ability to make right decisions. When Solange closed the door on him, she had made the right decision for both of them, no matter how painful, perhaps for her as much as it was for him. He would not return, not to Ste-Marguerite-des-Lys-Gran'ville, not to Solange, nor to Sophie or Madeleine, no matter how much he might desire it. The final break, clean and swift. Solange had deserved that much at least.

Now he faced the uncertain future of a marriage to a woman he had once loved with all his being and who professed to love him still. How could he be certain? And how could he rekindle within him the fire that once burned and had been all but extinguished by Solange? Can love, like a rose that has bloomed, its petals faded and dropped to earth, come into bud again? He thought of *Roseland* and the rose garden. There, as far as he could remember, the roses bloomed once, in late spring and into June, and if they survived the winter, did not bud again until the following spring.

He looked back on the past two years. They had been the rose time of his life, a time to love and now, a time for love to die, perhaps to be reborn with Athena. Or perhaps to die forever, as he might in the coming weeks and months when he returned to Flanders, to the front.

In a cloud of white steam and black smoke that reeked of soot and sulphur, the train pulled in and screeched to an asthmatic, clanking halt. He took his seat in the carriage and stared out of the window, forcing himself into a proper frame of mind to greet his fiancée and become a married man. Notwithstanding his fall from the moral high ground since leaving Washington, he was free to live up to his promise to Athena, to be a loving, caring and faithful husband. And, one day perhaps a father again.

*

Rhodes drove Athena to Truro and remained with the Daimler on the station forecourt while she paced back and forth in front of the ticket barrier waiting for Harry's train to arrive. The Great Western Railway steam engine whooshed past her towards the end of the platform as if it had no intention of stopping. Then at the last moment the chocolate and cream carriages screeched to a hissy-fit stop. Doors banged open. She caught herself jumping up and down and clapping her hands when she saw Harry alight from a first class compartment.

A porter took Harry's two battered leather suitcases and a small trunk and piled them onto his barrow. She saw him look up and down the platform, as if searching for somebody. She told herself to remain calm. This is England, she reminded herself, though she could scarcely believe she was actually there. No jumping up and down allowed. No shouting. Don't show emotion in public. "It's simply not done, old girl," Ernest had told her that morning when he'd caught her looking excited. "Not dignified." Pompous ass, she'd thought at the time and had had no reason to change her opinion since. Against all her desires, she took a step back and stood in the shadows of the brick archway over the ticket barrier.

"Hello, stranger," she said, when Harry passed through the barrier with the porter in tow.

Harry whirled round. "My God! Athena! I wasn't expecting you for another day or two."

Athena rushed into Harry's outstretched arms. "Pleased to see me?"

"Of course."

Athena didn't seem to notice his slight hesitation. Not exactly a lie, but less than the whole truth.

If only this had been Solange.

"I arrived in Liverpool on the *Mauretania* the day before yesterday. Then it was a mad dash to get here in time to meet you. I spent close to a week surrounded by nearly two thousand Canadian soldiers."

"No loss for company while at sea, then?"

"I'm trying to make you jealous, Harry. They were all most polite and attentive, as you can imagine. There were only three civilian women other than me on board. We shared a cabin. We girls, I mean. Not with the soldiers, though I think a couple of the girls were tempted. Plenty of choice. If there had been an orchestra I'd never have been without a dance partner."

"We're causing a bit of an obstruction here." Harry picked her off her feet, swung her around and carried her out of the way of the crowd. "God, you smell so good." He buried his face in her hair tumbling around the nape of her neck and smelled her perfume. Solange, he remembered, had only worn perfume once, the night they had dinner and made love for the first time. The rest of the time she smelled of rose-scented soap, clean, healthy and natural. He dragged his mind back to the present. "I remember that perfume from the first time we met. From a middle-aged man of your close acquaintance, if I recall."

"And you smell so... so... I don't quite know what."

"Rugged? Masculine? They don't immediately leap to mind?"

"You smell like a soldier."

"It could be worse, I suppose." He shrugged. "But you look so beautiful, so radiant, so… American. Even more beautiful than the day…" He choked back a lump in his throat. He knew it was for Solange, beautiful, red haired Solange in the farmhouse kitchen with their child, little Madeleine smelling of baby and nappies, asleep in her arms. Her image burst into his mind then flared out as quickly. The affair was over. Dead and essentially buried the day Madeleine had been born, though he couldn't know it then.

The future lay with Athena, as he'd known all along it would be no matter how long and how hard he had clung to the notion of a future with Solange. First, he would have to get to know Athena again. Then he'd see what transpired. He knew he was no longer in love with her like he had been. Perhaps he wasn't in love with her at all anymore. Some things he could disguise or hide, but outright deceit would probably be beyond his meagre acting talents. Don't rush me, please, Athena. Take it easy. Baby steps. He collected his thoughts, filed away the one that must lie forever buried, and directed his mind to Athena. And, oh God, was she ever more beautiful, radiant, smiling and confident? It wouldn't be hard to fall in love with her all over again.

"…than the day you waved goodbye to me from the pier in New York," he finished.

"I never took my eyes off the liner until it was out of sight. I kept waving, hoping you could see me, but not my tears."

"I waved to you until we disappeared around the end of Long Island. If I knew then how long I'd have to wait before I saw you again, I might have dragged you to the altar before I left and brought you with me." That may have been true then, but did he mean it now? He was not so sure, but he couldn't dash her hopes. He would do his duty and hope that it would become much more than that in time.

"I wouldn't have put up any resistance, you, caveman brute!" Athena gave him a broad grin and wrinkled her nose. "I like the moustache, by the way. Does it tickle when you kiss girls?"

"They all say it does and complain like crazy. Then they throw themselves at Major Cassegrain, a womanizer par excellence, who has a far more luxuriant growth than I'll ever have." He dropped his voice. "I think Cassegrain had me lined up for his recently-widowed sister in Paris. Her husband was a colonel of artillery at Verdun who sacrificed himself for the glory of France. Cassegrain's words, not mine. Not a chance. Cassegrain said his sister was overcome with grief and in need of solace. I never found out which was true, but I suspect the latter rather than the former. And in case you're wondering, I didn't make it to Paris."

"I should hope not! I knew I should never have let you out of my sight, Major Haig-Mallory." She dug him in the ribs. "Let's not stand here gossiping. We're making fools of ourselves, and Rhodes is waiting for us with the Daimler."

"And I'm sure he'll keep his eyes glued to the road ahead and avoid the rear view mirror."

"But kiss me, anyway. Here. Now."

When he put her down, Athena looked at him seriously. "I know I can't make you promise never to leave me. I won't even ask. But please promise me you'll do everything you possibly can to come back to me in one piece."

"The Germans may have other ideas, but I promise to do everything in my power to thwart their evil intent."

"I see you've moved on from Jane Eyre. Mary Shelley?"

"Mary Who?"

"Shelley. Frankenstein?"

Harry looked blank.

"Never mind." She linked her arm through his and drew him nearer. "Do you want to know something about Jane Eyre?"

"What?"

"She was a stuck up, sanctimonious, conniving, virginal, little prig. No one's that perfect. She acts holier than Joan of Arc."

"You're none of those. Were you ever?"

"Virginal. Once. A long time ago and an ocean away."

All the way back to *Roseland* they sat at opposite sides of the back seat, holding hands in the intervening gap. Rhodes slid the glass partition closed as soon as they pulled away from the station forecourt. Even so, Harry dropped his voice and looked sideways at Athena. "We're still on for Saturday?"

"Unless you have other plans."

"No change of heart." The next lie. When would they stop? He could not, in all conscience, send Athena back to America with an apology for falling in love with another woman while Athena was in America, and having a child, his child, by her.

Harry kept a straight face for the benefit of Rhodes, whose eyes Harry could see reflected in the rearview mirror never wavered from the road ahead.

"If a telegram comes between now and Sunday, promise me you won't open it."

"I promise."

Athena squeezed Harry's hand. "It's a pity my mother and father couldn't be here for the wedding. They were afraid of another *Lusitania,* but I told them I wasn't waiting another minute." She opened her handbag and handed Harry an envelope. "Take it. It's addressed to you."

Harry looked at the unfamiliar handwriting and slid a thumb under the flap. He pulled out a sheet of bond writing paper and unfolded it with a frown.

"What does it say? Read it to me."

Harry cleared his throat. "It's from your father."

"I know, silly. I recognize his handwriting, and he gave it to me to give to you."

He leaned away from Athena and read the letter to her.

*Dear Harry,*

*At last we have the son we have always wanted to lead our daughter through life. We could not have asked for Athena to have chosen better. We wish you both a long and happy life together. Our daughter has expensive tastes, as you may already have discovered. The enclosed may come in handy, and we offer it from both of us in the knowledge that you will use it wisely and well. As your banks are probably as untrusting as ours on receiving a check from an unknown source, I will wire you the actual funds as soon as you send me, in confidence, your account details.*

*Good luck. God bless you both. And please visit us in Cleveland whenever you can. Our door is always open to you both.*

*Ralph and Minnie Fenhagen.*

Harry glanced at the unsigned and undated cheque with Sample Only scrawled across the front and turned his head away.

"What is it, Harry?"

Without a word he handed Athena her father's cheque. She took it and gasped.

"I know," Harry said. "It's way too generous."

"We can't refuse it. Father would be terribly hurt."

"But five million dollars?"

"Father is a man of means. He won't miss it. He did say I have expensive tastes. I prefer to think of them as exquisite. Especially in my choice of husband. Besides, at the present rate of exchange, it's only a little over a million pounds. Am I right?"

"Only is hardly the word for it."

"Ernest will inherit *Roseland* one day. This will buy a very nice estate where we can raise our own family once the war's over, Harry. My parents will approve. And I'm sure they'll come and visit from time to time."

"But…"

"No *Buts*, my love. This is his way of welcoming you to our small family."

"I shall write to him this evening."

"Wait until after the wedding. I don't want him to think you've opened his gift early." She linked her arm through Harry's, pulled him towards her and squeezed his hand before moving back into her corner.

"I'll invest it in Gilts until the war is over. They yield four percent at the moment. The income alone will keep you in the Mayfair dress salons for as long as you wish. I'll write and thank your father as soon as we return from what passes for a honeymoon these days."

"Where are we going? I'd be more than content to spend it at *Roseland*."

"With my father and Ernest hovering over our shoulders? The Marquis of Butte has lent us his summer home and staff in Torquay for a couple of days. I've been there before. It's very nice, but quiet."

"Quiet's what I want. A desert island with you would be even better."

"They have sand beaches at Torquay, and palm trees, but I'm afraid it's no exotic tropical island."

The entire household, from Mrs. Tregarrick to the scullery maids, took time from their duties to turn out on the front steps to welcome Harry home as if he were royalty. His father was away, as Harry suspected he would be, but his stepmother made a fuss over him, clinging onto him every bit as hard as Athena did.

"I say, steady on, Mother," Harry said as she gave him a kiss on the cheek.

"I will not be deprived of my son. I know, I know. You are not my son, but I have always regarded you as my little boy."

"Welcome back, Harry," Ernest said as they shook hands. "How long will you be here?"

"Three weeks. And I'm spending every single day of them here, except for our wedding night and Sunday night. Everything arranged for Saturday?"

"Three o'clock at the church. The reception will be here. Immediate family and a few close friends. And the photographer."

"Exactly as we wanted. Thank you."

Harry gazed about at the gathering. "Many familiar faces seem to be missing, Ernest," he said. "The young footmen, the grooms. Have they all joined up?"

"Every last one old enough to fight."

"At least you're still here to run things."

"I volunteered, but pudgy, one-eyed soldiers are not in great demand. I think they've put me in the *Only If Desperate* column."

"After the butchery last month on the Somme, they may yet be desperate, particularly if things keep going as they have the last little while."

"The newspapers reported sixty thousand casualties on the first day alone," Ernest said. "Is that true?"

Harry grimaced. "No exaggeration. An army wiped out. Massacred. I don't know what went wrong. I doubt if the generals do. The best troops in the Empire couldn't budge the German line one inch. I've no idea where we go from here or how long it will take to recover. But given the numbers, I think one thing is clear."

"What's that?"

"If I'd been there I probably wouldn't be here."

# 15. ENGLAND'S PAWNS

Harry and Athena spent most of the journey to Torquay in silence, holding hands and staring out of the car's windows. On their arrival, Athena stepped aside as a footman picked up their valises and headed for the door. "I can hardly carry you over the threshold," Harry whispered. "It's not our house."

"You can carry me over the threshold into our bedroom if you like. I won't object. And I suspect the staff have a good mind what will be going on in an hour's time." She hesitated. "They won't have put us in separate rooms, will they?"

"Butte knows why we're here. And I know Butte. I'm certain it'll be the best bedroom in the house, private bathroom, all modern conveniences and the biggest bed you've ever slept in in your life."

"I wasn't planning on sleeping much, Harry. Not tonight anyway." She swept up her skirt and followed him up the steps and into the house.

"Welcome, Sir," the butler said, and bowed. "My name is Grieves. If I may introduce you to the staff?"

The butler went up and down the line of servants, naming each one. With the introductions made, he turned to Harry and gave a slight bow. "If you will follow me to your suite, Sir. Madam." Harry and Athena followed Grieves up the stairs. They stopped outside a door at the top of the stairs. The butler unlocked the door, pushed it open and handed Harry the key. "If there is anything you need, Sir." He turned to Athena. "Or Madam, please ring down. The housekeeper is Mrs. Menzies. She will make sure your stay here is most comfortable." He turned to Harry. "Breakfast on Sunday is at nine, unless you prefer it earlier or later." He turned to Athena and offered a slight bow. "You will be brought your breakfast in bed, Madam. Perhaps you would let Mrs. Menzies know what you would like in the morning." The butler stood aside to let Harry and Athena pass through into the bedroom.

"Thank you, Grieves."

"Your valet is Tomlinson, Sir. He has already unpacked your valises. Will you be needing him tonight?"

"I rather think not, Grieves. I think I can manage for one night. Perhaps you can have him attend at half past eight, after my bath."

"Very good, Sir." He turned to Athena. "Your lady's maid is Fairhead.

She serves the marchioness when she is in residence."

"Thank you, Grieves," Athena said. "And as my husband…" She stopped. That was the first time she had referred to Harry as her husband. "I shan't be needing her tonight. Perhaps she can run my bath in the morning after breakfast?"

"Certainly, Madam. I will tell her. Will nine-thirty be too early?"

"Not at all. Thank you, Grieves."

The butler bowed in acknowledgement and turned to Harry. "Then I will bid you and Mrs. Haig-Mallory a good night and wish you a pleasant stay."

When Grieves turned his back and headed for the stairs, Harry picked up Athena and carried her into the room. She had long since shed her wedding gown and wore a going away outfit of white pleated blouse, a long navy blue skirt and matching jacket. Harry kicked the door shut behind him and looked around. The electric lights were on and, as Grieves had mentioned, the valet had already unpacked their cases and put their clothes away. It was dark outside. Heavy damask curtains were drawn part way cross the open window, partially blocking the lights of the town beyond. The massive four poster bed with its drapes drawn back and tethered to the posts with matching damask loops, sat against the long wall of the large room. The counterpane had been turned down on both sides, ready for them. The fireplace had been prepared but not lit. The night was warm, and the scent of climbing roses drifted in through the window.

"I should probably put you down," Harry said. "But there doesn't seem to any place to put you, other than that uncomfortable-looking settee by the window." He swiveled around. "Or that rather imposing bed."

Athena tightened her grip around Harry's neck. "I could stay in here forever, Harry," she whispered in his ear.

"In this house?"

"In your arms, silly. I want to live at *Roseland.*"

"You're as light as a feather, but if I don't put you down soon my back will complain."

"Then there's only one solution, Major Haig-Mallory. That bed over there will make a good headquarters until circumstances require us to vacate."

Harry carried Athena over to the bed, leaned forward and dropped her, legs kicking, in the centre. "Which side do you prefer?" she said.

"The same as Washington with you on my left."

Athena looked up at Harry standing over her. "This isn't Washington, Harry. I don't know if we can ever go back to those days and nights again."

A puzzled frown creased Harry's forehead. "Are you having second thoughts, my love?"

Athena smiled. "No. Never. But we're no longer the people we were in Washington. We've changed. You probably more than I have, given what you must have been through these past two years. We'll need to get to know each other all over again. It'll be fun."

Harry reached down and tickled her ribs. Athena squealed and thrashed around on the bed cover. "Still ticklish," he said with a laugh. "At least that hasn't changed."

"My mother warned me about men like you. So did my father. I want to see if they had good reason. Are you going to lock the door and close the curtains? I wouldn't want the whole of Torquay watching me undress without paying for the privilege."

"Oh, you are a wanton little hussy."

Harry crossed the bedroom and locked the door. When he closed the curtains, he turned to face Athena. "I know this has been thrown together in a hurry," he said. "You've only just arrived. If you're tired. Or would rather sleep, I understand. I don't wish to presume…"

"You sound like a minister giving his spiritual and practical guidance talk to the bride-to-be. Of course, I want you. Now. More than anything I've ever wanted in my life."

"You were right just now. We have changed since Washington. Inwardly mostly. A little outwardly." He fingered his moustache and offered a wan smile. "Mostly we come to each other as a married couple tonight. We were having the time of our lives in Washington."

"And that night in New York before you sailed, don't forget," Athena added hurriedly.

"And in New York. Who could ever forget New York? But we've committed ourselves to each other for life. It's serious now."

"And it wasn't before? It was frivolous fun? I was a toy, a plaything and now I'm not? Is that what you mean?"

"No. That's not what I meant. We can be fun together, have fun together, laugh together but underneath there's a current of, I don't know what… Being different, being serious in our commitments to each other, starting a family together rather than trying to prevent one." He raised his arms from his sides and let them drop again. "It doesn't change the way I feel about you. I love you, Athena. I have ever since the day I met you, June the twenty-third, nineteen fourteen. I don't ever want to stop loving you. But it's deeper now. It has a real purpose. And I promise I'll be the best husband you could ever wish for. Or better, if that's possible." Harry knew she needed to hear those words. Even if they were slightly less than completely honest. The memory of Solange and the children returned. His eyes glistened. He had to dismiss Solange from his mind. She was the past. Gone. Forever. He would never see her again. Or Sophie or Madeleine. That was the way the world was, for better or worse. Perhaps this was the worse and things would get better in time. And he had promised Athena in front of a church full of witnesses only hours before that he would love her, for better or worse, in sickness and in health, until death do them part.

Solange had turned her back on him. He now had to turn his on her. He had promised himself he would, but he hadn't. Not really. Not finally and irrevocably. He needed time to get over her. And time was one thing he did not have, not with a woman who was now his wife. He would learn to love Athena again. How could he not? He had done it before, the kind of head-over-heels love only the young are supposed to know. She was beautiful. The most beautiful woman he had ever seen, anywhere. And she loved him. That had to count for something.

Tears pooled in Athena's eyes and tumbled down her cheeks. "I've always known I love you, Harry. I still do. I always will, no matter what. I was afraid… I was afraid you might have changed your mind about me while I was away. Two years. Two years is a long time at the beginning of a relationship. I didn't know if it would survive." She sat up and wiped the tears with the back of her hand. Harry handed her his handkerchief. She dabbed her eyes and blew her nose on the cotton before she shoved it beneath a pillow.

"It will," Harry said. "We will make it survive and thrive as never before, and let nothing come between us, no matter what. I promise."

"And I promise, too." She swung her legs over the side of the bed and stood. She placed the palm of her hand on the starched front of his cambric shirt and found his nipple beneath the cloth. "Now, Major, as I don't have a lady's maid here, will you help me out of my clothes? Or must I do everything myself?"

Harry shot her a quizzical look.

"Everything but that. I think I can rely on you to make sure tonight will be memorable for all the right reasons."

*

They lay in bed in the summer darkness with only a sheet covering their skin. Harry had drawn back the curtain fully. The slender sliver of moon cast a tiny, cold light all but lost in the yellowish glow of the town lights. His eyes accustomed to the night, Harry lit a cigarette and passed it to Athena, then lit one for himself. They smoked in silence for a few minutes, their hands touching beneath the sheet.

"This reminds me of our first night together, in Washington," Harry murmured.

"Except we had Champagne then, and you licked it off me as I remember. All the way down."

"How could I forget? You tasted so good."

"Was it better that first night? Better than tonight?"

"Different."

"How different?"

"You don't have Champagne in your navel tonight."

"How do you know? You haven't licked me there."

"I was just coming to that." He stubbed out his cigarette in the ashtray on the bedside table and threw off the sheet. Athena squealed. Harry lay on top of her and kissed her with passion on the lips, her throat, her breasts, working his way down her body. "I'm right," he said, breaking off his kisses.

"What do you mean?"

"There's no Champagne in your navel tonight. And we don't have any in the room. I shall have to have a word with Butte. Not up to the standards of the Hay-Adams when it comes to providing Champagne in bed.  But all is not lost."

"What do you mean?"

"This tastes even better than bubbly," he said as he burrowed his head between her thighs.

"Oh, Harry. Do you really love me?"

"Mmmph."

"As much as before?"

"Mmmph."

"Oh, Harry, don't stop."

He was a soldier. It was second nature to do as he was told.

*

The day after they returned from their abbreviated honeymoon a telegram arrived at *Roseland*. Athena took it from the silver tray in the dining room where they were having breakfast. She tried to hide it behind her back, but Harry saw her.

"You promised," she said as Harry reached a handout for it.

"You're right. I did. But only until Sunday. It's Tuesday. But go ahead, open it and let me know if I should read it." He chewed silently on a piece of toast. "Bad news? That's all that seems to come by telegram these days."

Athena tore the envelope open. "It's addressed to Lt. Colonel H.C.A.E. Haig-Mallory." She looked at Harry with a puzzled expression. "Did you know you'd been promoted?"

"I had no idea. I certainly wasn't expecting it. Go on."

"It reads, CONGRATULATIONS ON PROMOTION TO REGIMENT COMMANDER STOP PROCEED 21ST INST HORSEFIELD BARRACKS FOR DEPLOYMENT STOP AUTH OC BRIGADE SHACKLETON."

Athena looked at Harry with a puzzled expression on her face. "But aren't you terribly young for all that responsibility, Harry?"

"I won't be the youngest regiment commander in the army, especially after last month at the Somme." He looked over at the butler, standing at attention with the tray still in his hand. "Please send a reply, Tregarrick. One word will suffice. Acknowledged."

He turned to Athena. "I shall have to get hold of my tailor and order new uniforms. At least they have my size. They should be ready for a fitting by the end of next week. Now to break the news to mother. I promised her I'd spend the whole of my leave here."

Athena kissed him on the cheek. "I'm sure your mother won't mind under the circumstances. She'll be thrilled to know her son's a colonel."

*

After Harry's final fitting and Athena's tour of the Mayfair couturiers, they strolled through Green Park and St James's Park, both green spaces crowded with men in khaki and navy, in pairs and in groups, some with women, and some without. Many of the men leaned on canes or limped along on crutches with nurses at their sides. A few were pushed like small children, only glum-faced, in three-wheeled bath chairs. Harry lost count of the amputees. Most had pain etched on their faces and their silent suffering dulled their vacant, staring eyes.

"This is the first time I've seen the human face of war," Athena said. They sat on a bench by the Serpentine, tossing chunks of stale bread for the ducks from a brown paper bag.

Harry said nothing.

"At least they're not buried in a field in France," she said. "They look so sad, though, when they should celebrate the fact they're alive."

"What we see is only the husk of the man we sent to France." Harry's face looked as grim as he sounded. "They call it shell shock. We'll send many of the poor blighters back to face more shells and bullets. Until we run out of men. Or the Germans do."

"Oh, Harry…"

"But I won't become like them, I promise. I've already promised to return in one piece, and when this is over we'll raise a family of our own, far from the guns. Then we can decide whether we want to stay in England. There's little to hold us here. Ernest inherits the estate eventually, which probably means he'll end up in the poor house. It's sad, but he hasn't a clue. Or we can go to America and be close to your family."

"That's too far down the road to contemplate, Harry. Where will you be sent? Do you know?"

"The Hussars are at the Salient, around Ypres. So unless we are withdrawn from the line for some reason, that's where I'll be deployed."

"It's terribly dangerous there, Harry. I'll worry myself sick."

"You have nothing to fear, my love, for my safety."

"But I do."

He patted her hands. "Don't fret. Colonels don't go over the top. We derive satisfaction, and far greater safety, by leading from behind, like the Duke of Plazatoro in The Gondoliers."

"I've never heard of him."

"A character in a popular operetta by Gilbert and Sullivan. The Duke found leading that way less exciting. We're like chess pieces. Far too valuable to sacrifice. That's what pawns are for."

"How unfortunate for the pawns."

Harry ignored the frost in her voice. "High or low, we are all England's pawns," he said softly as he crumpled the empty bag of bread crusts. "Shall we move on?"

*

When he arrived in Flanders, Harry's regiment was resting, well to the rear of the front lines, at the time bogged down around the old wool centre of Ypres. Ste-Marguerite-des-Lys-Gran'ville lay a few miles from their position. So relatively near to Solange, Harry thought as he made his way through the canvas flap that served as a door to the Headquarters tent. And Sophie and Madeleine. But thankfully far enough away that he wouldn't be tempted to see how they were managing. That door was closed. He had heard Solange bar it, physically as well as metaphorically that night. In sliding the bolt home, she had made it plain he wasn't welcome back in her life.

"Glad to have you back, Sir," Merryweather said, as he snapped a salute to his side.

"Good to be back," Harry said, casting an eye around him at the relatively primitive conditions of his new surroundings in the reserve camp. "In a way. A bit of a change from my last posting. Not much use for mess kit here. What's our strength?"

"We took a mauling on the Somme. I imagine you saw the figures before you left. Three hundred and sixteen casualties out of a complement of a little over five hundred officers and other ranks. One hundred and twelve dead, eighteen missing, one hundred and eighty-six wounded. About half are Blighty ones. We expect perhaps a hundred back eventually. We've received eighty-one replacements so far. Not up to standards yet, Sir, but we're working them hard."

"Total strength?"

"Three hundred and seventy-one officers and other ranks."

"Officers?"

"We lost Major Kerslake on the first day of the offensive. And Major Smith-Bingley a day later. Both killed. Each troop has a lieutenant. Some of them are old enough to shave. Apart from me, only two of our originals survived the offensive. Captain de Beynac is acting adjutant. Captain Snow is in command of A Squadron. The other two squadrons are commanded by lieutenants. None has battle experience. All told, we lost three quarters of our officers, plus half our NCOs and other ranks. And that leaves me, acting major and CO until about two minutes ago. Not pretty, Sir."

Harry pulled a grim face. "No. Not pretty."

"Believe it or not, Sir, but we're better off than many. Some regiments suffered up to ninety per cent casualties. We keep chipping away at the Hun. It's not over yet but I have to say that enthusiasm to continue the offensive on the Somme is ebbing faster than the tide in The Wash. Still, we're here now, though I'm not sure if the Salient is the frying pan or the fire."

Harry shook his head. "Show me to my quarters, Merryweather, and let me have a full briefing. Then have the officers attend the mess at eighteen hundred hours. I shall want to meet them all." He stopped for a moment and gave Merryweather a fleeting smile. "Glad to see you made it through that ghastly affair, Merryweather. Carry on."

*

The officers assembled in the mess tent and stood to attention as soon as Harry entered, for most their first glimpse of their commanding officer. He strode purposefully through them, searching for familiar faces until he reached the front and rounded the dining table. He looked the officers over, checking for smart uniforms and polished boots, a hallmark of good morale and discipline. Merryweather, Snow and de Beynac he knew. The other dozen? He drew a blank. Could it really have been this bad? He nodded. "At ease, gentlemen."

"You there." He pointed with his swagger stick at a lanky young man with a wry smile and a wispy moustache that made him look even younger. The young officer stood to attention, licked his lips and shuffled his feet.

"Sheppard, E. Dexter," he said. "Second Lieutenant."

"As I can tell from the scarcity of badges of rank on your uniform, Mr. Sheppard," Harry said. "What drove you to become a Hussar officer? Surely you can't be tired of living yet, not like the rest of us here." A light laugh rippled around the officers gathered in the mess tent.

"I read divinity at Oxford." Sheppard shifted his weight from one foot to the other and back. He offered a rueful smile. "The war put a halt to my career in the Church. I was not very subtly invited to join the colours. It might have been a bit of a relief, actually. I'm not sure I'm cut out to be a man of the cloth."

"Hostilities only, I take it? Not a career path for you, am I right?'

"Quite correct, Sir. The day after the last shot's fired I'll be on my way home. That's what they promised when I signed on."

"We all need something to believe in, Sheppard, but surely you didn't believe that load of codswallop?"

"Not for a moment, Sir."

"If you did, I'd send you off for a psychiatric examination. Welcome to the King's Imperial Hussars. We need an officer in charge of hope and machine guns. Congratulations on volunteering, Padre." Harry shook hands with the young man. "I'm sure you know our last official padre didn't see it through the Somme. He was a good man. Through no fault of his own, he has responded to a higher calling. Let's hope you have better luck. Much better."

Harry went through his officer cadre one by one, questioning here, probing more closely there, seeking weaknesses in men he and his regiment would need to rely on in the weeks and months to come. It was worse than he thought. Most had been rushed through basic infantry training before selection for what must pass for officer training these days. Six months ago they had been civilians, some plucked from the Officer Training Corps at University before they had time to finish their degree, others from their desks. Beneath the outward keenness ran a current of nervousness, of fear. Would they be up to the task of leading men in battle? It was up to him to see that they were. Some, inevitably, would be found wanting. Those he would need to weed out before the first attack. He looked over their expectant faces and found he had nothing more to say. Despondent at the task before him, worse than the optimistic Merryweather had made out, he glanced at the adjutant, Captain de Beynac, and nodded.

"Attention!" de Beynac called out. The dozen young men snapped to attention. "Dismissed."

The men parted like the Red Sea as Harry made his way through them, intent on reading their files in his tent. He was only a few hours back in command and already the effects of the monumental task ahead left him confronting his own inadequacies.

# 16. CHRISTMAS EVE

The war on the western front crawled from the meat grinder of the summer of The Somme to a virtual standstill by December. The prevailing mood throughout the country, from palaces to slums, descended from gloom to resentment at the casualty figures which by now had a human face that affected nearly every community and family in every corner of the realm.

As if a mirror to the general mood, Christmas Eve at *Roseland* in 1916 was a subdued affair. Cecilia, Ernest and the earl came down from London to join Athena and Anne-Marie, the Countess St Austell, for two days. After handing out the bonus envelopes to the staff the earl offered his arm to the countess.

"The Guv'nor and the governess," Ernest whispered to Cecilia, not quite softly enough. Their father's back stiffened for a moment, interrupting the regal slow march toward the dining room.

"She's my mother," Cecilia hissed. "And I love her. And you'd better lay off the wine, Ernest, or you'll fall flat on your face into your soup. You've had more than enough sherry already."

Athena watched and listened to the exchange. The earl's cool indifference to her since she'd come to live at *Roseland* failed to mask what she believed was his contempt for her. And, she thought ruefully, probably for all foreigners, including his wife. It seemed unless the countess gave him grounds for divorce, or suffered a fatal accident like her predecessor, they were stuck with each other. She felt sorry for her mother-in-law, stuck in a loveless marriage to her significantly older husband.

She missed Harry desperately. The daytime she could write off to Harry being at work. Like most husbands. But the nights? She slept fitfully between crisp, cold linen sheets in their equally cold, draughty bedroom. The mahogany-handled, brass warming pan between the sheets did little to remove the damp left by the winter mists that swirled in from the sea or swept down from Bodmin Moor. In spite of closed doors and windows, the bone-chilling damp managed to seep into the house down chimneys, through walls and from beneath the floors. The sea fogs that seemed to have hovered over the house since her arrival showed little inclination to disperse.

Cleveland, in spite of its autumn gales off Lake Erie, never felt so damp, or the skies so uniformly gloomy which combined to match her mood. They would have had snow at home by now, squalls and flurries off the lake, with a lot more to come. But their house had always been warm, physically and as a place in which to grow up and live. It had been built to withstand Ohio winters. There was usually cheerfulness, and the sound of laughter filling the house, from her parents and from the few staff they employed. It was a happy house, a home filled with love and kindness, respect and understanding. As a girl, she had never encountered conflict or tension between her parents, or they with her.

*Roseland* seemed far from happy. Cecilia, she could tell from the way she distanced herself from him, despised her father. Neither did she have much time for Ernest who, Athena concluded, was more than a sandwich short of a picnic. The earl seemed as totally indifferent to his wife as she to him, each barely tolerant of the other, civil when they had to be in public, otherwise only too glad to be left alone. Unlike her parents, the earl and countess slept in separate rooms whenever the earl was at *Roseland*, something which Athena could not contemplate with Harry and her. In any case, Harry's father, she calculated, might only spend two weeks a year at *Roseland*, and those two weeks spent grudgingly away from London; a couple of days at Christmas, the same at Easter and a week during the summer. And the sad thing was, no one seemed to mind his absence in the slightest. It was as if he didn't really exist yet still managed to cast a dark shadow of fear and loathing over the whole household. Was Harry the only normal one?

While Athena waited for her turn to enter the dining room, Ernest leered at her as if she was a candy cane and he desperate for a sugar high. She edged away. He held out his arm for her to take. She shook her head and took her place behind Cecilia as the newest and lowest addition to the family hierarchy. More an appendage than a member, she thought. Whatever Ernest had on his mind it did not involve her. She pitied the poor serving girl whom he had no doubt selected as his personal Christmas gift — from him to him. And if Ernest was as stupid as she believed, an unwanted pregnancy would cause the admiral to suffer an apoplectic fit strong enough and loud enough to shake *Roseland* to its very foundations. She smiled. Perhaps it would be worth it. Take one for the team, young servant girl, as they say in baseball. Such a fit could just finish off the earl. In Athena's opinion, to judge from his florid complexion and the dark veins that ran like cracked glaze across his face, her father-in-law did not seem to enjoy the most robust of health. That would mean Ernest would be the earl sooner rather than later. Better a twit than a tyrant, a reflection she kept to herself.

"I'm with Harry," Athena said. She didn't smile or offer any explanation, apart from, "Wherever he is tonight." She strode resolutely into the dining room, leaving a perplexed Ernest gaping like a fish out of water.

*

Athena was half asleep beneath several layers of blankets and an eiderdown, trying to warm herself with a hot water bottle at her feet. She found it with her toes and sighed heavily when she discovered it was no warmer than her feet. Maybe colder, if that were possible. A few embers still smouldered in the grate but gave off little heat. The fire would be dead long before the tweenie came to relight it in the morning. Athena wore a shawl draped around her shoulders over her flannel nightgown. The unflattering nightdress had not formed part of her trousseau. Rather, she had bought it in Truro once she discovered how cold hers and Harry's bedroom was come October. She was glad of it now, and not altogether unhappy that Harry couldn't see her in it.

Behind her closed eyes in the cold of her dark bedroom she saw Harry. They stood on the station platform before he climbed aboard the train for Dover at the end of his short leave that passed for their honeymoon. They kissed and hugged. Then he pushed her away until he held her at arms' length.

"If we do that again I won't get on the train," he said.

She flew back into his arms and clung to him. "Then let's do this all over again and then you'll miss the train and you won't have to go back to war because it's the last train that'll ever go to Dover. Then you can be with me forever."

"It's a terrific idea, but it probably won't work. I have to go. They can't win the war without me." He smiled and plopped a final kiss on her lips.

Reluctantly she let go. "Off you go, then," she said, and pushed him away gently. "I'll pray for you."

"If you think it will help." He looked serious. "I'm sorry. I didn't mean to offend you."

"Prayer might make all the difference between you coming home to me and staying in France. Forever." She burst into tears. He kissed her forehead then turned and climbed the step into his first-class compartment. The guard blew his whistle and waved his green flag. Through the carriage window she watched Harry put his cases on the overhead rack and take a seat in the middle of the compartment. She could see his face in profile. As the train lurched forward he turned. He gave a slight nod and a grim smile.

She relived that scene, alone in bed, this night and every night since August And she vowed she would relive it every night until he came home to her.

She heard a slight noise from the landing and turned over to face the door. Probably Cecilia or Ernest, she thought, tiptoeing to the bathroom. Her bedroom door opened. She stared, wide-eyed, at Ernest in his nightgown, silhouetted in the doorway with a lighted candle in his hand.

"Go away," she hissed.

"Shh," he whispered, and shut the door quietly behind him. He advanced towards her bed. She tried to edge away but the weight of the several layers of bed clothes prevented her from moving more than a few inches. "You're cold," he whispered. "I've come to warm you up." He reached out and put a hand on Athena's shoulder.

"Touch me again and I'll scream, so help me, Ernest," she hissed. "I'm not kidding. You're drunk."

"I've had a couple," Ernest said, as if casual conversation were called for in his sister-in-law's bedroom at one in the morning. "But I'm not drunk. I've come to keep you company. There's no one else who can do that for you. You're alone at Christmas. You're lonely. So am I, if truth be told. So, we're both in the same predig…predic…boat."

He sat on the edge of the bed. Athena squirmed. In a flash Ernest slid his hand under the bed clothes and found Athena's breast. She opened her mouth and took a deep breath. To scream. Then changed her mind. Her mouth closed over Ernest's forearm and she bit as hard as she could.

Ernest pulled his arm away and clutched it. "Christ, Athena," he gasped between clenched lips. "That hurt."

"Get out of my room or I'll do it again. And scream. And don't ever think of coming into my room again. I don't even want to see you again, let alone speak to you. If you so much as look at me the wrong way I'll drive your fucking balls up through your throat and scratch your other eye out."

Ernest grabbed the candle holder and spilled hot wax on his hand. "Ouch," he managed before Athena hissed at him, "Get out. Get out. Right now. Or you'll wish you'd never been born."

"Jesus Christ, you've got a foul mouth. Perfect for an army wife."

"Out," she hissed. "Out this instant." She pointed at the door.

"All right. All right. I'm going. All I wanted was a little company at Christmas."

"Then go find a willing sheep on Bodmin," she snarled. "And don't let the door hit you on the way out."

She heard the door close with a soft click. There was no key. There had never seemed a need for one. She would ask Mrs. Aitchison, the housekeeper, for the key in the morning. She pulled the covers over her head and burst into tears. She wouldn't tell Harry. He'd probably murder Ernest, which is probably what Ernest deserved. But Harry would go to jail for the rest of his life. Or the gallows. Ernest wasn't worth that. Regardless of the provocation.

What a family I've married into, she thought. Weird? Fuck. She opened her eyes and looked around the dark bedroom. No one had heard her think that word. Or had she mouthed it? But not out loud, surely? She smiled and wiped her nose on her sleeve. She closed her eyes again. Yeah. Weird, the lot of them. Except Harry. And his stepmother. And maybe Cecilia. I'm not totally sure about her. I've hardly seen her since I arrived. At the wedding for a few hours. She was back in London before we returned from Torquay. And today. She's loud. She's brash. She'd make a good American if she put her mind to it. Athena smiled inwardly. But there's something awkward about her.

I don't know what it is. Everyone knows she calls herself a socialist. Maybe it's today's cause. Or maybe she's serious. She's a contrarian, the sort of person who would turn up for her deb ball in an exquisite gown and army boots to make a statement. Athena smiled at the thought. But I could slaughter Ernest. You're gross, you entitled, fucking creep. I could kill you with as much feeling as I'd have stepping on an ant. And I hate ants.

She pulled the covers tight over her head, as if they could form a barrier against assault from an enemy. You're delusional. Of course, the covers can't keep a creep like Ernest away. And the way his father kept looking at me over dinner was plain spooky. I'm glad I didn't vomit all over the sorbet, as much as I wanted to. Or say anything. 'Not done, old girl,' Ernest would have said. 'One doesn't speak ill of the pater. Or puke on the food.' God, what a pathetic, sniveling asshole. Like father, like son, only from what little I've seen, Ernest isn't a patch on his father in any respect. She shuddered. I hope Harry doesn't turn out to be like either of them. Maybe he's really, really good at hiding his true colours. No. That's unfair. I take it back, Harry. I won't ever doubt you. I feel sorry for your stepmother, though. She's been really nice to me ever since I arrived. Without her I don't know what I might have done. Tried to fit in? With what? Your family? The County set? Cornwall? Pheasant shooting, fox hunting and fly fishing? Changing dresses three times a day? What I've seen of the aristocratic way of life, Harry, I don't like. I miss Cleveland, the city, the office, working. I was useful there. I'm just an ornament here. Colonel Haig-Mallory's wife. Not a real person in my own right. Maybe Cecilia has seen through the whole charade. The world of the Haig-Mallorys and their like must be drawing to a close. It's already over in the States. Could you ever want to live in Cleveland? I don't see it somehow. You're too English. Not like your father is English. Or some of the others I've met here. They don't seem to give a damn about their tenants or servants. Or anyone else. No different from the rich in the States, for that matter. Except for papa. He's different. If he was like the rest of them in his business, he'd be a lot wealthier, and a lot poorer for it. And you're different, too, Harry. You're compassionate. You care for people, for your men. And you seem to like the staff here. To you they're not just servants. I think you see them as people first, who happen to work for your father. You're more like Cecilia than Ernest, thank God. Underneath the stern, aristocratic exterior could you be a secret, wealthy, silk-stocking socialist? Like your sister? The champion of the working man? The anti-aristocrat? The opposite of all you seem to stand for? You're a lot like papa, but more modern. And younger and better looking. And not going bald. They say every girl wants to marry her father. If he's good, and decent, and kind. Did I marry my father? No. But you're very much like him, dearest Harry.

Her angry, ragged breathing slowly returned to normal. She calmed. The more I see of the English, and the aristocracy in particular, the more I like and appreciate Demelza. You were right, Harry. Demelza is a dear. I've never been around a dog before. She took one sniff of my ankles as soon as I got out of the car when I first arrived and followed me everywhere. She must be a good judge of character. I'm surprised she doesn't sleep on my bed. They probably wouldn't allow it. Another of those 'Things that are just not done, old girl.' But I wouldn't mind. In fact, I'd quite like it. She'd be someone to talk to in the middle of the night when I wake up, scared and alone and in need of a good listener. And she wouldn't hold anything against me. Or snitch. I'll ask you next time you're home on leave, Harry, if she can at least sleep in the room with us.

A little happier, she drifted into an exhausted sleep interrupted by dreams she couldn't remember a minute after she woke up the next morning to a cold room, a dead fire — and her bedroom door opening. She snatched the bed clothes up to her chin. She took a peek. It was the tweenie coming in to relay and light the fire.

"Oh, it's you," Athena grunted.

"I'm sorry to disturb you, My Lady," the tweenie managed to say between bobs and curtsies made more difficult by the coal scuttle she lugged between her legs. "I won't be a jiffy."

"I thought it was time to get up."

"It's just gone five, My Lady."

"It makes for a long day for you."

"I'm used to it now, My Lady. And they're good to me here. I don't know where I'd be without Mr. Tregarrick. And Mrs. Tregarrick." She busied herself with paper and kindling. "There." She struck a match. Within seconds the paper had caught and the kindling crackled into its brief life. The tweenie waited a couple of minutes until the fire drew well up the chimney before she tipped coal from the scuttle onto the flames. "It's well banked up now, My Lady. That should do it for two or three hours."

"Thank you, Lily."

The maid looked around as if expecting someone apart from Athena might be in the room. "It's only Lily below stairs, My Lady. It's Broad, upstairs. Mr. Tregarrick insists."

"Thank you, Lily. I'll call you Broad whenever Mr. Tregarrick's listening. I don't want to embarrass you by appearing familiar."

"I hope you don't mind me saying this, but I love your accent, My Lady."

"I think you might be the only one here who does, Lily."

Lily left the room and closed the door behind her with a soft click. Athena sat up in bed with her knees hunched up to her chest and her hands clasped around them. She shivered, not only from the cold but, she knew, from fear. Fear that Ernest might try something again. She could never let her guard down. She tensed, aware of the fast beating of her heart and shallow breathing. She tried to calm herself, but the tension would not go away. She asked herself if this is how it's always going to be whenever Ernest's in the house. Is this any way to live until Harry comes home? Constantly on guard?

She stared at the fire burning brightly in the grate. Lily had done a good job but it failed to dispel the gloom that filled her heart, or the sense of dread at what might happen next, to her or to Harry.

# 17. TRENCH RAID

While Athena shivered between the sheets in Cornwall, trying to find sleep in a cold, empty bed, in Flanders it was Harry's third night on the latest tour of duty at the front. The temperature hovered a degree or two above freezing and the moonless night closed in, blacker than a bat's arse.

Word had filtered back of a new German regiment in the line. Intelligence needed to know its identity and strength, which could best be accomplished by interrogating prisoners snatched from the enemy front line trench. Trench raids were an unenviable and risky task, usually assigned to volunteers, the poor sods who could not dodge out of the squadron corporal major's line of sight quickly enough.

"Never mind standing orders for once," Harry told Lt. Sheppard. "I'm going with you tonight. I can't ask others to do what I won't do myself."

"The colonel and Mr. Sheppard will be with you tonight," the squadron corporal major told the four reluctant volunteers from C troop rifle section. "The colonel says as this is Christmas Eve, and seeing as he has never been to Germany, he wants to know how the Germans celebrate Christmas. And if they decorate their Christmas trees the same as we do. So look sharpish, do the job and don't leave the officers behind. I don't imagine either of them wants to spend next Christmas in Germany, or the one after, any more than you do."

The men in the Middlesex Regiment wished them luck when they passed through into the front line in the drizzle, though the looks they gave Harry's men all seemed to say, *Rather you than us, chum. And have a merry fucking Christmas while you're at it.*

Beyond what passed for the British front line, battered to oblivion by the German artillery during the months following the Battle of the Somme, lay no man's land. On this half a mile of shell-cratered killing fields spread the stage between the theatre's wings where armies fought, died and were destroyed. Separating the two front lines, sharp, rusty and deadly barbed wire, German, British and French, stretched hundreds of miles from the Alps to the North Sea.

The drizzle provided perfect conditions for a raiding party, and the six men who climbed out of the trench and over the parapet were as good as invisible from six feet away. They passed through the gap in their wire around one in the morning of the 25th and crossed into the churned-up quagmire of no man's land. Crouching low, they skittered like monkeys from shell hole to shell hole until they reached the half-way mark. Then it was down on their bellies, slithering in the mud until they reached the first coils of German wire. It began to rain in earnest. "Perfect," Harry whispered to Sheppard. "It means Fritz will be paying more attention to staying dry than looking out for a small group of bastards like us bent on evil." He saw Sheppard's white-toothed grin. "Sorry, Padre. I shouldn't use such language in front of a man of the cloth."

"Nearly, Sir," Sheppard whispered back. "But not quite. If I live long enough, I'm considering teaching. The hours are shorter and the pay slightly better. And I can leave my piety in the kitchen every morning instead of taking it to work with me."

They found a gap in the wire, silently drew the strands aside and crawled to the sandbagged lip of the parapet. A slow, careful recce of their immediate front revealed a deserted section of trench. They slid over the sandbags and dropped silently into the German trench. Once their feet touched the duckboards the group spread out, scouting for enemy lookouts.

Around the first corner of the trench they found a sentry with his back to them, stamping his feet to keep warm. Trooper Trudel crept up behind him, clapped his hand over the German's mouth and plunged his bayonet into the man's guts. He twisted the bayonet and drove it upwards. The long blade sliced through the aorta. The troop Lewis gunner, Lance Corporal 'Windy' Gale, grabbed the sentry's rifle before it clattered to the duckboards, and the German slumped soundlessly to the bottom of the trench. A pool of blood widened beneath him and dripped through the boards into the black water beneath.

When the German stopped twitching, Trudel took his bloody bayonet and cut off the dead man's regimental identification patch from his shoulder. He left the body propped against the rear wall of the trench, out of sight from any casual observer. Gale gave Trudel a thumbs up before they advanced soundlessly along the trench. A rat scuttled out of their way with a scrabble of claws on the duckboards and vanished around a corner. Their nerves already stretched to breaking point, to a man they inhaled involuntarily and held it until it was apparent the rat had not alerted a German sentry.

Harry cocked his head. He heard a different noise, low, soft and close by. He raised his hand. The raiding party froze. Harry remained statue-still with a hand to his ear until he signaled for them to close up. The group of five gathered around him, nerves taut, alert to any sound or movement. Snoring. Harry let out his breath and saw it form as mist in the chill night air. He pointed to a length of sacking that hung over what appeared to be the entrance of a dugout that led at a right angle off the main trench. In single file behind Harry the men made their way stealthily towards the entrance. They stopped outside, and waited, listening for anything to suggest they had unwanted company.

A star shell lit the night sky overhead. They shut their eyes and held their breath, pressing themselves into the recessed shadows of the fire steps to escape the blinding white glare. Silence. No trigger-happy soldier fired blindly into the dark. The star shell flared out. Pitch blackness replaced the light. They strained their ears for the sound of boots on duckboards. They heard nothing but the snores from the dugout.

On a hand signal from Harry, Sheppard pushed silently past the sacking, his revolver in one hand and a torch in the other. Gale slid into place and edged along the wall away from the officer with the Lewis gun pointed in the direction of the snoring. Trudel slipped in and held his bloody bayonet in one hand and a Mills grenade with the pin still in place in the other. The other two members of the party stood guard outside.

Harry ducked under the sack. In the total darkness behind the curtain Harry couldn't count the number of Germans in the dugout. He crouched, held his Webley revolver in front of him, blocked the doorway and nodded to Sheppard. Sheppard switched the torch on and pointed the beam at the roof of the concrete bunker. Gale held up four fingers. Harry nodded. Sheppard aimed the beam into the eyes of the nearest German. The man gave a loud grunt and sat up in his cot, blinked several times and rubbed his eyes. "Jesus," the padre whispered. "They've even got beds. It's cozier than bachelor officer's quarters at Horsefield for Christ's sake." Sheppard pointed to the German and held a finger to his lips.

Trudel tapped the three sleeping Germans with his bayonet until all four were awake and staring uncomprehendingly at the raiding party.

"*Gutten Abend, meine Herren,*" Trudel said quietly and like Sheppard, held a finger to his lips. "*Stehen Sie auf! Hände hoch! Schnell!*" The four Germans stood, mouths open and raised their hands above their heads. "*Sie kommen mit uns. Sie fahren nach England. Für Ihnen, ist der Krieg vorbei.*" With the bloody tip of his bayonet Trudel pointed in the direction they wanted the German soldiers to go.

The Germans filed out of their dugout in their stockinged feet, hands clasped behind their necks. Gale with his Lewis gun, and Sheppard with his Webley, covered the Germans as they left. Outside in the trench, one of the men propped a wooden scaling ladder up against the front wall. Trudel climbed the ladder first and searched around through the rain and darkness for any sign of their discovery. When Trudel signaled the All Clear, Sheppard pointed to the top of the ladder with his Webley. Like sheep the Germans followed Trudel and another trooper over the lip. Harry, Sheppard and the last two raiders clambered up the ladder after the Germans and slid over the parapet. They crawled on their bellies through the gap in the wire as far as their rendezvous point, a large shell hole a hundred yards beyond the German wire.

A star shell burst overhead, eerily diffusing the low clouds with the light of the flare. Harry's men flattened themselves against the sides of the crater and pushed their prisoners to their stomachs. "Do you think they've spotted us?" Sheppard whispered.

"Probably routine, Padre," Harry whispered, "but it's too close for comfort and I'm no believer in coincidences." A recollection of Clap saying something similar flashed through his mind before the flare drifted to earth and faded without machine gun fire breaking the stillness of the night. Behind them Harry heard a distant gramophone scratch out, *Stille Nacht* while several voices softly accompanied the carol. A lump formed in Harry's throat. What in hell's name was he doing at two o'clock on Christmas Morning in no man's land with a bunch of frightened German soldiers in tow? For a moment he was tempted to hack off their regimental identity flashes and send the men back to their trench. He suppressed the urge to be humane. Four Germans out of the war meant four fewer Germans still alive to kill his men. He shook his head and took a deep breath. The stench of cold, foul water in the bottom of the shell hole returned him fully to his senses.

A minute passed, then two. Darkness returned, and with it their night vision. *Stille Nacht* ended. A moment later he heard another familiar carol but could not put a name to it. German voices sung, more loudly this time, oblivious to the war going on around them. Three or four miles away another star shell lit up no man's land, followed by red and green flares from Very pistols and a brief exchange of small arms fire.

"I'll have a quick shufti, Sir," Trudel told Sheppard when the gunfire ceased and no man's land once more fell quiet. He eased his body up the shallow slope of the side of the shell hole.

"All clear, Sir," Trudel whispered. "Not a Hun in sight, except for this miserable lot."

"Right, let's go," Sheppard said. "After you, Sir." He indicated to Harry.

"It's all right, Padre. You lead. I'll bring up the rear. It's your show. Well done."

They crawled out of the crater and slithered on their bellies across no man's land. The Germans proved co-operative prisoners, taking hand directions from whichever of Harry's raiding party each was assigned. They had nearly reached their own wire when another star shell burst high above them. Before they could stop him, one of the Germans, braver or more stupid than his comrades, leaped to his feet, waved his arms and yelled. The blinding magnesium glare from the flare seemed to hang forever below the cloud layer, outlining the German's silhouette as plain as day before the flare drifted down through the rain. Before anyone could tackle the man and pull him to the ground, machine guns from both trenches opened fire. Without another sound the bloodied German fell in a crumpled heap and lay still. Harry looked up from the small shell hole in which he crouched and, in the glare cast by the dying star shell saw Gale in open ground a few feet away. Blood oozed through the Lewis gunner's battledress blouse and pooled in the mud. Gale moved and groaned, made it to his knees then collapsed onto his chest.

As soon as the light from the star shell died and some semblance of his night vision returned, Harry motioned to Trudel and pointed at Gale. Trudel slid across the short distance, grabbed the Lewis gun in one hand, hooked his arm under Gale's and around his webbing belt, and dragged the unresponsive man towards their front line trench

Harry instinctively looked up as a trench mortar bomb whined and whistled its way towards them. He saw Trudel dive into the nearest shell hole and lose his grip on Gale. Harry flattened himself against the side of the small shell hole. At the same moment the mortar round hit the waterlogged ground between them and exploded in a shower of mud and shrapnel. The explosion lifted Harry off his feet, held him aloft for a second then threw him back to earth on top of Trudel and Gale. The impact drove the air from his lungs and left his ears ringing.

The trio lay in a tangle of arms, legs, torsos and guns for several seconds, unable to breathe. Trudel was the first to stir. He reached out. "You seem to have something sticking out of the back of your shoulder, Sir," he said to Harry. "Looks like a piece of shrapnel." Harry struggled to his knees, then slumped back into the mud. He clamped his jaw shut to stifle the urge to scream.

"Hang on, Sir. I'll get you back." He grabbed Harry and slipped a hand around his waist, searching for the leather Sam Browne belt beneath the greatcoat. "Here goes, Sir. Might hurt a bit, but I'll do my best to see you come to no more harm."

"Thank you, Trudel," Harry gasped between clenched teeth. "I can manage from here." But when Harry tried to stand, his legs buckled and he all but slipped from Trudel's grasp. "You're a bit slippery with all this blood, Sir," Trudel said. "It'll have to be a fireman's lift. Not very elegant, Sir, but effective." He grunted as he bent and levered Harry over his shoulder.

"Shit," Trudel muttered.

"What now?" Harry gasped through clenched teeth.

"The Lewis gun, Sir. It's at my feet. I can't leave it here."

"We can replace a Lewis gun, Trudel."

"More easily and cheaper than a colonel is what I'm guessing you're suggesting, Sir. I'll come back for it later. We're only fifty yards from our wire. No sweat." With another heave, Trudel adjusted Harry's body over his shoulder and staggered with his burden through the mud to the wire. He eased himself through the narrow gap, gasping and heaving with the exertion and sucking in lungsful of frigid Flanders air. "Shoulder wound," he gasped. "Easy does it." He slipped Harry off his shoulder into waiting hands and without looking back, turned and headed towards the gap in the wire.

Encouraged by the bayonet points of the remaining troopers, the three surviving Germans crawled to the frontline parapet and disappeared over the lip into the waiting arms of the Middlesex Regiment soldiers.

Harry's head swam and spun with stars and planets swirling. He grabbed the nearest sandbag of the parapet to steady himself.

"Where the bloody hell do you think you're going?" Harry heard an NCO shout, and Trudel's voice, "Our Lewis gunner's wounded. I'm going to get him."

"You do and you'll be on a charge," he heard the NCO snarl. "You hasn't got the friggin' brains your mother born you with."

Harry tried to say something, but his tongue stuck to the roof of his mouth. He heard Trudel call out, "Back in half a jiff, Sir. And I'll fetch your hat an' all." Then the world turned black.

*

Lieutenant Sheppard stood on one leg doing an impression of a flamingo. Trudel stood on both legs at Sheppard's side, looking as if he would rather be charging the German front line alone than anywhere near his commanding officer, even one dressed in hospital pyjamas. Harry was propped up in a cot. He turned his head stiffly towards the pair blocking the entrance of the big Red Cross tent. "No one told me we had a German speaker among us, Padre."

"I didn't know either, Sir."

"That man there," Harry called out, and beckoned to Trudel to come over.

"You wanted to see me, Sir?"

"I didn't know you spoke German."

Trudel twisted his fingers in front of him and eased his weight from one foot to the other and back again in a slow dance. "I don't really, Sir. My grandfather was Austrian and my father grew up speaking German at home, but me mum, she never took to it. I picked up bits and pieces from listening to me dad and grandad."

"It was a pretty damn good imitation of German if it wasn't the real thing. What did you say to them?"

"They seemed to understand the *Hands up* bit easily enough. I don't know about the rest. I made it up as I went along. It might have been Mr. Sheppard's Webley and the bloody steel pointing at them what convinced them. Or the Mills grenade, or the promise of a free trip to England."

Harry uttered a brittle laugh, high pitched and feverish, and slumped back against his pillow. With an effort he slowed his rapid breathing. He gathered his strength and returned his attention to Trudel who stood mute, shuffled his feet and examined his toecaps. "You went back to fetch the Lewis gunner."

"Yes, Sir. He was a gonner, Sir. But I brought his gun back."

"Trudel, isn't it?"

"Yes, Sir."

"What you did was stupid and courageous. And against standing orders.

We don't stop for the wounded, ever." Harry took a breath and winced. "Some days you're the pigeon, Trudel, and some days you're the statue. I'm not sure which you are today, but I'll see your prompt actions in saving your CO's skin at the risk of your own are duly noted. And given your fondness for the Lewis gun, you are hereby promoted to lance corporal and in charge of the Lewis gun." He turned to Sheppard.

"Extra ration of rum for that man, Mr. Sheppard. Take his name and number and put it in your journal. And see he gets the stripe sewn on. Carry on."

Once Sheppard and Trudel left, a nurse filled Harry's arm with morphine and he passed out. When he regained semi-consciousness a day later he discovered his shoulder tightly bandaged. He tried to move only to find his arm tethered by a thin rubber tube to a metal post while a blacksmith took a hammer to his skull. He put his hand instinctively to his head and touched the bandage wrapped around it. He inspected his red-smeared fingers in dull incomprehension. A wave of nausea overwhelmed him. He closed his eyes and buried the back of his head in his damp pillow. Sweat soaked his body and a rivulet ran from his forehead onto the pillow. "I don't have a pillow," he mumbled. His hands touched cotton. "Or sheets." A great pain he could not explain lanced through his shoulder. He passed out again.

Seconds, minutes, hours later, he could not be certain, he heard a nurse say to him, "You've got an intravenous saline drip in your arm and a catheter into your bladder. Move too much and you'll pull out the drip and wet the bed. We don't want either to happen, do we, Sir?"

Harry opened his eyes to see a major in the Royal Army Medical Corps with a nurse at his side observing him as if he were a laboratory specimen.

"It's what you get for disobeying standing orders, Colonel, if I might be bold enough to venture." The man sounded foreign to Harry. German? No, not in an RAMC uniform. Australian, or South African perhaps given the distinct nasal accent.

"You may not, Major." Harry tried to raise his head but the blacksmith returned to use the anvil inside his skull as kettle drums.

"You're pumped full of morphine, in case you want to know, and you're not going anywhere without the brigadier's say so. Those are my orders."

"Where am I, and who are you, you insubordinate Colonial?" Harry managed half a laugh and winced with the pain shooting through his shoulder.

"Field hospital, about ten miles from the front, in the grounds of the Château Gran'ville. Nice, quiet spot, Colonel. A good place to recuperate. They brought you here from the regimental first aid post. I'll tell Brigade you've regained consciousness even though you're not quite compos mentis yet. That should get the ball moving. If you need anything, call for Sister McLeod."

When the RAMC major left, the nurse bent over and whispered in Harry's ear, "As soon as you can manage a few steps, Colonel, I'll take you to the commode. You'll find it more comfortable than a bedpan."

It was not what Harry wanted to hear.

# 18. A TELEGRAM

Brigadier Shackleton stood at the foot of Harry's cot the next day. "Good job you missed the Somme, Haig-Mallory," he said. "But there was no need to make up for it like this." He ruminated for a moment. "Bit of a bind. Damn good raid, and all that. Lots of good gen from the prisoners, so they tell me. But I doubt if we can get you anything for this little escapade. It would only encourage others to disobey standing orders."

The morphine cleared sufficiently for Harry to grasp Shackleton's meaning. "A trench mortar, so they tell me. Never heard it coming. I should pay more attention if I'm going to stray outside the wire to welcome the men back".

Shackleton tapped his chin with a finger. "Good thinking. As you were never officially on the raid," he said slowly, "I'll see Mr. Sheppard gets something for his leadership. A Mentioned in Dispatches, perhaps. I doubt if I can get much more. I gather he's your machine gun officer. A good man? Lots of initiative?"

"Yes, Sir. But by his own admission a terrible horseman. Good show for the Padre and Trooper Trudel."

Shackleton looked Harry squarely in the eye. "The Padre?"

"It's unofficial. Sheppard was snatched from Oxford in time to join the fray before he could begin a career as a curate or bishop or something. But the men seem to think he brings them luck. Clear line upstairs when they find themselves in a bit of a jam, I expect. It can't do any harm, and it's good for morale."

Shackleton cleared his throat. "Yes, well, next time, Haig-Mallory, and there won't be a next time, you hear, stay at home where we need you. Good officers are bloody hard to replace. By the way, I have something for you to take home. A couple of gongs. The Frogs awarded you the Chevalier of the Légion d'honneur medal. I can't read the citation. It's all Greek to me. Hope you can make head or tail of it. The other one's from our side. Distinguished Service Order. Well, you can read the citation for yourself. You must have really done a good job for Clap to have recommended it."

"Protocol, Sir. Clap wouldn't have done it if the French hadn't forced his hand."

"I doubt that. Well done, Harry." He reached into his leather dispatch case and handed Harry two small boxes containing the medals and the matching ribbons. He gave Harry a firm handshake. "I'll have your batman sew the ribbons on for you before you leave. You're going home for a month, medical leave, no argument. I'll see you when you get back."

He turned away. "Major Barrington?" he called out to the RAMC officer hovering nearby.

"Sir?"

"Can this man stand up by himself?" He spoke loud enough to be heard half-way across the tent.

"Yes, Sir, just about."

"Good. Then kick him out of here. No good having a perfectly good cot go to waste when some other poor blighter could use it. We'll not have any malingerers here, privates or field marshals. The sooner we get Colonel Haig-Mallory patched up and out of here the sooner we get him back on the job." He winked at Harry.

"Report to Brigade HQ as soon as the medical bods consider you fit enough to travel. Your travel warrant will ready for you by then."

"A moment before you leave, Sir, if you would," Harry said.

Shackleton regarded him with a puzzled expression.

"The trooper who pulled me to safety, Sir. Trudel. He deserves more than *Good Show* and an extra rum tot. I'll write up my recommendation before I leave. A Good Conduct Medal at least. Perhaps a Military Medal. He's a good man, Sir. Very dependable. Shows lots of initiative and promise. He's one of us, part of the Hussars family, even if he is part Austrian."

"I'll see what I can do. Pass it on to me, for my attention."

Shackleton turned and marched across the duckboards with the RAMC major in tow, skirting medical equipment and ducking under lanterns strung from the ridgepole. Harry watched him stop at several cots and speak briefly to the occupants. He knew there was nothing like a visit from the Brass to boost morale, particularly at Christmas. Harry closed his eyes and surrendered to the effects of the morphine.

*

Two days later a note in pencil reached Harry in the field hospital.

*Dear Sir. I am glad to hear you are better now. I promise not to do it again. And thank you for recomemding me for a medal. Yours faithfully Number 1698903 L/Cpl. Albert Trudel.*

Harry took the note and folded it into the breast pocket of his battledress blouse, the first note he had ever received from an anything-but-ordinary soldier.

"I'm glad you're on my side, Corporal Trudel," he whispered. The nurse gave him an enquiring look. "It's from one of my men," Harry said. "I'd hate to be a Hun."

He scowled at the syringe in her hand. "You can put that down, nurse. I don't need any morphine."

The nurse ignored him.

*

The RAMC major with the antipodean accent did not deem Harry fit to travel for another ten days, so he was stuck where he was, getting underfoot and growing testier by the minute.

Eventually, having demanded his release, travel warrant in hand and barely able to walk without the help of a cane, Harry caught his train. As he planted himself in a seat in the compartment, light-headed and breathing hard, he wondered if the doctor may have been right when he said that discharging a patient, even a wooden-headed colonel, before he was ready, was medically unsound. "You're the worst patient I've ever had the misfortune to treat, Colonel," he'd said. "Believe me, I never want to see you in my hospital again."

"And believe me, Major," Harry had said. "You won't."

Major Barrington turned away without saluting. "Famous last bloody words," he muttered, just loud enough for Harry to hear.

*

The telegram carrier leaned his bicycle against the wall at the servants' entrance to *Roseland* and rang the bell. A woman's voice from inside yelled, "See who it is, Elsie. We're not expecting any more deliveries today."

Footsteps clacked on the stone floor as Elsie scampered down the corridor and opened the door. She took one look at the man in front of her in his wet raincoat and hat and knew who it was, if not by name, or even by sight, but by occupation. Her hand flew to her mouth and her face blanched. She turned her back on the man and yelled down the corridor, "Mrs. Aitchison. Mrs. Aitchison. It's the telegram man."

As fast as dignity allowed, the housekeeper bustled down the corridor from the kitchen where she had been enjoying her elevensies; a mid-morning cup of tea and a slice of Mrs. Tregarrick's Madeira cake. "Thank you, Elsie. You may go." She turned to the telegram man. His face was sombre. He held out the telegram. "It's for a Mrs. A. Haig-Mallory, mom," he said. His hand trembled.

Mrs. Aitchison extended her hand slowly, knowing without a shadow of doubt what the telegram contained. "I'll sign for it, Bryce. And I'll see Mrs. Haig-Mallory gets it immediately."

"I'm sorry, Mrs. Aitchison. I always seem to be the bearer of bad news. Please convey my condolences to Mrs. Haig-Mallory. The colonel was always a gentleman, much liked in the village. He will be sorely missed."

"Perhaps we really should shoot the messenger, Bryce. That way there would be no more bad news."

The telegram man's face reddened. Mrs. Aitchison shook her head. "All excepting you, Bryce. You're a good man in an unfortunate position. When the war's over, the way it's going it may be possible we'll need more staff. Something to consider. Keep it under your hat."

She closed the door and retreated along the corridor to the kitchen, holding the envelope by one corner as if it were red hot. Four grim faces greeted her as she came through the door. All knew what she carried. None but she knew who was named in the telegram. She turned to the cook. "I need Mr. Tregarrick. As soon as he can be found." She clasped the envelope to her chest. Tears filled her eyes. She grabbed the back of a chair and held on tight.

"Sit down, Mrs. Aitchison," Mrs. Tregarrick said, "before you fall down. It may not be as bad as all that. Who is it for?"

"I shouldn't say, Mrs. Tregarrick. I'm sure it's private and personal. There'll be a formal announcement shortly, I've no doubt." She burst into tears. The envelope fell to the table when she reached for a handkerchief tucked under her sleeve. Mrs. Tregarrick saw the name and quickly turned the envelope over, face down on the table. Tregarrick entered the kitchen and raised his eyebrows.

"A telegram," his wife said.

Tregarrick stopped in mid-stride. "For whom?" he said.

The housekeeper dabbed her eyes and handed the envelope to the butler. He took a quick glance at the name and reached for a silver tray. "If there is an announcement to be made," he said. "I shall make it when all the staff are gathered. Meanwhile, as we do not know the contents of this telegram, and as it does not concern any one of us directly, I suggest you all return to your duties immediately and without gossip or speculation. Idling and gossiping was a flogging offence when I was in the Royal Navy, may I remind you. And fortunately for you, none of you would come close to being a sailor if you spent your lives trying."

The grim faced but implacable butler paused for a moment then turned on his heel and, reorganizing his features as he went, headed for the stairs to the main floor where he had last seen Athena in the morning room.

Athena put down her coffee cup and saucer on the occasional table beside her as soon as Tregarrick entered the room. She saw the look of gloom on the butler's face, a look he had failed to hide completely behind the mask required of his position in the household.

"Yes, Tregarrick?" She knew instinctively what lay on the silver salver. The morning post had already been delivered. There had not been a letter for her. There hadn't been one from Harry in nearly a month. Not since before Christmas. She was fully determined not to betray any emotion at what she knew could only be bad news — the very worst news possible. She would honour Harry, and the news, with a stiff upper lip, as she knew he would if their roles were reversed. He would be proud of her. She would grieve, mourn and pretend she was managing. Then, as the widow of an Englishman without title or fortune, and no longer a member of his family, she would return to Cleveland to lead a normal, American life. And life at *Roseland* would return to the new normal, without them.

Tregarrick approached and bowed with all the dignity and solemnity he possessed. "A telegram for you, My Lady," he said quietly, and offered her the tray with the envelope and letter opener. Athena knew she was only entitled to be addressed as Mrs. Haig-Mallory. Or Madam. That Tregarrick had called her *My Lady* seemed most unusual. Then again, she had always treated the servants with respect and with thanks for the service they provided. Maybe, she thought, this was his way of showing additional respect in return.

Athena reached for the buff envelope, silently cursing the slight tremble in her hand. She took the letter opener that lay beside the envelope. "Thank you, Tregarrick," she said as calmly as she could.

Tregarrick took a step back, head up, eyes fixed straight ahead. Athena slit open the envelope and drew out the telegram. She read it once, carefully. Then read it again. Tears reached her eyes. Her upper lip trembled. Her resolve to be thoroughly English in the face of disaster evaporated. She pulled a lace handkerchief from beneath the sleeve of her day dress and dabbed her eyes.

She took a deep breath and steadied herself. To her surprise, her hand no longer shook. "Colonel Haig-Mallory will return home shortly on leave, Tregarrick. It doesn't say when he will be here, or for how long. He has been wounded but is expected to make a complete recovery. He will convalesce at *Roseland* until he is fit enough to return to duty." She let out her breath.

"That is indeed better news than we could have expected, My Lady." He bowed.

"Perhaps you would be so kind as to inform the staff. I will give the news to the countess personally."

"I believe she is in the drawing room, My Lady."

"Then I shall go there directly. And perhaps you could bring us a couple of brandies on your way to inform the staff. I need one, and I suspect the countess will need one, too. If not, I'll have them both." She laughed as the tension ebbed. "I'm sorry, Tregarrick. Not very ladylike of me. I must practice my stiff upper lip routine." She stood. "Oh, and Tregarrick."

"Yes, My Lady?"

"Make mine a generous, free pour double."

"Yes, My Lady."

Demelza followed Athena from the morning room to the drawing room. It was as if the old dog knew instinctively that something was not right and that Athena needed comfort and her unquestioned support. In Harry's absence, the clumber spaniel had taken upon herself the role of Athena's constant companion, at heel when Athena walked, sitting when Athena stood or sat. She now spent the nights in Athena's bedroom, curled up on a rug on the floor beside her bed. Her short legs and sturdy body did not favour the high jump onto the top of the bed and Athena did not insist. Demelza, she decided, deserved her dignity and had earned it over her long life. To jump up on beds was definitely not ladylike, especially for an elderly dog.

Athena spent the next three days in a desperate search for Harry's whereabouts. She knew no one in London who could help. She tried the Hussars' Barracks in Bristol. The man on the other end of the phone was able to confirm that Harry had been posted as wounded in action, but there was no word of his current status. Or where he was. Or how severe the wounds were. Or when he would be home. She thanked him and hung up. She knew more than the army did. Which, she thought, was not all that difficult in the chaos of wartime. She left messages for Cecilia, her father-in-law and Ernest, all in London. Only Cecilia returned her call late in the afternoon.

Three days of frantic telephone calls produced not a scrap of further information. It was as if Harry had vanished down a hole, *Somewhere in France*, like Alice, and failed to re-emerge.

*

While Athena ran around in circles, getting nowhere with the military establishment, Harry endured a snail-like train journey to the transit camp. There he waited three days until he could find transport to Calais, and two more days in a converted dockside warehouse waiting for a hospital troop ship. When he reached the quay at Dover, he cadged a ride in the front seat of an ambulance to the military hospital where he cajoled the matron into letting him telephone Athena.

"All I knew was you were wounded," Athena wailed, in a voice that bordered on hysterical. "I didn't know if it was a scratch, or if you lost an arm or a leg, or were going to die."

"I'm sorry. They sent the telegram from the hospital before they discharged me. I should have sent a telegram as soon as I left the field hospital. In my rush to get home to see you I didn't think of it. I won't do it again."

"I should hope not. I don't want you getting wounded as soon as I let you out of my sight."

"It was nothing, really," he insisted to a still weepy Athena. "Only a few scratches and a dent or two. I don't know what all the fuss is about."

"The fuss is because it's you," she snapped. "I love you, in case you forgot. I don't want to lose you."

"The other ranks get a week's leave a few miles from the lines, Paris if they're really lucky, then back to mud and bullets. I get a month's home leave. It doesn't make any sense."

There was so much he wanted and needed to say, but the stern face of Matron prompted him to interrupt Athena's tearful pleadings on the other end of the line. With a sag of his shoulders and a promise he would see her within a day, two at the most, he hung up. He grimaced as he handed the phone back to Matron.

"Thank you, Colonel," she said. "As you see, there are others waiting and I'm grateful to you for not taking up their time." A nurse guided the next in line, a captain in the Buffs, his head and eyes swathed in bandages, to the phone.

"Look, Matron," Harry said while the captain spoke quietly on the phone. "There are others who have a higher claim on my space here. Please inform the commanding officer I'm discharging myself forthwith. Thank you for your kindness, consideration and patience. I could never do your job. You deserve a bloody medal."

"You've not done so badly yourself, Colonel." She briefly touched the ribbons of the DSO, the MC and the Légion d'honeur heading the two rows of medal ribbons.

Harry gave her a rueful smile. "I can see myself out, Matron. Thank you again."

*

Harry arrived late at the Marlborough Club in Pall Mall and slept in, exhausted, in the most comfortable bed he could remember. He washed, shaved and dressed himself the next morning for the first time with an arm in a sling and without outside help. Each movement provided its unique challenge, but he managed, slowly and not without considerable discomfort. He followed his nose and the smell of bacon to the club dining room. He glanced quickly around the familiar room, a carbon copy of dining rooms in officers' messes from London to Calcutta. It seemed like a home away from home, with standard issue dark wood furniture and wainscoting, the obligatory hunting prints on the walls — for all he knew they could be the same as those in Shackleton's office at Horsefield Barracks — photographs and oil paintings of military scenes and battlefields. The dining room was nearly full of men in khaki; small groups conversing in hushed tones or buried singly behind a newspaper. He sidled up to the long sideboard to discover he was not alone with his arm in a sling. "I'll hold, you shovel," he said to a captain with the end of one sleeve pinned to his tunic. He seemed little more than a boy, barely old enough to grow a moustache. He took the young officer's plate and waited while the captain helped himself to bacon and eggs.

"Thank you, Colonel," the captain said, sounding embarrassed. "I'll get used to it eventually, I expect, but it's a bloody inconvenience at the moment. I still think it's there, until I realize it's not."

Harry noticed the young man's eyes burned bright in dark sockets and saw the pain etched deep within them. The captain smiled weakly. Harry watched him limp away with an awkward, lopsided shuffle to an empty table. Harry knew he was lucky. Lucky his wounds were only relatively light, lucky he possessed all the limbs present at his birth. Lucky to be returning to his wife, and lucky to be able to return to the front, to the war, where and when he might not be so lucky next time.

"I'll hold. You shovel, Colonel." A one-armed major standing in line behind Harry smiled and took a plate from the pile with his remaining hand. Harry helped himself to kedgeree. When he finished, he placed his plate on the buffet top.

"And allow me to return the favour," Harry said.

"Bowen-Jones," the major said. "Welsh Guards." He stopped and looked at his empty sleeve. "Career Guardsman. Was, most likely, I don't think they'll have much use for me like this. At least my wife will be happy I'm out of it. And you?"

"Haig-Mallory.  King's Imperial Hussars. Trench mortar in the early hours of Christmas Morning. That's the official version. There's no unofficial version." Harry grinned. "Officially."

"Not very sporting of the Hun on Christmas Day."

"A small return for what we did to them half an hour earlier. Not very sporting of us either."

"Life's like that at times," the Welsh major said. "Good luck."

# 19. TREVELYAN

While the silver-haired, uniformed Rhodes stood by the Daimler in the cobbled forecourt of Truro station, Athena waited impatiently at the ticket barrier. Harry dropped his suitcases on the station platform as soon as he saw her. She cast aside her inhibitions and ran to meet him.

"Only an American would throw decorum to the wind in such a manner." Harry buried his face in the crook of her neck. Athena's perfume drifted through her silk scarf and fox stole and up into his nose. It reminded him as it always did of their first encounter more than two years ago. Through the heady perfume he detected the first faint stirrings of the same love he held for her back in Washington. He held her closer, this time because he wanted to.

Athena grabbed him around his waist and held on to him so tightly he could scarcely breathe. He held his bad arm and shoulder out of the way when Athena reached up and kissed him.

"I'd almost forgotten what it's like to be this close to you," he said when Athena finally released him. "To feel the warmth of your breath on my face, to smell your perfume, to touch your hair, your skin, your body."

"And I'd quite forgotten how a soldier smelled in slightly damp khaki."

"Rugged and masculine still don't come to mind?" He raised his eyebrows. She shook her head. "It's chilly standing here, even with you draped over me like an overcoat," he said. "Let's go home."

Rhodes drove them home to *Roseland*, never taking his eyes off the road ahead even to glance at the rear-view mirror. Athena seemed content only to snuggle up to Harry and rest her head on his good shoulder. The bandage was off his head. The neat stitching of the nasty gash on his scalp left Harry not looking as gruesome as he had feared. Not that he cared particularly for his sake, but for Athena's — what was the word? — Sensibility.

He dozed off, waking only when Rhodes pulled up in front of the main entrance to the rambling, Elizabethan manor house. The household staff turned out to greet him, and their genuine warmth and affection left him touched. His stepmother gushed. Ernest managed a smile.

"Cecilia not here?" he said to Ernest.

"In London. Studying." Ernest pronounced the word as if it were a concept totally alien. "Nursing." He seemed unsteady on his feet. His eyes were watery and bloodshot. His breath smelled of whisky. It was still two hours to the dinner gong.

"Of course," Harry said. "I remember."

It promised to be a good leave even though the weather turned as sour and miserable as only Cornwall in winter can be. It was the 11th of January, 1917. The war seemed so distant, a page in an unfinished book set aside for the moment. Only a bookmark remained to remind him of where he'd left off. He was home, not in a manner of his choosing, but he was home. He was with Athena, with a chance to build on their relationship, once so hot and now only tepid, at least on his part. But if his reaction to Athena at the station were anything to go by, that would change for the better. He would let nothing come between them again. Athena deserved that. More than that. He looked around the familiar hallway and noted his bags had already been taken upstairs. Demelza sidled up to his side to greet him with frenzied wags of her stumpy tail. Then she went over to Athena and sat at her side. "She's yours when you're home, Harry," she said. "And mine, it seems, when you're away. I don't think she was expecting you back so soon."

He was at *Roseland*, with his family, and he counted himself lucky to be alive, even with the pain in his shoulder. And, he told himself, that would go away eventually.

*

That evening Harry passed out at the dinner table. "Tired," he said once he regained consciousness. "I apologize for disrupting dinner."

"Nonsense," Athena said. "You should probably still be in hospital. Did they give you anything for the pain?"

Harry shook his head. "I have to set an example. No shirking behind a fog of morphine. It's scarce, and there are many who need it more than I do."

Two elderly footmen, supervised by Tregarrick and accompanied by a worried Athena, helped the barely conscious Harry up the stairs and into their bedroom. The shoulder wound had reopened and bled into his wool undershirt. Athena removed his mess jacket and gasped when she saw the dark crimson patch on the back of his starched white shirt. She dismissed the footmen. With tears in her eyes she undressed him, careful not to jolt him as she removed each bloody garment. When she came to remove the blood-soaked dressing, she hesitated. "One rip, or a tiny bit at a time?"

"One rip. I don't feel up to death by a thousand tugs."

"The blood's still oozing. At least I won't be pulling the scab off. Ready? Here goes."

She teased a corner of the adhesive dressing from Harry's back.

"Ouch."

"Sorry. Are you sure you want me to grip it and rip it?"

"A hair came away when you lifted the corner. I wasn't expecting that. Go ahead. Do your worst, Doctor Haig-Mallory."

Athena took the corner and, in one motion, ripped the dressing from Harry's skin. Harry slumped forward without a sound and passed out on the bed covers. Several seconds later he groaned. Athena grabbed him by the shoulders and buried her face in his hair. "I thought I'd killed you," she wept. "I'm so sorry."

"I don't know what came over me," he gasped. "It was nothing like that when it happened. I'm all right now."

"No, you're not. Lie still while I sponge the blood from your back and apply a new dressing."

When she finished cleaning the wound, she said, "I'll send for Dr. Wetherall. The bleeding's stopped but there's an ugly gash. He may need to stitch you up again."

"No need," Harry grunted. "It'll heal itself in time."

"I'm calling for him anyway in the morning. No argument." She shook her head. "A scratch and a dent, I think you said."

"A scratch on the head and a dent in the shoulder. I didn't want to alarm you. A good night's sleep is what I need. I'm sorry. I won't be of much use to you as a husband tonight."

"I can wait as long as you can. I'll dress the wound for now and I insist we call the doctor in the morning." She rang for her maid and before long she had Harry's wound hidden beneath a compress and bound to his shoulder.

*

The pain diminished with each passing day. In time Harry stopped snapping at everyone. His facial muscles no longer twitched. He treated the staff with his customary courtesy. By the end of three weeks Harry was as cheerful as ever as he walked Demelza around the grounds and into the village with Athena on his arm.

A few days before Harry was due to return to the front, Tom Trevelyan, the first footman, asked to see him. "Have him see me in the estate manager's office," he said to the butler. "Any idea what it's about?"

"None, Sir."

"*The mystery thickens*, as they say in the Sherlock Holmes novels."

"I believe it is, *The plot thickens*, Sir."

"I believe you're right. Either way, we shall find out what's on his mind shortly, and probably without the help of Dr. Watson." Harry pulled out his pocket watch. "Ten minutes, Tregarrick? That should give Trevelyan time to flick an imaginary speck of dust from his livery, don't you think?"

"Always immaculate is Trevelyan, Sir. I shall see that he is there promptly."

Ten minutes later Trevelyan knocked on the door of the estate manager's office. "Come," Harry called. Trevelyan stepped through the doorway and looked around the office before he settled his sight on Harry.

"What's this about, Trevelyan?"

"I want to join up, Sir."

"Why in God's name would you want to do such a thing?"

"I'm forty-seven, and I know I don't have to join up if I don't want to, Sir, but I want to do my bit. What I mean is, Sir, if I volunteered for your regiment, would you take me on as your servant? I'd be proud to serve under you if I could, Sir."

"Well, Trevelyan, you have caught me by surprise." Harry leaned back and lit a cigarette. "Are you sure you want to do this? It's not a picnic over there for men half your age." He blew the lungful of smoke to the ceiling.

Trevelyan watched the smoke spiral from the ashtray for several seconds before he spoke again. "I've made up my mind, Sir, if you'll have me. Otherwise I'll stay here and look after the youngsters until they go, and anything else required of me in His Lordship's absence. But they don't need a full staff at *Roseland* under the circumstances. And I was a good shot in my day. I spent ten years in the Infantry before I came into service. I ended up as mess corporal." He drew himself up to his full, if unspectacular height. "I served in South Africa against the Boer. Perhaps you didn't know, Sir."

"I had no idea. Well, if you really have made up your mind, we'll go up to the Hussars Depot in Bristol tomorrow and you can sign on the dotted line. I'll square it with the CO. Once you've completed the thirteen weeks of hell known as basic training you will join me as my soldier-servant. You're a bit under regulation height for the Hussars, but I doubt they'll be fussy given the circumstances. One advantage of being shorter is you present less of a target to the enemy."

"Thank you, Colonel," Trevelyan stammered. "I didn't know how you would take it, my joining up, I mean. I won't let you down, Sir. I'll be proud to serve you, and the regiment."

"You've got until seven tomorrow morning to change your mind. In the meantime, think about it very hard. And if you do decide to go through with it, you may live to regret it."

"I won't change my mind, Sir. But I'd be grateful if you didn't mention this to anyone, not even to the countess or to Mr. Tregarrick until after I've signed up. If you don't mind, Sir."

Harry nodded. "No doubt you have your own reasons for not telling anyone. Take the rest of the day off, Trevelyan. Perhaps you'd like to head into St. Just to say your goodbyes personally if there's anyone there who might miss you."

"That's all right, Sir. There's nobody there for me."

"See you at seven tomorrow, then. Make sure you've eaten a good breakfast. Mum's the word. And I'm glad to have you aboard at my side. I couldn't wish for better. Thank you for the compliment and your trust, Trooper Trevelyan." Harry rose and extended his hand. The footman grasped it and shook it, then took a step back and snapped up a quivering salute.

"Carry on."

*

Harry rose early without waking Athena and took breakfast alone in the dining room. Shortly before seven Trevelyan showed up at the open door of the estate manager's office. He knocked and stood back, waiting to be admitted.

"Come," Harry called.

Trevelyan stood framed in the doorway, a brown paper parcel tied with string tucked under an arm. Harry squinted hard at the man then recognized him.

"Ah. Fooled me for a moment. I see you've had the local barber butcher your hair, but don't worry. The army will take off most of what's left anyway. It's easier to find the lice in short hair and believe me, you'll find plenty of lice."

"I hadn't forgotten about the lice, Sir." He grimaced. "I'm ready when you are. Perhaps we can simply leave quietly. I don't want any fuss or bother with the staff. You can tell anyone who asks when you get back, if you don't mind, Sir. And I'll sit up front with Mr. Rhodes on the ride to Bristol."

"I won't hear of it, Trevelyan. I'd be honoured if you would sit in the back with me."

Several hours later, Rhodes dropped Harry and Trevelyan off at the guardhouse at Horsefield Barracks. Harry made his way over to the commandant's office in the main officer's mess building. He handed the CO a letter of introduction and waited in silence while the colonel read it.

"Not an unusual request, Haig-Mallory. Every officer of a certain rank should have a personal servant from within his own household. Stands to reason when things get a bit sticky one can rely on a family retainer to stand firm, eh? Not cut and run like a man may be tempted to do in an ordinary regiment. I take it your servant is one of us. Family?"

Harry nodded. "He's been in our employ for fifteen years, Sir. He's our first footman. He's wiry but tough, and he's a hardy Cornishman by birth. And I think you'll be well pleased with his marksmanship."

"Leave it with me, Haig-Mallory. I'll personally see to it he's posted to your regiment as soon as he's finished basic training."

Sitting in the back of the Daimler on his way home to *Roseland*, Harry relaxed. The shrapnel wound that had left such an ugly scar on his arm and shoulder had closed up and healed and gave him little more than background pain. It would take a while, he knew, before new bone grew over the hole left in the scapula by the shrapnel, but he wouldn't milk it and shirk his responsibility as a soldier. Apart from the wrench of leaving Athena and the family he relished the chance to get back to his men, to what he knew deep down he did best — soldiering.

He arrived home late to find Athena and his mother in the drawing room about to get ready for bed.

"I apologize for not letting any of you know where I was today. I'm glad you're both still up so late so I could give you the news together. I went up to Bristol with Trevelyan. He's enlisted." He waited for the information to sink in.

"So that's why Tregarrick was in such a tizzy all day," Harry's mother said. "No one knew where Trevelyan was. He was nowhere to be found. Nor you, when we looked for you. Well, what a turn of events, I must say."

"He'll join me as my batman as soon as he's finished basic training. I have to admit it'll be good to have someone from the household I can rely on no matter what. It was his idea entirely, and it took me quite by surprise. Yes," he paused for a second, "With any luck I'm sure it will work out very well."

*

Harry and Athena spent the last night of his leave at The Dorchester hotel in London. After they made love they smoked in silence, propped against giant pillows. "I don't know why you choose to spend time at my father's house rather than return to Cornwall," Harry said. "I know Cornwall can be a bit dull at times, especially when the weather's not the best, but at least you won't have my father to contend with."

"I haven't finished shopping, yet," she said, and he heard the tease in her voice. "Besides, I don't expect to spend much time with him. He's always so busy at the Admiralty and I know he won't want to follow me around the shops. The time will fly by. By which time the weather will have improved, the flowers will be out and the birds a-wing."

"That does sound poetic."

"Something I remember from my days at Vassar, but I've no idea who wrote it."

"Then perhaps it's a Fenhagen original."

"I'm a Haig-Mallory, Colonel. And don't you forget it. No more Fenhagen. I've even got my signature down pat, though I've yet to sign a check. And I still spell it C-H-E-C-K. Not the weird way you do."

Harry laughed. "One day you'll change, once you discover the letter U in the alphabet." He regarded Athena in the darkened room. His eyes roamed all over her body until his gaze settled on one spot. Athena watched him. "This?" she said, touching a nipple.

"Mmm. Or the other one."

"They're twins. You're not allowed to have a favourite."

"I don't. They're equally enticing. I want them both."

"Then start with this one. It's nearer."

Harry bent his head closer and took the nipple in his mouth. Athena closed her eyes and let him explore her body for the second time that night. When she judged the time was right she rolled over and straddled him. "I know you like it like this," she whispered. "So do I."

Harry grunted his pleasure.

*

After she had seen Harry off on the train from Charing Cross to Dover and eventually back to war, Athena took a taxi the short distance to her father-in-law's house in Belgrave Square.

"I'm glad you could make it," the earl said to Athena on his return from the Admiralty building in Whitehall that evening. "I'm sorry I wasn't here to meet you, but it couldn't be helped."

His greeting was polite, if not heartfelt. To be expected of the admiral, Athena thought. At least he hadn't grumped and made her feel unwelcome in his house. "Cornwall in winter can be a bit dull and dreary, and not only the weather. A month or two in London, if you can stand me that long, is what the doctor ordered to chase away the blues of Harry being back in France." Athena glanced at the carriage clock on the mantel piece. "He should be there soon, and it'll be months before I see him again." Tears pricked the back of her eyelids and she fought them back. "At least as a colonel he won't be going over the top and leading the charge. That's what he assured me anyway. Unless he breaks the rules again."

"And he's perfectly correct, my dear. Unlike the navy, where if your ship is caught up in an action, every man jack is equally involved. This isn't Balaclava and, *Into the valley of death rode the six hundred.* Colonels are the last to leave the trench, usually when the objective is secured. Don't worry. He'll be perfectly safe, you'll see."

He patted her arm — patronizing, Athena thought, but didn't recoil at the touch — and turned to leave. Then he stopped. "I won't have time to spare to show you London. I work long hours. I'm often away at conferences for days at a time. Plymouth, Chatham, Portsmouth, dull places like that. I'm afraid you'll have to amuse yourself as best you can. The British Museum, the National Gallery. Westminster Abbey." He paused, as if to let the culture tour sink in. Athena nodded. "When I'm at home we have dinner at eight. Otherwise, let Mrs. Hume know when and what you'd like to eat."

"I know how busy you are," she said. "And I don't want to be a distraction. I'll eat breakfast in the dining room. I've never enjoyed balancing a breakfast tray on my lap in bed. It reminds me of the few occasions when I was sick as a child and made to stay in my room and take all my meals there. And I don't wish to be a burden to the staff."

"You are no burden, my dear. It is why they are here and why I pay them to wait on us. You would best forget whatever you did in America and adapt to how we do it in England." He paused and looked at her sternly. "If you intend to stay."

Athena bit her tongue and buried the deserved retort. "I've been here six months and I'm getting the hang of it, Admiral. In another six you won't know I'm American."

He gave her a fleeting, insincere smile. "I have a meeting with your ambassador and the prime minister on Monday evening. A soirée. May I prevail upon you to accompany me? It's at the American Embassy. It will be an informal affair as it seems most of these occasions are these days. No glittering ballroom or dancing. Canapés, I expect, not a full dinner. It's to be a working meeting to which wives and such have been extended an invitation to see what it is their husbands do all day."

"Of course, Admiral. I'd be delighted."

She called him *Admiral*, not *Father*. "I'm not your father," he told her when she first arrived in England. "I don't intend to take his place, or even try. What you and my wife decide to call each other in public and in private is up to the two of you. To call me, *My Lord* is too stuffy in a family setting. You may find, *Admiral*, more to your taste."

"Maybe I should call Harry, *Colonel*," she wanted to retort, but bit her tongue. The admiral did not expand on the suggestion, nor offer any alternative. At least he didn't insist on *Father*, for which she was thankful.

Harry's stepmother had a suggestion. "I'm not Harry's mother," she said, "but I act like it and he treats me as if I were. He doesn't call me Maman any longer. I must confess I miss it, but he's far too old for that now. My given name is Anne-Marie, but nobody but my husband ever uses it, and then only in private. If you feel comfortable with *Mother* I'd be delighted if you'd call me that. But not Mother-in-law. *Belle mère en français.* That sounds formidable. Hideous. Like an ogress."

# 20. AMBASSADOR

On Monday evening, Athena and the admiral attended the gathering at the American Embassy in Great Cumberland Place. Unlike the Midsummer Eve's ball at the British Embassy in Washington, as her father-in-law had said, this time there was no receiving line, no banquet and no orchestra in the large reception room. But there were other ladies present, the wives, and such of the attending officers. The American ambassador, Walter Hines Page, spent most of the evening huddled at one of the large round tables, engaged in earnest, hushed discussions with the prime minister, with Field Marshal, The Viscount French, and with senior staff from both sides of the Atlantic.

At one point during a break in the discussions, the Prime Minister, Lloyd George, beckoned to the admiral to join them. "Mr. Ambassador, may I present Rear Admiral, the Earl of St Austell, and his American daughter-in-law, Mrs. Athena Haig-Mallory. The admiral heads our naval procurement division."

The ambassador rose, peered over his half-moon glasses and down his nose at Athena. A flicker of recognition crossed his face. "I believe I know the name," he said.

"You are correct, Mr. Ambassador," Athena replied. "We have exchanged correspondence about America's non-involvement in the war. You are acquainted with my father, Randolph Fenhagen."

The ambassador took a step back. "Ah, yes. I remember. You wrote me on several occasions. I'm afraid nothing has changed since our last correspondence." He scrutinized Athena for a moment before recognizing her. "Well, I'll be! Little Athena Fenhagen. How you've grown. I'd forgotten how long it's been since I last saw you. You were in braids if I remember. So, now you are married. Who is the lucky man?"

"Colonel Haig-Mallory, at present in Flanders as officer commanding the King's Imperial Hussars."

Field Marshall French coughed. The ambassador turned to him with a frown, then back to Athena. "It seems as if the business of the day must interrupt our reminiscences, Mrs. Haig-Mallory. Another day, perhaps." He turned to the men at his side. "A moment, Gentlemen." He turned back to Athena who by now was the object of thunderous looks from her father-in-law.

"We must get together over lunch one day soon, Mrs. Haig-Mallory.

Perhaps if you call the Embassy and ask for my secretary she can arrange a mutually convenient date." He smiled. "I shall try and persuade Mrs. Page to join us. Now, if you will excuse me, I must return my attention to the reason for tonight's meeting." He smiled, a genuine smile, Athena thought, not a diplomatic one. Ambassador Page turned to the men at the table. "I can assure you, Gentlemen, I will do everything in my power to persuade President Wilson to see things your way, but ultimately Congress and the Senate will decide…"

With a loud grunt, the admiral left to talk to some senior naval officers and Athena returned to their table, resigned to another boring interlude with service wives and others, and their small talk.

A tall, dark haired, red-tabbed brigadier detached himself from his group and approached. He stopped in front of Athena and bowed.

"I believe I overheard the admiral introduce you to the American ambassador as his daughter-in-law and the wife of Colonel Haig-Mallory."

"I am. And you are…?"

"Brigadier Shackleton. I was honoured to be your husband's commanding officer before he left for Washington, and again on his return through the campaigns in Picardie and Flanders. He now has my old regiment while I languish in Whitehall under General Horrocks-Smythe where I try to appear useful."

"It's a small world, Brigadier. My husband worked under General Horrocks-Smythe when he returned to France in nineteen fifteen. We were able to be married as soon as his assignment ended. Unfortunately for us he had to return almost immediately." She offered Shackleton a smile. "Then, of course, he was wounded at Christmas."

"It was unfortunate, being wounded at Christmas especially. Unofficially, he was leading by example, as is expected of all Hussar officers, and disobeyed standing orders. As he has learned the hard way, we have those for a reason."

"He didn't tell me how it happened, and I didn't like to ask."

"If he didn't tell you, I won't either. I'm sure he has his reasons. By the way, it was I who gave him permission to marry you. I was bitterly disappointed when the first wedding invitation failed to arrive. It couldn't be helped, I suppose, as we were both in France and neither of us able to attend."

"Not half as disappointed as I was, I can assure you."

"And again, I was busy in Flanders and couldn't get away when you eventually tied the knot."

"He's back in the front line I expect, knowing him." Athena's mouth tightened to a thin, grim line.

"And left you idly kicking your heels in London and attending Embassy soirées with your father-in-law."

Athena wrinkled her nose. "It's a chance to spend some time in London rather than in Cornwall."

"Perhaps you'll allow me to show you the sights in London, should you find yourself at a loose end one day. Are you staying in town?"

Athena bristled and shot Shackleton a flinty look. "I am staying at my father-in-law's London house in Belgrave Square. If I understand you correctly, Brigadier, I don't think a meeting such as you suggest would be entirely appropriate."

"I meant no disrespect, Mrs. Haig-Mallory, and nothing of the kind crossed my mind. It is, however, a standing offer, should you wish to take it up one afternoon. There is a lot of London to see that is not on the tourist maps."

"I'm sure my father-in-law could show me the sights if he has a mind to, without setting tongues wagging. You know what idle gossips women can be who have nothing better to do than to spy on others." She looked pointedly at the women and their sour faces, taking in her exchange with Brigadier Shackleton while pretending to ignore it.

Shackleton smiled, bowed and kissed the offered gloved fingers before returning to his table. The admiral returned at the same moment, sat down with a grunt before he turned and glared at the troika at the large round table behind him. "What a dreary and doleful looking man your ambassador is if there ever was one," he mumbled behind his hand. "He makes the prime minister look like that dreadful matinée idol in the motion pictures."

"Douglas Fairbanks?"

"I wouldn't know his name, but I could swear your ambassador has found sixpence and lost a guinea."

"He's a very successful businessman and obviously well regarded in Washington circles, or he wouldn't be here. But you're right. He is a most miserable-looking man."

The admiral snorted. The Prime Minister, Field Marshal, the Viscount French, and the ambassador stopped talking and glared at him. The admiral turned his back on them. "By the way, who were you were talking to just now?"

"Brigadier Shackleton, Harry's most recent commanding officer. Harry's taken over his command in France."

"He certainly cuts a dashing figure. Had you met him before?"

"No. Harry's spoken of him, naturally, but he's not a bit how I imagined him."

"It seems people never appear as we imagine them. Probably a good thing, all told, or there would be no mystery to them."

*

A week later, Athena sat opposite Ambassador Page in his spacious office. Bookcases lined the walls. His wall calendar said April 2, 1917, as did his desk calendar. The wall clock ticked loudly with each pass of the pendulum. The carriage clock on one side of the ambassador's large, intricately carved and inlaid desk indicated the same time — 11:47 a.m. Their lunch was set for noon and she had arrived early, terrified of being late and showing disrespect for the ambassador. Instead of being kept waiting in an anteroom a woman, whom Athena judged to be about the same age as her, immediately stepped forward.

"Ambassador Page is expecting you," she said, and showed Athena straightaway into the ambassador's office.

The ambassador rose when they entered and indicated the chair in front of his desk. Without a word, Athena sat. The ambassador returned to his side of the desk and sat also, with the desk separating them forming a deep barrier. She noted that her chair was lower than his, probably, she supposed, to symbolize lofty power on his side and to emphasize her lowly status, in line with all his other supplicants.

Athena had dressed in the modern manner of women of business. This would be a business meeting, she presumed, conducted in a civilized manner over lunch with a famed and important diplomat. The young woman left the ambassador's office and returned with a pot of coffee, cream, sugar and two cups and saucers.

"Thank you, Mrs. DeBrouwer," the ambassador said.

Alone except for the coffee and the ambassador, Athena eased her weight nervously in her seat. She sipped the coffee and put the cup down. "Thank you for seeing me, Mr. Ambassador," she said. "And for this excellent coffee. By far the best I've tasted since I arrived in England."

Ambassador Page smiled. "We have long enjoyed a special relationship with the British," he said. "Unfortunately, it doesn't seem to have extended to coffee. Theirs is terrible, don't you agree?"

Athena smiled in agreement and at acknowledging the first words he had directed specifically to her.

"I'm delighted to meet you again, Mrs. Haig-Mallory. My spies inform me that, as we speak, your husband is languishing in relative comfort far from the front. The accommodation is less than he would desire, I'm sure, but better than any available to those of less than general rank."

Hardly able to believe her luck when the ambassador had asked her to lunch a week ago, Athena was delighted to learn that Harry was safe — for the present, and that the ambassador had thought to enquire. Now that she was face to face with him, she was equally determined to press her cause, to help America join the war, if she could. And without seeming hysterical. Not that she expected to have the remotest chance of influencing the ambassador, any more than she had convinced anyone in New York or Washington, but at least if she failed, it would be with her head high, knowing she had done the best she could. In her pep talk before she set out that morning she told herself repeatedly not to allow herself to be intimidated by the ambassador's rank within the American hierarchy. She had prepared her speech, memorized it and she was going to deliver it, come hell or high water. She cleared her throat.

And immediately departed from her prepared script.

"Thank you for inviting me to lunch, Mr. Ambassador," she said. "It is an." honour"

"The honour is mine, Mrs. Haig-Mallory. And I hope I may also honour your father by spending this short time together."

Athena felt the blood rise to her cheeks. She folded her hands in her lap and took a breath. Here goes, she thought. No backing down now. "Mr. Ambassador, in spite of our differences over the past hundred and forty years, I believe America and Britain to be the closest friends and allies on the planet. The daughters of many of America's most prominent families have married into the British aristocracy, as I indeed have."

"And I am sure you do your husband great honour and credit, Mrs. Haig-Mallory, as I expect all our Anglo-American wives do."

The interruption flustered her. She almost forgot her place in her speech. She started again. "For obvious reasons I could not plead my case last week, and I thank you for taking the time out from your meeting to listen to me then." She took a deep breath. "My husband and his men are fighting for their lives in Flanders, as are millions of other Englishmen and Frenchmen, while we Americans sit idly on the sidelines, watching from a distance, like vultures waiting to pick over the bones and carcasses of the dead." She took another breath to calm her nerves. "I'm sure you recall it was the French, who were at war with England during our War of Independence, who virtually guaranteed our victory. And even then, it was no sure thing for a long while."

"How do you explain that, Mrs. Haig-Mallory?" He steepled his fingers and leaned forward.

The question, the interruption to her flow of argument, set her back on her heels. She gathered her senses. "If it were not for the French engaging British forces on land and sea all those years, Britain could have sent tens of thousands of soldiers across the Atlantic and defeated Washington's army at a time and place of their choosing. And if it weren't for the French, Mr. Ambassador, right now much of America would be part of Canada and the rest Mexican and French. We wouldn't exist. Not as a country. Perhaps not even as an idea. We owe it to France, in gratitude and in return for their good deed. And we owe it to England now. If America wants to run the civilized world, she needs Britain and France on her side, not Germany."

The ambassador folded his hands. "A pretty speech, Mrs. Haig-Mallory. I take it you are a student of American history?"

"I majored in English at Vassar, Mr. Ambassador. My final year thesis was on the writings of Jane Austen and the Brontë sisters within the context of the social and political history of the period."

"I see."

Athena took another deep breath. "I am a patriotic American. Our fence-sitting is uncharacteristic of a brave nation. Even un-American. And that does not make me proud." She hesitated. She saw from the scowl on the face of Ambassador Page her words had hit home. Before she could continue, the ambassador spoke.

"Strong words indeed, Mrs. Haig-Mallory." He steepled his fingers again, lowered his head and gazed at her over the top of his half-moon glasses.

This, she realized, was not going as she had so carefully planned. She had overplayed her hand. In fact, she knew she had done worse than that. In her handling of the meeting thus far, she had turned the ambassador against her. And in so doing she had let Harry down. There would be no help from America. Not today. Not next month or next year. If sinking the *Lusitania* couldn't bring America into the war, not much else would, least of all the prattles of a young American woman who had clearly outstayed her welcome in the Embassy. And certainly, he would cancel lunch with her. Her fault, she knew, and the penalty to be paid for interfering in business that clearly was not hers.

She resisted the urge to shift her position in her chair. The ambassador could only interpret it as squirming and a sign of weakness and indecision. She searched the ambassador's face for any sign that what she had said had registered with him. The scowl told her the ambassador had replaced his friendly countenance with his professional diplomat look that gave nothing away yet still conveyed politeness to his guest, as demanded by unwritten protocol. Ambassador Page regarded her for several moments while he fiddled with his fingers several times.

Her stomach lurched as the seconds of silence stretched to a minute or more. She knew she'd lost her battle. She'd failed. In a moment she would be escorted out of the Embassy, disgraced. No doubt her father would hear of it and not be pleased, personally or professionally. But there was no way she'd be the one to break the silence.

The ambassador took a breath. Here it comes, Athena thought, and steeled herself for the words of dismissal. "You may not know this, Mrs. Haig-Mallory, but I am an anglophile of long standing. It is my dearest wish to see America help our closest friend and staunchest ally in her time of greatest need." She waited for the 'but' to come, for the other shoe to drop. With an effort she held her tongue.

"Everything I've worked for since Britain declared war on Germany has been to that end. I have met countless times with Britain's Prime Ministers, past and present, and with the Chief of the Imperial General Staff. I have returned to Washington several times to plead Britain's case directly with President Wilson. He is, I can assure you, sympathetic. He sees and understands the big picture. But the common voter? The man steeped in his own self-interest? He remains unpersuaded. President Wilson has assured me that he will do everything in his power to steer the necessary legislation through Congress and the Senate. But only when he feels the time is right, when he has the hearts of the American people, whom he serves, which means the public and, yes, the voters, in his hands."

"And when might that day be, Mr. Ambassador?" No harm now, she told herself. One parting shot to prove I'm not dead, that I'll go down fighting for Harry. Even if he does think me unthinkably rude

The ambassador pulled out his pocket watch and glared at it. He glanced at the carriage clock and lastly at the wall clock. Athena did likewise. 12:04. He returned his attention to Athena. "I'm afraid I won't be able to have lunch with you today, Mrs. Haig-Mallory," he said in a voice that sounded like a death knell ringing from a church steeple.

That's it, then, Athena thought. You had it coming to you. Dismissal for being rude, pushy, undiplomatic. American. Her hand edged for her purse.

Whether he saw her movement or not, Ambassador Page continued, "I had hoped that we could. We have much in common to discuss. I'm sorry."

Athena stood. "I quite understand, Mr. Ambassador. I have been unforgivably rude for which I apologize. I won't take any more of your time. You have been more than gracious to have granted this interview." She picked up her purse —— handbag, she remembered the British called it. The meeting was over.

"I don't think you understand, Mrs. Haig-Mallory. I haven't finished what I started to say. Please sit down."

Athena's face turned scarlet. Now the ambassador was about to level a dressing down at her, the likes of which she had probably never received in her entire life. And, she admitted candidly, she deserved it. Not knowing what else to do, she sat, obediently and on the verge of tears.

"When I invited you to lunch I had every intention of enjoying a pleasant hour or two in the company of the daughter of one of my oldest acquaintances. More than that, a friend. Unfortunately, I have received news that now makes it impossible. It has nothing to do with what you have said today. I appreciate your frankness and persuasive language in arguing your point. Refreshing candour is generally lacking in diplomacy."

Athena made to interrupt. He held up his hand. "Please allow me to finish." He checked his pocket watch again. "What I am about to say will probably come as something of a surprise. Maybe shock is a better word."

Athena sat rigid, waiting for two Marines to appear and remove her bodily from the Embassy.

He slipped his pocket watch into his waistcoat pocket. "If you wish to stay, what I am about to tell you neither Mrs. Page nor Mrs. DeBrouwer knows about. It must go no further than the walls of this room. I warn you, if it does, we may see fit to have you extradited to the United States to stand trial."

Athena's lip trembled. She felt the tears prick behind her eyelids and her stomach lurched. She had an almost uncontrollable urge to wet herself. Or worse. She tightened her abdominal muscles and fought down her nausea.

"Why?" Her voice quavered. The blood rushed to, then drained from her face. "I've done nothing wrong."

"You haven't, I assure you. But it concerns your husband, if only indirectly."

Harry? What could the American ambassador possibly hold over Harry? She was about to ask when Ambassador Page held up a hand. "If you do repeat a word of what I am about to tell you, you could find yourself in a prison cell for a very long time. Do I have your word? Or do you wish to end this meeting now?"

Athena swallowed hard. She tasted coffee on her tongue and in her throat as she subdued the urge to be sick. This was not a game; that much she knew. But whatever it was, she had no idea of the rules. Or what to do. She did the only thing she thought sensible.

She nodded. "I promise never to breathe a word to soul. Not even to my husband," she whispered.

Ambassador Page waited for seemed an eternity before he spoke. "Last night I received a signal from Washington. From President Wilson himself." He paused. Whatever was in the message must be supremely important, Athena realized, for the ambassador to take her into his confidence and make such a fuss about it.

"It is still a little after five in the morning in Washington. Although neither the Secretary of State, Mr. Lansing, nor the German Embassy know it yet, the Secretary of State will summon the German Representative in Washington at nine, Washington time. You may not be aware of this, but the German ambassador, Graf von Bernstorff, was recalled to Berlin in early February over Germany's intention to embark upon unrestricted submarine warfare. He has not since been replaced. Mr. Lansing will inform the current head of the diplomatic mission that a joint bill will go before both Houses of Congress today and, when it passes, a state of war will exist between the United States and Germany and her allies."

Athena let out the breath she only then realized she'd been holding.

"I have told no one but you."

"I see." She could think of nothing else to say.

"It will take a few days for the bill to work its way through Congress, but I can assure you it will. With little more than token dissent, the Senate will rubber stamp it. The first of our troops will be on their way the day we make a formal declaration of war, most likely within the week."

He sat back. "Now you understand why I have no time for our lunch today. But I would dearly love to reschedule it for when things are a little less hectic and we can enjoy an hour or two together. Perhaps with Mrs. Page. After all, it wouldn't do to be seen spending more than a few minutes alone with a beautiful young woman, no matter how innocent it may be."

Athena gave him an uneasy smile and nodded.

He leaned forward and regarded Athena sternly. "I will hold you to your promise, Mrs. Haig-Mallory, believe me. You are in possession of the world's most closely guarded secret. One word, one hint of a word, ever, that you were aware of the secret… We are not playing games."

Athena said nothing for a long while. "I see," she said eventually. She pushed her cup towards the ambassador. "I think I would like another cup, if there is one."

The ambassador poured a single cup, added cream and a single cube of sugar and passed it back to Athena. "As a precaution," he said, "you will remain in this room until the German Representative in Washington, a First Secretary I believe, has been informed. For your convenience, there is a washroom off." He pointed to a door. "I will have lunch sent up on a tray. It won't be what I had planned, but it will be something. We are not subjected to rationing at the Embassy." He smiled. "This will be common knowledge within a few hours and in all the newspapers by tomorrow. You will be free to leave once I receive confirmation from State that the German Representative has been informed of our intention. I expect that to be before four this afternoon, London time. If I'm not here to say good-bye, Mrs. DeBrouwer will show you the way out. Do you have any questions?"

She had none. The ambassador rose. Athena extended her hand. The ambassador kissed the offered fingers. He paused at the door from his office with one hand on the doorknob. He turned to face Athena.

"Now that we have an understanding, may I call you Athena, as I used to when you were little?"

"Certainly, Mr. Ambassador."

"I must confess that I have been aware of these developments for some days. It has been a most difficult secret to keep. Secrets make for great loneliness, but I accept that they come with the position." His face seemed less doleful. He stood taller. "My regards to Colonel Haig-Mallory next time you write, and to your father-in-law. And of course, to your father back in Cleveland. He is made of stern stuff. I can see where you get it from." He paused. "Perhaps I shouldn't say this, but I will anyway, and please forgive me if you should take offence."

"Certainly, Mr. Ambassador."

"Regarding Mr. Bryan. You made the right decision."

Athena took a step back. "How did you …?"

"The Secretary of State's security detail reports daily. Less frequently on the activities of those close to him. You were in our sights for a short while, as were all Mr. Forrest Bryan's friends and associates. Believe me, nothing good would have come of any sort of relationship with him, as I am sure, many would testify."

Without giving her a chance to reply, he passed through the door and closed it behind him with a soft click.

Red-faced and angry, Athena downed her coffee in one long swallow.

# 21. PERSONA NON-GRATA

Three weeks after Athena's meeting with Ambassador Page, Hobbes, the admiral's butler in Belgrave Square, silver salver in hand, glided into the drawing room after lunch. He offered the engraved card on the tray to Athena.

"An officer, Madam, of General rank, has called."

Athena read the card. Brigadier D.E.S. Shackleton, DSO. The Priory. Walton-on Thames.

"What shall I tell him?"

"Tell him… Tell him… All right, Hobbes. Tell him I shall receive him here. Perhaps some seed cake and a glass of Madeira in a few minutes. I'll ring if I want it."

"Very good, Madam."

Hobbes returned a few moments later with Shackleton in tow. "Will that be all, Madam?"

"For now, Hobbes."

Athena remained seated when Shackleton entered the room. She regarded him with a stern eye and offered him her hand. Shackleton kissed the fingers and straightened. "To what do I owe the pleasure, Brigadier?"

"The pleasure is mine, Mrs. Haig-Mallory. And it will be an even greater pleasure if you will agree to dine with me this evening, unless of course you have other plans."

"I thought I made it quite clear, Brigadier, any arrangement would be unseemly and inappropriate. You, of all people, would understand what even a whiff of scandal could mean to the career of a Hussar officer. Or two."

Shackleton coughed lightly. "I shall be dining with my sister and her husband, Commodore Sir Victor Canning, at their Knightsbridge home. It is where I stay while I'm at the War Office. It's more convenient than Walton-on-Thames and more comfortable than my club. I hoped you might join us. Nothing extravagant. My sister keeps a simple house, and with rationing she thinks, they both think, they should set an example by keeping a simple table as well. Their cook, however, performs miracles, and regularly turns a sow's ear into a silk purse."

"And your sister has agreed to this?"

"She has. She impressed upon me not to come alone."

"The admiral will be out tonight, Brigadier. You may call for me at seven, if it's not too early. It'll give me time to meet my hostess without being rushed."

"I shall be delighted, Mrs. Haig-Mallory. And perhaps we could be on first name terms for the evening. We don't want to appear stuffy. After all, my sister is a sailor's wife."

"Athena," she said.

"Most people call me Des. From my initials. DES."

"Des."

"It's also my Christian name, Desmond. I shall be in civilian clothes. White tie. The gown you wore the other night would be perfect. It sets off your eyes so well. Or something simpler if you prefer. No need to go to town on our behalf."

"In keeping with your sister's desire to keep a simple house."

*

After dinner with Victor and Julia Canning, Athena leaned back into the padded, black leather upholstery of a cab heading toward Belgrave Square. Brigadier Shackleton sat next to her, close enough that a casual observer might remark that they seemed to enjoy a cozy relationship. Athena's proximity to Shackleton served two purposes — to gather warmth from the cool, blustery late-April weather, and to take in his masculine smell. Since Harry's return to France she had not smelled a man, responded to a touch, or the scrape of a bristly chin against her neck and shoulder as a prelude to…

Harry had managed to make love to her while he was on leave, on their last night at the Dorchester Hotel. She thought back on the occasion. It had been vigorous, heady and on the surface, satisfying. She had been more than willing to do anything he wanted, but beneath it all she had come to the unfortunate conclusion he had done little more than go through the motions to satisfy their needs. His lovemaking had lacked the passion of their days in Washington. She could tell his heart really wasn't in it. It was as if he danced with her so she wouldn't have to dance alone, not because to dance with her was what he wanted most in his life. He had left her faintly disappointed and, days later, wondering whether he still loved her. He said he did, but did he mean it? Had he lied to her about his true feelings? He clearly wasn't fit to go back to active duty, but he had insisted. When he took his shirt off his scars were obvious, the wounds barely healed. Surely those wounds must have scarred him inside, like some of the soldiers and sailors they had seen in Green Park. And it had been more than two months since he had gone back to France — closer to three. Not really long at all, far less than the two years they'd spent apart before their wedding, but at the same time much too long. And it would be months before he returned. If he returned. Why did Des have to be so damn good looking? She remembered Lester Morgan with a shiver and wrapped her fur stole around her neck.

"Chilly?"

"A bit. It always seems to rain whenever I'm out."

"It's what you can expect in April." Shackleton edged closer. Their hips and shoulders touched. Shackleton wrapped an arm around her shoulder and placed a hand on her thigh. She looked down, at the hand, then at his face. The hand edged higher. She put her hand over it and stopped any further progress.

"No." She was married. Des was not brash, cocky Lester Morgan. Lester was a boy among men by comparison. Des was only a few years older but far more mature. Not to mention more urbane and debonair. A burst of adrenalin surged through her. She gulped and swallowed. "Not here," she whispered, unable to believe she had suggested there might be something more, elsewhere.

"The Dorchester?"

"No. It's where Harry and I stayed the last time we were in London."

"Claridge's," he whispered.

"Mmm." It was too late to retract it, even if she wanted to. Her heart beat hard and fast and the blood rose to her cheeks and neck. She was under no illusion regarding Des. They both knew what they were doing, to Harry, perhaps to their marriage. Harry must never find out. She was sure she could trust Des never to say anything. She would try her best not to let anything slip. She knew it was different for a man; it should be expected he would stray from time to time, but not for a wife. She admitted she didn't know if Harry would forgive and forget, assuming he discovered her secret. If it were Harry seeking comfort while far away, with his life in danger of imminent forfeiture, would she understand and forgive? Though it would pain her, she thought she would. But if Harry found out about tonight, would he ever trust her again out of his sight? She wouldn't blame him if he didn't. She told herself not to give him any reason. Back out, you little fool. Des would understand it was an error of judgement. Blame it on the wine at dinner. We could part without complication. And never see each other again.

"Des?"

"Yes?"

She edged closer and smelled his cologne, the faint aroma of man sweat and the warmth of his body. She needed him. She wanted him. Her breath came in shallow pants. Her resolve vanished like a card in a conjuring trick. "You will be careful, won't you?"

He patted her hand. "Leave it to me," he whispered in her ear, then gave the cabbie their revised destination.

*

At the hotel, the front desk staff did not so much as raise an eyebrow when Athena and Shackleton checked in without luggage and ordered Champagne to be sent to the room.

Standing at the reception desk with their backs to the lounge, neither of them noticed the group of frock-coated elderly businessmen making their way towards the lobby. Trailing the group was Rear Admiral, the Earl of St Austell. He stopped. "My hat," he said quietly to his nearest neighbour. "I've forgotten it. Go on without me. I'll catch up with you at my club." He turned and hid behind a pillar in the deep shadows of the darkened and shuttered bar at the rear of the lounge.

He watched a young page hold the lift door open and Athena and Shackleton entered. The door closed and the lift rose silently. It stopped at the seventh floor. A few minutes later it descended again with only the page inside. The earl waited ten minutes. Neither Athena nor the brigadier reappeared. He asked the desk clerk to check the register. Satisfied, he left the hotel.

In their room, once the Champagne had arrived, Shackleton popped the cork and poured two glasses. He handed one to Athena. She turned to him. "You must think I'm some cheap tart, Des. Rented by the hour and paid for in champagne."

Des looked startled.

"I'm sorry. That slipped out, but you know what I mean. I can imagine what it would mean for both of us if it ever got out."

"Then we must be extra careful this night remains our secret."

"I don't know how, or why I let you talk me into this. I drank too much. And this doesn't help any. I'm not sure this is a good idea."

"We both need it."

"It's not been three months since Harry went back to Flanders. Even when he was home he... he was too injured and exhausted to... I've been as virtuous as a nun since the day he and I met." She crossed her fingers behind her back. It was at least half true, if not completely so, thanks to Lester Morgan.

"Then you must have been bored stiff all that time in Washington and Cleveland."

"Is that a pun, Des?"

"If it was, it was unintended. And I had no intention of offending you. If I did."

"You didn't. And how Harry and I conducted ourselves in Washington is above reproach." She wondered why she had just lied to Des. But then it was none of his damn business what she and Harry got up to in Washington pretty well every night. "It's been worse than living in a convent with Harry away. London or Cornwall, it's pretty much the same." She wrapped her arms around her shoulders. "It must be like wearing a straight-jacket."

"I don't think some nuns are as virtuous as they would wish the world to believe."

"Maybe you're right."

"All the more reason to enjoy the night as a fallen nun."

Athena rested her palms on Shackleton's lapels. "I know this doesn't mean anything to you. If it's any consolation to you or Harry, it's no different for me. I'll get up tomorrow morning as if tonight never happened. I'll block all memory of it from my mind, and I'll never do it again. Harry will never know unless you tell him."

"I'd be the last person to do such a thing. I don't want a bayonet thrust in the nether regions." He placed his hands on her shoulders and bent towards her to kiss her. She turned her head away.

"Don't," she said. "Anywhere but on the lips. A kiss is personal. We're both here for one reason only. I don't love you. And I know you don't love me. Which is fine for why we're here. I don't want…Don't let's complicate matters." She took a step back. "Des?"

"Yes?" He sounded eager.

"You promise to be careful. I couldn't explain a pregnancy."

"I promise." He pulled out a small, silver foil-wrapped square from his pocket. "See? Boy Scout. Always prepared. Not that I thought in my wildest dreams we might end up here, but you never know your luck."

She turned her back on him. "It's not luck. I suggested it. I knew what you wanted the first time we met. Only the time and place was absent from the invitation card." She paused, collecting herself. "I've never dishonoured Harry."

Shackleton's smile was lost on her back. "Don't think of it that way. We're both adults, Athena. We both need and want each other, especially after what you must have gone through."

She touched the plunging neck of her gown, then fanned her face with her hand. There was no doubt in her mind she wanted Des. Physically. But not emotionally. Men like Des were never faithful. And now neither was she. She was about to commit adultery with her husband's former commanding officer. She was here willingly. In a hotel. At her suggestion. Without exception where all her illicit lovemaking had taken place. Des hadn't seduced her. It had been her idea, impetuous and brazen. Unforgivable. But she knew how desperate she was for what Des offered. Other than that one night at the Dorchester, it had been August of last year since she and Harry had been intimate. Des would be different from Harry. She knew she was about to find out just how different. If she didn't call a halt to it, right then.

Would Des give her what they both knew she so desperately wanted? Did Des know how to gratify a woman? Or would he please himself and leave her, abandoned on the bed, unsatisfied and ruing the night more than anything she had regretted in her life?

Des stepped closer and undid the top button at the back of her gown. The second button came undone. The ache in her groin intensified. A small flush of moisture seeped into her flimsy, sheer silk underwear. *I want it. I need it. I must have it, the release. Oh, please Des, make sure.*

When he met no resistance, Des continued until he had undone all the buttons. The gown slipped to the floor. He palmed her silk underwear over her hips. Without a word she stepped out of the growing pile of clothes, a willing accomplice to her adultery. He unlaced her corset and let it fall. She stood naked with her back to him, shivering. He drew her close. She shut her eyes. She felt his body against her back, his hands as they gently cupped her breasts, her nipples swollen and nut-hard. His breath fanned the nape of her neck. He was warm against her skin. She wondered if he would be rough with her. Did she want that? Or gentle? She turned to face him, undid his white bow tie and pulled it away from the collar. She dropped it on top of her clothes. *How easy it is to discard our clothes,* she thought. *As easy as discarding my honour and my marriage vows for a few minutes of illicit, snatched pleasure, not unlike the visceral thrill of shoplifting a candy bar on a dare.*

Shackleton picked her up, cradled her in his arms and kissed her naked body from neck to toe before he lay her on the bed. He stripped off the last of his clothes and turned off the electric lamp beside the bed. He lay beside her in the dark, propped up on one elbow. He stroked her cheek and her hair, tumbling over the pillow. "You are beautiful, Athena," he whispered.

"You can't see in the dark," she said.

"But I remember."

She turned on her side and ran her fingers through his chest hair. She touched a hard nipple. "You like that," she whispered.

Des grunted his reply.

*

Athena fell into an exhausted but fretful sleep and woke only once, in the small hours, not knowing where she was. She opened her eyes and recognized — nothing. The bed felt strange; not the one in *Roseland,* certainly. And not the one in Belgrave Square. The room seemed different. She saw the curtained window and didn't recognize it as any she had seen before. She stretched an arm out from beneath the covers and felt the hard edge of the bedside table. On it sat a heavy ashtray. There was no ashtray beside their bed at *Roseland.* And none in Belgrave Square. She never smoked in bed, except with Harry, and only when they were in a hotel. Or that time in Torquay in the Marques of Butte's place. Was she still in Torquay? No. She definitely remembered leaving and returning to *Roseland.* So, she must be in a hotel. Which hotel? Where? Why? She didn't know. She couldn't remember.

She turned over onto her back and ran a hand over her skin. Skin? She was naked. She never slept naked. Not these days. Not since Washington. Was she still in Washington? In the Hay-Adams? She couldn't be. And certainly not in the Martha Washington. Heaven forbid! Surely she hadn't travelled back in time in some sort of machine that she had no recollection of entering. Her hand roamed further down her body and stopped. She felt sore. And wet. Down there. How could…?

It came to her like a jolt of electricity, in all its clarity. Des. The Dorchester Hotel. No. Claridge's. She had made love to Des Shackleton in a hotel room in London while Harry was in Flanders, fighting Germans

The skin on her scalp crawled. She was barely able to prevent herself vomiting at the thought of what she had done. With Des. She rubbed her arms. What should have been warm beneath the bedclothes was cold and clammy and smelled of uninhibited lust satisfied. And then some. Then came waves of disgust and fear — disgust at her actions and her weakness, and fear that she might somehow be discovered in shameless abandonment of her marriage vows. She had to admit that Des was certainly an accomplished lover, more so that Harry, especially of late, and she had responded with all the pent-up desire of long abstinence. Had it been worth it? On the surface, yes. But deep down, absolutely not. Now she lay awake with Des asleep at her side, rather than Harry. An adulteress, and she loathed herself for it. She fell asleep again only as the first pink and mauve fingers of dawn crept into the eastern sky.

Athena woke once more to an empty bed and discovered Des and his clothes gone. Her clothes lay over a chair. Des must have put them there. Thoughtful. Considerate. And a fitting end to their brief entanglement. They would never see each other again — or if they should by accident meet, it would not be as lovers. Not that Des would want a repeat performance. After all, she was hardly an accomplished lover: nothing more than a convenient wayside stop, eager but lacking a breadth of experience. She had egged him on. And he had obliged, had come to her like an eager retriever responding to a whistle. Were all men like that? Was Harry?

She knew she had no amorous feelings for Des. He had satisfied a need, an urge, no more. But at least he could have said goodbye or left a note. A gentleman would, wouldn't he? Or was that only in Regency novels?

She got up and took a long bath to wash the smell of their lovemaking from her body. She dressed. Conscious of her appearance at eleven in the morning, a time when only high-class prostitutes wore evening gowns, she went to the front desk to check out, only to find her account already settled. A note on Claridge's hotel stationery waited for her. With trembling fingers she picked up the single sheet of paper and held it up to the light.

*My dearest Athena,*

*It will to be to my lasting regret that I enticed you to dishonour Harry. I promise it will never happen again. If our paths should ever cross in the future it will be as if we had never met before. I will always remember last night, and you, but I will convince myself it was a dream. It never happened.*

*Des.*

Athena folded the note and was about to slip it into her handbag when she thought better of it. Last night never happened. There must never be a trace of evidence connecting her with Des. Harry's father saw them together, of course, at the American Embassy, if only for a few moments. But Harry and his father rarely spoke. Besides, Harry was in France. Hobbes saw Des come and leave, and knew Des came in the taxi to take her to dinner. And Barclay helped dress her and do her hair. Damn! Why did deceit have to be so complicated? She tore the note into confetti and gave the pieces to the hotel clerk to drop in the wastepaper basket. So, this is what it is like to betray someone, she thought, and barely managed to stop herself retching.

Pale faced and with shaky legs, she arrived by taxi at the house in Belgrave Square twenty minutes later.

"I am not well, Hobbes," she said. "I took ill last night and stayed over at Lady Canning's house. I should have sent a note, or telephoned, but I was too ill to think of it. Tell Barclay I will spend the day in bed. If I need her, I will ring. If I feel better I may be down for dinner. Tell Mrs. Hume it will be very simple. Some soup, perhaps, and some cheese and crackers."

"Very good, Madam."

Athena climbed the stairs to her room. She went into the bathroom, was violently sick and, still shaking from the effort of throwing up as well as from shame, took another long, lavender-scented bath. Then she drew her bedroom curtains closed and climbed into bed, praying Harry would never suspect and that she would let nothing slip. She did not want to know what he was up to in France, or with whom, even if it meant keeping secrets from each other for the rest of their lives. And if there is someone else, Harry, please never tell me.

As she tried to sleep, her temples throbbed in rhythm with each heartbeat. She could not put last night out of her mind. She prayed the memory would diminish with time, as it already had of her first time while at Vassar. Was it only half a dozen years ago? Last night was different. Now she was married, with her promise at the altar to remain faithful lying in tatters, fit only for the rag and bone man's cart. She knew she loved Harry with all her heart, an unshakable love. But still, last night's episode would haunt her all her days unless she could somehow block it from her memory.

She slept most of the day, in part to make up for lost sleep the night before, and in part because she could not face Barclay or Hobbes who must surely suspect her infidelity. They would be honour bound to tell the admiral, their employer, who would, in turn, tell Harry. But, she reasoned, the secrets of the family were inviolate. The sanctity of the confessional ranked no higher. If they knew, or even guessed, please, God, let her secret remain safe with them.

Athena came down for dinner. Hobbes met her with a silver tray on which rested a carved ivory letter opener and an envelope bearing a crest.

"This came for you, hand delivered, Madam, at four o'clock. I was assured there was no need to trouble you and no need for a reply."

Athena took the envelope and looked at the handwriting. She did not recognize it, but it seemed to be a feminine hand. She slit the envelope open and took out the single sheet.

*Dear Athena,*

*Victor and I were delighted to meet you last night and were so sorry you took ill while at dinner. I wish you had let my husband drive you home this morning rather than take a taxi, especially in this weather.*

*We hope you have by now regained your strength and are well on the way to a full recovery.*

*Victor and I look forward to seeing you again when you are next in town.*

*With my best wishes,*

*I remain,*

*Yours sincerely,*

*Julia Canning.*

"It's from Lady Canning with whom I dined last night, Hobbes."

She fought to keep the relief from her voice and resisted the temptation to fan her flushed face with the letter.

"Mrs. Hume tells me a light dinner will be ready in half an hour, Madam."

"Thank you, Hobbes." As he glided out of the drawing room she wondered why she thanked him. Her secret was safe with Hobbes, if indeed he so much as suspected an impropriety. She reread the letter. Des must have put his sister up to it and she'd played along. She wondered how often his sister covered for him.

To be on the safe side she left Julia Canning's letter on the writing desk where Hobbes would be able to find and read it and reassure himself there was no impropriety.

*

The earl returned home to Belgrave Square as Athena was finishing dinner.

"A word," he said, when she folded her napkin, leaving her with no illusion that this was not a request but a command. He guided her into the drawing room and shut the door behind them. Confusion clouded her face. She caught herself twisting her hands.

"You can wipe that innocent expression off your face, young woman," he snapped. "I know where you were all last night, and with whom."

"I was at Sir Victor and Lady Canning's house in Knightsbridge for dinner," she stammered.

"And afterwards?"

"I fell ill over dinner and Julia Canning graciously invited me to spend the night there rather than take a taxi home." She crossed to the writing desk and grabbed the note. "See?"

The earl snatched the sheet from her hand and tore it into pieces. "You are an incompetent liar. I hope you enjoyed your tryst with Brigadier Shackleton at Claridge's Hotel last night. It's what I expect of actresses and American women unable to keep their knickers on as soon as their husbands' backs are turned. It's all one can expect with marrying a foreigner. He's a fool to have become entangled with someone like you in the first place."

Athena's face turned white. She staggered sideways and clutched the back of a wing back chair for support. She opened her mouth to speak.

"No point in denying it, you little trollop. I was there at the hotel. I saw you enter the lift. Your room was on the seventh floor. I checked the register to make sure. I don't know how often this has occurred behind my son's back, but it will never happen again while you are under my roof. You will pack and leave first thing after breakfast. I don't doubt there are hotels in London that exist principally to accommodate your behaviour." He pointed at her. "I will not forget this incident, but unless you cross me, I will not tell my son about the tawdry affairs of his wife. Of a man it may be expected. Of a wife, never. I bid you good night. I do not wish to see you again before you leave." He paused. "It might behoove you and my son to seek alternative accommodation if you choose to remain in England. I leave it to you to tell my son why and see what he makes of the foreigner he married."

Athena's legs turned to jelly. Bile rose in her throat. With a supreme effort she managed to avoid vomiting her supper over him. He held the door open. She passed through the doorway as if she were a ghost, her face white except for two red blotches on her cheeks that betrayed her anger and her shame. Her personal reputation lay in tatters at her feet and she was beholden to the admiral, her father-in-law, to keep her marriage intact. All because, without scarcely a second thought, she knew she had acted like a cat in heat.

She knew what might happen if her deceit, her adultery, was discovered. So these were the consequences. In her heart she hoped Harry would forgive her. Not that she deserved his forgiveness. And now this — her life with Harry held firmly in his father's hands.

Athena dragged her weary body upstairs to her bedroom, threw up in her bathroom then crawled into bed, fully clothed. Ernest she could handle. But the admiral? She had no idea which way to turn. Would he keep his word? Or would he feel duty bound to report her to Harry? What a shambles, she thought. What have I gotten myself into?

She pulled the bedclothes over her head and drifted into an exhausted sleep.

# 22. PASSCHENDAELE

Six months after his return to active duty following the trench raid Harry could smell it in the air. Something big lay around the corner, another major onslaught on the enemy's positions most likely, though no one at Brigade had included him in their confidence. Perhaps this latest push would turn out to be another Somme, the one in which his luck would run out. If not, if fate should spare him, he would live to fight another day, another week, another month. Or possibly, though improbably, see the war through to its end. The thought passed with his summons to Brigade HQ and the briefing.

The next day the regiment moved into the front line. Beneath an umbrella of British artillery shells Harry assembled his officers in his dug-out.

"As you are undoubtedly aware," he said, "what's left of the village to the front of us is called Passchendaele. Behind it is Passchendaele Ridge. By this time tomorrow there will be nothing left of the village but rubble and a lot of dead Germans. That's the objective as outlined by the General Staff who plan these things. Of more importance to us, individually and collectively, is that we all come out of it in one piece with the ridge, captured and held."

Harry heard loud mutterings and a couple of cheers from the younger officers. He raised his hand for silence.

"We attack along a line at first light." He pointed with his swagger stick at the map hanging from the wall of the dugout. "From Ypres to Sanctuary Wood."

He let his words sink in. "In the great scheme of things, this is the big push. It's what we've trained for this past two months, the push that will win the war if everyone, from Field Marshal French to the newest recruit trooper, does his bit to ensure its success."

There's no backing away now, he wanted to say, but to have suggested it would not have been fitting for a Hussar officer, let alone their commanding officer. A twinge of acid gnawed at his stomach. He surveyed the sea of pale faces in front of him. Who would survive this attack? Perhaps none of us. It wouldn't take much to cock it up. The Somme had proved that. No doubt they were as scared as he was. It was time to allay their fears.

"Never before, gentlemen," he said, "has such a formidable array of fighting men been assembled to fight the enemy. Our Cavalry Division has the honour of occupying the centre of the line. To our left and right we have the Scots, Highlanders for the most part, shoulder to shoulder with us." He paused. "This may be your best chance to learn what a Highlander wears under his kilt."

He heard a round of laughter and someone with a Scottish accent call out, "It's called a Ghillwillie, Sir. Otherwise known as a jock south of Hadrian's Wall. But we only wear it during the thistle harvest." This elicited another round of laughter.

"I take it you've been peeking up a Highlander's kilt when he bent down and his back was turned, presenting you with his best view, Mr. McInnis." More laughter. "Where was I?" Harry turned serious. "We are proud, skilled, seasoned, battle-tested men. A generation from now Englishmen will look back on this battle and will see it as the turning point in the war. We are ready to take our place in this moment of our island's history."

Many of his officers, the more experienced, he noted, avoided eye contact with him. "We are ready to attack. All we wait for is the word to go over the top one final time and seize the high ground from the Germans. We will take the ridge, and we will hold what we have taken. Then we will drive the enemy back, all the way to the North Sea, east to the Rhine and beyond, to Berlin." He tapped the top of the map with his swagger stick. "The war will end before Christmas."

He knew it was a shamefaced lie. He had asked his intelligent officers, men who placed their trust, and their lives, in his judgement, to have faith, to believe in what was patently untrue. There were some who still believed in miracles, even after three years of carnage. He did not believe any stood in front of him now. He examined their faces and saw only skepticism, even in the most junior cadre of his officers. Infused in the smell of damp khaki packed into the warm, humid dugout he smelled fear. No. They didn't believe him either. He couldn't blame them.

It couldn't be helped. This was their job, why they were here. They served no other purpose but to fight and, if necessary, die for England until victory was theirs. He took a deep breath and suppressed his desire to agree with them. He wanted to go home, to Athena, to live in peace far from the sound of guns and the sight of a German uniform. No doubt to a man they did too. He cleared his throat. "If you think what you have heard from our artillery this past two weeks was the barrage to end all barrages, you won't believe your eyes and ears come three o'clock tomorrow morning. Our artillery will pound their defences as never before. It will blast their rows of wire like cotton thread. It will devastate their trench system until it ceases to exist. Destruction will be total."

He set his jaw and stared at the faces of his officers, defying any of them to disagree. "We will advance behind a creeping barrage." He kept quiet about his own thoughts of the efficacy of a creeping barrage. "Our primary objective is the German front line trench. Once we have cleared the trench, we move on to their second line trench, clear it, and hold it. Our second wave will leapfrog us and take their third line, communications trenches and their reserve trench. From there, they tell me, we will have an unobstructed view of the Rhine."

Harry raised his head and looked down his nose. "A bit fanciful, perhaps," he said, which brought a titter of nervous laughter from his officers. "Unless the earth really is flat." He paused for effect.

"At three fifty tomorrow morning, we go over the top. You will have about an hour's advance notice because of..." he cupped a hand to an ear.

"… The rats," the gathered officers chorused.

"The rum ration will come around twenty to thirty minutes before the off. Make sure each of your men has a tot, even the non-drinkers if there are any left. Have your NCOs inspect each man's rifle, and his pack for rations, water and ammo. Bayonets fixed, full clip and one up the spout, cocked and safety catch on until we're over the top. It's downhill all the way from there to Berlin."

He waited a moment, scrutinizing his officers, searching for weakness. "Any questions?"

There were none. And why should there be? Their orders were simple: advance and die. Any poor sod could do it. He remembered Clap had said something like that on his first day under his command. Even an Australian like Captain Benaud, who had turned out to be a likeable, efficient, and utterly unambitious sort.

"Get some sleep tonight, if you can," Harry said, bringing the briefing to a close. "Last letter pick-up is at nineteen hundred hours. Reveille will be at o-three hundred hours. That is all, gentlemen. Good luck and God bless."

All night the artillery barrage continued without let-up. The first trickle of rats scurried over the parapet shortly before reveille. By the time the men were fully awake and at their posts, the trickle had become a stream. The stream turned into a river, then a torrent as squealing rats, gorged from feeding on the corpses in no man's land, cascaded over the sandbag parapets into the trench. From there they sprinted for safety around the men's ankles and down the communications trenches to the rear.

The rum ration came round at 3:30 a.m. At 3:45 nervous men fingered their rifles or relieved themselves where they stood while they waited for the whistle blasts to signal the start of the assault, to send them over the top. For some it would be their first time. For others their last. And for some poor sods, both, if they were unlucky. Or perhaps lucky.

For the past hour, the artillery barrage had reached and maintained an eardrum-shattering crescendo. The ground shook beneath the men's boots. Water pooled beneath the slats of the duck boards trembled and shivered in wavelets. Normal conversation became impossible. Occasionally, the voices of NCOs rose above the din, repeating, "Ten in the mag. One up the spout. Look to your front." Up and down the trench, pacing like sentries at Windsor or at Horse Guards Parade.

At 3:50 a.m., as the first pink-grey smudges of approaching dawn crept into the eastern sky, the order came: "Fix bayonets." Four hundred and forty-six NCOs and men snapped their bayonets over the muzzles of their Lee Enfield rifles. The officers checked their Webley revolvers one final time. The men snatched surreptitious sideways glances at the man on either side of him, wondering which of them wasn't going to see the next sunrise. Your turn this time, chum? Or mine? Just hope it's quick and clean, one through the head or the heart, not left to bleed slowly to death in no man's land, or die of gangrene from festering, amputated limbs. Or in the agony of lockjaw.

A minute later the first shrill whistle blasts ran the length of their trench. In response, men scrambled up the scaling ladders and made their way through the lanes in their wire the sappers had cleared overnight. They fanned out as soon as they reached no man's land. Some ran, some jogged in a half crouch over the churned and pock-marked ground toward the enemy front line trench.

As Harry topped the scaling ladder and stepped into danger a fleeting reminder of the last time, he found himself in no man's land settled over him. This time, though, the surface was dry and reasonably firm, so different from last Christmas. Was it only eight months ago? And today it was dawn, not pitch black like last time. The sun would be in their eyes once it was fully up, making them perfect targets for the German infantrymen, but by then they would be in the German trench anyway.

He glanced to his left. Trevelyan jogged by his side clutching the cage of pigeons and his Lee Enfield. The assaulting troops ahead of him made good progress towards Pilkem Ridge. With Harry hard on their heels, the first wave reached the abandoned German front trench without casualties or a shot fired. They continued unopposed to the second line trench. The first man into the trench looked around him, searching for signs of the enemy. A second, then a third followed. Harry caught up with them within seconds and dropped into the trench beside them.

"There's no one here," one said, in amazement.

"We throw a party and nobody comes," grumbled another.

"Do you think they were expecting us?"

"What, after crapping on them for two weeks solid? What do you think?"

"Perhaps Haig sent them an invitation, but it never got delivered."

"Well, he can drag his drinks cabinet over here and set it up. I'm thirsty already, and it ain't even breakfast time."

"We done a day's work already. Time to knock off and head for the pub."

"Pub don't open till eleven, you daft sod."

"Pie and a pint is what I fucking want. And a doorstep, a wedge of cheddar and a pickled onion."

"Piece of fucking cake, this. Berlin here we come."

As if waiting for them, the storm clouds returned, piled like anvils overhead in banks of funeral grey and black. "It'll be fucking raining soon," one optimist groused as he stood guard beneath the broken parapet of the German second line.

"You a fucking weather forecaster, or did you look up, lick a finger and stick it in the air?" came the grumbled reply.

"Seaweed's wet. Any fucking idiot could tell it's fucking raining. Twat."

"Glad their trenches are drier than ours. Have you found their latrine yet? I need to pay my respects to the Kaiser."

"Down the communication trench, what's left of it, a short way and turn left. Have one for me too, while you're at it."

"By the time I've finished I doubt if you'll still want one."

"The Hun did a good job of building their trenches," one trooper said. "They even got concrete dug-outs."

"Looks like they intended to stay a while," the other grumbled. "High and dry."

"Maybe they even have a cinema."

"It probably only showed Kraut pictures."

"Ever had a piece of German crumpet?"

"Can't say as I have."

"No different from any other bit of skirt."

"How the fuck do you know?"

The soldier tapped the side of his nose. "If you don't know by now you daft twat, you'll never know."

Harry took heart from the banter, the break from the tension they must all have felt when they took their first steps into no-man's land. The expectation of death, dismemberment or blindness at any moment had their nerves stretched to breaking point. Now that an equally unexpected anticlimax greeted them, their release turned to boldness. This, Harry liked to see, and hear. Cocksure banter by men who could now proudly proclaim that they had crossed no-man's land and captured the enemy trench. Their objective was theirs without a scratch and it was hard for anyone not to believe they were on their way to Berlin. The second wave, Canadians of The Loyal Edmonton Regiment, went through their positions and occupied the reserve trench without opposition. The Hun was on the run, though few dared share the thought out loud. Harry knew never to whistle past the graveyard.

Then the rain came, not an ordinary summer shower, but a deluge that caught the men without their rain gear on. Within minutes what was once firm ground became a sea of slippery mud. With sixty-pound packs on their backs, the men slithered around like salamanders, trying to gain a footing in the ooze. Too late, they unbuckled their ground sheets and pulled them around their shoulders. Perfectly timed with the downpour, the Germans launched a counterattack with an artillery bombardment that made it plain to even the dullest of soldiers the British artillery had failed to take out the German guns. The Loyal Edmontons fell back to join Harry's regiment.

"Shit! That was too fucking close!" a trooper yelled as mud rained down on him from a shell burst right behind him. He pressed his body against the trench wall.

"Look to your front," an NCO shouted. "The other front, you daft bugger. The way the Hun's coming from!"

The banter ended. The German bombardment hammered their trench system, softening it up before they launched their counterattack.

As soon as the bombardment lifted, the first counterattack hurled itself against the British defenders. At two hundred yards range Harry heard his NCOs up and down the line repeat the words, "Pick your target. Hold your fire." Harry checked his service revolver and snapped it shut. He glanced at Trevelyan and nodded. Trevelyan cocked his Lee Enfield and slipped the safety catch off.

At one hundred yards came the command, "Single round, open fire." A volley of .303 ammunition swept through the advancing wall of grey, cutting them down like scything through tall grass in a hayfield. The Germans fell to their stomachs and slithered towards their communication trenches. Above the noise Harry heard the squadron corporal major yell, "Independent fire at will." Moments later the first wave of Germans poured out of the communication trench and into the line held by Harry's men. Men in field grey and khaki screamed and died. Harry recognized Trudel with the Lewis gun firing a long burst at the advancing Germans. Half a dozen fell, their blood splattered over the trench walls as they died, twitching, screaming, or in silence.

The Germans retreated down the communication trench. A trooper tossed a Mills grenade after them. Mud, blood, body parts and shreds of grey uniform erupted into the air. They all heard it — the scuttling of feet, only this time it wasn't rats but the sound of Germans on the run. An unnatural silence descended over their section of the trench.

"Good work," Harry called out. He turned and nodded to Trevelyan on one side of him and at Trudel on the other.

"Casualties!" Harry heard an NCO shout, just as they had at Le Cateau. And probably ever since Hastings.

*

The rain didn't let up for three days. Sleep proved impossible, even underground in the Germans' deep concrete bunkers. No reinforcements arrived, nor any replenishment of rations or ammunition. When food ran out they scavenged from the dead and the dying without compunction. And when there was nothing left, they went hungry and thirsty. Artillery fire from both sides shredded the field telephone cables early in the assault. Pigeons occasionally got through. Sometimes a runner made it through the slop of no man's land to deliver a message. More often than not he died in the mud and his message with him.

Harry's regiment spent those three days doing whatever it took to stay alive. They sought cover behind obliterated parapets. They lay flat against the rims of the craters where once a trench existed. And all the time it poured, both rain and German shells. One slip too far into the depths of a shell hole and the careless or unfortunate bastard slid uncontrollably and inexorably downwards, sucked into the slime and ooze at the bottom. There he drowned, unnoticed and in silence.

The Hussars and the Loyal Eddies, as the Canadians liked to be known, held their ground. From shell holes and improvised sections of trench they beat back every counterattack and endured the German bombardment that preceded each one of them. On the fourth day the rain stopped, but the German counterattacks continued without cease. The British artillery, bogged down in the mud behind their own lines could not move far enough forward to be of help and the German artillery withdrew out of range of all but the heaviest calibre guns. One barrage tore up a temporary German cemetery, a hastily dug mass grave immediately behind the German reserve trench. For several seconds an unidentifiable soup of mud, shreds of grey uniforms, decomposing flesh, bones and entrails rained over and around Harry's men. Anyone caught out in the open became drenched with a stinking deluge of human viscera. The stomachs of the hardest of men churned and heaved, though by then they had nothing left to vomit.

On the fifth day, a runner reached Harry with unequivocal orders: abandon your position and retreat to your original jumping off points in the British front line. Harry's shoulders slumped. He shook his head slowly. The offensive was effectively over, for now, perhaps forever. Dejected, they obeyed, and retreated across the churned mud of no man's land without harassment by German artillery.

Upon his arrival at the British front line, Harry called a briefing of his officers in the HQ dugout. Before he took the floor, Trevelyan handed Harry a newly polished Sam Browne and spit-polished boots. "Thank you, Trevelyan," Harry said quietly. "One must set a proper example if one expects it to be followed."

He turned to the assembled group of officers. "I'm glad you all made it back, more or less in one piece. Something of a miracle, given the mauling we took. You can all thank the padre, Mr. Sheppard, for your safe delivery. I need casualty numbers for my report to Brigade."

The officers in turn gave Harry the figures of the dead, the wounded and the missing. "We have no immediate orders, gentlemen, other than to hurry up and wait, so, any questions?"

Captain de Beynac spoke, as much to himself as to the assembly. "We give up all that hard-earned ground and God knows how many casualties for what?" A brooding silence fell over the assembled officers. "Why?"

"So Haig can report back to Lloyd George we continue to press the enemy hard in Flanders and elsewhere on the Western Front," another officer muttered.

"They haven't even been near the front," a third grumbled.

Harry heard the rumblings of agreement. "Quiet," he barked. When the assembly fell silent, Harry said, "In the big picture, of which we are not aware, I'm sure it wasn't an easy decision, gentlemen. And I'm glad it wasn't mine to make."

He regarded the sea of faces and counted his blessings. He stopped for a moment. He could only think of one. He still had his full cadre of officers. At least, he thought, this wasn't a repeat of the Somme.

"That is all. Dismissed."

He clasped his hands behind his back and squeezed them tight, willing the trembling to stop. His knees shook, as they had before his father caned him for failing his Dartmouth entrance exam. He took a deep breath and screwed his eyes shut for a moment. He inspected his hand. He had torn a nail without realizing it.

That stupid little nail hurts, he thought. But it told him he was alive. The dead feel no pain. His turn would come, of that he was sure. Only the time and place had yet to be determined. He suspected he was wrong earlier about the offensive being over. Although he could not know it, there was time yet — the battle for Passchendaele had barely begun.

# 23. ARMAGEDDON

Foul tempered, the British army licked their wounds for eleven days before they attacked again, this time without artillery support.

With rifles carried at the high port, Harry and his men advanced in line across the slop of no man's land. They slipped and slid in the mud, dodged from shell hole to shell hole and stumbled their way towards the German wire. Those who survived the lethal steel curtain of the machine guns, the mortars and the German shellfire in front of the enemy trenches, cut the wire in full view of the German pointblank rifle and machine gun fire. They pulled aside lengths of rusted barbed wire that still bore the remnants of clothing and body parts from previous failed assaults. Into these narrow corridors they filed, crouched low, firing from the hip. Then it was down into the trench and a hand-to-hand fight with bayonets, entrenching tools, rifle butts, boots, barbed wire and clubs; anything they could lay their hands on. No rules existed for this kind of combat. Kill or be killed. Die silently, die whimpering or die screaming, but always die bloody. Neither side showed mercy. Neither side took a prisoner. Chivalry — decency and honour, if they had ever existed in the filth and slime of Flanders — died at Passchendaele.

Again and again, for three weeks the men of Harry's regiment fought back and forth over the same few waterlogged acres. Each time they failed to dislodge the Germans or gain an inch of ground. Orders to fall back to their original jumping off point in their own lines followed each failed attack. Stretcher bearers carted the burnt, bloody wounded officers and men alike to forward first aid posts to be patched up as best they could. Or die. At each retreat they left behind the dead in the bottom of the German trenches. Or, gutted like fish and bled white, abandoned khaki-clad bodies dangled like washing on the line on Mondays, headless and limbless, their entrails spilled from torn bellies as their mortal remains hung tangled and snared in the German wire. Recruits became veterans in days. New, replacement officers, callow young men, most still fresh from their Officer Training course, possessed neither the savvy nor the experience to avoid being picked off by snipers. Harry learned few of their names and remembered none. What was the point?

*

In the evening of August 26th, Harry briefed his remaining officers once more.

"The big push is on for tomorrow, gentlemen." He glanced around at the pale, anxious faces and bloodshot, sunken eyes of his troop and squadron commanders staring back at him. He realized he barely recognized half of them. All the good ones, the reliable ones, lay dead, or in hospital. Those unaccounted for were still somewhere out there in no man's land — rat food.

"Our objectives are Glencorse Wood and Inverness Copse." He tapped the wall map with his swagger stick and gave the map references. "In spite of their names, neither is in Scotland. And as you will note from aerial photographs, there is neither a wood nor a copse there anymore. So there should be nothing to hinder our view of the retreating enemy."

Brittle, nervous laughter greeted his words.

"We will advance this time behind a creeping artillery barrage. So don't get too far ahead of your men."

Another thin laugh met Harry's attempt at gallows humour.

"We take up our jumping off point tonight. We attack at first light. Any questions?"

Silence greeted him. "Very well, then. Last letter pick-up is at nineteen hundred hours. Reveille at o-three hundred hours. Good luck and God bless."

They reached their jumping off point at 11:00 p.m. and stayed there fifteen hours without food, sleep or explanation for the delay, and without an order to attack. The rum ration arrived at 1:45 in the afternoon. Fortified with a little Dutch courage, everyone knew they would go over the top any moment. Would this time be any different? Would they capture their objective and hold it as a springboard to victory? Or would the attack be another futile effort that ended in death for no discernable reason?

Harry listened to the familiar call of the NCOs up and down the line, "Ten in the mag, one up the spout, and don't fucking drop it, you 'orrible little man." He took two nips of Scotch from his hip flask and promised himself another when they secured their objective. He tucked the pigskin covered flask away in the outer thigh pocket of his battledress trousers and patted it. There would be no refill until they were back behind their own lines, resting or in reserve. And then only if the mess had any.

He glanced at Trevelyan's calm, expressionless face. In one hand he held the familiar cage of homing pigeons, the communications system of last resort; in the other his rifle. Harry nodded. Trevelyan nodded back. No need for words. The runner from Brigade arrived breathlessly at 1:55 p.m. with the order to attack. Harry checked his watch. Attack at first light? Ten hours had passed since then. He raised his arm. At 1:57 p.m. he brought his arm to his side and blew his whistle. All along the line his officers blew theirs. The first of his men climbed the ladders and, crouching low, took their first tentative steps through the gaps in their wire.

A few yards from the lip of their frontline trench, the ground resembled a quagmire, waterlogged from all the August rain. The Germans sprayed the killing field with withering machine gun and rifle fire. British and German mortar and artillery rounds churned the ground between the two front lines into a sea of ooze. Eruptions of liquid earth drenched everyone close to the explosion with deluges of mud, blood and body parts. The mud had its own distinctive smell: to a man they recognized the acrid, eye-watering stink of cordite overlaid by the nose-clogging, stomach-churning stench of decomposing flesh and foul drains. "How can anyone become used to this?" Harry wondered aloud. Within minutes his mind obliterated the smell as his brain, and he, concentrated on the task at hand — staying alive long enough to reach and seize their objective.

Through the smoke of battle, Harry watched the men in the first wave of the attack dodge from shell hole to shell hole. Closer to the enemy wire they slithered and crawled or lay flat on their stomachs in the hope they might avoid a bullet. Two minutes out from their own trench the attack had already bogged down, barely halfway to the German line.

The men forced their way through the slick, boot-sucking morass. Unidentifiable, decomposing body parts from long dead infantrymen clung to every surface of man, uniform and piece of equipment. With each passing minute the British barrage pulled further and further ahead of Harry's first wave of troops. Once the barrage passed beyond the forward German positions, a gap opened up. Enemy machine gunners retook their positions in their sandbagged and concrete-reinforced pill boxes. From these, the Germans fired at will at the exposed British flank, using Harry's Hussars for live target practice.

Tight-lipped, Harry motioned to Trevelyan to stay close. With his batman at his side, he strode forward, picking his way as best he could around craters and through the mud. He held his shooting stick in one hand and his Webley revolver in the other as he tried to appear unconcerned.

Harry stopped to catch his breath. "It's important to be visible, Trevelyan," he shouted over his shoulder. "It inspires confidence and heart in the men. But truth be known I'm sure they have other, more pressing concerns than the fate of their CO." He let out a wild laugh. "Only a blithering idiot would walk around a battlefield as if he's on a training exercise then back to the mess for drinks before dinner."

"I suspect the silverware will need a bit of a polish when we get back, Sir," Trevelyan shouted. "And I've heard tell from the wine steward our stocks of claret are running low." Harry saw Trevelyan grin, and he was never more reassured to have a reliable man at his side.

"As long as there's still some Scotch left when we get back." Harry patted Trevelyan's arm. "Let's go," he said. "We still have work to do."

Harry turned and faced the enemy wire. He plodded forward as best he could through the slippery, shell-cratered mud. A hundred yards further on, he stopped. Mouth open, he gazed around in bewilderment. Soundless and jerky like a motion picture show, men around him stumbled and fell. As far as he could see, only he and Trevelyan still stood. Trevelyan grabbed Harry and pulled him into a small shell hole. The sound of battle returned. Harry heard the bullets crack past his head with a sound like tearing calico in a haberdasher's shop.

"Bloody hell, Trevelyan!" he shouted. "They're shooting at me. How dare they?"

"Nothing personal, I'm sure, Sir." Trevelyan gingerly raised his head to the level of the crater's lip and motioned to Harry. Harry followed the line of Trevelyan's finger and saw the sandbagged machine gun nest well dug in a few yards in front of the German trench. Only the barrel of the machine gun and the helmet of the gunner were visible.

"He's the bastard who shot my men," Harry said. "It stands to reason. I can't see any other bloody gun emplacement around here. And he's still firing at me. It makes me so bloody angry. Bugger them!"

Harry checked his revolver to make sure it was still fully loaded and thumbed the safety catch off. "Provide covering fire, Trevelyan," he said, and climbed out of the hole. With a rapid rate of rifle fire Trevelyan kept the head of the German gunner down while Harry strode over the mud to the machine gun nest and shot the two Germans at point blank range. One moved and struggled to raise his rifle. Harry shot him again. The German fell back and lay still on top of the other. Harry heard bullets whizz and buzz all around while he bent and gathered up the hand grenades he found at the bottom of the pit.

He stood and gazed about, getting his bearings. He swatted at the irritating bees that buzzed around his head. Invisible children tugged at his clothes. Birds pecked at his battledress blouse. The world fell silent for a moment and nothing made sense. He searched for the birds, the children and the bees. They had vanished. To his left he spotted another German machine gun nest a hundred feet away. He slid back down into the German pill box and pushed the two dead Huns and their Spandau machine gun aside.

He counted twelve hand grenades. Four looked like British Mills grenades and eight of the German style with a wooden handle. The machine gun stopped firing at his position. He counted to ten then stood up and in one movement tossed the first of the four Mills-type grenades in the direction of the German machine gun nest. The grenade exploded and seconds later the machine gun fired a short burst. He ducked and calculated the range and direction. As soon as the bullets stopped tearing holes in the sandbags around him, he stood and threw the second and third grenades.

He ducked again as a long burst of machine gun fire raked his position. When it stopped, Harry counted to five, sprang up and in one movement tossed his remaining grenade. He scrambled to the bottom of the pit on top of the dead Germans. He vaguely heard the explosion. The machine gun stopped firing. The sound of battle returned to Harry's ears but his anger didn't diminish. He stooped and grabbed a German-style grenade, pulled the pin and tossed it at the machine gun emplacement. It exploded in the heart of the pill box. He gathered the seven remaining grenades and stuffed them down the front of his battledress blouse. He climbed out of the hole and strolled back to Trevelyan in the shell crater.

"Very well done, Sir," Trevelyan said. "But perhaps next time you'll let me do the honours. It's a job for the rank and file, if you don't mind me saying so. Not a colonel."

Harry regarded his batman as if he were a stranger. He shook his head. Reality seeped through the fog in his brain. "They made me so bloody angry, Trevelyan. It wouldn't have worked with you. They would have recognized you as a soldier and you wouldn't have gone two steps before, well, you know. Stupid of me, I know, but I probably caught them by surprise. Best not to mention it to anybody. Let's get going. We've got them where we want them this time, on the run. Time to get out the mop and bucket and clean up."

Harry and Trevelyan resumed their slow but steady progress diagonally towards a gap in the enemy wire. "Over there," he called out to Trevelyan, pointing with his shooting stick through the smoke. "Come on. Next stop, Berlin." Harry turned back in time so see Trevelyan clutch his chest and drop the pigeon cage as he crumpled without a sound to his knees. An explosion close behind Harry threw him into the air and dumped him back on the ground a couple of yards away. Dazed, with his lungs emptied of air and his ears ringing from the explosion, he picked himself up and stumbled over to Trevelyan. He slung Trevelyan's rifle over one shoulder, hauled his batman over the other and picked up the pigeon cage.

He staggered through the gap in the wire and into a section of captured enemy trench. "Stretcher! Stretcher!" he yelled, until he was hoarse. Harry stood over the prostrate body of his batman until a stretcher and two bearers arrived. "He's bleeding badly from his chest," Harry told the stretcher bearers. "The right side. Might have got him in the lung. Looks pretty clean, Get him back to a dressing station. I can't afford to lose him."

The medic ignored Harry. "Looks like a blighty one. Lucky sod. No more going over the top for him. His name, Sir?"

"Trevelyan, Thomas. Trooper. My batman."

The stretcher bearers picked Trevelyan up and bundled him onto the stretcher. The batman groaned and opened his eyes.

"You're going to be all right, Trevelyan," Harry said. "We've seized our objective. The second wave has leapfrogged us and consolidated their position. We've buggered them for sure this time. We'll have you back to our own lines and tucked up cozy in a hospital bed in a jiffy."

Trevelyan managed a smile.

"And after they've patched you up, you're going home. This is a young man's war. You've done your bit, no question. The next time I see you will be at *Roseland*."

Harry took his silver cigarette case from his breast pocket, lit one and placed it between Trevelyan's lips.

"I don't smoke, Sir," he said, "But thank you. If it helps me heal quicker, perhaps I'll take it up."

"We won't be able to get him back with only the two of us," one of the stretcher bearers said. "You've seen it, Sir. It's worse'n a Dartmoor bog. We'll up to our waists in a minute." He turned to Trevelyan. "If you don't want it, mate, I'll have it." He took the cigarette from Trevelyan's lips, pinched the glowing ash off the end and stuck the remains behind his ear.

Harry looked about him. "You, you, and you two." He pointed to four men. "I'll have no idlers and shirkers in my regiment. Help these men take this wounded man back to our lines. Then rejoin your troop. Move!"

Harry followed the six men to the dressing station and watched while a medical orderly pressed a compress over Trevelyan's wound and taped it. When they finished, the troopers picked up Trevelyan's stretcher and started on their way back to their own lines, no doubt glad to be out of the fight for a few hours.

"Now your wounds, Colonel," the orderly said. "Let's have a butcher's."

"What wounds? I'm not wounded."

"Begging your pardon, Sir, but you are. This is your blood, not his."

"Well, I'll be damned," Harry said.

"We probably all will be, Sir."

"Be what?"

"Damned."

"I had no idea. I never felt a thing. Are you sure?"

"Yes, Sir. Bill, help the colonel off with his blouse." The orderly unbuttoned Harry's battledress blouse and slipped the braces off his shoulders.

"I do believe you're right," Harry said. "It is a bit of a mess, isn't it?"

"I'll say, Sir. Can't understand why you didn't feel them."

"Them?"

"Well," Bill said, "Let's see. There's one through your side, here, a bit below the ribs. Then there's one in your arm below the shoulder. Doesn't look like it hit the bone, though. There's another one creased your shoulder." He examined Harry's back and shoulders. What do you reckon, Nobby?"

"I count six holes in the top of your shirt, Sir. Not bullets. Maybe small pieces of shrapnel from a grenade or a shell. There's quite a bit of blood. Your pack's shredded. Looks like it stopped the worst. Some bits and pieces must have gone through it and into your back. They don't look deep. Then there's the two in your thigh. It's bleeding pretty badly, Sir. We'll have to get you back to the field hospital and have a doctor look at it."

"No chance." Harry gritted his teeth. "Fish out what you can then bind it up good and tight. I'll try not to put too much weight on it. I've come this far, I'll be damned if I'm going to bleed to death before we've finished what we started."

"The bullet might be in there for a long time, Sir," Bill said. He inspected the bloody mess high on Harry's inner thigh. "It's pretty close to the femoral artery. Sever the artery trying to fish it out, and you won't last ten minutes." He bent down and wrapped his hands around Harry's battledress trousers.

"Scotch, by the smell of it," he said. He pulled out Harry's hip flask and held it up. "You might want to finish it, Sir. We're a bit short of morphine. I'm sure the Hun what put the bullet hole in it and your thigh will apologize. Here."

Harry took the flask, drained the last couple of mouthfuls and regarded the orderlies. "It was a blend. I'm glad I didn't waste a decent single malt."

"I'll take a blend any day, if you don't mind my saying so, Sir," said Bill. "If it's offered."

"Sorry. All gone."

"Just my luck. I suspected as much."

"I'll keep the flask as a souvenir." Harry gritted his teeth again as a wave of pain bit. "But I won't hold my breath waiting for an apology from the Hun. He's dead." The medics finished bandaging his arm and leg and helped him to his feet.

"I can manage, damn it!" Harry swore. "Point me towards regiment HQ."

"Major Merryweather, A Squadron, is down the hall, Sir. First door on the left. You can't miss it." Through the mask of dried mud on the soldier's face Harry saw him grin.

Harry squinted down the trench. Merryweather's face peered around the corner. Harry waved and reeled over to him like a drunkard.

"Glad you made it, Merryweather," he said. "Pass the word to stand by for a counter-attack. And I'll set up regiment HQ here. Have the adjutant report with casualties."

"Captain de Beynac went down, Sir," Merryweather said. "He's still out there, somewhere. Mr. Moncrieff in B Squadron is the next most senior. A good head on his shoulders. Steady. Not too excitable. Been with us since Christmas."

"Pass the word for Mr. Moncrieff, Major. Have him report to me as the new adjutant."

German artillery blasted the two front line trenches for twenty minutes. Then the first field grey wave of screaming Uhlans in their spiked helmets poured over the parapet of the forward trench and overwhelmed the defenders. Rifle fire and grenade explosions followed the retreating Hussars down the communication trench. The first German rounded the corner of the trench and died in a hail of bullets.

More Germans poured into the trench. Grenades exploded. Lewis guns fired sporadic bursts Men screamed foul oaths in English and German as they died. Others died wordlessly. The Hussars stood their ground. Then they charged as the enemy retreated and drove them back to their third line trench. In their fury Harry's men raked the two hundred yards of open the ground between the two trenches with machine gun fire until not a grey-uniformed German still breathed.

"Look to your front," came the order from NCOs and officers. "Reload. Wait for the word."

The men scrambled onto hastily scraped fire steps and waited. The next attack came less than an hour later. The Germans poured once more into the second line trench. Then, like water surging through the sluice gate bottleneck of the communication trenches, they swarmed into the front line. Hand to hand, Harry's men beat them back. The mud and duckboards beneath their feet ran red.

German artillery rained down on the trenches all afternoon. Harry's men sought cover in the concrete dugouts. As each barrage ended, the Hussars returned to the fire steps hacked into the rear walls and waited for the next counter-attack. Wave upon wave of field grey fell upon them. Ducking, weaving, crouching, the Germans fired from the hip as they slipped and stumbled over the sodden ground and dead bodies. When they reached the trench they poured over the lip like an army of bloated grey rats. And there the Uhlans fell, cut down by the accurate, determined, rapid fire from the Hussars' bayonet-tipped Lee Enfields.

As the last of the Germans retreated to the relative safety of their reserve line, Harry stood, feet apart, over the bloody abdomen of a bayonetted German soldier, the tunic and shirt over his chest ripped open. Two bayonet thrusts, in then up, had cut through the cartilage between the man's ribcage and breastbone but had failed to sever the aorta. The German's entrails hung by his side, leaking visceral fluid into the earth. The soldier's stomach contents dribbled into his body cavity. Harry stared in a detached way at the dark, shiny liver partially hidden beneath a thin layer of fat, and at the man's lungs as they expanded and contracted with each laboured, gurgling breath. He watched the heart beating as it pumped arterial blood into an ever-widening pool around Harry's boots. The Vikings used to do this, Harry thought as his mind returned to an earlier age when he wore short pants and had a history teacher with a vivid vocabulary. Hack the cartilage down the sides of the breastbone with their battle axe, tear the rib cage apart and pull the organs out to lie on the man's chest. They probably laughed or boasted as they stood over the unfortunate wretch dying in agony. What did the Vikings call it? The butterfly? The flying angel? He couldn't remember. He would have to ask his history teacher. What was his name? Woodhouse. That's it. His mind snapped back. A thousand years later are we any more civilized?

The German soldier stared at Harry through clouding eyes.

"*Bitte,*" he gasped.

Harry cocked his revolver, took aim at the German's head, and squeezed the trigger. Click. He fired again. Click. Click. Click. He broke open the Webley and ejected the six empty casings. "Sorry," he said. "*Désolé.*" He scrambled to remember the German. "*Es tut mir.*" His mother used to say that a lot. He hoped that was right. Harry reloaded his revolver with six bullets and cocked the hammer with his thumb. He extended his arm and took aim at the man's head. His finger moved off the trigger guard, preparing to shoot. He hesitated. As he watched, the German's heart stopped beating. His jaw grew slack, his mouth gaped, and his head rolled to one side. Harry eased the revolver hammer back and thrust the gun into his holster. He slumped against the side of the trench and forced his knees to stop shaking.

"I would have," he croaked in a voice he hardly recognized, as much to reassure himself as the dead man. "Only I was too late."

# 24. A TIME TO DIE

The fighting dribbled to a close, the end of a round in an interminable boxing match. During the lull, Harry sent off pigeons requesting reinforcements, medical supplies, food, water, ammunition and artillery support. A trickle of fresh troops arrived from a Scottish regiment, but no medical supplies, no food, no water and no ammunition. To stay alive Harry's men robbed the dead and the dying of everything they could use, Englishman and German alike. There was never enough.

As dawn struggled over the battlefield on the second day Harry ordered his men to abandon the German second line trench and shorten their perimeter with their remaining troops concentrated in what was left of the front line trench. For two days it poured; rain, shells and mortars rounds. For two days the Germans counter-attacked with unrelenting ferocity. And for two days Harry's men killed Germans in bloody, savage hand to hand combat. But without reinforcements, the British line grew shorter as one by one the Hussars died, or were too wounded to fight on.

The rain stopped. With the second nightfall an eerie, ghostlike calm settled over the battlefield, as if only the dead dared venture abroad. Then, through the silence, a feeble and ragged chorus of wounded and dying men rose, ululating, then grew fainter and less frequent during the black hours. Some called out in English. Some in German. Sometimes silence echoing through the night followed a single gunshot. The living understood the implication. Then the cries for help arose again, begging for water, for morphine, for stretchers, their comrades, their mothers, for an end to their suffering.

Twice more Harry was wounded, a bullet in the shoulder and a bayonet thrust below the ribs that he managed to parry with his arm before it could do much damage. That German died — his throat ripped out by a bullet from Harry's Webley. Waves of pain seared through Harry's body until he could hardly think clearly. His body screamed out for something to deaden the pain, but he refused to allow the medics to inject him with the last of the morphine. The drug, he knew, was a two-edged sword. It would relieve the pain but also numb his senses and render him useless as a soldier and commanding officer. Then the effect of the drug would peter out and he would be back where he started. Or worse.

Harry hobbled about, leaning heavily on his shooting stick. He visited every squadron, every troop and every section with his Webley in his hand and his last rounds in the chamber. He spoke with his men and comforted those who, though wounded, were still able to man their posts. He sucked in a lungful of air. In his nose, his mouth, his throat he tasted the smell of battle — not cordite, though the ever-present, acrid stink lingered — but the sickening stench of human corruption, of veins and arteries and intestines split open by bullet, bayonet or shrapnel and the slime seeping into the mud beneath his boots. English. Germans. It doesn't matter, he thought. We all smell the same when we're dead.

He found Trudel on a fire step with his Lewis gun cradled in his arms and his head swathed in a bloodied bandage. "Glad to see you're still with us, Trudel," Harry said. "Our luck has not deserted us completely."

Trudel turned slowly, his exhausted eyes sunk deep in their black sockets and stared at his commanding officer. "It seems like we've been in this pickle before, Sir, only this time we're a bit farther from our own lines. You wouldn't remember, of course, seeing as you weren't there. Officially." A maniacal laugh escaped his lips before he clamped his jaw shut.

"You're right. I wasn't." A star shell burst near their position, high overhead in the clear night. Harry looked over Trudel's shoulder and stiffened. Something moved. He stared at the corner of the trench. It moved again. Harry drew his revolver and pointed it. A German? A Hussar? A rat? He advanced towards it. It moved again. He brought his Webley up to aim, then stopped, seeking a better target. The target froze at the same instant. Harry moved again. The target moved with him, swaying with each movement Harry made. The star shell burned out and the object vanished. After a moment, Harry relaxed. Only a shadow, or his imagination playing tricks. He holstered his revolver and breathed again. He desperately needed to sleep. He couldn't allow it. Not while his men depended on him.

"We'll pull through, Trudel, never fear. Keep up the good work. It's men like you who are the backbone of the Hussars."

"Thank, you Sir."

"Carry on." Light-headed, Harry hobbled on down the trench. The cries of dying men grated on his nerves. He gritted his teeth. "Carry on, Haig-Mallory," he muttered. "The men must see you in their midst."

Another dawn crept towards the eastern horizon with the Hussars at stand to. The cries and whimpers from between the trenches had ended overnight. At sunrise a barrage of German artillery shells rained down on their position. The German infantry pressed their counterattacks following on the heels of each bombardment, ducking and weaving like boxers only to stumble and fall at the fists and rifle butts and bayonets of the Hussars. Men bled and died on the parapets, or in the trench, or snagged on what shreds of barbed wire strands remained. By the end of the day not a Hussar had a bayonet unbloodied or a round of ammunition left. German and English blood soaked every English uniform.

As first light crept into the sky after three interminable days and nights of savagery, a runner from Brigade reached Harry. "Orders from Brigade, Sir," the man panted. "You are to retire immediately to original positions. Leave all non-walking wounded. Stretcher bearers can't make it through in this mud, Sir. Orders are to bring prisoners."

Harry could not suppress a hollow laugh. "Prisoners?" He waved an arm wildly at the carpet of dead Germans at the bottom of the trench. He winced as pain knifed through him from his wounded arm. He pointed at the ends of the communication trenches where dead Germans lay piled two and three deep and half a dozen high like human sandbags, blocking the entrance to the Hussars' position. "What prisoners? We took no prisoners."

"Officers are to report to Brigade HQ at twelve hundred hours, Sir," the runner stammered.

"My compliments to the Brigadier, but I don't have any officers left," Harry said quietly. "They are all dead or too badly wounded to make it back. Tell him I'm down to fewer than half my NCOs and men, and most of them are wounded." Harry returned the runner's salute. The man scuttled out of the trench and made it a hundred yards through the mud before he was cut down by German machine gun fire.

Merryweather and Sheppard lay on makeshift litters on top of several German corpses. "Orders, gentlemen," Harry said. "Walking wounded only. I'm sorry, but we have to leave you here." He regarded Merryweather's blood-soaked battledress trousers and the three bullet holes in a neat row down what was left of the front crease.

"It's broken, Sir, but I think I can manage on my own." He elbowed his body into a sitting position and immediately fell back onto the litter. His eyes shone bright with fever. His pale, grey-green face gleamed with sweat.

"Perhaps not," he said. "You know, Sir, my maternal grandmother was German. I remember her from when I was a child. She scowled a lot, but she wasn't a bad sort at heart."

"Nor was the Queen Consort, Prince Albert," Sheppard said through gritted teeth. "Or so I've heard. I'm sure the majority of them are decent human beings. I don't doubt they will treat us well."

"I don't doubt it either, Padre. I'll see you both after the war." Harry stepped back and saluted.

Sheppard's eyes, wild with pain, closed. "I would stand and return the salute Sir, if it weren't for the arm. And the shoulder. And whatever else is missing."

Harry inspected Sheppard. "Everything you arrived with still seems to be there, Padre. The leg doesn't look too straight, though. I've no doubt it will mend." He smiled. "I'm sorry there's no morphine left."

"Not to worry, Sir. I can't feel much in any case." He took a breath and winced. "In spite of all this, Sir, I still believe in a just and merciful God."

"I know you do, Padre," Harry said quietly. "I'm sure we all do in our own way. God bless both of you. Good luck."

Harry, the squadron corporal major, and Trudel were the last out of the German trench.

"Senior NCOs can't lead a retreat, Sir," the corporal major growled. "It's not dignified."

"Quite so, Corporal Major."

"And someone has to look after you, Sir," Trudel said. "Especially as standing orders say we don't stop for the wounded, ever. And colonels don't do trench raids, especially not one as big as this."

Harry grimaced and pointed at the spiked helmet in Trudel's spare hand. "A souvenir, Trudel?"

"Yes, Sir. I picked him off when he slid over the top of the trench. I got his mate, too. A pickelhaube, my grandad says it's called." He held the helmet up. "He was an officer. I've kept his Luger too." He patted his thigh pocket. "The helmet will go nicely on the mantelpiece back home, if me mum lets me keep it."

Harry grinned, then grimaced as a spasm of pain lanced through him. Leaning heavily on his shooting stick, he put one foot in front of the other and began his snail's slither through the boot-sucking mud. He told himself every tortured, agony-filled step took him further away from the enemy, and closer to Athena. He shut his eyes briefly and saw her, her face, her hair, her clothes, and smelled her perfume. Odd, he thought, but he didn't see Solange. He opened his eyes to see Trudel regarding him with curiosity. Smarten up, Haig-Mallory, he admonished himself. This is no way to lead.

"Thinking of a nice cup of tea, Trudel," he said, hoping the lie went undetected. "With a splash of milk and a teaspoon of sugar."

"That would be nice," the corporal major muttered.

"A nice cuppa," Trudel said. "Something to look forward to I dare say when we get back."

"See what you can manage, Trudel. I'm going to need a new orderly when this is over. Perhaps you might consider it. I rate at least a corporal of horse."

"And part with Lucy here?" Trudel gave the Lewis gun a friendly pat. "Thanks, but no thanks, Sir."

Trudel on one side of Harry, and the squadron corporal major, his waxed moustache tips pointing skywards and his swagger stick under his arm on the other, accompanied Harry back to their lines. Harry dared not look over his shoulder at the abandoned ruins of the German line shrouded in smoke. All the time, fully exposed to the Germans on the ridge behind them, he expected the Germans to fire on them. At any moment a German would kill them in vengeful fury for the casualties his men had inflicted upon their own. At every step he anticipated a bullet from a shot he would never hear slam into his back between his shoulder blades, a bullet that in less than a heartbeat would shatter his spine and snuff out his life. And when death came, he wouldn't blame the man for doing his job. He knew before going over the top this would be his last time. Death would meet him on its terms, not his, as he always knew it would. He only prayed it would be swift and clean.

But the Germans held their fire. Perhaps, he thought as he staggered through the gap in the wire of the British front line, not even the Hun considered it sporting to shoot a defeated, retreating enemy in the back. And perhaps, as the padre said, they were decent men at heart.

He fell into waiting arms and blacked out.

*

Harry woke briefly. He thought he detected the hazy outline of a kerosene lantern overhead, or the sun, or the entrance to Heaven burning in his eyes like a bright halo, but he couldn't be sure. The light died. He knew nothing more until he heard distant voices. He recognized the nasal twang of the antipodean major. He couldn't remember his name. He searched his memory: Barrington. That's his name, the man who oversaw his recovery from the trench raid at Christmas. He opened his eyes wide to see a rubber tube dispensing fluid into his arm from a bag hanging overhead. Daylight, diffused by the heavy white canvas above him, and powerful electric lamps, lit his world. He heard the rattle and click of metal on metal; rifle bolts being worked. Puzzled, he saw nurses moving around him with carts loaded with kidney basins and surgical instruments, and realized he was alive. And if the voice was Barrington's, he wondered if he could be back in the grounds of the Château Gran'ville. He smelled chloroform and heard female voices. He could not place the voices. None sounded like Athena. Or Solange. He lost consciousness again.

*

"Brigadier's compliments, Colonel," a nurse said during a moment of relative lucidity. "He will see you at o-eight hundred hours. Perhaps a shave before he comes?" Without another word she lathered Harry's face and shaved him as expertly as any barber. Before the brigadier arrived two orderlies propped Harry up on pillows.

Recalling Sheppard's words, Harry said, "I would salute, Sir," when Shackleton arrived at the foot of the cot, "but someone seems to have bound my arm to my chest and taken my uniform away." He barely recognized his voice. It sounded high pitched, fevered and disembodied, as if he only mimed words spoken by someone else. "And you caught me by surprise. I wasn't expecting you back here."

"I arrived yesterday. No need to stand, Haig-Mallory, even if you could. How are you? "

"A bit stiff and sore, Sir, but otherwise in pretty good shape."

Shackleton regarded the tubes running into and out of Harry's body. "Not according to the medical bods. By all accounts you ought not to be alive. They tell me they're doing everything possible to prevent blood poisoning and gangrene. So far, so good." He paused while he glanced at Harry's chart hanging from a clipboard at the foot of his cot. "Let's cut to the bit where the fox goes to earth, shall we? I've received a full report of your actions from your squadron corporal major. He says you have no officers left in your regiment. Is that true?"

"Unless any made it back through our lines I don't know of, Sir. All my officers were killed or too badly wounded to be moved."

"It's unusual to lose all one's officers in a single engagement, but these things happen from time to time. The Somme…sometimes it can't be helped."

Harry tried to swallow but his swollen tongue stuck to the roof of his parched mouth. A dribble of saliva ran down his chin. "You and I came over with the first of the Expeditionary force," he said slowly, and with difficulty. "We're the only officers left. And Merryweather, if he's still alive."

"We check the hospital admissions as a matter of routine," the voice of the RAMC major interrupted. "If anyone turns up, we'll let you know."

"I don't know how many of our original complement are still with us," Harry said. "It can't be many."

Shackleton scratched his chin. "I can't think it can be more than a handful. We should thank our lucky stars we're still here to ask the question."

"We should never turn our backs on luck, Sir, no matter how fine the leadership is. Sometimes luck's the only thing that separates the quick from the dead."

Shackleton paused, his chin resting in his hand. "We're transferring you to a more substantial hospital as soon as your wounds permit," he said. "Should be in a day or two. Boulogne, I expect. Then we'll see about getting you back to a real hospital in England, get you up and walking properly again. You'll be as right as rain in no time."

"I expect so, Sir." Harry glanced around and took in the rows of beds and the heavy canvas sides of the hospital tent. Nurses bustled around. He smelled ether and antiseptics, and the sickening stench of rotting flesh, of gangrene. "The accommodation here is close to the standards of the Savoy or the Dorchester, especially after the trenches. Where exactly are we, Sir?"

"We're in the grounds of Château Gran'ville."

"I wondered as much." There was no getting away from Ste-Marguerite. "And Brigade HQ?"

"In the château. Most pleasant accommodation all round. I would give you a guided tour when you are up to it, but you undoubtedly know the château blindfold. Anything else before I leave?"

"About informing my wife, Sir?"

"Already done. Telegram sent. Wounded in action. Expected to make a full recovery. How's that?"

"I'm sure it will allay her fears."

"I'll write to her as well." Shackleton lowered his voice. "Another thing, Harry. Your squadron corporal major? Good man, is he?"

"Utterly reliable. One of the best ever to have served with us. I can't speak too highly of him."

"Not prone to exaggeration, is he? Flights of fantasy, that sort of thing?"

"Not him. A man largely devoid of imagination or humour. A Boer War veteran. Came over with us in nineteen fourteen and he's been with us ever since. Always in the thick of things and never so much as a scratch."

"Good, good. I wanted to make sure his report was full, complete and accurate. Intelligence needs assessments without embellishment. I've asked for written reports from your other senior NCOs as well. They're never happy higher up the ladder without paperwork. I've also put you up for a bar to your DSO for your leadership under fire."

"Thank you, Sir. You'll have my report before I leave."

"Anything else?"

"No, Sir. Well, yes, there is something else. My batman, Trooper Trevelyan. Did he make it back? He was wounded during the attack."

"I don't know. Trevelyan, you say? I'll ask around."

"One other thing, Sir."

"Yes?"

"Is it still raining?"

# 25. THE ABBEY

The letter from Shackleton arrived at *Roseland* by the first post on a rainy Thursday morning. Athena recognized the buff, army envelope in which Harry's letters always arrived, but not the handwriting on the front. Puzzled, she took the envelope to the morning room before opening it. Her face turned ashen as she read the words. She staggered backwards and found the arms of a chair. She sank into it, breathing heavily. With the uncanny knack of prescience that is the hallmark of the perfect butler, Tregarrick arrived at the door and knocked.

She held the letter up. "He's been wounded. Why didn't they send a telegram, Tregarrick?" she sobbed. "At least he's alive! Nothing else matters. He's alive. Maybe he'll come home for good this time."

She collected herself. "I must share the news with the countess."

A terrified-looking maid bobbed and curtsied before she handed a telegram to the butler without raising her eyes from the floor.

"Steady as you go, Jesse," Tregarrick scolded. He turned to Athena. "A telegram, Madam."

Athena tore open the envelope and read the brief message. "It's from the army hospital in Midhurst," she said in a hoarse voice. "An update on my husband's condition." She burst into tears and crumpled the sheet of paper in her fist.

"Have the telegram man wait for the time being, Tregarrick. Perhaps Mrs. Tregarrick might offer him a cup of tea. We shall need to send a telegram reply shortly." She took the letter and the telegram into the drawing room.

"I've received these," she said to her mother-in-law and passed her the letter and the telegram. "He's in Midhurst, wherever that is. And it doesn't look good."

"It's in Sussex, south of London," the countess said. "You'll have to go and see him right away. I'll come with you. A lady doesn't travel alone."

"Honestly, Mother, there's no need."

"He's my son. I should see him. You can stay at the London house in Belgrave Square. You can take the train every day to Midhurst."

Athena turned white. "I wouldn't want to bother the admiral. I'll go straight to Midhurst and stay in a hotel."

"I'm sure my husband won't mind if we stay with him," the countess said.

"I wouldn't think of it. I want to be by Harry's side, day and night if necessary. But I'll be glad of the company on the journey if you still want to come. And you could stay with me in Midhurst if London proves too fatiguing."

The countess looked hard at Athena, then shrugged. "I shall stay at Belgrave Square. The food will probably be better than at a country hotel."

*

"He looks terrible," Athena said as soon as her mother-in-law came to the phone in the Belgrave Square house. "He's black and blue where you can see what bits of him aren't still covered by bandages." A catch in her voice threatened to undermine her resolve to be detached, like a newspaper reporter.

"Otherwise, how is he?"

"Not good." She paused. "I'm calling from the only telephone in the hotel. It's in the lobby and there's absolutely no privacy. I don't like to talk in front of the staff or the other guests." She paused again, for longer this time. "The doctors say he's had a relapse. He's barely conscious." She sniffed loudly. "I don't think I can hold it in much longer."

"Do come back up to London."

"I can't."

"Why not?"

"It's the admiral."

"What about him?"

"He and I don't get along."

"I'm hardly surprised. As I'm sure you have already suspected, none of us gets on with him, except perhaps for Ernest. Between the two of us, I'm only too glad to see the back of him every time he returns to London."

"It's worse than that. I think he regards me as—"

"Let me guess. An actress? He's used that word before. I think sometimes he regards me as one, though I've given him no reason since we married."

"That and worse. An American. A foreigner. I think in his eyes all foreign women lack basic morals." She crossed her fingers. In truth she had acted no better with Des than an actress. "I think he quite dislikes me especially."

"Why?"

"We had a showdown last time I was here. Raised voices. A frank exchange of views. I wouldn't back down. As far as the admiral's concerned, I'm persona non grata in Belgrave Square, and I'm not welcome at *Roseland* either, but at least I can still stay there. It's Harry's home after all and I can make myself scarce when the admiral is down. I expect Harry and I will have to move up to London after the war, if not before."

"Worse than I imagined. But my husband's not here at the moment. He'd never know if you stayed a night."

"Hobbes or Barclay or Mrs. Hume would be duty bound to tell him."

The countess sighed. "You may be right. Go on about Harry."

Athena hesitated. "Frail. He looks frail, haunted, as if he's lost the will to go on," she sobbed.

"He'll get better. I know he will. Harry's tough. He's the bravest man I know."

Athena's voice cracked. "He hardly recognized me. I held his hand, but he didn't hold mine. It simply lay there. It's as if he's no longer human inside."

"Give him time to heal. Then he'll be back to his usual form, you'll see. He needs to be home, with you and with family, not in a hospital."

At the other of the line Athena composed herself. "Thank you for your kindness. Seeing him today it's hard to imagine what he was like immediately after it happened." She dabbed at her nose with a handkerchief and took a deep breath. "I'll return to *Roseland* on Sunday and pack for a longer stay. I'll come back to Midhurst on Monday or Tuesday." She paused. "I know what you're thinking. I'll travel on my own. I know. More like an actress than a lady, but it can't be helped. Besides, I'm a foreigner, an American. We do things differently, don't we?"

"I admit even I have come to terms with the changing times. One day no one will think twice about travelling alone. And even drive a motor car like Cecilia, though I don't think I'd like to." She paused. "I'll come down tomorrow, just for the day. Then I'll return to *Roseland* with you on Sunday. If you don't mind, of course."

"I hope Harry will be up to seeing you by then, Mother."

*

On Tuesday evening Athena returned to the hotel in Midhurst after seeing Harry briefly in the hospital. "I'll do whatever you need," she promised her barely conscious husband, "until the officer-in-charge here says you're fit enough to travel home. And I'll be here with you every day."

Night after miserable night she lay half-asleep while she tossed and turned in her uncomfortable single hotel room bed. She longed for Harry to be beside her, to hold her and to comfort her. And more than anything else, to promise he would never return to Flanders.

In the early days she sat with him by his bedside with his cold hand in hers while he lay motionless beneath a red blanket in a white painted, iron-framed hospital cot. His dreary room had only a single, sealed window, a folding screen and a wash basin. This, she thought, was all a colonel was entitled to. At least he had privacy of a sort to go with his catheter and bedpan. She shuddered to think what a lower ranked officer's room was like.

As the days passed Harry was able to sit up, propped against his pillows. A week later later, with Athena's help, he managed the two steps from his bed to the armchair in the corner of his small room. Athena sat with him on an uncomfortable, straight backed chair, holding his hand in silence, as if the effort of moving had left him too exhausted to speak. Once the doctors deemed him strong enough, Athena wheeled his huddled form, swaddled like a newborn and slumped in a bath chair, along the hospital's gravel paths. "From my first day in Flanders till the last it always seemed to be raining," he commented, once. "I'm sure it didn't, but it's hard to remember a sunny day there."

The bandages came off his body one by one. His face, unscarred by the battle, remained hollow-cheeked, lined and grey. Athena had to admit she hardly recognized Harry as the man she'd married little more than a year ago, before he became the man she pushed daily around the hospital grounds in Sussex.

On Sunday evening a month after she first arrived at the hospital, the colonel in charge declared that Harry was as fit as he would ever be under their care and could be discharged in the morning. Athena phoned Belgrave Square and received the news that the earl was not in residence and not expected back for several days. With Harry tucked up in his hospital bed Athena returned to London for the chance of a decent night's sleep. Too bad if the earl found out, she thought. "Bugger him, as Harry would say," she muttered as she boarded her train to Victoria Station, and immediately covered her mouth. The worst he could do would be to tell Harry, and her secret would be out in the open. She had come close to changing her mind and stayed down at Midhurst, but there was one more thing she had to do, something that she could only do alone. She needed to give thanks for Harry's return to her, and that she would do in London, at Westminster Abbey.

*

The Belgrave Square morning room overlooked a small park bordered by leafless trees and shrub beds. Through the window Athena watched the Rolls-Royce draw up in front of the house. An impossibly young footman staggered out of the front door with her suitcases and loaded them onto the rear of the motor car. He wrapped the cases in a tarpaulin and strapped them to the rack. Athena turned her back on the window and bade goodbye to the staff who had gathered to see her off. "Stay in the hall, Mrs. Hume," she said. "There's no need to go out in this drizzle." The footman held a large black umbrella over her head as she crossed the wet pavement. She thanked the footman for holding the passenger door open, then climbed into the car. When she was seated comfortably, she leaned forward and knocked on the glass partition to gain the chauffeur's attention.

Her mind went blank for a second. What was his name? Heath? Yes, that was it. "Heath?"

"Yes, Madam." He touched the peak of his hat and turned to look over his shoulder.

"The Abbey, Heath."

A few minutes later the car stopped near the great west door of Westminster Abbey. "Wait for me," Athena said. "I shall be about an hour." The drizzle ceased, the clouds parted and the sun broke through, casting a thin, late autumn light over Westminster. She hung back for a moment, watching the sparse crowd move slowly about the Abbey precinct before she gathered herself and joined them. She passed through the heavy wooden portal, hundreds of years old, and entered the Abbey, conscious of her insignificance and intimidated by the building's size and magnificence. She made her way a few steps up the nave of the greatest religious building in England. She stopped, slipped into a pew and took her place among the sombre, grey-faced islands of humanity dotted singly, in small clusters, or strung out like archipelagos throughout the body of the church.

Perched on one of the string-seated, straight-backed chairs with her hands clasped in front of her, uncomfortably aware of the constriction of her corset against her ribs, she gazed upward in awe. High above her head threadbare flags and tattered banners marched the length of the nave. Each torn, proud battle honour marked a victory or a defeat dating back through eight centuries, to the time of the Abbey's consecration. A tear clouded her eyes as her sight rested on the faded and ragged banner of the King's Imperial Hussars. She wondered how many had given their lives over the centuries defending its honour. And how many more would follow before the insane slaughter ceased, before the swords of Isaiah could be beaten once more into ploughshares?

She turned her head to take in the tombs of monarchs and martyrs, poets and playwrights, philosophers, prelates and politicians whose mortal remains lay enshrined in Westminster. Some, she noticed, were memorialized grandly in white marble or polished pink or black granite. Others lay beneath unpretentious flagstones on the floors of the nave, apse and transept, their worn inscriptions now barely legible after countless feet had scuffed over them down the centuries.

In the half-light of side chapels, the lives and deeds of other ghosts lived on, remembered in modest wall plaques hidden by choice or by happenstance from the light of magnificence cast by the stained-glass windows. Equal in death, side by side lay the bones of royalty and commoners, heroes, rogues and churchmen whose lives and legends were but a few threads in perhaps the richest tapestry the world had ever known.

Soft, thousand-year old plainsong and the faint shuffling of feet broke through the hollow, echoing quiet as the choir took its place in their stalls for the morning service. A pale, early December sunlight flooding through panes of plain glass high above massive stone pillars cast a checkerboard of light and shadow on floors and walls, yet failed to illuminate the deepest nooks of private, intimate lady chapels. Separated from the main body of worshipers by black, wrought iron railings and screens, the scent of beeswax candles wafted through the grillwork from the dark recess of the nearest side chapel. Athena glimpsed black-cloaked, black-veiled women praying for husbands or sons, brothers or lovers who would never return home. With this realization came a rapier thrust of guilt. Capricious fate had spared Harry while others, his brother officers and men, were less fortunate. They would never see England again. Many, she knew, would lie forever in the mud of Flanders, unidentified, unclaimed and unburied.

A single shaft of dusty sunlight slanted across the nave and fell upon the cross of St. George, narrow red on a white field, the flag of England. Next to it, with the cross of St. George forming the greatest part, hung the white ensign of the Royal Navy, the senior service dating back unbroken a thousand years to the Saxon king of England, Alfred. Beyond those two flags, and slightly above them, hung the red, white and blue crosses of the Union Jack, the flag of Great Britain and of all the countries, great and small, which comprised the British Empire.

Athena strained to hear the muted voices of the choir that drifted high into the intricate fan vaulting. She recognized the words of a psalm. As it washed over her, echoing off the stone walls, it calmed her bruised spirit. With each intake of breath, she absorbed the dust motes of centuries, the treasure hoard of English history and heritage that lay everywhere around her in the Abbey. This, she understood intuitively, was what the great Abbey church of Westminster meant to Englishmen. This was, above all else, an English church, the home of all Englishmen, of every estate, of Englishmen like her husband. Harry's words returned to her: *High or low, we are all England's pawns.* Her lips moved with the unspoken words, *No, Harry. You will never be anyone's pawn.*

In that hour of tranquil contemplation, a distant glow, an aura that came before the dawn of understanding, rose over the rim of darkness to reveal a side of Harry until then hidden from her. She sensed a veil lift from her eyes. She came to see more clearly that, for Harry, to serve England was not a burden nor an obligation of the nobility into which she married. Service was a privilege, an honour conferred on those who, without the need for fanfares or declarations of patriotism, truly loved England no less than she loved America. The surge of emotion that flooded through her brought tears to her eyes. In part to hide her lack of English self-control she knelt. With her handkerchief balled in her gloved hand, she whispered her thanks for her husband's deliverance, then recited The Lord's Prayer and the 23rd Psalm.

Comforted by the time-worn cadences of those ancient words, she rose from her knees, the allotted hour of solitude at a close. Humbled, and with eyes downcast, she left the Abbey through the same west door by which she had entered. As she made her way down the path, the clouds closed above her and with a chill gust of wind a light rain slicked the pavement.

"The Hospital for Officers in Midhurst, Heath," she said, once seated comfortably in the back of the Rolls. With her mind now clear and focused she remembered the chauffeur's name without difficulty. Heath engaged gear and with scarcely a sound eased the Rolls into the traffic.

She sat back as a gloom to match the weather enfolded her. After Christmas at *Roseland*, what did the future hold? In the New Year, she knew she would have to face the sight of Harry's back as he descended the steps to the waiting Daimler. Then, with a wave and a slight, reassuring smile he would raise his swagger stick in acknowledgement, and return to Flanders, to the killing fields, to the savagery and the butchery. Then she would settle down to the routine of *Roseland* while she steeled herself for the arrival of the telegram. She prayed nightly that the dreaded summons to join the grieving ranks of the veiled women in black in one of Westminster Abbey's lady chapels would never come.

An hour and a half later Athena came face to face with Harry's gaunt, haggard figure. He gripped in his trembling hands, not the shooting stick he took with him to the front in the spring, but hospital crutches. He paced constantly, one step forward, one step back without seeming to realize what he was doing. She wondered if his physical wounds caused this unrest. Or was he afraid she would see him, a man not whole, a man still scarcely able to feed and clean himself? And how would she react to a man startled by every slightest noise and unexplained shadow; a man in shell shock?

She held him fully in her embrace for the first time in what seemed like a lifetime, her arms wrapped around the boney body beneath his uniform. His body trembled slightly. He stiffened and tried to disengage himself from her arms, but she refused to release him.

In her arms she held her husband, but the man who held her in return without passion was unrecognizable, for now at least, perhaps forever, as the man she had said goodbye to in February. But she refused to allow sadness at his plight overwhelm her. She knew the physical wounds would heal in time, and the scars eventually fade, but the man into whose dull, expressionless eyes she gazed hardly recognized her today, little better than he had on her first visit to the hospital.

And when she looked into those eyes, she knew Harry might never speak about what had happened. He might decide to keep the truth and the details of the grim place they called Passchendaele locked inside him forever. If it was what he wanted, she promised she would spare him the torture of reliving it.

"I've come to take you home, Harry," she said softly, and touched his cheek with a light kiss.

"Home? What day is it?'

"It's Monday, Harry."

"Which month?"

"December. December third." With relief she saw a flicker of a smile cross his face. She linked her arm through his. "We're going home for Christmas."

# 26. POPPIES AND BIRDSONG

As December wore on, Athena soothed and comforted Harry during his sweat-soaked nightmares. She helped him dress and undress and bathe. On days when the weather was dry and mild enough to allow slow, short walks, she accompanied him around the grounds of *Roseland*, muffled in greatcoat and scarf. Demelza plodded contentedly at his heel.

"You've no idea how morbid hospitals are," he said, during one morning walk. "And how restorative home is." Athena could scarcely contain her glee at this first positive acknowledgement that he recognized and appreciated his surroundings. "I was dying. I'd given up hope. In my more lucid moments at Midhurst I knew I was slipping away, and I didn't care. I had come to terms with my death. I was in no physical pain. I suspect they had me pumped full of morphine. I think they recognized the truth and allowed me to die on my own terms and in my own time."

Harry stopped and took in the broad, dark leafed rhododendrons and spindly azaleas at the back of the flower borders. The gardeners had dug out the tender dahlia bulbs and trimmed the flowering shrubs, cut back the rose canes and turned over the soil for the winter. He returned his attention to Athena. "I had no fight left," he said in a hoarse voice barely above whisper. "One time, I saw Flanders, the trenches, the battlefields, the churned-up mud, running red with blood. It looked for all the world like endless fields of poppies in May. I heard a noise above the sounds of guns. For a moment I didn't know what it was. Then I recognized it as birdsong, though no birds sang or flew over the battlefields. I found the source of the sound, a speck, rising, always rising in endless circles above the destruction. It was a lark singing as it flew, ascending above the chaos left by man and machine in search of a calm, peaceful place. I saw myself as that lark, high above the earth, looking down, and wondered if it was my soul leaving my body. A hand touched mine. I smelled your perfume and I knew whose hand held mine though I couldn't see it. I knew then I was still alive. I turned the corner that day. I opened my eyes and saw your face. I saw you gaze at me for the first time in months, and I wanted to live. Your touch gave me renewed hope. I wanted more than anything on this earth to spend the rest of my life with you, to grow old together." He coughed and choked back a catch in his throat. "I want to thank you for giving my life back to me."

Athena took him gently and, with tears in her eyes, held him to her.

"When I saw you that day in Midhurst, I knew you were close to death. When I held your hand that morning, I prayed you would somehow pull through and that one day I would reclaim my husband, even if he was no longer exactly the man I married, but pretty darn close." She stood on tiptoe and pecked him on the cheek. "You can have a rain check on the kiss and a proper hug when you're up to it."

Harry walked a little further and for a little longer each outing with Athena and Demelza always at his side. A week before Christmas he abandoned his crutches for a walking stick that replaced his shooting stick, a casualty of war left behind in that grim place called Passchendaele. His muscles recovered some of their strength though there was still work to do to accommodate his new stride. His limp became less noticeable. His face gradually regained its colour and his cheeks filled out. A smile found his lips.

*

The morning post on the Friday before Christmas brought a letter for Harry, a sturdy, official-looking envelope postmarked Whitehall, London W1. He regarded the envelope with grave misgivings and set it aside. The envelope remained unopened on the tablecloth while he demolished his buttered kippers and spread his toast with marmalade. He rose from the table and poured himself a second cup of coffee from the pot on the sideboard.

By now Athena could bear the suspense no longer. "Aren't you going to open it, Harry?"

Harry swallowed his slice of toast and dark, bittersweet marmalade. He turned to face her. "It can wait until after breakfast. He pointed to the marmalade jar. "We don't get this in France. I want to savour every morsel while I can, undisturbed by the War Ministry." He took another bite and closed his eyes. He was teasing her and they both knew it. She grabbed the envelope before he could stop her and picked up a knife covered in butter, marmalade and toast crumbs. She held the knife close to the top corner, poised to open it, her turn to tease him.

"*Pax nobiscum?*" he said.

Athena looked puzzled. "Does that mean truce?"

Harry nodded and tackled another slice of toast. She handed the envelope to him.

"Mmm." Harry kept his hand over the envelope until he swallowed. "Perhaps you could pass me a clean knife."

He slit open the envelope and glanced briefly at the content. Then, slumped in his chair, he reread the letter carefully. He put the letter down on the tablecloth and closed his eyes. Athena saw his hands tremble slightly, the same tremble she often noticed when he was tense and which he always tried to hide. Harry pushed the single sheet of neatly folded bond paper over to her. Hesitantly and fearfully, she picked it up and scanned the lines briefly.

*"Dear General Haig-Mallory,"* she read aloud, as if doing so would give the

words a truthfulness she could not believe.

*"I am commanded by His Majesty, King George V, to inform you that he has condescended to award you the Victoria Cross for your gallant action during the attack at Passchendaele on August 25th of this year, and subsequently in holding the position which you had gained despite being gravely wounded. His Majesty further commands me to inform you that he has condescended to award you a bar to your Distinguished Service Order in recognition of your dedicated and outstanding leadership during the Passchendaele campaign in August of this year, culminating in the attack on the 25th.*

*His Majesty commands that I inform you that you will be invested with these awards personally by His Majesty at a ceremony at Buckingham Palace on Tuesday, March 19th next at 11:00 in the forenoon.*

*I am further commanded to inform you that, on orders from Field Marshal, The Viscount French, you are by this present informed that your promotion to the substantive rank of Colonel has been published in the Gazette, such promotion effective August 25th of this year.*

*Upon your return to active duty you will assume the duties of Officer Commanding, His Majesty's 16th Cavalry Brigade , Ypres, as Brigadier General. Your promotion to the rank of Brigadier General is effective as of the date of this letter. Such notice will appear in the Gazette forthwith.*

*I am commanded by His Majesty and Field Marshal, The Viscount French, to offer their congratulations.*

*I remain, Sir,*

*Your obedient and respectful servant, etc.*

"The letter's signed by the Principal Secretary to the Minister of War. Does it mean what I think it means? You're now a brigadier?" Tears welled up in Athena's eyes and she could no longer hold them back. Harry stood and wrapped an arm around her. He held her tight against him as her shoulders shuddered and heaved and he stroked her thick hair until she calmed and her sobs subsided.

"I don't know whether to be happy for you, or what." Athena looked up at her husband, her face powder streaked with tears. "Why do you have to go back? Haven't you done enough already? You've been over there virtually ever since the first day of the war. How much more can they ask of you? Of any man?"

"I have to go back." Although he had tried to sound reasonable and conciliatory, it came out sounding grumpy. "It's not over. I can't shirk my responsibilities."

"Can't let the side down, you mean?" Athena snorted, with anger and frustration fighting for the upper hand as she pushed him away. "Harry, you're not a schoolboy and it's not a game of rugby at Marlborough School, followed by a hot shower and tea with the opposition, all jolly good chaps really and we must play you again next year."

"You're an American," he said, sounding exasperated. He wiped his lips and placed his table napkin on the cloth. "You can't understand what it means to be English, or the obligations in turn England places on an officer and a gentleman."

Tears glistened in Athena's eyes. "I most certainly do know!" she snapped. "And I object to your suggestion that I'm only an American so I can't possibly understand what it is to be patriotic. Or loyal. Next you'll say I'm only a woman. And, do you know something? I seriously question your sanity, and at times I wonder why I ever agreed to marry you."

Harry's mouth gaped.

"And there's no need to look like a fish. It shouldn't come as a surprise. You're not the man I met in Washington. Not anymore. And I'm not the woman who couldn't resist your English charms. The war has changed both of us. We're going to have to adjust to being married to someone we neither of us knows as well as we once thought. We're going to have to fall in love all over again, if we can, or our marriage will be a sham."

Harry heard the blood hiss in his ear. He was certain his cheeks smouldered. He couldn't decide whether Athena had somehow discovered his affair with Solange, or if it was a shot in the dark. Or something less sinister. "I… I don't know what to say. I can't change what I do. For the future of England, of Europe and the Empire we must win this war. Until then I will continue to do my duty as I swore when I received my commission. I won't let England down, or the men who serve under me. And least of all will I let you down." He patted her back. "It's what I do. It's who I am, and if that's not enough…"

Athena clung to him fiercely. "I just wish you weren't so stupidly, impossibly brave, but I love you all the more for it."

"I've lived with fear since the day war broke out, my own and the collective fear of my men. Being afraid of dying on the battlefield is something we all confront daily. Only the insane don't fear death. But I'm most afraid that one day, when I can't help it, I'll give in to my fear and do something shameful."

"Oh, Harry. You won't. But can't you persuade the Germans to leave you alone?"

He grinned. "I'll suggest it next time I see them."

"You see? You're making light of it again." She looked away. "I hope there won't be a next time." Athena stood on tiptoe and kissed him. "You told me colonels don't go over the top, but you did. In a minute you'll tell me brigadiers don't go over the top either, and this time I shan't believe you. And I'll question everything you say, wondering if you're lying to me to spare my feelings or to stop me from worrying. Or to keep secrets from me. I don't ever want that to happen." She pushed him away and held him at arm's length. "I'll always worry about you. But look at you. You keep coming home shot full of holes, bloody, bandaged and barely able to stand. What am I supposed to make of you? I didn't ask to be married to a hero. All I want is my husband back, safe and sound, in one piece so we can have a family of our own. You can't even promise me that."

"As far as I know, everything still works the way it's supposed to in the owner's manual. I'm just waiting for a chance to prove it." He turned serious. "I won't let our marriage come apart. I married you because I loved you. I still do, more deeply and completely than I can say. The war won't change that. But you're right. Three years has changed us, in ways we never thought possible, but not so much that we can't fall in love again. And differently. I'd rather like that, if you'll let me."

She buried her head in his chest. Her body gradually relaxed before she let go of him with a playful shove.

"I still love your perfume," he said quietly. "I imagined you would have run out of it by now."

"I've had no reason to wear it while you were away so I still have lots left." She took his hand. "Come on, we have news to share." The smile returned to her face. She wiped the tear streaks in her face powder with her table napkin and dusted her cheeks with a new layer from her compact. "There, that's a bit better. We can finish our coffee in the morning room. Look, the sun's come out."

Athena put her arm through Harry's and led them out of the dining room. His stepmother looked up as they entered the morning room. She put down her coffee cup as Athena handed her the letter. She read in silence before the tears trickled down her cheeks. She placed the letter next to her cup and saucer.

"I don't know what to say, Harry," she said once she regained her composure. "At least you are safe, for the present, and I thank God from the bottom of my heart." She smiled at Harry, then her face clouded. "I wish I had news from the staff. I have heard nothing from any of those who have gone off to serve, but then I didn't suppose I ever would. It is not as if I were their mother or wife or anything. Still, it would be encouraging to hear how they are faring."

Harry cleared his throat. "I only know of Trevelyan. He was with me during the last attack in August. He was badly wounded." The images returned, unbidden as always. He fiddled with his fingers then laced them as he glanced anxiously from his stepmother to Athena. He thrust his hands into his pockets, but he could not hide the unease in his voice.

He took a deep breath. "We got him back to a field hospital and I've received no news of him since. I don't know what happened to him. I wasn't in a fit state to start making enquiries. I'll attend to that as soon as Christmas is over." He offered a weak smile. "Trevelyan mentioned to me when he enlisted he'd ask for you to be notified as next-of-kin in case he was killed. If nothing has arrived from the War Ministry, then perhaps we should regard it as no news is good news."

His stepmother took the news in silence. She looked up at Harry and gave him a small, thin smile before she glanced at the letter from the Ministry sitting on the side table. She handed it back to Harry without a word.

"As your stepmother I insist on taking my place ahead of His Majesty and Field Marshal French when I offer my congratulations on both your medals and your two promotions." She rose and kissed him on the cheek. "Stay safe this time, will you? I don't want you anywhere near the front again."

She turned to Athena. "You must be very proud of him, my dear. I know I am." She put her arm around Athena's shoulder. "He is still my little boy. He always will be. I will always only be his stepmother, but I love him as if he was of my own flesh and blood. I think you are very lucky to have him as your husband, but then I am highly biased, so please forgive me if I let my prejudice slip occasionally." She gave Athena a light kiss on the cheek.

"I definitely got the better half of the bargain, Mother," Harry said. "All Athena got was a beaten-up soldier with a body full of scars. I'll probably be crippled with rheumatism before I'm fifty. Mark my words, this is the last time the Hun is going to use me for target practice. Brigadiers definitely do not go over the top, no matter how much they may want to lead from the front. Please believe me when I say I promise not to break with tradition."

*

The rain that started after breakfast the next morning set in for the day. Under a black umbrella in front of the Truro Cathedral Deanery, Rhodes held the car door open for Athena and the countess. "I don't know why the Bishop continues to invite me to his annual Christmas luncheon, Rhodes," the countess said. "He knows I am Catholic."

"Perhaps it's because you represent the family, My Lady, rather than any desire on his part to open doors to conversion."

"You are probably right," she said, heading off any debate on the merits of either religion. "Still, I have done my duty for another year, as have you, my dear."

"My family's Episcopalian," Athena said, "which isn't much different from the Church of England, except, for obvious historical reasons, prayers for the Royal Family."

The countess knocked on the glass partition. "Home, Rhodes. If you step on it you can be back here in time to pick up His Lordship and the family at the station."

Athena and the countess pulled their fur coats closer around their shoulders as Rhodes merged the Daimler into the sparse traffic.

"You'd think they'd put a heater in the car," Athena grumbled. "There's one in my father's car. It keeps us as warm as toast in a Cleveland winter."

"I won't suggest the British are made of sterner stuff, my dear, because I don't suppose for an instant they are. But I believe there's a heater in the Rolls in London, although that doesn't help us today."

They drove in silence east through Truro, crossed the narrow estuary at Tresillian and took the St. Mawes road towards St. Just. As they approached Trewithian Athena glimpsed a figure in khaki trudging up the incline ahead. He carried a canvas kitbag slung over one shoulder and seemed bent as he huddled beneath a greatcoat. Rhodes slowed and pulled out to pass the man.

"Stop the motor, Rhodes," Athena said as they drew alongside the soldier. "Let's at least find out where he is going in this weather. He must be soaked through and half frozen." The soldier turned to face the car as it passed and rolled to a stop a short distance ahead of him. Athena stared at the soldier's face a few steps away.

Before Rhodes could open the door, Athena stepped out of the car. "Trevelyan? Surely it can't be you!"

"It is, Madam."

"I am so glad to see you're still alive. We've heard nothing since you enlisted. Have you walked all this way from Truro station?"

"Yes, Madam."

"That's a long way."

"Only a short route march by Hussars' standards."

"May we offer you a lift to *Roseland*? We are on our way there."

"It's very kind of you, Madam. If it would not be too much trouble. I was on my way to see the Colonel, if he's at home."

"He's a brigadier now. We received the news yesterday."

Rhodes came around the side of the car and took Trevelyan's kitbag.

"Put it beside you, Rhodes, if you would. Mr. Trevelyan will ride in the back with the countess and me. I'm sure we have a great deal to catch up on."

Rhodes' eyebrow twitched fractionally. The countess scowled and turned her attention to Trevelyan. "No point in standing around in the rain, is there?"

Athena eased herself back into the car and sat in the middle seat. Trevelyan climbed in and sat next to her in the corner. The smell of wet wool from his army greatcoat permeated the interior of the Daimler. She took a deep breath and decided she rather liked the masculine odour that blended so well with the polished leather. And, she thought, not at all like the smell of Demelza's fur when she was wet and stank out the drawing room while she dried herself in front of the fire.

Rhodes closed the door and took his place behind the steering wheel. As the Daimler eased away from the side of the road Athena turned to Trevelyan. "I heard you were wounded, Trevelyan. Have you been discharged from the army? Or do you have to report back shortly?"

"That's what I wanted to see the brigadier about, Madam. I've been discharged on medical grounds, but if the brigadier needs my services again, I'm prepared to reenlist."

"I'm sure you have done more than your fair share," the countess said. "You have earned the right to spend the rest of the war recovering fully from your wounds."

Trevelyan opened his mouth to respond. The countess gave him a stern look. "You are not a professional soldier, unlike my son. It is his obligation to return to active duty as soon as he has recovered."

"And as a brigadier now," Athena added, "he assures me he won't see any more front-line action. Which was what he also said when he was promoted to colonel. Still, if you're determined to return, I am sure he won't stand in your way."

"I'll see what the brigadier has to say, Madam."

They turned away from each other to stare out of the window. "I've missed this," Trevelyan said, pointing at the leafless oaks, elms and beeches that towered above the hazels in the copses. "There's nothing like this left in Flanders."

"I'm from Lausanne," the countess said. "Even though I am Swiss, and I miss the mountains sometimes, there is nowhere like Cornwall."

"And it's quite different from Ohio," Athena said. "And I miss it sometimes."

An awkward silence descended for several minutes before the countess turned to Trevelyan. "You left without a word of warning, Trevelyan. I confess I was more than a little upset you did not think to inform us of your intentions. Or Mr. Tregarrick. It rather left us in the lurch."

Athena glanced sideways at the bedraggled, hunched-shouldered man. She fancied she saw a spot of colour on his cheek. Perhaps her mother-in-law had embarrassed him. But the rebuke, she decided, if such was how he took it, had evidently struck a nerve.

Trevelyan clasped his hands in his lap. "I'm a simple man, My Lady." His voice was scarcely audible above the crunch of the tyres on the gravel road. "I did what I believed I had to, without making a fuss about it."

The countess leaned across Athena and touched his fist for a second, then patted it. "I am sorry if I sounded harsh. I did not mean to." She replaced her hand in her lap and cleared her throat. "I do hope you will consider staying at *Roseland* rather than go back into the army. We will all draw great strength from your heroism."

"I don't like to leave the brigadier without his orderly, My Lady."

"I shall speak to my son as soon as we arrive."

"And I will do whatever he asks of me."

The car pulled up outside the front door of *Roseland*. Rhodes got out quickly and held an umbrella over Athena and the countess's heads. Trevelyan picked up his kitbag headed towards the rear entrance of the house.

"If what my husband says is only half true, I'm sure your old room will be warmer and dryer than Flanders" Athena said. "And it is reassuring to see you back again." She smiled and turned toward the steps to the front door and did not see his salute.

"And indeed, it is good to see you back again, Mr. Trevelyan," Rhodes said. "I'm sure we all hope you'll be staying with us for a long time."

"As I do. If you'll excuse me, Mr. Rhodes, right now I have to see Mr. Tregarrick and arrange for a billet for the night, then I have to see the brigadier."

"You will never guess what," the countess gushed, as she burst unceremoniously into the drawing room. "Trevelyan's back."

Harry looked up from his newspaper at his wife and mother, still in their fur coats. "Really? Is that true, Athena? That's better news than I could ever have wished for."

"We gave him a ride home in the car," Athena said. "He was soaked through, poor man."

"He wants to speak to you about reenlisting and going back to France with you as your orderly," the countess said. "I thought I should tell you so you won't be surprised when he asks."

"Did he tell you if he has a medical discharge, Mother?"

"Yes. He has."

"Then I suspect he's out of it for good." Harry looked hard at Athena, as if daring her to contradict him. "The army will do anything to avoid a medical discharge."

"So I've heard," Athena said pointedly, returning Harry's look with one of her own.

Harry cleared his throat. "I doubt very much if they will take him back. The least we can do is offer him his old job back."

Tregarrick padded soundlessly into the drawing room and coughed deferentially.

"Begging your pardon, General,"

"What is it, Tregarrick?"

"Trevelyan has returned to *Roseland*. He is in the servants' hall enjoying a cup of tea and a slice of Mrs. Tregarrick's Victoria sponge cake."

"So I have just this moment heard. I would not wish to interrupt his first decent cup of tea in a long while, or his enjoyment of Mrs. Tregarrick's fine cake. But please pass the word that, when he has finished and has a moment, I should like to see him."

"Very good, Sir. I shall send for him." The butler bowed slightly and left as silently as a cat.

A few minutes later a knock of the drawing room door announced the presence of Trevelyan and the butler. Harry rose with extended hand.

"Trevelyan. Welcome back. My wife told me she and the countess stopped to pick up a half-drowned otter. Was that you?"

"It must be, Sir."

"Well, I'm delighted to see you're still in one piece."

"Not half as pleased as I am to breathe good Cornish air, sir. Nip and tuck for a while, they told me in the hospital. And you, Sir?"

"Much the same as before. Nothing vital missing. Back in the saddle shortly. And you with a medical discharge, I hear."

"Only one fully working lung to do the work of two, so I get a bit puffed climbing stairs and the like. The army doesn't want me back."

"I should hope not. You've done more than your bit." Harry looked sheepish. "I put you up for a Good Conduct Medal. I'm sure it would have been more had you not been wounded."

"I have received the medal, Sir." He pointed to the ribbon on his tunic. "Thank you."

Harry turned to the butler. "Tregarrick, have you offered Trevelyan a room here and a roof over his head?"

"Not as yet, General. It is not for me to decide, but his old room is unoccupied and available."

"Good. Have Mrs. Aitchison make up for him. I hope Trevelyan will stay for a long while." He turned to Trevelyan. "You are definitely not going back in the army, Trevelyan, under any circumstance. Mr. Tregarrick needs a dependable first footman. What do you say? First footman again? I know it's my father's prerogative to grant employment at *Roseland*, but he's not here, so I shall have to do in the interim. I'm sure we're short-staffed, right, Tregarrick?"

"Indeed so, Sir."

"I won't be here forever, Trevelyan, but until my overlords need me again, would you consider serving as my valet in addition to first footman? We can discuss compensation privately."

"I'm deeply obliged, Sir." Trevelyan's face was a study in embarrassment. "It will be an honour and a privilege."

"I wouldn't go quite than far. But it is good to have you back on board. Take the rest of today off. You must be tired after your journey."

"Not too tired to serve at table tonight, Sir. If you don't mind, of course."

"Not at all. We still have his livery, don't we, Tregarrick?"

"Indeed, Sir. I expect it will still fit with some minor alterations to accommodate the army diet."

"Good." He turned to Trevelyan. "I shall dress for dinner this evening. Mess kit. Miniature medals. No spurs. Seven o'clock?"

"Seven it is, Sir."

# 27. BITTER CHILL

For the first time since Harry's and Athena's wedding the whole family was together for Christmas Day. Rhodes, with a quick turnaround at *Roseland* made it to Truro station in time to meet Cecilia, Ernest and the earl off the Penzance train. The earl cold-shouldered Athena whenever the two were in the same room together, which was as infrequently as she could arrange. She wondered if Harry noticed his father's brusqueness with her but as Harry didn't mention it, with considerable relief she let it pass. His mind seemed elsewhere so much of the time, preoccupied with God knows what. The mind, she had read, was often the last place to heal, long after the body had recovered. His must still be in tatters, like her nerves. He'd never admit to shell shock, but Athena was certain that was what kept him awake at night. Whatever it was he was keeping from her she wouldn't ask. He would tell her in his own time. If he ever did.

Her mother-in-law noticed, however, and an enquiring look came Athena's way after one brief, and largely one-sided exchange between Athena and the earl while Harry was in the billiards room giving Ernest a lesson in how to play snooker. Athena settled her gaze on her mother-in-law, set her lips in a straight line, but said nothing. What would she do if the earl didn't keep his word and told Harry about her tryst with Shackleton? Or dropped so much as a hint? Come clean. She'd have to. She couldn't lie. She was terrible at it in any case. She wouldn't try and justify what she'd done. That would be futile as well as disingenuous. Repent. And accept the consequences. A return to America acknowledging a failed marriage, if it came to that, would be better for both of them than enduring a loveless one, like her mother-in-law.

After thirty-six hours scarcely daring to breathe and her nerves in shreds, Athena came down to breakfast on Boxing Day, sick with dread. To her relief, breakfast passed in virtual silence without more than an irritated rustle of the Times newspaper from the earl. Harry seemed more distracted than usual. He hadn't slept well that night, tossing and turning in bed, grunting and trying to say things which were unintelligible to her. Ernest was red-eyed, looked decidedly hungover and said little. And Cecilia arrived just as Athena and Harry rose from the table.

With no more than an ill-tempered grunt from the earl whom they both ignored, they took their coffee into the morning room.

"Your father seems out of sorts today," Athena said.

"No more than usual when he's down here, I'd say," Harry said. "He can't stand the place. He'll be merely grumpy by the time he reaches Paddington. I pity whoever has to share the compartment with him." He studied Athena's face. "You look a bit peaky yourself. Everything all right?"

"I'm just a bit tired. I hardly slept. You were restless most of the night." Harry picked up a copy of The Tatler magazine and flipped through the pages. Athena let the matter pass without further comment, relieved that Harry really hadn't noticed his father's gruff manner. In half an hour his father would be gone, back up to London, and she could breathe more easily. If nothing was said or happened in the meantime. Half an hour, that's all. Please, God, get me through this next thirty minutes.

She looked up when, a short while later, the earl and Ernest joined Athena and Harry in the morning room but made a point of sitting as far away from them as possible in the large, airy room. As soon as he finished his coffee the earl pulled his pocket watch from his waistcoat and consulted it. Moments later he called for Tregarrick. "Have Rhodes bring the motor around to the front shortly. I have to catch the 11:00 o'clock to Paddington, and I don't wish to be rushed."

"Very good, My Lord."

"I'm ready to leave as soon as you say the word," Ernest said as he drained the last drop of coffee from his cup and rose from his armchair. "I can drive you, if you like. I'm heading that way."

"Oh? Why?"

"I was planning to take in the start of the hunt at Furlong's place up Kenwyn way."

"And what do you plan to ride, Ernest?"

"Oh, I wasn't going to ride. It's only to be sociable. A stirrup cup or two, lunch if it's on offer and back in the afternoon."

"I take it from your innocent and offhand tone of voice there is a young filly somewhere in this tawdry tale of stirrup cups and box lunches. Furlong's daughter, by any chance?"

"As a matter of fact, pater… How did you guess?"

Harry's and Athena's heads swiveled from the earl to Ernest with each question and answer as if they were watching a tennis rally.

"You are transparent, Ernest. I see through you. I gather that's the reason for the extra close shave this morning and smelling like an Italian barber's shop."

"The cologne is the best there is. Don't you like it?"

"Some people bathe rather than splash themselves with perfume."

"Oh, I bathed too, to be on the safe side. And on firmer footing with the delectable Clarissa. She's a looker all right, but a bit on the haughty side. She needs to be brought to heel." He brayed and slapped his thigh. Demelza gave him an enquiring look before returning to her nap in front of the fire. "She thinks she owns the County and everyone should bow down to her. I mean, her father's only recently been made a Lord. She needs a jolly good spanking, if you ask me. Should do the trick, what?"

"To spank her you would have to catch her, Ernest. You are pudgy and unfit. You couldn't run a hundred yards. And has anyone reminded you lately you are no Rembrandt portrait? Eh? Eh?"

"I know nobody would mistake me for Douglas Fairbanks, but I have my good points."

"Which you can count on the fingers of one hand with several left over."

"I say, steady on, pater. But if you're looking for an heir, I could be your man. Clarissa's blood is blue enough, and I dare say she'll suffice. And if she closes her eyes she won't see my eye patch." He touched his eye patch and chortled. "Or she could imagine me as a swashbuckling pirate king."

"Only in your dreams, Ernest. Still, Harry here's taking his time getting round to fatherhood." He nodded to Harry. "And if anything happens to him, which seems more than likely given his recent history, you're all I have to rely on to keep the earldom alive."

"Point taken. If it can't be the Honourable Clarissa I may have to set my sights a little lower." His father winced. "I'll be back in good time. Unless I strike gold with Clarissa and snag an invitation to stay for tea." His father rolled his eyes.

"I don't think anyone else is planning to use the motor today," Ernest continued, now that he was on a roll and the goal in sight. "I cut a more dashing figure behind the wheel of the Daimler than the Lanchester. It might help press my case. Let me drive, unless you want to."

"If you insist, but I'd be happier if Rhodes drives. I can berth a dreadnaught without a nudge, but I don't know one end of a motor car from the other."

"Ah. I can help there. The steering wheel is near the front, behind the motor, and—"

"The luggage goes aft, Ernest. Sometimes I despair. I hope Clarissa is not too much on the bright side."

Ernest got his way. The family saw them off from the front steps of *Roseland* with the earl in the rear seat of the Daimler and Ernest behind the wheel. With a firm hand the earl slid the glass partition closed as the motor car drew away.

*

Two hours later, a constable arrived on his bicycle at the back door of *Roseland*. On hearing the purpose of the constable's visit, Tregarrick took the barely coherent man to the study.

"What is it, Tregarrick?" Harry said as he appraised the butler and the ashen-faced policeman's face.

"The officer brings news, My Lord, of the worst possible kind." Tregarrick nodded to the constable.

"My Lord," the policeman stammered. "It is my duty to inform you that there has been a fatal motor car crash near Truro Station." He hesitated and licked his lips, produced a notebook from his tunic breast pocket and flipped it open to a page. He scrutinized the page carefully. "We have preliminary identification that the two occupants of the motor vehicle, a Daimler bearing a number plate HB 147, were killed instantly when the vehicle was struck by an up-bound goods train at the railway crossing right before the station. From personal identification obtained at the scene we believe that the deceased persons were the Earl of St Austell and the Honourable Ernest Haig-Mallory." The constable took a deep breath and replaced his notebook with a trembling hand.

Harry took the news in stride. Death was no stranger to him. Rather, for the past three years it had been his companion. He accepted the constable's brief account with a nod and thanks. Unlike the officer's, Harry's hand did not tremble. Nor did his knees. His father and older brother were dead. His stepmother was a widow and he the new earl. He felt nothing. He thought for a moment. Surprise, perhaps, but no more. He wondered if the war had killed his ability to feel for other people as it had killed so many he once knew and no longer missed. How might he have reacted had it been his stepmother? Or Cecilia? Or, God forbid, Athena?

The constable interrupted Harry's thoughts. "We will need someone from the family to make a formal identification of the deceased, My Lord," he said, as he shifted his weight awkwardly from foot to foot.

"I will attend to it personally," Harry replied. "The Royal Cornwall Infirmary in Truro?"

"Yes, My Lord."

"Twenty miles. I should be there in an hour."

The police officer left with alacrity to retrieve his bicycle. Harry broke the news to his stepmother, Cecilia and Athena in the drawing room, then called for Tregarrick.

"You were present when the constable delivered the news. I have no doubt the entire household is aware of our new circumstances. As you've said before, not much fails to pass through the green baize doors."

Tregarrick's face remained as unchanged as stone. "I took it upon myself to remove speculation among the staff as to the purpose of the constable's visit. You and the family have my deepest sympathies, My Lord. I shall attend to matters below stairs and inform the staff, unless you wish to do so."

"It's only proper that I do that myself, Tregarrick. Meanwhile, if you would have Rhodes attend in the library. I have to go to Truro immediately. And before you go, stiff brandies for the ladies, if you would, and call for Dr. Wetherall."

"Certainly, My Lord."

Moments later, Rhodes presented himself. "The Lanchester, Rhodes,"

Harry said after he had given him the news. "Thank goodness we have two motor cars, otherwise we'd be in a real pickle."

"Very good, My Lord. And the dowager countess?"

"Tregarrick has sent word for the doctor. Shock, I expect. He can administer to all the women, including any members of the staff who may need his services. I shall notify the staff immediately. It won't take me long. I'll see you out front in a few minutes."

In the servants' hall Tregarrick gathered the staff before Harry gave the white-faced servants the news.

"You have our condolences, My Lord," Tregarrick said.

"Thank you." Harry allowed a brief smile of encouragement. He knew the staff would never turn down the offer of brandy, whether for medicinal purposes or not. A tot would do the trick. Two would be even better. It was no secret to Harry that neither his father nor his brother was well liked below stairs, but the servants knew better than to express their feelings in public. "Trying times are upon us, Tregarrick. We must all rise to the occasion."

"I shall see that we do, My Lord." He bowed lower than usual as Harry left.

*

The joint funerals took place at St. Just's church a week after the accident. At Harry's strongly worded suggestion, his stepmother did not view either body before the undertakers screwed down the coffin lids. "Remember Ernest as he was, bright and cheerful, full of beans," Harry told her. "And father's dignity. Believe me, there was nothing Underhill's could do to make either of them presentable."

"It is at times like these, Harry," the countess said quietly over a cup of tea at breakfast before the funeral, "that I am glad I have not completely abandoned my Catholic faith. It provides a measure of comfort, and indeed hope in dark times." She put down her cup. "I know. It was never seemly for a peer of the realm to be married to a Roman Catholic, although the Dukes of Norfolk have managed it for centuries without, for the most part, losing their heads."

"True," Harry said, and the conversation moved on other topics.

A handful of dignitaries made the journey down from London and occupied the pews of St. Just's-in-Roseland church immediately behind the family members. The servants from *Roseland* came next in line, occupying much of the middle of the church, and the few villagers from St. Just who chose to attend filled the rear.

Shackleton, in the dress uniform of a major general, arrived at the last minute and sat next to Cecilia with the family in the front pew. When she saw him, Athena felt the blood drain from her face. The last person she expected, or wanted to see, was Des. Stay calm, she told herself. Polite small talk if and when required. No one here knows I've ever met him. God, I hope he's true to his word and doesn't say or do anything to give us away.

Speculation as to the identity of a ridiculously young and handsome general spread through the church before the dreary service began. Of course, the congregation nodded knowingly, the war had spared no one, and rapid promotions were commonplace in the officer ranks, if one were lucky enough to survive and had connections. Word soon passed around: it stood to reason he must be Lady Cecilia's beau, although none had seen or heard of one. By the end of the service, however, the consensus was they were engaged to be married, which only stood to reason, or else why would a complete stranger, and a general no less with no apparent connection with the family, attend the funeral with her?

At the graveside the new Dowager Countess of St. Austell dropped a holly and cedar wreath onto Ernest's coffin as it was lowered into the ground. Harry watched the clods of earth, heavy with rain, hit the coffin lid, and turned away from his brother's last resting place. The gathering dispersed and the villagers made their way either on foot, in a cart or by bicycle to the St. Austell Arms for the wake. "Send the account to my attention," Harry told the landlord. "And make sure the constable turns them out at closing time, if he can still stand."

Harry, accompanied by Athena, his stepmother, Cecilia and the dignitaries made their way to the family's private dock in the Carrick Roads where the Royal Navy Pinnace waited to carry the coffin of the late admiral to the English Channel and his burial at sea.

The chill wind and the cold waters of the English Channel froze most of those on board to the marrow. The immediate family, however, swathed in heavy coats, remained on the exposed deck until the coffin slid into the embrace of the oily swell from which it sank from sight without so much as a bubble to mark its passage. The dowager countess shivered beneath her fur coat. Cecilia and Athena each wrapped an arm around her.

"Chilly, Mamma?" Cecilia asked.

The dowager nodded. "It is especially bitter today."

*

"This is the last of my father's pre-war Champagne," Harry said, as part of his toast when the family and dignitaries returned to *Roseland*. "I am sure my father could not have wished for it to be enjoyed in finer company, if not for this reason." He raised his glass. "To my father, and to my brother, Ernest."

"Harry?" Harry heard the words behind his back after the toast. He and Athena turned to see Shackleton and Cecilia, all smiles.

"So sorry about your father and you brother. May I offer my condolences?"

Harry nodded. "Thank you, General."

"We're off duty. It's Des, as you know," Shackleton said. "So now you're the new Earl of St. Austell, if not exactly how you anticipated it. Or would have wished it."

"Completely unexpected."

"Quite. Let's all hope you remain the earl for a very long time. We'll have to see if we can persuade the Hun to leave you alone."

"Athena," Harry said. "May I introduce you to my former commanding officer, General Shackleton?"

"The new Countess St. Austell. And your mother-in-law now the Dowager Countess."

"Yes, General. And I'm sure my mother-in-law shudders at the very thought of being the dowager of anything," Athena said before turning pale and looking away.

Harry turned to Athena. "Are you all right?"

"Perfectly," she replied. "A little overwhelmed by everything, perhaps. You know, I've never been to a funeral. I think I need a cigarette."

Shackleton pulled a silver cigarette case from an inside pocket, flipped it open and offered Athena one. "You sound American," he said. She fumbled the cigarette as she accepted it without a word, not daring to look Des in the face. Shackleton lit the cigarette and she inhaled deeply.

"That's better," she said, exhaling. "Thank you, General. I haven't had one in ages." She offered a fleeting, wan smile. The slight trembling in her hands stopped. She glanced swiftly at Harry. He seemed not to have noticed anything amiss. "And yes, I'm American."

"She's the one you gave me permission to marry in fourteen." He beamed at Athena. "My one and only."

Shackleton turned his attention to Harry. "I remember you mentioning something along those lines when you sought fit to return from America." He turned serious. "Although I didn't know either your father or your brother personally, Harry, I'm here as a friend, not as your former CO. I read the news in the Times. Clap's away for a couple of days and he doesn't know I'm here. He'll discover my absence tomorrow when I don't show up for work. Perhaps I should send him a telegram to let him know before he throws a tantrum. "

"What Athena calls a hissy fit. Perhaps you should."

"Other than you and Cecilia, I don't know a soul here, so I'll stick close to your sister and regale her with tales of your valiant soldiering."

Harry turned to Cecilia. "It will be all lies, and if there is a kernel of truth buried somewhere, it will be embellished beyond all recognition."

Harry regarded Shackleton with a puzzled look on his face. "I probably shouldn't talk shop, but I'm curious to know how you ended up in Whitehall."

"We pulled out of the line in early September, after Passchendaele. I received a summons to Divisional HQ. I expected a rebuke, but I was wrong. They sent me back to London as a temporary acting major general. We held a party. Things got a bit out of hand."

"I can imagine, though I'd prefer not to. I hope the lady involved took it well."

Shackleton winced.

"Sorry. Perhaps she didn't."

"There was a penalty — four months in the detention room at the War Office. It was supposed to be six months to a year, but I think Clap let me out early and put me on probation, or something. These things happen from time to time. You know how it is."

Cecilia slipped an arm through Shackleton's. He put his hand over hers. "He's promised to be careful." She turned to him. "Haven't you, Des? I'm not sure which is the more dangerous. The women or the Germans."

"The Germans by a long way. I've sworn off women."

"Except me, I hope."

"Absolutely, Cecilia."

"What's next for you?" Harry asked, steering the topic towards more familiar and less controversial ground.

"Back to Flanders any day I expect. I can't say I'll miss Whitehall. Too much gold braid around for an honest soldier's liking."

"I couldn't agree more," Harry said. "It was bad enough working under Clap in France."

Shackleton smiled. "The Division's taken over our old Brigade HQ, the château where you spent many happy days, taking life easy on Clap's staff when not lying on a stretcher. It's closer to the front. Still perfectly safe for wives and children to spend their holidays there these days, in case you were thinking of taking the countess over for a brief visit." Shackleton looked thoughtful for a moment. "When are you back at work?"

"I report to for deployment at the beginning of February. Sixteenth Cavalry Brigade. I'll know more then."

"I'll be gone by then. I should warn you, though. I think he wants to keep you for himself in Whitehall, you lucky man."

Harry grimaced. "Not my idea of soldiering."

"Hopefully we'll bump into one another over in Flanders every so often."

Harry smiled. "I hope so, too." He glanced from Shackleton to Cecilia, attached to his arm like a limpet. "How did you two meet?"

"In London. We were introduced by a mutual friend," Shackleton said. "She went out with him. I took her home."

"Straight to the Westminster nurses' residence, Harry," Cecilia said. "No stops along the way." Harry thought she winked, a slight twitch of one eye. He had no doubt Shackleton's reputation would have filtered back to Cecilia, who had probably ignored it for her own benefit. He hoped she would be happy, and if so, good for her, but if history repeated itself, he doubted if it would be for long. He cleared his throat. "Now, if you will forgive me, Des, I ought to circulate."

"Of course. I've taken up too much of your time already."

Leaning on his walking stick and with Athena on his other arm, Harry limped away.

*

The order to report to 16th Cavalry Brigade Headquarters, Ypres, was rescinded in late January.

"Whitehall," Harry snarled when he read the telegram before showing it to Athena. "No reason given. What did I do to deserve this?"

"You became an earl? You're too valuable to return to the front? You're no longer a pawn? You're not medically fit to assume the duties of a Brigade command? I don't know, Harry. Any one of a number of reasons. Or all of them. But at least you'll be safe in London, even with the Zeppelins dropping the occasional bomb."

The Dowager Countess interrupted any further discussion by entering the drawing room. "I have decided to move into the dower house," she announced. She regarded Harry and Athena with a flinty gaze. "As is customary under the circumstances. And as you can see, I am no longer wearing black. A month is long enough for widow's weeds."

"There is no need to move out, Mother," Harry replied. "We'd love you to stay here."

"I know you would, but I have made up my mind." She looked around the room. "This house does not hold many fond memories for me. I have never liked it. Besides, it is your house now, Harry. Yours and Athena's. I hope it will become a happy home once more, full of love and laughter. And perhaps children's voices again one day."

"If that's your final word, Mother, I'll have Tregarrick organize the move."

"I already have. You can move into your father's rooms, and mine in a couple of days. I shall be quite cozy in the dower house. My maid will join me. In a way it will be refreshing to shed the shackles that have bound me all these years."

"But you will join us for meals, Mother?"

"My maid tells me her mother taught her to cook before she left for service. But lunch on Sundays, if that is all right? And special occasions."

# 28. FOR VALOUR

On the first Monday in February, Lt. General Horrocks-Smythe welcomed Harry to Whitehall. "Sorry to hear about your father, by the way. I would have sent a telegram, but Admiralty stuff rarely leaks over to Horse Guards until too late to do anything about it. And congratulations on your VC, and the bar to your DSO." He cleared his throat noisily.

"You may be wondering why you're in London rather than at the front with a Brigade command." Harry knew he wouldn't have to wait long for the revelation. "You're not fit enough for those rigors. Not yet. One day, perhaps. If you weren't a career soldier, you'd have received a medical discharge by now." He paused, long enough for his moustache to bob like an angler's float. "Frankly, we can't spare men like you over there. We need our best and brightest minds here in Whitehall."

"But, Sir," Harry began, the disappointment as evident in his voice as in the sag of his shoulders. Damn Clap.

"General Shackleton has already left in your place. I'm sure you're aware of his reputation as an outstanding soldier."

"I know him well, Sir."

"You will do well to move to town while you're at Whitehall. Your club is hardly the best arrangement. And persuade your wife, the countess to join you."

"I can stay at my late father's house in Belgrave Square," Harry said without thinking. "It will give the staff something to do. That is if you insist on me staying in London rather than a field command."

"The Chiefs of Staff insist, Haig-Mallory. And I'll be glad to have somebody I can depend on to get the job done under difficult circumstances, not someone who disappears for half a day without reasonable excuse. There's usually a woman involved when that sort of thing happens on a regular basis."

Harry wondered what Clap knew or suspected about Solange. Whatever it was, he left Harry with no illusion that he certainly disapproved. Harry tried one more time. "If it's all the same, Sir, I'm a soldier first. I'm really not cut out to do Headquarters work. As the adjutant I struggled to keep the mess accounts up to date. You can ask anyone."

Horrocks-Smythe ignored Harry's protests and pressed a lever on his intercom. "Have my ADC report to my office." He released the lever. A few seconds later a slim, sandy-haired and moustached officer in immaculate

Number Two uniform appeared in the doorway.

"Don't look surprised, Haig-Mallory. You know Colonel Benaud. I tend to keep my best officers, when Whitehall allows." Horrocks-Smythe paused. "As you'll be here for some time, you'll need a soldier-servant. We can provide one, unless you have someone in mind."

Harry hesitated. "My batman in Flanders was badly wounded at Passchendaele. He's received a medical discharge, but he has indicated he would reenlist if I could take him on as my servant."

"A good suggestion, but if he's already been discharged on medical grounds, I see no reason to second guess the medical bods. Any other suggestions?"

Harry thought for a moment. "One of our Lewis gunners, Lance Corporal Trudel, if he's still alive. I'd like to give him a chance. It might even prepare him for civilian employment once the army has no further use for him. A good man, one of the best, and good with kit. He saved my life once. It's something I can do in return. He'll do very well, if he's willing."

"Leave it with me. I'll see to it. And one other thing."

"Sir?"

"Keep a spare uniform and shaving kit in your office. We don't work bankers' hours here, but don't overdo it at first. The time will soon come when you'll be working sixteen hours a day like the rest of us here."

Horrocks-Smythe turned to Benaud. "Show Brigadier Haig-Mallory to his office."

Alone in his new office, Harry closed the door and cast a critical eye around it. Other than the plaster work on the ceiling and the ornate crown moulding, the room looked like every other government office he had seen in Whitehall. Bigger than most, he admitted, but the same gloss, eau-de-nil and cream paint adorned the walls. On one wall, next to an aquatint portrait of King George V, a large Government-issue clock in dark wood ticked away the seconds with maddening loudness. On one long wall of the office hung a large map of the Western Front, tacked to a cork backing. Pins with small flags littered the map in apparently haphazard fashion until Harry inspected them more closely. On one, southwest of Ypres, at Ste-Marguerite-des-Lys-Gran'ville, he saw his brigade's name, part of Shackleton's division now, on a paper flag, and the capital letter R. In reserve, he noted. Doing nothing of any particular value. Like me.

He pulled open a drawer of a filing cabinet and found files. A bottle of single malt Scotch left by Shackleton would have been a welcoming present. No such luck. He removed the thickest file and slammed the drawer shut. A fine trickle of dust drifted down from the chandelier.

Harry yanked the door open and saw Benaud lounging against a wall at the far end of the corridor, engaged in earnest conversation with a young female clerk.

"Colonel Benaud," Harry called.

Benaud snapped upright and hurried down the corridor. "Sir?"

"Pass the word to the cleaning staff. My chandelier is dusty. I have yet to inspect the rest of my office, but you may inform the staff I shall inspect it daily and act accordingly."

Benaud's face turned red, though whether from embarrassment or anger, Harry could not tell. "That is all."

Harry shut the door, reminded himself to control his temper. He resumed his visual inspection of his office. A large mahogany desk occupied a third of the room with its chair back to the window, no doubt to discourage daydreaming while watching the traffic pass down Whitehall. On the desk sat a large blotting pad, a pen and ink desk set, and a telephone. He placed the file on the desk, sat himself down on the swivel chair and pulled it up to the desk. Not uncomfortable, he noted, but not designed for long stays either. He pulled open a desk drawer. It was empty. Not even a pencil, note book or paper clip rattled around in it. Each of the five other drawers was as void of content as the first. In short, there was nothing in the room, or the furniture, to provide a single clue as to the identity of the last occupant. The name plate on the door now read, Brig. St Austell. He still hadn't had time to become accustomed to using his title. He felt like having the name plate changed to Haig-Mallory but decided against it. He would still be known as, and answer to Haig-Mallory, no matter what the name plate read. He would let Clap know of his wishes. And when it comes time to move on, Harry thought, this office will look exactly as it does now, except for the name on the door.

Harry picked up the telephone and rattled the bar several times. He heard a female voice on the line. "Sir?" Harry gave her the number and a few moments later Tregarrick brought Athena to the phone.

"I'm here for a while," Harry said. "Probably a long while. Presumably someone higher up the ladder than me doesn't think I'm fit enough to go back to soldiering."

"At least someone in the army agrees with me." He heard Athena's light laugh from the other end of the phone.

"I'd give anything to be back in the field, where I belong."

"Over my dead body, Brigadier."

"Clap has suggested strongly that you join me for the next little while in Belgrave Square. The staff's doing nothing to earn their keep other than washing clean windows and polishing already glistening silver."

Athena's heart thumped. Her father-in-law was dead but what did Hobbes and Barclay know? Or dear Mrs. Hume? Would they say anything to Harry? Even if they suspected the truth she would have to rely on their discretion, on their unwritten Trappist vow of silence as household servants, a trust as sacred as the Catholic confessional. She had no option. She couldn't refuse to come to London. Harry would surely suspect something. Or was that just her guilty mind leaning on her?

She calmed her breathing. "Are you sure? Wouldn't I just be in the way if you have to come and go at all hours of the day and night?"

"I'd love nothing more than to have you with me. And I'll be home every night unless there's a major flap, and there haven't been many of those recently. Please say you will."

"Give me two days to pack the bare necessities to see me through until the spring fashions appear," she said brightly, "and I'll be there. No need to interrupt your busy day. Heath can collect me from Paddington Station and drive me to Belgrave Square."

"See you in a couple of days, then?"

"You got it, Brigadier."

*

Harry spent the rest of February stewing at his desk between frequent and interminable meetings.

He studied his wall map for the umpteenth time that day. The Fifth Army Brigade, part of Shackleton's division of the Second Army which included the King's Imperial Hussars, was headquartered in the Château Gran'ville. He visualized the grounds, the tent hospital — and the farmhouse where Solange Grenier lived with her young family.

Christmas 1914. Was it only three Christmases ago? Sophie would be six by now. Her little sister, Madeleine, someone for Sophie to play with and look after like a little mother, had already turned two. She may even be out of nappies by now. His mind drifted to Pierre-Auguste, who even now looked over his shoulder from his grave like an unwanted newspaper gawker. Strange, he thought, but he couldn't remember ever seeing a photograph of him in the farmhouse. He wrenched his mind back to the present. Solange would receive a small widow's allowance from the Government. It would not be enough. It would never be enough to support her and two children. But she would find a way to make ends meet. Perhaps even now she had remarried or taken a new lover and protector. Harry was forced to admit she still had not left him completely. Perhaps she never would. He silently wished her, and the children, good luck before he turned his mind to Shackleton, and wondered what he was doing. He read Shackleton's reports after Clap had finished with them, and tried to grasp any meaning between the lines that might have escaped the censor's attention, but came up with nothing but the usual army jargon. Shackleton, he decided, had become as circumspect about his military activities as he had about his personal affairs.

*

"I have some good news, Haig-Mallory," Horrocks-Smythe said one morning late in February.

"Sir?" Harry dragged his thoughts away from the map.

"Two of your officers you were forced to leave behind at Passchendaele have resurfaced."

"Who might they be, Sir?"

"A Major Merryweather and a Lieutenant Sheppard."

"Reggie Merryweather. A good Leicestershire man. They're both good men. Merryweather and I crossed the Channel together in August of fourteen. And Sheppard joined us after The Somme. His father's a clergyman in Hampshire."

"Merryweather's back with your old regiment as acting lieutenant colonel. I gather he still has a bit of a gimpy leg, but he insisted on returning to the front. Sheppard's still convalescing in hospital but should be released before long."

"I'm sure the padre — Mr. Sheppard that is — will pull through. He's a lot tougher than he looks. He said he plans to be a teacher when this is over. How did they get back?"

"The next attack was successful enough to get beyond the Hun reserve trench. They found Merryweather and Sheppard in a German forward first aid post along with some other chaps and a bunch of Huns. And you'll be pleased to know that Lance Corporal Trudel will be here any day. Apparently, they had to drag him away from the front-line kicking and screaming about having to give up his Lewis gun. I think the promise of a corporal of horse's stripes and the extra pay may have done the trick. Well, time to get back to work."

Harry studied the wall map and mentally stuck a pin with Merryweather's name on it west of Ypres.

*

General Horrocks-Smythe regarded Harry with a critical eye. "Best bib and tucker, I see."

"Only the best for His Majesty," Harry said.

"You do the Hussars credit, Haig-Mallory. I knew the first time I set eyes on you I could depend on you to get the job done, whatever the personal cost."

"You'll be at the presentation, Sir?"

"Of course. I'm not going to miss a Victoria Cross ceremony. They don't happen every day. The war can look after itself for a couple of hours."

"Thank you, Sir." Harry paused for a moment. "I've never met him, you know," he said. "I have to admit I'm a bit nervous. I received the other medals at third hand."

"Simply do as you are told, like any soldier, and you'll do fine. The equerries know what they're doing, even if you don't." Horrocks-Smythe broke into a rare smile. "The car's waiting downstairs. You don't want to be late. It wouldn't do to keep the King waiting. And don't look so glum."

"Sorry, Sir. It's just that I can't think what I might have done to earn the medal." He hesitated. "For Valour," he said with a catch in his voice. He paused for longer this time. "I can't think what I did was exceptional, or even particularly valiant. If I deserve the medal, so does every man who was there."

"You do yourself no credit with this negative self-talk, Haig-Mallory. If anyone deserves it, you do. After the ceremony take the rest of the day off. Share it with your wife and your mother."

The staff car dropped Harry off at Buckingham Palace where crowds outside the gates already stood ten deep in the wan sunlight, waiting for the appearance of the king and medal presentation ceremony. He searched for Athena and his stepmother and spotted them in a place of honour near where the ceremony would take place. He smiled at them and half raised an arm to acknowledge their presence. Athena beamed and waved back.

The equerries scurried around the recipients, getting them into line and issuing last-minute instructions. "Address His Majesty as, *Your Majesty*, the first time he speaks to you, Brigadier," one said quietly to Harry. "Then, *Sire*. No need to step forward. He will approach you and pin the medals on your chest personally. When he has finished and steps back, you may salute. Any questions?"

Harry could not think of any. Call him *Your Majesty*, then *Sire* when spoken to. Salute when finished. Got it. I hope. He needed to urinate, like he did before going over the top. Nerves. He overcame the urge, as he always had. A little while later he noticed a slight flurry of activity in the distance. A voice bellowed, "Parade!"

Harry snapped to the At Ease position.

"Parade!" The regimental sergeant major, now visible, paused before bellowing, "Atten-shun!"

The king appeared at the head of his entourage and the band of the Coldstream Guards struck up the National Anthem. When the last chord died away, His Majesty made his way briskly across the Palace forecourt and stopped in front of Harry in the place of honour at the start of the line. An equerry handed the king a square wooden box.

"Our thanks, St. Austell," he said. The use of the title took Harry by surprise. He had been known as Haig-Mallory since his first day at his preparatory school, or by his rank until a few minutes ago when Clap had taken his leave of him. "We know of no one who deserves this more than you. You are an example to your men and to the whole of Britain." The king pinned the length of wine-red silk ribbon from which hung the bronze Victoria Cross onto Harry's tunic. "We are sorry to hear of your father. A tragic loss, both personal and to the country."

"Indeed, Your Majesty. And most unexpected."

The king nodded. "Our condolences to the dowager countess and your family."

"Thank you, Sire."

"And the bar to your DSO." The king opened a second box and pinned the bar to the ribbon of Harry's Distinguished Service Order. "No doubt you would prefer to be in Flanders, but we are glad to see you in London. You are too valuable to us here."

"As my wife frequently reminds me, Sire."

The king suppressed a laugh. He extended a hand. "It is an honour to shake your hand, St. Austell." Harry took the offered hand without thinking and felt the king's firm, genuine grip. *This isn't in the script. Help. What do I do now?* The king released Harry's hand and took a step back. "Carry on, St. Austell."

"Sir!" Harry snapped up a salute, held it for the count of three, and snapped it down to his side. The king moved on to the next recipient.

*

"I'm so proud of you, Harry," Athena said when they met for a quiet moment together after the presentations. "I'm sure the whole country must be as proud as I am." She linked her arm through his and kissed his cheek.

"And so am I, Harry," his stepmother said and slipped an arm through his.

"Steady on," Harry growled. "We can't appear to be human, not yet, not with all these people around. Besides, I haven't offered my congratulations to the other men here. I'm sure they must be equally deserving of their medal, and in most cases more so than I."

"You underestimate yourself, and your bravery," Athena said. She pulled him tighter to her. Harry looked at her and saw the glimmer of a tear forming in the corner of an eye.

"What is it you Americans say? *Aw, shucks. It was nothing.* Did I get it right?"

Athena laughed. "Perfect." She took out a dainty handkerchief from her handbag and dabbed at her eye. "Except for one thing."

"I know I can't do an American accent. What else?"

"It was anything but nothing. It damn nearly cost you your life. If you were a normal human being it would have done. And I would have lost everything I hold dear."

Harry looked embarrassed. "Well, it didn't, although it cost the lives of too many people I admired. But I wouldn't swop places with them." Arm in arm the three meandered through the dispersing crowd towards the Palace gates and the waiting staff car.

*

At Belgrave Square the extension phone rang at Harry's bedside. He switched the lamp on and glanced at the clock. 5:17 in the morning. It could not be good news, not at that time of the day. He answered the phone on the second ring.

"Yes, Sir," he said, wide awake now. "I'll be there shortly."

Harry ran a quick bath, unsure when he might have a chance to bathe in the next few days. He dressed hurriedly, kissed a sleepy Athena and took a taxi to the War Office.

"It's a major offensive along a long line, east of Ypres, Haig-Mallory," Horrocks-Smythe said as soon as Harry arrived at the office. "It started a couple of hours ago. Our front line around the Salient has already yielded ground and has fallen back to our reserve lines. It doesn't look too promising."

The phone rang. General Horrocks-Smythe picked it up himself and grunted into the mouthpiece a few times. He replaced the earpiece and regarded Harry with a solemn face. "Shackleton's dead," he said without preamble. "The château is damaged but still in our hands. A long-range shell apparently." He shook his head. "A good man wasted." He looked at Harry. "No," he said. "You're not going over there to replace him unless the king personally orders it."

Harry looked glum. "I think I'd be of more use there than here, Sir," he said.

"That's for me to decide, Haig-Mallory. Now, get to work. I don't expect either of us will be going home for the next few days. Perhaps you should inform your wife."

Shackleton. Dead. The two words swirled through his mind. They had had a professional relationship, one which would have bordered on friendship had the army allowed such familiarity between officers of differing ranks. He had to tell Athena. He picked up the phone and asked to be connected to his home. Athena came to the phone immediately.

"Des is dead," Harry blurted out. "Killed in shelling early this morning. He must have been fifteen miles from the German line. I didn't know they had anything with that kind of range." He wanted to say it was a numbers game with casualties projected on a blackboard. Acceptable losses. Only it wasn't a game. It was real. And death came to visit far too many families. But he held his tongue. He was tired already, tense and irritable. No need to take it out on Athena.

Harry heard nothing from the other end of the line. "Athena? Are you still there?"

"Yes, I'm here."

"Are you all right?"

"I suppose so. It came as a complete shock. I don't know what to say."

"I know you only met him at the funeral, but he was my CO for a long time. And at the end, my friend." He paused to catch his breath. "There's a hell of a flap on. I expect it'll be days before I can get away."

"I'll break the news to Cecilia, Harry."

"Yes. I suppose she had better know."

"She knew him better than you think."

"What do you mean?"

"She's expecting in August. Des' child."

"What? They hardly know each other."

"It's true nonetheless. She confided in me a month ago. She asked to keep it a secret until she told Des. He doesn't know. Now he never will."

Harry heard the stifled sob down the telephone line.

"I'll tell her, Harry. You've enough on your plate. And I might do it better than you."

"Thank you." He paused. "It's getting too close to home." He felt a catch in his throat. "If anything happens, remember I'll always love you."

"More than Demelza?"

"Even more than Demelza." He put his hand over the mouthpiece as Colonel Benaud entered the room.

"Meeting with the Imperial Chiefs of Staff at thirteen thirty, Sir. Second floor conference room. I'll have a sandwich sent up to you for lunch in a jiffy."

Benaud closed the door behind him. "I have to go," Harry said. "The flap has only just started, or so it seems. Call me if you need anything, all right?"

"I will, don't worry." They hung up.

# 29. UNFINISHED BUSINESS

"The tide has turned at last Haig-Mallory." General Horrocks-Smythe tapped the map that took up much of one long wall in his office. "You've read the reports. It's taken two months since we turned back the German offensive. Now the mopping up has begun. The end is in sight."

Harry flicked an imaginary fleck of dust off his lapel. Horrocks-Smythe suppressed a phlegmy cough while Harry studied the excellent spit polish of his toecaps, courtesy of Trudel, unsure if this was to be a dressing down, or something more sinister. He was tired, wearier than he could remember, even in the trenches. Baggy pouches puffed beneath his sunken, dark rimmed eyes. It took an effort to stand upright. His attention span had diminished as his intolerance of others increased. He was testy and moody. He slept badly and woke frequently, as often as not only to find Athena's hand on his brow, whispering to him. He didn't know how Clap had the stamina to continue. He was twice Harry's age yet seemed tireless.

Harry shifted his study to the wall map and its pins. "We've driven the front forty miles east of Ypres," he said. "With the Americans over there at last there's little chance of a successful Hun counter-offensive."

"Our job's nearly done. So the next step is…?"

Harry hesitated, wondering what Clap was up to. Whatever it was, Harry knew it would involve him, willingly or not. "To bring in the local civilian authorities to exert control, rounding up looters, herding refuges to resettlement centres, and providing food, medicine and other essentials. None of those is the army's job."

Horrocks-Smythe dragged on his cigarette before rubbing a finger over his nicotine-stained moustache. "What do you suggest?"

"In terms of sheer numbers, I think the biggest problem will be the refugees, Sir." Harry coughed diffidently. "I doubt if the local authorities can handle hundreds of thousands of displaced persons, perhaps as many as a million, without the army's help. And that's just in Flanders. Then there's the rest of France, especially those parts that have been under German occupation."

In response Clap raised his eyebrows and squinted down his beaky nose. "Continue."

"My wife thinks it's the children, especially the orphans who are in greatest immediate need. After I'd listened to her argument, I'm rather inclined to agree with her. She says there's no one to look after them. They get into trouble, they steal food, and they fight. The girls get raped, even the youngest. Some of the boys probably do too." Clap grimaced. "The girls get sold into prostitution by their own mothers. It's how they survive. I've seen it at first hand. It's all they know. The Military Police can't very well lock them all up and the local police don't seem interested except for the worst cases. The whole social system broke down long ago. Nobody wants someone else's children to feed when there's not enough food to go around as it is. The war's not the children's fault."

"Do you, or the countess, have a solution?"

Harry took a breath and exhaled loudly. "Possibly, in a small way, Sir. My wife's been approached by an orphans' charity to become their patron. I know she wants to do something positive to alleviate the suffering of the children. We've even discussed making a trip over there after the war to see what we can do."

Clap's eyes narrowed. "And where do you fit in with this scheme?"

"I don't, Sir. It's my wife's decision entirely if she wants to work with the charity. I'll lend a hand if she asks, but I honestly don't know what use I could possibly be. I'm a career soldier, not a nanny. One thing's certain, though — the orphanages in France and Belgium will be chock full of children in need of a new home. I doubt if either country can meet the need. That leaves England and America to pick up the slack."

Horrocks-Smythe clapped his hands together. "Splendid idea, Haig-Mallory. I commend you and the countess for your humanitarian gesture."

Harry's head snapped up. What idea? What humanitarian gesture? Since when did Clap give a fig for anything humanitarian? And what scheme might the old bugger be plotting?

He didn't have to wait. The answer came immediately. "Why wait until after the war? You look a bit peaky, Haig-Mallory. You need some fresh air. Some time away from your desk. A week or so in Flanders will bring the colour back to your cheeks. I'm sure we can spare you for a few days."

Harry hesitated. Harry touched his burning cheeks. A command? A brigade in the field? At last. This time he snapped his shoulders back and assumed a soldier-like stance.

"Check out the orphanages, or wherever they've herded these children," Clap continued. "Pick out a handful you think most in need of a new start in life and bring them back with you. You could do worse than Ste-Marguerite-des-Lys for starters. You know the place well enough. We have a history there."

We? I did. You hardly left the château the whole time you were there. You know, don't you? About Solange. Nothing ever escapes you.

"You could spread some cheer on a bleak future and at the same time tie up some loose ends on behalf of the Brigade."

Tie up loose ends? God knows how. But the look in Clap's eye told him the old bugger definitely knew about Solange. And probably Madeleine too. Harry offered a non-committal grunt and snapped his gaping mouth shut.

"We'll send over an official photographer to take pictures, and a reporter from The Illustrated London News to write it up." Horrocks-Smythe spread his hands as far apart as his massive wingspan would let him. "Banner headline. VICTORIA CROSS WINNER RETURNS TO FLANDERS TO RESCUE ORPHANS. That will cheer up the great British reading public. What do you say?"

"And once I've rescued them, Sir?"

"Why, bring them back to England, of course, where they will be celebrated as little heroes, fêted and photographed, and probably invited to tea somewhere grand. The Palace even. A chance to meet the king and queen." He didn't give Harry time to formulate a response, let alone an objection. "And adopted. You and your charming wife may even decide to adopt one or two of them as your own as a gesture of solidarity with our French and Belgian allies."

"I see," Harry said, his voice heavily laden with doubt. "I'm not sure how my wife will take to becoming the instant mother of a bunch of refugee orphans. Even one. Or me, for that matter."

"She's a woman, Haig-Mallory. Take it from me. Like a duck to water as long as you don't interfere. The children would be right at home in your household. You speak French. Your stepmother speaks French. She'll have children to speak French with while you're in Whitehall and up to your neck in paperwork. She could even stay with you in town until they're adopted. Or take them down to Cornwall. It's a damn good idea of yours."

My idea? Since when had a rescue mission to Flanders complete with reporters and photographers been my idea? "We intend to start our own family once the shooting stops and I can safely become a parent without being a target for the Germans," he said, clutching at straws.

Clap looked at Harry sternly. "I didn't suggest your wife stay with you in London simply for the shopping opportunities." He cleared his throat. "And, by the way, I can assure you, Haig-Mallory, you won't be going back to France in any other than a staff capacity. I have that on authority of Field Marshall French. Even if you're not pleased, I'm sure your wife will be."

He regarded Harry as a schoolmaster might at a boy who was too dull to parse a simple Latin sentence. "In the meantime, there are children in Belgium who are in great need. You're free to defer the issue until after the war, mind you. Or even refuse, if you choose." Clap's tone rose with the last words and left them to dangle. Harry knew refusal, or deferment, was not an option.

Clap paused to let this sink in. Harry knew a suggestion from Clap was as good as an order. He was snookered. He grasped his last straw. "I'll think about it and talk it over with my wife." He barely managed to suppress his nervous stammer. "It will be her decision."

Clap frowned. "Not if she's to be the patron. She must be seen to be proactive. There's no time to waste. I can have a photographer, a reporter chap and a couple of cars lined up and ready to go in forty-eight hours. Have your soldier-servant drive. He can drive, can't he?"

"So I believe, Sir. I gather he built motor cars for a living before the war."

"Splendid. I'll liberate some cash from the contingency fund to help with expenses while you're over there and I'll assign someone as ADC."

"Perhaps Lieutenant Sheppard as ADC, if you know his present whereabouts. I'm sure he must be out of hospital by now. He might be eligible for a medical discharge but if he's available he might be persuaded."

"Leave it with me." Horrocks-Smythe hesitated, then looked Harry steadily in the eye. "You exercised sound judgement in the field, Haig-Mallory, at least sometimes. I don't doubt you'll do so in this latest project. Choose wisely."

"A week, you say?"

"At the most. No need for mess kit. It would set the wrong image. We want humble, but stiff upper lip, doing the right thing for our allies, for their children, orphaned through no fault of their own. The ones most in need. I'm sure you won't let us down. Or the children."

"I catch your drift, Sir. I'll practice my speech and break it to my wife tonight."

"Good show, Haig-Mallory."

"Yes, Sir. She won't be happy to hear I'm returning to Flanders, even for a week. But it would be the right thing to do." Grim-faced, he returned to his office and snarled at the pile of paper in his in-tray.

*

At dinner that evening, Harry's hand shook slightly. He put his cutlery down on his dinner plate and folded his hands in his lap where Athena wouldn't notice them. Athena picked up on it right away.

"What's on your mind, Harry?"

"Nothing," he said, trying, and failing, to sound nonchalant.

"Nonsense. I can read you like a book. Is it going back to Flanders?"

Harry nodded and swallowed the mouthful he had been chewing without enthusiasm. He picked up his wine glass and stared at it moodily. He put the glass down without drinking. He picked up his knife and fork from his half-finished plate and tried to finish the course. A mouthful, and he set the cutlery down again. "I've quite lost my appetite. I'm sorry." He looked at Athena. "I'm being sent back to Ste-Marguerite-des-Lys-Gran'ville. I was there twice. Four times if you count my hospital stays." He explained Clap's proposition. "I'm to round up orphans and bring them home so they can be put up for adoption." He threw his napkin on the tablecloth. "I'm a soldier, not a bloody nanny. If this is all Clap thinks I'm good for..." He left the rest of his thought unspoken.

"If you want to know what I think," Athena said, "it's that it's grossly unfair of the General even to ask you to do this. You're right. You're a soldier, not a public relations expert, and right now I'm not sure which I'd prefer you to be." She smiled. "But you'll go. At least it's not to fight. You'll acquit yourself brilliantly as usual. And on your triumphant return to London the general will congratulate you, and the British public will regard you as a great humanitarian. And most importantly a few lucky children will be spared an unimaginable life. We can't rescue them all but we can at least start with a few. I'm sure the public will fall over themselves to adopt them. We may even have to start a lottery system. You have my blessing. There! I've said it."

"I'll only be gone a week and if it's any consolation, no one will to be shooting at me this time. It'll be like a TEWT." Athena looked blank. "A tactical exercise without troops. I'll be back before you notice I've been away, I promise."

"And with a couple or orphans in tow I expect. Girls or boys?"

"I haven't the foggiest. Whoever seems most in need, I suppose. Anyway, that's the only plan I've been given. And, however vague, that's the only plan I'll execute. But how? I've not worked that out yet."

*

Though Athena took the news better than Harry thought she would, if she really meant it, it did nothing to quell the disquiet rumbling through his innards. The return to Flanders, to Ste-Marguerite-des-Lys-Gran'ville promised to be a battle for which he had neither been trained nor one which he had had an opportunity to rehearse. It lacked a plan of attack, if there was a plan at all, a secondary objective and a fall back option. If anything could go wrong, in typical army fashion it would. He should never have agreed to go. He knew that when he accepted Clap's suggestion. But it was too late to back out now. How could he return to Ste-Marguerite and not come across Solange and the children? In a village that size word of his arrival would spread in minutes. Perhaps she would hide at the farm for a few days. Or if Solange were forced into a situation where she couldn't avoid him, perhaps she would act as disinterestedly as she had the last time they were together, before she shut and barred the farmhouse door on him.

The thought of her name produced a blip in his heart rate. He suppressed the gnawing pit in his stomach before anyone noticed the look on his face that accompanied it. If he found Sophie, would she recognize him and give the game away? Probably not, he decided, but she would be six now, so it wasn't out of the question. But he knew he would have to go to the farm, to check on their safety. When they met, he decided, he would treat Solange with courtesy and respect, as if she were someone with whom they had conducted business while they were billeted at the Château Gran'ville, which they had. Nothing more. No dredging up old times. It would be too uncomfortable for both of them. And all the better for it, now that he had Athena, his foundation on which they would build their lives once the war was over.

*

"Good to see you again, Padre," Harry said two days later. "The arm holding up well?"

"Nearly lost it, they said. Still a bit wonky but I can manage a salute, if not exactly conforming to the Hussars manual." He grinned. "It's good to be back, Sir, and doing something useful other than sitting around waiting for a discharge. Not fit for active service, they told me. Light duties only."

"Let's all hope the next few days count as light duties, at least in the physical sense. And Trudel you know. He'll be driving the other car. You can drive, I take it?"

"Fortunately, the gear lever is on the left so I can manage just fine."

*

The two commandeered staff cars, with a photographer, a reporter, Sheppard as his aide-de-camp in one and Trudel behind the wheel of Harry's vehicle, they arrived at the battle-scarred remains of the village of Ste-Marguerite-des-Lys-Gran'ville.

"I was here, off and on, gentlemen, from December, nineteen fourteen until last October," Harry said to the reporter and photographer. "The large, partly damaged building over there is the Château Gran'ville. It's been in the Gran'ville family for generations, dating back to the fifteenth century. We established our regiment headquarters there in fourteen, and it was where I was aide-de-camp to General Horrocks-Smythe in fifteen and sixteen." He pointed to several nearby craters. "There was a field hospital over there, where I was an unwilling guest on a couple of occasions. It's where my former commanding officer, Major General Shackleton was at the start of the German spring offensive. General Shackleton was killed in the shelling. I had been slated to be here. Wounds got in the way and he took my place. It could have been me buried in a military cemetery instead of him." He thought for a moment. "It probably should have been me."

Harry turned to the reporter. "Did you get all of that? This place is special, to me. Now step this way, gentlemen."

With trepidation at what he might discover, he led the men to what remained of Solange's farmhouse. A mound of stone, mortar, lath and plaster no higher than the nearby shell-blasted barn walls covered the ground where the farmhouse once stood. Harry's stomach lurched. What had befallen them? Had they survived the shelling? Or had they...? He didn't want to contemplate the alternative. He took a deep breath. "If I'm not mistaken, though it's hard to tell now, a war widow lived here," he said. He placed his feet apart on the rubble while the photographer took pictures.

"Dramatic," said the photographer to the reporter. "And don't forget determined."

"War widow," Harry snarled. "Did you get that?"

The reporter grunted and continued scribbling in his notebook.

"Her husband was the mayor of Ste-Marguerite-des-Lys-Gran'ville before he volunteered for the infantry. He wanted to set an example for the young men in the village. He died in a German prisoner-of-war camp of wounds suffered at Verdun. Verdun," Harry repeated. "Fighting for France."

"What became of the woman?" the reporter said.

"I don't know. She had a young child, a daughter, I recall. If they're still alive after all this..." He swept an arm dramatically while the flash went off. The photographer reloaded his camera with another plate.

"Do that again and hold it, please, General," the photographer said. Harry pointed theatrically at the ruined farmhouse. The flash lit in a puff of smoke and blinding light. "Got it. Thank you." The photographer turned to the reporter. "That's a good one, Clive. I need more like that."

Harry scowled. "We may be here to play a game for the British reading public, but I'm here on a mission. I hardly need remind you I won't leave Ste-Marguerite without at least an orphan or two to satisfy your readers. My general has insisted on at least two."

"It's the human-interest side my magazine is most interested in, General," Clive, the reporter, said. "Stories about your time here, and the orphans, of course. Our readers lap it up."

Harry shot the reporter a withering look. "I'm sure they do. Ask away. I'll try to oblige. Now, shall we move on?"

They returned to the cars and piled in. "Perhaps they can put the orphans in the boot," the photographer said.

"That'd be a laugh, Godfrey," Clive said, and they broke into laughter.

"Well, there's no room for them in here with all our stuff, and I'm not walking back to Calais, not with all this camera equipment."

"And I have to file my story to meet the deadline. So, somebody's going to have to walk."

Harry glared at them.

"Sorry, General. Having a bit of a laugh. It's been a sombre day. I'm glad I wasn't here then."

"There must be a million Englishmen who were here who would have shared your thought, had they lived, and another million or so Germans." He turned his back on the newspapermen. "As it's Sunday," he said to Sheppard. "It's a good day to visit the church and the vicarage, if they're still standing."

# 30. ORPHANS

Harry gazed out of the car window as they passed through what was left of the village and shook his head. Nothing moved — not another car, not a cyclist or a pedestrian. Not even a cat slunk from one house to another in search of food.

The two cars pulled up beside the mound of rubble where the church of Ste-Marguerite-des-Lys once stood. The vicarage and parish hall next door seemed to have escaped the worst of the shelling. Some of the vicarage roof remained, enough to provide a measure of shelter from the elements. Although there was not a pane of glass left in the windows, the stone walls stood defiant, pockmarked with bullet holes and shrapnel scars.

The two men from The Illustrated London News, Sheppard and Harry left the cars and viewed the devastation. "The parish priest used to be a Father Migot," Harry said. "We had a couple of left-footers in the regiment who attended mass here from time to time. I've no idea if the priest is still alive. Let's find out, shall we." The flash went off behind him as he picked his way over the rubble-strewn road. Another flash went off as Harry paused, his fist poised as he prepared to knock on the vicarage door. An elderly woman in black came to the door in answer to his knock. She scrutinized Harry with deep suspicion as she tied her head scarf tighter under her pale, whiskery chin.

"I am looking for the parish priest, Father Migot," Harry said. "Is he still here?"

"Yes. Wait one moment." She disappeared inside. A few moments later a gaunt, elderly priest wearing a plain black cassock and a wide brimmed black hat appeared in the doorway. Harry hardly recognize the man as the plump, middle-aged parish priest of only two years ago. He must have aged a dozen years since then. The photographer's flash went off behind Harry. The priest shielded his eyes.

"*Monsieur le curé? Père Migot?*"

"Yes. What do you want?"

Harry removed his hat. "Do you remember me, Father? Captain Haig-Mallory. I was here at the Château Gran'ville for a while, early in the war."

The priest peered at Harry's face, then put on his spectacles for a better look. "Yes. I remember you."

"May I come in?"

"Who are they?" He pointed at the three men behind Harry.

"They are with me. I am a General now, and a General is not allowed to travel alone. Army rules. But they're clean, and I promise they won't steal anything."

"Come in. But I warn you, I have nothing to offer and even less to steal. We have no food. Not even a glass of communion wine."

"We seek only your gracious hospitality. We've brought food for the orphans, if you have any."

"Orphans? We have so many. There are six here under our care and many more in the village. It will take more than a few loaves and fishes to feed those under our roof." He laughed. The high-pitched cackle Harry did not remember ever coming from the old man caught him by surprise.

"And we have brought a little wine to go with the feast. A few bottles of vin ordinaire only. Perhaps a blessing will change them into something better." He turned to Sheppard. "Fetch the provisions from the boot, Mr. Sheppard. Have Corporal Trudel lend a hand."

"Sir!" Sheppard saluted and scuttled away.

The priest held the door open, removed his hat and hung it on a nail. Harry, with the reporter and photographer in tow, crossed the threshold into the darkness of the unlit vicarage. Harry removed his hat and pressed it against his side with his arm. The priest eyed him warily. "You did not come to Ste-Marguerite-des-Lys-Gran'ville simply to have supper with an old parish priest, General. What other business brings you here?"

Harry smiled. "You could always see past the obvious, Father. I have an ulterior motive. These two gentlemen are from the English press. They are here with me to record my travels and my mission. At the suggestion of my general, who used to be in command at the Château Gran'ville when I was a major, I am here on his behalf do something to help to help the village and the people. And the orphans. Especially the orphans."

"I never once met the general while he was here," the old priest said. "So I am suspicious of his proclaimed desire to do something for the village. As for the orphans, how does he intend to help them?"

"He has given me the task of offering a new life in England for one or two of the orphaned children. Perhaps even permanent adoption, if no adoptive parent can be found here. Along with a cash donation, to help with the expenses of raising those not fortunate enough to accompany me."

"How much?"

"How much is a child worth, Father?"

"A good question, General. Some of our children are quite sickly and all are undernourished. They will undoubtedly die without proper medical attention, which is impossible to obtain locally. Besides, we have no money to pay for medicines. Others are healthier, and will probably survive, at least until the next winter. Then, who knows?" He spread his hands and shrugged. Harry suspected the old priest was salting the mine. "No doubt the Four

Horsemen of the Apocalypse will revisit us, along with the torment of lesser plagues."

"And it is the sick ones you would like me to offer to take? Those most in need?"

"If it would not be too much of a burden, General."

"Perhaps we could meet them. Then after the introductions we can all eat together while we decide."

The priest clapped his hands. "Violette!" The door opened and the old woman appeared. "Get the children washed and ready for the General's inspection. He will take some of them back to England with him."

"Only a couple, Father," Harry said. "My general insists on two."

Without a word or a nod the woman disappeared. Harry heard the squeaky sound of the pump in what he imagined was most likely all that remained of the kitchen, followed by the slosh of water in a basin. The sound of children's piping voices echoed around the bare room. A few minutes later the woman reappeared ahead of a line of children, dressed in rags, but with their hands and faces clean. All girls, Harry noted. He quickly scanned the line and recognized Sophie Grenier immediately. She showed not a flicker of recognition, even with his hat off. The child next to Sophie with the runny nose, the one whose hand she held, was undoubtedly Madeleine. She had Solange's thick red hair, though perhaps a shade darker, braided to her shoulders, and her mother's freckles and green eyes. He continued his inspection down the short line. Half a dozen waifs between two or three and ten or eleven years old, he guessed, grubby and undernourished but who otherwise seemed outwardly healthy.

"Are all the parents missing or known to be dead?" he whispered to the priest.

The priest nodded. "All."

Harry's stomach lurched. If it were the case, it meant Solange was dead as well. He tried to show unconcern.

"Do you know their family names?"

"Yes. The two on the end are Grenier, Sophie and Madeleine. They are the youngest, six and two." He pointed to the next pair, also holding hands. "Those two are Catherine Bourgeois and her sister, Hélène. Eight and six. Then there is Adèle Fournier." He dropped his voice to a whisper. "She is nine. As far as I know, her parents never married. Her father is rumoured to be of German descent, from Alsace. He left Adèle's mother soon after the child was born. Neither, of course, is the fault of the child. The name on the child's birth certificate is Adelheid. Her mother called her Adèle. Fournier is her mother's family name." He paused. "You know how it can be sometimes."

Harry nodded and hoped his wan smile revealed nothing but neutrality at the information.

Father Migot brightened. "And last, we have the oldest, Jacqueline

Marois. She is eleven and acts quite the little mother to them. But I warn you, she is vulnerable, emotionally fragile. She is old enough to know what is going on, and she is suspicious of adults. She does not seem to adapt to change very well."

"I can hardly blame her."

"She will soon be in need of a mother figure. I think you know what I mean."

Harry thanked the Lord that task would not fall to him.

"I know nothing of her father. He is listed on her birth certificate as Unknown. Jacqueline and her mother came here as refugees from Brussels. Alas, Ste-Marguerite proved no safer."

"No boys, I see."

"The boys can be put to work in the fields, and elsewhere, as can the older girls. Nobody wants the younger girls. They are just an extra mouth to feed when there is no food to spare and nothing in return." He sighed. "These are all we have left in the vicarage at the moment, the ones no one can use or wants."

"And who are the trouble makers?"

"Undoubtedly the Grenier sisters."

"It must be the red hair." Harry clapped his hands and laughed. "And which are most in need of medical treatment? They're all skinny, perhaps, but nothing some wholesome food, a bath and a loving mother wouldn't cure."

"The Greniers," the priest whispered. "They have worms. And lice. They all have lice. And without good food they are all in danger of getting rickets. And scurvy."

"Nasty," Harry whispered back. The old priest was laying it on a bit thick, Harry thought, but he let it pass. "The lice are the easy part."

"We have tried but look at that thick red hair. Try getting a fine comb through those manes after a carbolic soap hair wash. It will take a sheep dip to cure them of the infestation."

"That can be arranged," Harry said, and shared a laugh with Father Migot.

"I warn you, they will spit and curse like a *poilu* if you try. We discourage it, but except for Madeleine Grenier, they can all swear fluently in French and Flemish."

Sheppard and Trudel interrupted further conversation by barging through the front door clutching a large wicker hamper between them.

"On the table," Harry said. He clapped his hands. "*Allons, mes filles! Mangeons!*"

The children jumped up and down and clapped their hands with glee. "We have cold chicken and ham to go with the wine," Harry said. "Cabbage and lettuce and carrots. And bread and butter and jam. Don't ask where the butter came from, Father. And for us, a pâté de foie. Alas, no oysters or Champagne, but we have fresh fruit, and cheese, and a pie for dessert. What we do not eat tonight we will leave with you. Oh, and a bottle of Cognac. For medicinal use."

And enigmatic smile creased Father Migot's face. "Worms cannot live in alcohol, General, but I think the children are too young to benefit from such prevention."

"I leave it, in case of need by the adults in the village."

As the meal neared its conclusion, the priest whispered to Harry, "I have all their documents. When do you leave?"

"Immediately."

"And have you chosen who to take with you?"

"You said the Grenier children are most in need of attention."

The priest looked hard at Harry, then smiled. "I recall you knew their mother."

Harry's cheeks burned. Here it comes, he thought. Unmasked as Solange Grenier's lover and the father of Madeleine. How on earth could he have ever convinced himself a secret could last in Ste-Marguerite-des-Lys? Not just snookered — check and mate.

"In passing only. She dealt more with our squadron quartermaster corporal who was in charge of provisions."

"Yes. I remember him. A dour man indeed." Father Migot's face gave nothing away.

Harry took a deep breath and looked closely at all the children and their eager faces. "It is too hard to choose."

Father Migot blinked. "They are all deserving. How can one choose between them?"

Harry took a deep breath, as if he were about to take a plunge into icy water from a high diving board. "Would it be too much to ask if I could take them all back to England with me?"

Father Migot smiled and spread his hands. "You are a kind and generous man, General. God will bless you."

"Although my wife and I are members of the Church of England, my stepmother is Catholic. We will bring up the children as Roman Catholics until permanent adoption. And we will do our best to see that adoptive parents are Catholic. In that way we can honour their parents and their religion."

"I cannot hold you to your word, General, but I thank you for it as a man of honour."

Harry smiled at the old man. "My stepmother will insist, I can assure you, Father." Game, set and match. Everyone wins. The girls, the parish, Horrocks-Smythe, the British public, the war effort. The list went on. Everyone, except perhaps, Athena. How would she take to six grubby, lice and worm-infested urchins living in Belgrave Square or *Roseland* until they could arrange for some of them to be permanently adopted by English families?

Athena could always say no, and even mean it. But how could she once she saw them? Lice-infested or not, they were beautiful. Perhaps Clap was right. Athena would want to mother them, in the same way he wanted desperately to be the father of the Grenier sisters legally, and in Madeleine's case in fact. He would rather die than abandon those two girls again.

He reached into the inside pocket of his tunic and pulled out his wallet. He withdrew a thick wad of banknotes and handed them to Father Migot. "For your trouble so far, Father. May God bless you and the work you have done with these children under such trying circumstances."

The priest's hand closed over the banknotes. Harry knew Father Migot would count his good fortune the moment they left, but Harry knew he had the better bargain.

Father Migot looked Harry in the eye. "Pierre-Auguste Grenier is the father of Sophie. Madame Grenier refused to divulge the identity of the father of Madeleine. Like Adèle and Jacqueline, she will go through life as illegitimate through no fault of her own, but I am sure a kind, forgiving God will not hold it against a child."

"Nor should any man, Father."

The photographer's flash went off several more times while the group gathered in front of the vicarage. Jacqueline clutched a small, battered suitcase containing all their worldly possessions, except for a rag doll, which Madeleine clasped to her chest.

"Say goodbye to Father Migot," Harry said to the six girls.

"Goodbye, Father," they chorused.

Sophie turned to Harry. "Papa?"

"She asked me the same question the first time we met," he said to Father Migot. "Her mother said she asked it of every soldier she saw. She could not remember her father, only that he was a soldier." A lump lodged in his throat and a tear pricked his eyes. He turned to Sophie. "*Oui, chérie. Ton papa.*"

Sophie grabbed Madeleine and squeezed her. "See? I told you papa would return one day." She ran over to Harry and hugged his leg. Madeleine held back for a moment, then ran up and hugged Harry's other leg. A flash from the photographer broke the spell.

Harry turned to the old priest. "What became of their mother?"

"Alas, their mother died during the German advance in March. It is a miracle the children survived unharmed. The rescuers found the girls frightened out of their lives behind the barn and their mother under the ruins of the farmhouse."

Harry's stomach lurched.

"She gave her life for her children," Father Migot whispered. "By all accounts the Bosche were not kind to her before they killed her."

"I understand. A truly brave woman." Harry choked back a lump in his throat. "And a devoted mother."

"Truly."

"And her grave? We should pay our respects before we leave."

"In the churchyard. With the others. Come, I will show you."

Harry and the children followed the priest. The small party stopped at a gravesite — the mound rudely sodded over. Harry clasped the small hands of the Grenier girls in his. There, beneath the irregular clumps of earth even now sprouting new shoots of grass and dandelions lay closure of a sort, but only of a sort he told himself. Sophie and Madeleine would be a permanent reminder of their mother and of his time spent with her at the farm on the outskirts of Ste-Marguerite-des-Lys-Gran'ville.

The photographer took several shots of Harry with the children in hand next to the priest. When he finished, Harry walked slowly and with sadness back to the car. The girls clung to his hands as tenaciously as Madeleine had the night he left the farmhouse for the last time. He stopped alongside the car and turned to the photographer and the reporter.

"Gentlemen, I suggest you prevail on Mr. Sheppard to accompany you as before. Military checks. You know how it can be for civilians on their own."

He shot a stern look at the Sheppard. "Go with these gentlemen, Mr. Sheppard and see they come to no harm."

He turned to the two newspapermen. "I'll see you in London, gentlemen, in time for the publication and a glass of cheer at your favourite pub in Fleet Street. I wish you both a good day and a safe journey home." He turned to Sheppard. "Carry on, Padre. See you in Whitehall the day after tomorrow."

Harry touched the peak of his hat with his swagger stick and ushered the girls inside the car. "If I sit up front with you, Trudel," he said, "there'll be just enough room to squeeze the six of them in the back. I'll shut the screen. It might offer some protection from the lice. Then on to Calais."

"Calais it is, Sir. We should be there in time for a hot carbolic bath."

"And see if you can arrange for some female help to go with it. I don't believe it's within my operational orders to bathe young girls."

# 31. A FAMILY CHRISTMAS

On the Saturday before Christmas, and with Whitehall nearly five hours behind him, Harry leaned against his seat rest with his back to the engine. They had the first-class compartment to themselves. He closed his eyes and listened to the rhythmic click and clack of the wheels of the Paddington to Penzance train each time it crossed an expansion joint of the track. Truro lay less than half an hour away.

A loud snore woke him and he looked around with a sheepish expression on his face. "Sorry," he said. "I hadn't realized I'd dropped off." He pulled out a briar pipe from a pocket in his uniform tunic and a tin of Three Nuns tobacco from another and began to fill his pipe.

Across from him, Athena stifled a yawn. "You're not going to smoke that stinky thing in here, are you?"

He looked at the pipe then at Athena. He grunted and put the pipe away. "Are you all right?"

"I'm fine," she said. "A little weary, that's all."

"You can rest as long as you like in Cornwall. And in clean, country air you probably won't catch that awful 'flu germ that's going around. It seems so much worse in the city. I'm sure it's the overcrowding that encourages it. I'll get a nurse and some extra help to look after you while I'm back in London."

"We won't catch it, I promise. And I don't need a nurse. I'm not a baby, Harry. I'm having one. I'm an American, and we American women can do anything we set our minds to. Besides, we have Nanny Lemay to help if needs be." She smiled and looked at the children. "In the meantime, we have this little treasure trove to look after."

Six girls, including the two red-headed, green-eyed, non-stop chatterbox Grenier sisters, all dressed in new hats and gloves, dresses, coats and stockings, gazed out at the train window at the woods and tilled fields of the rich Cornish countryside. Crumbs from the Chelsea buns Harry bought for them at Paddington Station buffet lay scattered on the floor. The girls chattered away like excited sparrows in a mixture of French, English, and occasional words in Flemish. They pointed at trees and hedges and livestock as the train chugged past farms and pastures. Harry wondered for the thousandth time what he had done to deserve them and Athena. As impossible as it seemed only a year ago, they were on their way to *Roseland* for Christmas — for the girls their first visit — to start a new chapter in their lives.

The lines on his face, and the grey strands, no longer flecks at his temples, bore testament to four years of war and the weight of the increasing burden of command. Now, he longed to be ordinary, to be able to melt into the vast multitude of Englishmen, devoid of badges of rank to mark him as somehow special, even exceptional, and thus placed above them. They, the rank and file — the common soldiers he so admired and appreciated — they were the exceptional ones.

He knew he was the inescapable product of his family, of the army, of England, but it also fell within his power to change the direction of his future, to forge a new pathway if he chose. And he had made that decision the day the war ended, not six weeks since. He'd told Athena of his intention to resign his commission and to return to Cornwall to raise his family. If called upon to do so he would sit as a  magistrate in the local court, and take up his duties as Lord Lieutenant of the County, his father's old post, once he became a civilian. He never thought he would admit such a thing, but he was done with active soldiering. Fate, or blind luck had given him a priceless gift, a second chance at life. He resolved to make the most of it, for Athena, for Sophie and Madeleine, for Catherine and Hélène, Adèle and Jacqueline, for his servants, for his tenant farmers and for his fellow Cornishmen.

He gazed at the familiar countryside and smiled with satisfaction. "*Regardez! Une vache.*" He pointed to a Guernsey cow ruminating contentedly in a field as the train sped by. "A cow, in English. *Répétez.*" The children pointed. "Cow," they dutifully repeated.

"*Et là-bas, un troupeau de moutons.*" He indicated the flock of sheep huddled in the lee of a barn in the adjacent field. "A flock of sheep."

"Ship?" said Sophie. "*Un bateau?*"

"I know. They sound almost the same. It's complicated, but it won't take long before you and Madeleine speak English as well as you speak French. Right, maman?"

Athena smiled. "*Exactement.*" The girls giggled at the way Athena mangled the word in her American-French accent.

I'm so lucky, Harry thought. He blinked and smiled at Athena across from him. He might accept a post as Honorary Colonel of the local militia, if it were offered. Next year. Or the year after, but not immediately. He'd promised Athena the day the war ended that he would never again set foot outside England in uniform. The war wasn't technically over, but the fighting had stopped with the armistice in November. He prayed that, when the powers eventually signed the peace agreement, everyone could breathe a collective sigh of thanks.

He'd shaved off his moustache before dinner on November 11th to show his resolve to become a civilian, a human being, a soldier no more. "It makes you look younger and more dashing," Athena told him that evening. "And far less grumpy."

He'd have to return to Whitehall after Christmas and remain there until such time as they no longer needed him, but with officers of brigadier and general rank falling over themselves trying to look indispensable there would be no shortage of qualified replacements. There'd be a job for Trudel as well, if he wanted it, though service didn't seem up his alley. Still, he seemed to have taken a shine to the governess, Mademoiselle Guilbeault. Perhaps she might influence his decision. He'd see.

And there was Cecilia. Now, with a three-month old, fatherless daughter to look after, life for her and baby Philippa had taken an unexpected turn, and probably not for the better. Shackleton had died in ignorance. Cecilia hadn't told his family either, and there'd be no allowance from the army who did not recognize unmarried widows, nor their orphan children as dependants. Harry accepted the fact that Cecilia had always had a stubborn, independent streak and before the baby was born she'd expressed her wish to make her own way in the world. He'd make sure Cecilia, and especially the baby, were properly provided for. They would be at *Roseland* for Christmas. He hadn't seen either Cecilia or the baby yet. Athena had, when Philippa was a few weeks old, and pronounced her niece beautiful. He smiled. That was Athena all over, always looking on the bright side, seeing the good and the beautiful in everything. How glad he was that they had married.

With their own baby on the way, he and Athena would have to postpone their trip to the Georges Cinq. Paris would still be there in a year or two. Perhaps Sophie and Madeleine might come with them. Or all of them if none were adopted. Or perhaps it might be better for them to stay at *Roseland,* with *mémé*, or Grannie as the girls sometimes remembered to call her whenever she visited Belgrave Square. He smiled inwardly. If that were the biggest problem he faced, he had very little to worry about.

He stretched and eased the stiffness and aches from his joints. Christmas Day was only four days away, and the staff would be busy decorating *Roseland* with holly and cedar and pine boughs. The tree would go up on Christmas Eve. They had bought electric lights for it for the first time this year. He was pretty sure none of the children had ever seen a Christmas tree and he wondered what their reaction might be.

This year the job of handing out the envelopes to the staff before dinner on Christmas Eve fell to him. His father had always performed that small task, offering his thanks and words of encouragement to the newest and youngest members of their household. *Plus ça change,* he thought. So much had changed in such a short time, but at least he would keep that tradition alive. They, the household staff, the gardeners, the stable lads, all appreciated his father's gesture at Christmas, as begrudgingly given as it was. The envelopes would be generous this year — a month's pay rather than the customary one week. So few had done the work normally carried out by so many.

Harry glanced at Athena and smiled. She caught his smile and returned it. She seemed happy, he thought, and after the past four years she deserved every scrap of happiness he could give her. Once, in their bedroom at Belgrave Square, she had said, "You know, in a certain light, Sophie looks a bit like you. I think it's the chin and the shape of her mouth." He had scoffed at the idea and told her it was nonsense, fanciful thinking on her part. And besides, Sophie would have been about three when he first arrived in France.

Athena had given him a funny look at his protestations. "But Madeleine is yours, isn't she, Harry?"

His mouth had gaped and a crimson blush spread up his neck. "There's no point in denying it," Athena said in a quiet voice. "It's the way you look at her. Only a father could look as adoringly at his daughter as you do at Madeleine."

Harry gulped and opened his mouth to speak. Athena held up her hand. "I don't want to know about her, but I can imagine she was very pretty if her daughters are anything to go by."

Harry nodded. "She was. She died in the shelling during the Spring Offensive. Somehow, I knew I'd never see her again when we parted company not long after Madeleine was born. I certainly never expected to see the two girls again."

"And you loved her, at least a little?"

He nodded again, tongue-tied as he tried to formulate the words. "Yes," he whispered, as he choked back a tear. "She was a widow. Her husband was killed at Verdun. I won't make excuses for what I ... we did. I didn't know if you still loved me or if the words in your letters were what you thought I wanted to hear. And I wasn't sure after all that time apart if I still loved you."

"And now we both know the answer. I love you, Harry, more now than ever."

"And I love you, too, more than I can say. I don't deserve you. I never will but I'll try to prove my love every day."

Perhaps that was why he'd grown to love her so much. Athena accepted him for who he was and stayed by him. He could not ask for more. Her knowledge of his affair in no way diminished the remorse he felt and would without doubt endure for the rest of his life. He knew it served him right. But he had learned his lesson and vowed never again to submit to such a moment of weakness. Solange could now remain buried in the churchyard in Ste-Marie-des-Lys-Gran'ville, and in a small place in his heart.

The rush to adopt French and Belgian orphans had failed to materialize. Perhaps in the New Year adoptive parents might come forward, but he had reached a point when he knew he could not bring himself to part with any of them. The children had been abandoned once. How could he, in all conscience, abandon any of them a second time? Harry thought Madeleine, out of all of them, had most easily glided into accepting Athena as her mother. She was the youngest, of course, and probably had no memory of her own mother, of Solange. One by one, the others had followed suit. Except for Jacqueline, and Harry thought she was gradually coming around.

Whenever Jacqueline looked at him with her deep brown eyes, they seemed to implore him not to send her away, to someone strange, and possibly unkind. Father Migaud had been right – she did seem the most vulnerable of the six and had taken the longest to settle into the London routine. She seemed to have grown to trust him — and Athena — at least a little over the past six months, and that trust could quickly and easily be betrayed. Although she hadn't come right out and said so, he suspected Athena might share the same sentiments about adoption. He would have to discuss it with her. Once the excitement over Christmas died down. He hoped deep down she felt the same way, but how could she? An instant mother of six girls? Still, she had been virtually that since May.

He caught Jacqueline's eye — not a hard thing to do as her eyes seemed to follow him everywhere. He leaned forward and mouthed, "*Reste tranquille, ma petite. Tu vas rester avec nous pour toujours.*" Jacqueline returned Harry's smile with a fleeting one of her own and lowered her eyes. Did she really have nothing to worry about? Was she really going to stay with them forever? Yes. Emphatically, was his answer, and he hoped Athena's too. He really was going to have to discuss it with Athena — or break the promise he'd just made.

Athena turned her head to look at Jacqueline next to her. The child was crying silently, tears running down her cheeks. Athena took her hand and squeezed it then slipped her arm through Jacqueline's and hugged her close. A lump came to Harry's throat and settled uncomfortably there. Athena was close to tears herself, and he was sure the cause wasn't her pregnancy.

"Harry?" she whispered.

He looked up.

"We can't give them up," Athena said, louder this time. "We can't leave them."

Harry tried to swallow but the lump in his throat prevented him. "I'd hoped against hope you'd say that. I was meaning to say something. After Christmas. I want them to stay with us forever, as our family."

"No more than I do. Or at least until they decide to leave, like on their honeymoon."

He laughed. "They wouldn't want us there. But you know what I mean. Shall we tell them?"

Athena nodded as she wiped tears from her cheeks. She clapped her hands. "*Faites attention, mes filles,*" she said. When they looked at her with varying degrees of astonishment, she said. "*Nous avons une annonce.*" She regarded their eager faces. "*Dès ce moment, et pour toujours, nous serons une famille, ensemble."* She paused. "There," she said, turning to Harry. "It's done. It's official. I hope I got it right."

The girls squealed and clapped their hands.

"They seem to think so." He chuckled. "I had no idea you could speak French as well as that," he said.

"I've been practicing that little speech for months. Besides, I took French at High School, but I never could see the point of speaking French in Cleveland."

"You never know when it might come in useful."

Jacqueline buried her head in Athena's shoulder. Her small body shuddered as tears coursed down her cheeks. Athena put an arm around her and hugged her until the tears stopped. "Thank you, maman," she whispered. She wiped her face and looked across at Harry. *"Merci, Papa."*

"She idolizes you, Harry," Athena murmured. "You have no idea how much this means to her."

Harry merely grunted.

"It's a crush. I recognize the symptoms. She'll get over it once she realizes you're only human and a far from perfect one at that."

He clapped his hands. *"Encore une annonce,"* he said. "No more meals in the nursery from now on. We eat together in the dining room *en famille*, as a family. And to heck with what the rest of the County thinks of that."

With a hollow rumble, the train crossed the bridge over the estuary. Truro Cathedral loomed into view then disappeared behind them. Soon afterwards the train slowed. The girls, the worm and lice-infested orphaned waifs Harry had acquired barely seven months earlier regarded Athena quizzically.

*"Nous arrivons bientôt, maman?"* Madeleine said.

*"Oui, chérie. Bien tôt,"* Athena replied, then looked at Harry, who smiled. "I hope she asked me if we were arriving soon."

The girls, except for Jacqueline who had declared herself much too old and sophisticated for crayons and colouring books, put them away and hopped and skipped excitedly as they waited for the next stage in their lives. Once the train had lurched to a noisy stop, Harry retrieved their hand luggage from the overhead rack and carried it out onto the platform. He helped the girls out of the train and reached for Athena's hand. She took his hand and stepped onto the platform. Trudel, Nanny Lemay and Mademoiselle Guilbeault alighted from a third-class compartment and joined the family, back on duty once more after a few hours off. A railway porter retrieved their trunks from the guard's van and piled them onto his barrow.

Athena spotted the familiar figure of Rhodes in his chauffeur's livery by the ticket barrier. She waved, and Rhodes made his way to her as fast as dignity and Demelza would allow. The girls, shepherded by Nanny Lemay and Mademoiselle Guilbault, rushed to the chauffeur's side and hugged the old, white-haired spaniel. With a smile the chauffeur watched the children and the dog exchange kisses and licks with squeals of delight.

"Welcome home, My Lady," Rhodes said. "It will be quite the full house this Christmas, what with these six and Mr. and Mrs. Fenhagen arriving the day after tomorrow."

"Thank you, Rhodes. A lot has happened in the past year, much of it sad. I'm truly glad nineteen eighteen is all but behind us. And it's wonderful to be home without the spectre of war hovering over our shoulders. We must do everything in our power to make sure it never happens again."

"I took the liberty of hiring two taxis, My Lady, when I heard how many of you there would be. I hope there will be enough room for all."

"Eleven, plus you, Rhodes. Three automobiles should be enough."

Harry stood back, taking in the greetings and listening to the exchanges with a pleasure he had not thought possible. His face clouded for a moment. Beyond the immediate future, what lay ahead? He frowned, trying to peer through a mental fog bank as impenetrable as any that had ever enveloped a lost sailor. He saw nothing but a grey wall, swirling lazily with the currents of time like eddies in a slow-moving summer river.

Then the creases in his forehead vanished, replaced by a smile.

"Sir?" Trudel said.

"Nothing, Trudel. Just a passing thought. What next?" He pointed to Athena and the children, the nanny and the governess. "Colonel Merryweather, then a lowly subaltern and I a captain, asked me the same question the day we stepped ashore in Boulogne in August, four years ago. Blowed if I know, I told him. Life is complicated, but it always sorts itself out somehow. With the unfolding of time, the future always becomes the present." He paused and allowed a fleeting smile to cross his lips. "And any competent Hussar officer can handle the immediate situation. Right, Trudel?"

"As you say, Sir."

# 32. THE FALLEN

"We're all that's left," Harry said. "Five hundred and forty-nine of us set foot in France fifty-four years ago. Twenty-three of us made it to Armistice Day. We're all that's bloody left." He eased his weight on his tightly furled umbrella and turned his lined face to Merryweather. "Two broken down old men, Reggie, old before our time." The wind gusted, sharp and cold, into his face, ruffling his wispy white hair. His rheumy eyes teared for a moment but he made no attempt to wipe away the moisture.

"The Padre's still alive," Merryweather said, "but looking very frail last time I saw him. Some of the others who joined us after Passchendaele are still going. But it won't be long before there's no one left who was there."

They stood in the shadow of the Menin Gate in rebuilt Ypres. A temporary steel mesh barrier prevented them from leaving the pavement and crossing the road. A knot of traffic passed them in a roar, the sound of their exhausts reverberating off the vaulted archway. The drivers and motorcyclist seemed oblivious of the presence of the two men leaning on their furled black umbrellas, dressed in navy cashmere overcoats, King's Imperial Hussars ties knotted at their throats and poppies on their left lapels. Neither wore a hat to ward off the chill.

"You'd think they'd make something of a do for the fiftieth anniversary," Merryweather said.

Harry looked around him, past Merryweather through the archway. "Perhaps it means nothing to them now. There can't be many still around who were here when it ended. And they have lives to lead. Still, I'd rather be here with you today than lost in a crowd at the cenotaph in London."

"Is it really only fifty years since the last gun fell silent? It seems like a lifetime," Merryweather said.

"For most it was, Reggie."

"I never expected to see the end, Harry. And I certainly never thought I'd still be alive today." He thought for a moment.

Harry shook his head slowly. "Mons."

"The Somme," Merryweather said quietly.

"Passchendaele," Harry said with a catch in his throat. "Three hundred thousand died here in four years, and at least as many Germans." He swept his umbrella around in an arc. A middle-aged woman in a grey wool coat scowled at him as she narrowly missed the ferrule on the end of his umbrella.

"*Pardon, madame,*" he muttered as she scurried by. "A hundred thousand missing, no known grave, no specific place for family to mourn. It's a shame. At least their names are here."

"You would think the world might have learned a lesson from that time," Merryweather said slowly. "Never again. Rubbish. They say that every time. We were back at each other's throats barely twenty years later."

"And now the Germans are on our side and it's the Russians we'll face, if we ever do it again."

The two old men fell silent, each lost in thoughts of a time when they were young before the cruelty of age and lingering effects of their wounds crept up on them.

"They'll blow the Last Post tonight at eight," Harry said. "Like they do every night. I doubt if many will be here to hear it."

A light rain began to fall as a clock sounded the first note of eleven. Harry and Merryweather stiffened and stood to attention. Once a Hussar, always a Hussar. When the final stroke of eleven fled across the square and echoed its way into the town, Harry spoke, softly, "We shall not grow old as those who are left grow old."

"At the going down of the sun and in the morning, we will remember them," Merryweather said in a voice that scarcely sounded above the background roar of the traffic.

Only after several moments of silence, did they relax and unfurl their umbrellas. The rain turned heavier, striking the black canopies audibly and dripping off the plastic tips of the ribs. "Bloody rain," Harry said. "Some things about this place never change. Time to warm up with a large Scotch before the train, Reggie?"

"Never known to say no, Harry. How's Athena?"

"The usual aches and pains. And Moira?"

"Grumbling at being left at home this time…"

# THE FALLEN

Our souls ascendant as the lark that soars
Above the meadows where in huddled rows
Close-ranked beneath the turf in death we stretch
From Ypres to the Somme and Passchendaele.
We are the wraiths uncounted of the dead
Unnamed, our broken bodies in French soil
Interred, our comrades' lives the currency
Of generals who bartered with our blood
Each step, each cratered inch of Flanders' mire.
Horizonless, our lives before us stretched
When we were whole, not measured by the day,
The hour or less before the whistle blasts
Drove us from trenches deep to charge across
The death-swept killing ground of no man's land.
No scything bullets can our courage shred.
Where once we fell and drew our final breath
Bled white upon the uncut wire. We sleep
While grass upon our graves brings life renewed.
Remember us, the unknown soldiers all
Who marched in khaki regiments to death.
We can no longer in our hearts revive
The pain inflicted by our wounds, nor grieve
With those who mourn their menfolk lost, the lambs
Who were for King and Country sacrificed.

Michael Joll.

# ABOUT THE AUTHOR

Born in what was left of Portsmouth, England in the last days of the Second World War, Michael Joll spent his early years in India and Pakistan. A return to England and boarding school at age nine served as a taste of life to come. A traditional English education left the author singularly unqualified to spend more than four decades in the work force. "Never volunteer" was one of several lessons he failed to grasp and which landed him in uniform on three occasions.

Attendance at university did little to improve his prospects of amassing vast wealth, and dreams of becoming a retired lottery winner failed to materialize. Between university and retirement, he spent thirty years on both sides of various courtrooms. His participation in several other occupations failed to change the course of world history.

After forty years and no longer gainfully employed outside the house, he started work on the first of dozens of short stories and a series of radio plays which were broadcast on Canadian Public Radio. In 2017 his first collection of short stories, *Perfect Execution and Other Stories*, was published. The following year a collaboration with four other authors produced *Our Plan to Save the World*. 2019 saw the publication of a collection of detective stories, *Inspector Masters Investigates Persons of Interest*.

*A Time to Love and a Time to Die* is his first novel.

Michael lives in Brampton, Ontario with his wife and a laptop (computer, not dancer).

**MORE BOOKS FROM MIDDLEROAD PUBLISHERS**
**ALL AVAILABLE ON AMAZON**

*"Making literature see the light of day."*

## Racing With The Rain
### By Ken Puddicombe

"Ken Puddicombe's brilliant novel...an historic political conflict in Guyana, during the Cold War and the cold cynicism and tragic irony of a state sacrificed to super-power hegemony." -Frank Birbalsingh, author of *Novels and The Nation: Essays in Canadian*

## JUNTA
### By Ken Puddicombe

"A gripping story (of) an imperfect democracy...the tension...builds increasingly from page to page."—Rico Downer, author of *There Once Was a Little England*

## Down Independence
## Boulevard And Other Stories
### by Ken Puddicombe

"A brilliant collection of stories telling the tales of people forced to leave their homes...craving the past, escaping from racial conflicts and dictatorship..."—Judith Kopacsi Gelberger, author of *Heroes Don't Cry*.

## Perfect Execution
## by Michael Joll.

"Michael Joll is a master of surprise endings, but they never seem forced. He always stays true to his characters and their worlds." —Nancy Kay Clark, author and editor, *CommuterLit.com*

## PERSONS OF INTEREST
### By Michael Joll

"Exotic and intriguing! Joll brilliantly captures the reader's interest with vivid imagery and a relentless sleuth." —Phyllis Humby, short story writer, poet and novelist.

## WITNESSES AND
## OTHER STORIES
### By Raymond Holmes

"Whether comedic or tragic, plunge his readers into vivid slightly askew worlds, where violins hold memories, suitcases vanish, ghosts abound and death waits behind every door."—Nancy Kay Clark, author of *The Prince of Sudland: Escape from the Palace*.